Far Away Hills

Jean Debney

Clink
Street

This book is dedicated to my mother Margaret.
Born 15.11.1919, Lidgett, Saskatchewan.

This is a work of historical fiction based on anecdotal notes
written for me by my mother 32 years ago, and some
genealogical research that I have conducted.

My thanks to:

Peter Huska
Tonya Ludwig and Meryle Iwanicki (RIP) for their
invaluable help for my historical research in Saskatchewan.

And Milt and Paulette Mastaad for keeping my
grandfather's cabin on their land.

Prologue

The Last Hope

She stood rigid to the spot, frozen in shock. Her eyes fixed on the crimson rivulet of blood which now trickled from his nose. He lay still and prone on the couch, his pale complexion in stark contrast to the rich red fluid which dribbled down his chin, the only sign of life the light rise and fall of his chest, hardly distinguishable as breath. All was hushed in the room. A woman crouched on the floor next to the boy, holding his hand and speaking in a low whisper into his ear.

"Come on Eddie, you know Mama needs you, you open your eyes now... open your eyes for Mama... please, my fine bonny boy?"

Her gentle pleas fell on deaf ears, ears too lost into unconsciousness to hear the desperation in his mother's voice. The little girl watched as her mother became more insistent and frantic with her son's lack of response, now beginning to stroke his head and his sleeved arms as they lay limp.

"Eddie, hear Mama... Eddie, wake up please?... Mama needs you... you can't sleep... Edward, you must wake!"

This last statement came as a command, an order; Mama only used big names when she was angry and determined that her charges would obey her at any cost. The little girl made a move to try and comfort her mother; in her little heart she knew that she was in pain, she understood she was hurting, she could understand she had already seen this despite her very young age. As she ventured forth a hand held her shoulder fast, a gentle hand that belonged to the figure which had stood considerately behind her, allowing her the space to see, to witness.

"No Rita, give your Mama a moment, let her talk to your brother."

The little girl looked up at the matronly smile, which belonged to the red-jolly face, the kind face of the gentle hand of Mrs Purdy, now stooped to give the little girl comfort, arms open. The little girl flung her arms around the large woman's neck, and felt the warmth of her corpulent frame, burying her face into the folds of bare flesh.

She turned again to view her mother and brother and as she did she surveyed the others in attendance in the room. The tall-suited figure who fumbled in his large black bag which was placed on the kitchen table, searching for some implement or medicament to alleviate suffering and cure the affliction. Doctor Cameron: a fierce and commanding figure, but he had the knowledge, he knew what to do, and all the grown ups respected him and paid him money, even if he did give nasty medicine which made you feel sick before you felt well.

Then there was the group of women gathered behind the table, three of them of all different shapes and descriptions. There was a fine lady with angel hair, not rich, just well kept, she was pretty like a kewpie doll; blue eyes and soft skin. Next to her stood a dark skinned old lady, her steel-grey hair swept back in a plait; she was old, her face had lines and crevasses, each indent like a deep memory carved on her flesh. That lady seemed to stand slightly back from the one either side of her, slightly aloof. The third woman was like Mama, she was old, but her hair was red and her eyes were green, her clothes were old like Mama's and she had that same weary haggard look about her face; someone who had started working the day that she was born and not stopped a day to rest.

There was another in the room standing in the other corner, a girl near the dresser, a grown girl of 12. She had mousy hair and grey eyes, and she too stood statue-like, frozen to one point unable to move or speak, staring at the couch which was the focus of everyone's concern. The doctor motioned forward to attend the large adolescent who lay oblivious to everything. The doctor felt for a pulse in his neck and opened an eye to look at the pupil within; he then held his stethoscope to the open-shirted chest which moved ever so slightly.

"I've done all I can do, Mrs Flynn," he declared in his most solemn tone. "It is in God's hands now, we should all pray that he will pull through."

The scared woman looked up at him pleadingly.

"Please Doctor Cameron, there must be something that you can do? I know God will look after him, but God sends men like you to help... we need your help... there must be something more that you can do?"

"I am so sorry Mrs Flynn, head injuries like this are not something that we can do much about, he has taken a lot of force in that last blow to his head, there is really little I can do except hope for a miracle."

Frantically, the woman turned back to her son, and clasped her hands gently but firmly to his cheeks, the nose still trickling life away.

"Eddie, please... please, Eddie, for Mama, you must wake up... you must... what am I going to do without you? You are my strong lad… you are the man of the family… I need you, bonny boy… I can't do this alone… I can't do any of this alone… Please remember the promise you made me… please remember you said it would be alright, that you would never leave me, that you would be there for Mama… please, Eddie, please…" With this she broke down into incessant sobs, trying desperately to rouse the life in her son, bringing back the animated figure that he was.

At this point the old dark-skinned woman began to hum and sing in a low melodic voice, of chants and guttural utterances. The angel-face that stood next to her genuflected and clasped her hands in prayer. These low moans and incantations were suddenly split by a high-pitched whine which heralded loud howls from the young girl in the corner, who stood visibly shaking, her hands at her sides. The woman with red hair rushed towards her and wrapped her arms around the girl's shaking frame, in answer to her loud show of uncontrolled emotion.

"There there, Cissie, don't take on so… your Mama needs you to be strong now… come on, calm yersel' girl."

This seemed momentarily to quieten the distressed figure, as she sniffed back the tears and wiped her nose on her sleeve.

The little girl surveyed all of this from her new vantage point, as by now Mrs Purdy had lifted her up and was holding her as toddlers are held. She gazed around the room, confused about all of the differing and conflicting emotions upon display; the stern authoritarianism of the doctor now softened in sympathy. 'Angel-face', eyes tightly shut, muttering and fingering her beaded necklace that she clasped in her hands, and the old lady with the craggy face empathically humming and chanting. Then she looked back at her sister; her sister was crying, why was she crying, what was she hurting for? And why was Mama crying? Eddie was just asleep, he would wake up in a minute, wouldn't he?

The little girl turned back towards her matron questioningly; her little voice squeaked out, "Cissie's crying? Why is Cissie crying?... Eddie's asleep?"

"It's alright Rita, Cissie's not crying, are you Cissie? And yes, Eddie is just asleep. Mama and the doctor will try and make him well."

But there was something in that voice, though it was said in a reassuring tone, something that did not feel right, that did not feel truthful, and you never told lies, Papa said you must never tell lies, he would make it alright when he came back wouldn't he, because that is what Papa did? Again the little girl insistently pressed on her carer.

"Papa will know what to do, won't he? When he comes home, he will know what to do?"

With that, Cissie burst into high-pitched screams and sobs from the other side of the room, which brought the red-haired woman to hug her tightly in a desperate attempt to quieten her rather than cause greater distress to Sal, who was now absolutely desperate to rouse her son.

"Eddie, you must wake... we can't manage without you... you must wake!"

Her inconsolable tears flowed like a tap down her grubby cheeks, cheeks which had seen far too many tears in her life already.

"Eddie, please... please... I beg you, for Mama."

The listless lad opened his mouth ever so slightly and a small breath eased out through the pallor of his lips. Sal froze; the doctor rushed forward. All the onlookers crossed themselves as one, Mrs Purdy uttering quietly under her breath, "Holy Mary, take this boy's soul."

Doctor Cameron laid Eddie's arm gently down.

"I am sorry, Mrs Flynn, he has gone."

A howl the like of which the little girl had never heard came forth from her mother, it was the howl of a dog caught in a gin trap and an animal in pain near death, it came from the very depths of her being and seemed to have no ending. As if to complement this deep pain Cissie screeched into the shoulders of the red-haired woman, unable to compose herself any longer. Mrs Purdy quickly placed the toddler on the floor; 'Angel-face' had rushed to the couch to try and console Sal, who heaved great screams from her heart.

Little Rita stood, scared and confused, all this pain, all of this crying, what was wrong? Where was Papa? Why wouldn't Eddie just wake up? Why wouldn't Mama stop crying?

"Sal, Sal, there there, God bless you my dear, your wee boy has gone, there there..." Mrs Purdy tried in vain to reach Sal's spirit to make contact with the deeply distressed soul, who cared nothing except for her lifeless boy so cruelly taken from her.

"No... no... Eddie! Wake up, Eddie! You must wake up!"

By now Sal was desperately shaking the lifeless corpse of her much-loved son in determined disbelief, the cacophony of sobs and screams punctuated by the dark-skinned woman's incantations, which had changed in melody from prayer to mourning. Mrs Purdy tried again to encourage Sal to let loose her dead boy and leave him to rest, while 'Angel-face' reached her two hands around her friend's grief-stricken shoulders.

"Sal, leave the boy be, let him rest now; there is no more that can be done."

"No... he will wake up... my lovely boy will wake up..." She tried shaking him again and then dissolved into deep sobbing.

The doctor packed his bag unnoticed, and discreetly headed for the door; wailing and mourning was not for him, he preserved life and brought relief to those who were dying, his job was done. Cissie was almost hysterical and was having to be held tightly to restrain her from hurting herself by 'Red-hair'. She too was showing the signs of breaking grief in sympathy with her charge.

The little girl stood motionless behind the voluminous Mrs Purdy, half forgotten in the melee of emotion and noise. She tried to stand on her tiptoes to get a look at her Mama over Mrs Purdy's shoulder, who by now was on her knees trying to comfort her friend's pain and encourage her to accept Eddie's passing. As Rita tried to get a better view of her mother, she lost her balance and fell gently into Mrs Purdy's back, muttering, "Oh," as she sat on the floor, her bare legs and black feet poking out beneath her stained pinafore dress. Mrs Purdy's arm came round her back to stimulate her to stand and come round to the front; at the same time she spoke to Sal gently.

"Eddie's gone, Sal... but little Rita needs you... don't forget little Rita..."

Rita stood looking pitifully at her mother, entreating her for a motherly hug or acknowledgement. Sal didn't even turn round, her hand swept round her back dismissively as she continued to wail in her despair.

"No... I don't want her... I only want my Eddie... just my Eddie... just my beautiful boy... oh God, please give me back my beautiful boy."

Part I

A Scottish Tale

Chapter 1 –

The Beginnings of Things

Of course the story, my story, had begun long before I was born, long before my mother and father had fallen in love and married. Although I knew of my paternal grandparents and their simple Irish backgrounds, it was the distaff side of my heritage that would have the most influence over my life and care. Good Irish stock, my grandmamma used to say; with a name such as Flynn that was obvious with my father, but my mother's Scottish name of McBride could be deceptive. Sal, or Sarah, McBride was born to stern Victorian parents: Peter, whose parents were protestant and hailed from county Antrim, and Bridget, whose ancestors had suffered the worst effects of the famine in Armagh. Both of the parents had been born and grown up within fifty yards of one another, Peter having lived on the High Street, and Bridget on the Saltmarket.

As much as my grandfather had come from one religious background, his wife made sure that he crossed the divide very quickly and they were married in St Andrews Cathedral on the 15th October 1875 as practising Roman Catholics; this was always Bridget's preferred place of worship and wherever they moved in the first half of their marriage, the procession as committed worshipers was always made to the cathedral. In good Catholic tradition they set to producing their family, despite the fact that their home consisted of renting rooms in one end of the Gallowgate or the other, or London Street, or anywhere they could get. All the areas that tolerated the Irish immigrants, who now began to arrive in wave after wave on the back of the famines that had wiped out a nation.

The young McBrides were hardworking and with great aspirations; Bridget had no intention of remaining in the drudgery and poverty in which her family had existed for generations, and Peter would turn his hand to whatever he could get, never an idle man. When they had met, Bridget had been working as a tartan weaver since the age of fourteen. She was bright, and would have loved to have continued her schooling – taking her lump of coal daily to the drunken school master in payment – but she had to earn a living; no one was going to keep her and she did much to support her parents. With a good head for figures and having learned her letters, she was able to retain the complex weaving patterns to memory, and claimed to be able to weave any of the tartans. Peter was illiterate at twenty, but willing to learn, and Bridget, by now eighteen, was determined to teach him. In between his general labouring and her duty to produce children, she set about educating him to read and write; they both knew that literacy was the key to breaking the cycle, to get themselves out of renting rooms in the Gallowgate. Their first child, Annie, born eighteen months after their union, was a sickly wee thing – probably unsurprisingly with their almost itinerant living, but that was the way with all families of that place and time; Darwin's theory of evolution where only the strongest survive was put into practice in these flea-ridden, rat-infested lodgings. Eighteen months later a boy was born: James, to carry the McBride name on. Sadly little Annie did not survive and passed within a few months of his birth.

Grandmamma used to claim she had thirteen children, although I knew of only eight that had survived, but I often remember listening to her prayers for the souls of those that she had not carried full-term which she had named.

"Holy Mary mother of God, bless my little Annie, Mary, Peter, Susan and Henry-John."

I used to reflect how sad that must have been to lose like that, but what struck me more is that it happened to most women; it was commonplace, yet grandmamma had named her lost 'wee bairns', there was a softer side to her.

Of her eight children that survived birth, my mother Sarah was number three, behind James and John. She was the first daughter, born on the 21st December 1885. It was a month after losing John in a freak accident, he had lost his footing on some stone steps in the ice that had gripped the city that year. He was found by a neighbour lifeless, having broken his neck. Bridget faced this with the same stoicism that every woman of that time did; losing children was commonplace, especially in the impoverished parts of Glasgow. Sarah came in with an icy blast on a Monday just before Christmas, and her childhood would be punctuated by the constant moving and changing, with two more brothers and three more sisters added to the brood as her parents made their progress out of their poverty trap. Sarah was a wilful girl, but always respectful towards her father and mother; she was what could be described as a strong personality, and certainly not the wallflower that her sister Katie would be.

Peter had become a general dealer and then a merchant, he would buy and sell anything. He realised that people needed things and that if he could get a good price for goods that he purchased and then sell them on at a profit, he would build up his assets. The one thing that was in desperate need in that part of Glasgow was clothes, and he would deal in the clothes and the rags that would get recycled from the more affluent areas through every echelon of society before turning up in the East End. Anything had a value, anything could be sold for something somewhere, if you were not too proud to deal in it. By the time he died, at the age of 70, he had built up quite an empire with a warehouse which stored his wares. That sort of labour takes a considerable amount of time, and Bridget had her hands full too, and was not beyond doing a little extra to bring the pennies in; their elder children would receive a good basic education, but as soon as they could be set to work to add to the household income, they would.

It is here it began for me. As the century turned, Sal was now a working girl in a thread mill; she was sixteen and beautiful, with her dark hair and pale skin like her mother, petite in stature but strong and feisty. The whole of her life was laid out before her like some unfolding mystery; what at first appeared to others to be her pre-ordained path through this world, she knew was not the case, for her own father was working his way to a better life. To Sal all things were possible, anything could happen and all she had to do was make it happen. The world around her was changing rapidly and people were changing, they were beginning to stand up for themselves and vocalise what they felt and what they were entitled to. Trains had opened up the whole country and could take you anywhere, messages could be passed by telegraph, everything was moving faster, getting bigger, and changing right in front of her eyes, and Sal wanted to be part of these modern times.

□ □ □

"Watch out henny!... you'll get yesel' killed!"

Sal felt herself lose her balance and she lightly stepped from the factory gates and lost her footing near the road; luckily the steadying hand of Nell saved her from the wheels of a passing motor car just in time.

"Sal, be careful!... You're nae good to me if yer' squished." Nell looked concerned and motherly towards her headstrong friend, but Nell would; she was the natural motherly type, slightly round and jolly, destined to make many children and some man very warm in bed at night.

"How am I ever going to get a husband if you are not around? They are attracted to you like flies to jam, sooner or later I will get one that gets sick of trying, but not if yer squished!"

Sal laughed playfully, but was a little lost and her head was full of confusion. A day in the mill, with its constant bang, bang, bang, of the spinners and the clatter of the belts and engines made her feel quite sick and confused; she always felt so tired and relieved to get out into the air only to be greeted with packed city streets, which seemed to grow more congested day by day. Where once a few cabs passed, now there were many and carts, and then there was the trams! Noisy, smelly and downright dangerous, there were accidents, fatal accidents all the time. If it was not some poor unsuspecting pedestrian stepping in front of one, it was a horse that lay suffering and dying surrounded by a crowd of onlookers, with some morbid fascination of death pangs. However, they were awfully convenient to get around and you could get somewhere else, out of the smelly, noisy parts of Glasgow, and into more salubrious surroundings. There you could witness how the other people lived and wish that you might be there yourself one day. You could even take a blanket and sit in a park and pretend to be like them; the trams made escape possible.

The centre of Glasgow had originally been the Gallowgate, the slums of which the McBrides had suffered ten years earlier. But as the wealthy had moved west, up the Trongate and George Street, they had left their vacated homes behind for others to take. If you were truly wealthy you could live in the large villas in the West End and that was the greatest of aspirations. But if you were really adventurous and wanted a better life, she had heard, you could take the train from Central Station and go out to Gourock 'Doon the wata', and there a simple ride in a steamer and you would be in Dunoon and the real wilder parts, but she had never done that but her mother was always talking about it. If her mother wanted something, it was going to happen: no one would argue with her, a more determined type of woman did not live anywhere; Bridget McBride was not going to let the grass grow under her feet!

"Sal? Sal? Did you hear me? Do ya ken?"

Sal was jolted back to reality and realised that she had not answered.

"I am sorry Nellie, just a bit tired that's all, don't you get like that after a day in there, or is it just me?"

"Nae, it's nae just you, we all get it, but it does get easier, dinna' forget, I have been there longer than you. You'll get used to it. Come on, we'll be late back and your Ma will hae' a word or twa' to say never mind mine, we have the bairns ta mind."

The two girls hurried down the back streets trying to avoid as much of the congestion as possible. They were coming from everywhere, a plague of people seemed to fill every available pavement and roadway as they swarmed out of the various textile factories which dotted the inner part of the city. Everyone finished work at the same time, which made the mayhem even worse as everybody seemed to be in the same place at exactly the same moment. The well laid grid pattern of the slum-cleared Glasgow funnelled all into the same popular bottlenecks.

Eventually they were in the Cowcaddens racing down the 'toon' to their homes, when Nellie let out a muffled yelp of excitement. Sal was somewhat surprised.

"Nellie, what's with you?"

"Oooo it's him, you know the one you keep pushing away, him…"

Nellie was quite long-sighted; Sal often wondered how she managed in the spinning trade, but she seemed to get along just fine. Sal followed Nell's gaze which was directed yards down the Cowcaddens at a figure Sal could barely make out in the distance, but she had a fair idea exactly who had raised such excitement in her friend, and this was the last person Sal wished to bump into right now, her mother would never approve.

"Please tell me it's not that John Flynn that you have got your unmentionables in a twist over?"

"The very same… but dinna' you think he's just beautiful?"

Sal shook her head dismissively, and looked on with dread as the tall figure was growing taller and more dis-cernable in her gaze.

"Sal McBride! You are just being stubborn! It's obvious he likes you and you dinna even smile at him, give him ta me, I will hae' for my henny, just you see if I do."

"You can, I dinna care, he is not fa me."

Just as the girls had finished their exchange, they were in earshot of the young man in question. Sal kept her eyes downcast so as not to attract attention in the hope that he would pass, but it was not to be, and even if he had decided to walk on anonymously Nellie had no intention of allowing him to.

"Well… Mr Flynn, I presume…" Nell put on her most seductive voice and manner, which was so sweetly done John could not help himself but respond.

"If it is not my two most beautiful young ladies… Nellie… Sal…"

Nellie smiled coquettishly up at the blue eyes as deep as the sea. Sal mumbled a hello under her breath and remained with her eyes fixed on his feet, which she thought to herself were rather large, mind you he was rather large, he stood a head high than the average man, which meant he towered above her.

"You are little bit forward John Flynn… your two beautiful young ladies… since when have we become *your* two young ladies?"

"Pardon Nellie, I only meant it in a nice way… you are two beautiful young ladies though…" John beamed at her with his wide smile, she blushed and became coy.

"You say the nicest things so you do… what have you under your arm?" Nellie enquired, looking at the large brown parcel tied up with string that John was carrying.

"Oh this?… Only some old boots that want patching, I am taking them to father's hame, after all work is work isn't it?… You got to get it where you can."

"Aye and your pa's a good boot-maker, so my father says."

"He is that, but it's not for me, I prefer to get out in the fresh air… working on the railways now… it's hard but it pays well… and they won't stop building the railways…"

All the time that this conversation had been carrying on between the two, Sal had stood unnoticed by them both;

she took the opportunity to take a sly look at John. She carefully raised her eyes up his frame, the length of his long legs in his rough workman's trousers, patched by his mother at the knees; they had probably been worn by his father a few years earlier. Then further up, his hessian shirt beneath his heavy jacket. His skin at his neck was smooth and pale, he had a good strong jaw and a winning smile. His cheekbones were chiselled and high, his nose in proportion to his face and those eyes; deep blue, almost as deep blue as the Clyde on a sunny day, like sapphires. He had a mop of tousled dark hair which crowned his strong face. She had gazed too long, he caught her spying; quickly she cast her eyes to the floor again, unaware of the conversation that had continued after she had lost herself in her discreet admirations.

"And you Sal? Will you be coming to the barras?..."

Taken aback by the question and embarrassed in case her subterfuge had been revealed accidently, she became tongue-tied in her response to John's question.

"Errm... y... y... es... I mean I think so..."

"Well that will be fine then, no doubt we will pass in the street, good day ladies." With that John strode on, leaving Nellie glowing with happiness and Sal unsure what she had agreed to.

"You are coming aren't you Sal?... on Saturday?... You are coming down the barras? I mean you normally do..."

"Oh right well... I dinna naw sorry, I forgot... Mother is helping father on that day, I have the wee weans to look after... and you know she dinna' approve of the Barras anymore... but if I dinna' tell her..."

"Perfect! You can come out then, she won't know, you can bring them with you."

"Nellie, she will know, if Jeanie or Katie dinna tell, Annie started to talk and she wont stop... Of course she will know, I certainly couldnae' go out without telling her first..."

"Shoppin' got to be done, she has to accept that you have to get meat... just tell her that... your Jeanie and Katie dinna' nae John fra Adam... come on yer hae ta, I canny ga without yer... anyway it's fa me not fa you... I telled yer, if ya dinna care then I won't waste my time, he's too good to lose..."

The girls walked on and parted outside number 10 George Street, the latest home that Sarah had known but so far the longest time the family had remained anywhere. The house was five stories high and three families lived there. The Lynch family of Mr and Mrs with seven children and a servant had the lion's share of the house. Then there was Mr McAllistair who lived on the top floor, he was a widower with a son, William, and two daughters, Robina and Isabella. The McAllistairs had a spare room and had let it out, as enterprising people did in those days, to two lodgers: a railway shunter and a ticket collector. Bridget and Peter had taken the lower floor and the basement, it was more noisy being just off the street. The basement rooms would get damp, and dirt would make its way in through any door or window that was left slightly opened.

They had managed to secure three bedrooms, a kitchen and scullery, and a front and back parlour; Bridget finally felt as though she was moving up in the world, even if she was still closer to the streets than she would have preferred. Her brood was now complete, Sarah and her much younger sisters shared one room, with two beds between them. There was Jeanie who was five and bright as a button, and quiet Katie who was four and sickly, but always making things. And then there was baby Annie Theresa, the last to be born, who was now two; she had been slow to learn to talk and had only just found her voice, but she had learnt all of the words and now had to use them, she would not stop talking, morning, noon and night and she was tiring everyone out.

The boys who were left shared a room, including James who at twenty-five was still living at home and was a grocers' assistant. James was able to have one bed to himself, while Hugh who was fourteen and working as an apprenticed furniture maker, and Peter who was thirteen and working as a shop assistant, shared the other bed. With five wages coming into the home, plus whatever Bridget could make, the family were no longer struggling and able to afford things and save for the home that Bridget wanted, somewhere in the country. She had her plan, her next move would be just out of the city and it would be their house; their roof, their walls, and they would have a garden. But her plans did not stop there, she dreamed of better things, of living where all the wealthy lived 'Doon the wata', her heart was in the Highlands, and as soon as it was possible that is where they were going.

Peter was a successful rag-woollen merchant, he was turning over a tidy profit and was beginning his ventures into the circle of businessmen who kept the economic cycle going in Glasgow. The city had strict religious divisions, and Peter was fortunate, for although the strong-minded Bridget had forced him down the route of conversion, and he had on occasions suffered a Sunday mass, he was known to be by birth from the other side of the cloth; in fact his name and his provenance stood before him, consequently, questions were never asked as to where his true allegiances lay by others in the business community. This left Peter free to be inducted into the tight network of freemasons who ran Glasgow for real, not the Corporation who believed that they ran Glasgow but in fact had very little power. Success breeds success: Peter knew this instinctively, and he understood that being among the really successful businessmen was the only way to progress his dealings, so he did. Bridget quietly suffered this swing; if she was privately disgruntled it was never voiced within earshot of anyone else.

As Sal walked towards the door in the entry, Isabella McAllistair was just leaving by the main door, she acknowledged Sal with a sideways glance and a brief 'hello' but that is all that it was. The McBrides were still climbing and were seen to be, and the snobbery that comes with an elevated position is sometimes the only protection from knowing there is a slippery slope back down to the gutter. Sal uttered, "Bella," nodding her head in her general direction before opening the door. The first thing that hit her was smell of cabbage boiling, a smell which always brought her to nausea and the second thing was the continual chatter from 'Wee Annie' to all and everyone, but none were listening, all had disconnected through numbness.

"Jeanie, play with me?... Jeanie, will you play with me?... Katie reading, can you see that Katie is reading?... Mama cooking in the kitchen and we will have tea soon... then Jeanie will read me a story, won't you Jeanie... James comes home soon, he is coming home, isn't he and Sal?.... And Papa... Papa come home soon then we will have tea..."

Nineteen to the dozen, barely drawing breath Annie went on, as Sal entered the back parlour. Jeanie was looking tired and playing with a raggy doll which had seen better days; she was totally oblivious to Annie who was standing next to her and jabbing her with her fingers every time she said something. Katie sat on a chair with a tatty bit of newspaper, pretending to make the words, copying Mama trying to read, she silently mouthed the words while using her finger to point, and then she would look puzzled. She had very little understanding of it, having only just begun to learn her alphabet.

"And where have you been, young lady? Dawdling again, were you? No doubt dragging your heels with that Nellie? You know I need you here in the evenings, I need to get other things done, we cannot afford help yet, we must do it, we are the women of the house, you and I. Really, Sal, I should not have to be telling you at your age."

The nagging had started, but it was not angry or irate nagging, that was distinguishable by her mother's descent into a broader Glaswegian accent. It had become very noticeable to Sal that over the last ten years, her mother had been 'improving' herself, modulating her voice, losing the broadness of her diction and use of words. The fact that every time Sal dared to utter a 'dinna' or a 'tae' in front of her mother and she received very firm and immediate correction.

"Sal is 'do not' or 'don't' not 'dinna', and please use 'to' not 'tae' dear."

As Sal had received the very stern welcome from her mother, it was perfectly worded and calmly delivered, totally dispassionately.

"Sorry mother, we did hurry but the streets were full I dinna... I don't know where the time goes, it seems to take longer and longer... here, let me, I will finish making the tea and look after the bairns."

Sal suddenly thought to herself, was bairn an acceptable word to her mother, or did that seem too broad too? It was not a word she seemed to correct but rarely used it herself.

Sal squeezed herself into the small kitchen and checked the pots on the range. Potatoes boiled in one as always, and the sickly cabbage in another. A scrag end of lamb had been chopped up for stew with some onion and carrots and was simmering it its own soupy broth. She knew what she had to do; lay the table in the parlour for the six wage-earners, and feed the 'wee ones' before.

"Bread and dripping, girls?"

"Yaay," Annie squeaked out, but that started her on a new mantra to torment Jeanie with.

"Bread and dripping... bread and dripping... bread and dripping... bread and dripping..."

All the time she tugged on Jeanie's sleeve, who tried to raise her arm above her head in order to loosen her little sister's grip.

"Leave me be Annie, I am tired."

It made no difference, Annie persisted as she always did.

Sal set to producing the three plates for her younger siblings, while juggling her pots of vegetables and stew, trying to avoid overcooking. Soon all of the boys and men were home and gathered around the table waiting for father to join them. Peter, tall and stern, entered and all talking stopped; the wee girls had been sat in the scullery. He took his place and nodded to Bridget to start proceedings. He was a man of few words, and generally when he was known to talk at home it was a severe reprimand given to one of his offspring or other. He was not going to be hypocritical by leading his family in the saying of a grace that he had limited respect for, those sort of things were left to Bridget, who was very much in charge of hearth and home.

Grace was said, tea was consumed silently and then once father had moved to the front parlour with his copy of the newspaper, the brothers would relax and chat, while it was left to Sarah and Bridget to clear the pots and plates to the scullery. Jeanie and Katie were helping as best they could, they were in training as much as Sal had been since she was their age. Bridget reminded her daughter of her responsibilities of care on the coming Saturday, to which Sal thoughtfully replied in a nonchalant fashion, so as not to reveal any pre-planning, "Mother, I noticed we are short of a joint for Sunday, I will take the girls up the barra…" She stopped, checking her pronunciation to ensure success in the answer.

"…To the market, they can help me." She waited for the reply.

"Yes Sal, that is a good idea, and you can pick up a block of carbolic soap while you're there, and be sure to get a nice joint of beef, do not let those butchers palm bad meat off on you."

With that Bridget left the scullery.

Sal stood stunned momentarily; there had been no contradiction, no cross-examination, no argument, this was not the reaction she had expected, she had made up a whole package of replies to the many possible quizzed responses and not one had come. She felt slightly guilty, she did not know why, after all she was only going because Nellie had insisted. It was Nellie who had set her sights on John Flynn, she herself had no interest in him whatsoever, had she… had she?

Chapter 2 –

Toil and Trouble

As she entered the market, the place was alive with shouts and whoops from the various stall holders trying to attract the passing custom. There was some livestock, a few hens and geese, and some penned lambs who were being harried by some stray dogs. There was no order to the stalls, food stalls were mixed in with fabric and rag stalls, and soap vendors; an iron monger had his sharpening wheel set up and was sharpening scissors and knives of those who had brought them, adding to the general high level of noise. She heard Nellie before she saw her.

"Sal… Sal henny… over here… oooeee…"

Sal looked through the thronging crowds across a vast stretch of the market; Nellie, as jolly as ever, was smiling broadly and waving frantically trying to attract her attention.

"Sal… oooeee… Sal…"

Sal waved in recognition and fought her way through, little Annie being buffeted by the adults as she was lost amongst the sea of legs that her elder sister dragged her through, Jeanie and Katie scuttling after her.

"Goodness! What a lot of people are here this morning, I hadnae' realised it would be this busy... I think I will only have a little time to get the things my mother wants..."

"I... I... am not sure you can leave that easily..." Nellie was looking past Sal back towards the Gallowgate with a strange smile. Sal was puzzled.

"Of course I can... what do you mean?" Sal turned to follow Nellie's gaze.

"Seems you have been followed."

"Good morning ladies, what a coincidence seeing you two here..." John sidled up to them both, his workmen's clothes changed for a slightly better assemblage of trousers and shirt; it could not be described as a suit, but was certainly his Sunday best, being worn for Saturday's rest.

"Dinna' be daft John Flynn... you knew we were coming... I telled you we'd be here." Nellie playfully rebuked him, Sal stood slightly stunned by his sudden appearance within minutes of her own, in quite a crowd, maybe he had followed her?

"I naw... but dinna' spoil the formality lassie... may I say, Miss McBride, you are looking very dapper this fine morning... I often sit a few pews behind you in mass on a Sunday... and I think how nice you do your hair up... just like today."

"Thank you, Mr Flynn... but dinna you think Nellie is looking rather fine today?..." She nodded and smiled at Nel, who laughed. "... You will have to excuse me both of you... I have chores to do for my mother... and my sisters need to be got home..." As if on cue, Annie perked up.

"We are shopping for tea... do you want to help, Nel? And you can bring the man with you..."

Sal had been thwarted. She had hoped to make her escape and leave Nellie to take her place and allow her to leave without problems. She felt distinctly uncomfortable; she had been overcome by girlish shyness and she felt herself colouring up and becoming tongue-tied. She did not know him, well, not really, other than passing him in the street. She did not want to know him, his family still lived in the Gallowgate, she knew what her family would say if she formed any association with someone from there. But at the same time, she felt very flattered by his attentions, and there was no denying he was very fine looking man, and today after a good wash and better suit of clothes, he looked very handsome.

"Of course we will help you and Sal. Annie… did you think we would leave you here?…"

Nellie was deliberately being mischievous, she had no intention of allowing her friend to escape, and beside which it would not be seemly for her to be seen alone with a young man, it was best to be together in numbers. Jeanie and Katie stood looking a little lost. John broke the ice.

"And who are these two beautiful young ladies, Sal?" Jeanie realised that he meant her and Katie and giggled.

"These are my sisters Mr Flynn, Jeanie, Katie and the wee one…"

"I am Annie!" Annie shouted out rather than have her name spoken.

John formally shook their hands and said, "I am very pleased to meet you, and please call me John." There were collectively chuckles from the younger sisters, but Sal was determined to keep the formalities.

"We are rather busy, Mr Flynn, so you will have to keep up." And with that she marched her charges to the nearest soap stall, being led by her nose and the strong odour of carbolic.

She had no time to reflect on his somewhat forward behaviour as she had dashed from stall to stall, very thankful that her 'new' friend had been there to help carry the parcels. She had hardly had a moment to consider his thoughtfulness as he entertained her younger siblings, keeping them giggling and distracted, allowing her the time to buy her wares. Neither did she take the opportunity to reflect about his care and concern for the whole party as he accompanied them back, carrying their quarry northwards up the High Street towards George Street – even though she knew he must have been expected by his parents in the Gallowgate. And not for one moment did she give a hoot about the way he had kept hold of her hand for longer than necessary, while wishing her a good day when they had reached the half way point of the street – a point he punctuated with a hope of doing this again, while looking deep into her eyes.

She had so much on her mind, as she had practically run the rest of the way up the High Street with little Annie having a devil of a job trying to keep up. Then Sal had set to, first settling her sisters down with the heel of yesterday's bread spread thinly with jam, then preparing vegetables: scraping, peeling and chopping in bowls of muddy water, before placing in pans to boil. A piece of brisket was carefully placed in a roasting pan and into the oven, and the table laid. Sal sat in the scullery; only then did she cast her mind back momentarily to her earlier meeting, then she felt a warm glow starting in her toes that seemed to travel all the way up to the top of her head. Indeed, he was very good looking, and charming, and good mannered, oh, but she could not even consider him as suitable – it would cause so much trouble, and she did not want to spend the rest of her life chained to a stove. She did not have long to lose herself in her thoughts before the rear parlour was full of noise, as her younger brothers had returned and were using the opportunity whilst their parents were absent to bang out a musical hall tune on the upright piano; something that would be disapproved of particularly by their mother; fortunately their father was tone deaf and unable to distinguish by tune, just by tempo, he held with 'holy music' only.

"Keep the noise down you two… you'll catch it if mother comes back!" Sal hissed at them, jealous of their freedom and time to play.

"Oh Sal… have a little fun… you'll be old before your time if you are not careful," Hugh said thoughtlessly, as he and Peter continued to vent their high spirits. Sal felt her anger rise, and then her common sense stayed her hand from any action. He was right, she would be old before her time, she might as well go into service; at least she would get a salary for her trouble, but that would definitely not go down well. Her mother was aspiring to better things, a daughter waiting on others did not fit with the greater vision.

The front door rattled as her parents entered the hall. Quickly, Hugh and Peter shut the piano and removed themselves to the dining table with looks of innocence on their faces. Katie and Jeanie, who had stood next to the piano dancing with little Annie, scuttled to the hearth rug collapsing in stifled laughter, just as the petite Bridget entered with her tall son and husband following. James looked knowingly at his brothers and winked furtively. Bridget looked down at her wee daughters.

"You three to the scullery now, please, so the adults can have our tea… Sarah, you may lay the food now please."

Sal dutifully complied, all the time her personal fear that she was guilty of something terrible, that she would be found out, hanging over her. Half nervous, half elated.

The following day, the solemn procession for Sunday mass made its way from George Street south to the river and St

Andrews. Bridget was flanked on either side by her youngest sons, James walking just behind, and Sal held Annie's hand with Katie and Jeanie walking either side. Sal was still lost in her guilt, which had not been of her design or intention, but was leaving her uncomfortable; her only too vocal little sister next to her. Peter was notably absent, as he had been for a number of years, an issue which Bridget had no desire to confront, or explain with her children; it was an accepted state of affairs.

The attendance at mass was not voluntary for the McBride offspring, it was absolutely necessary; not only was Bridget a devout Catholic and cared deeply for the eternal souls of her children, but it was a social gathering of those of the faith, a chance for family to eye family to view their social progress. Bridget's family had been from the earlier wave of Irish immigration and, due in most part to her own determination, they were rising quickly; now with the recent influx of jobless, starving Irish, many were not so fortunate, hence the Gallowgate had become such a run-down part of the City infamous for the vice and crime which seemed to pervade every door and alley way - yet only ten years previously the family had been as much part of the Gallowgate as any other Irish family. The further you lived away from here seemed to chart your family's rise in social stature in Glasgow at that time; it even affected how close to the pulpit you sat in the Cathedral; the McBrides were now halfway from the front.

After the passing of social niceties, the family were seated and reciting their catechism as one. Annie had to be corrected once or twice to keep very still and very quiet, she knew that this was a place where she could not talk and had felt severe reprimands previously when she had, however, the rhythm and incantations of the mass were very musical in tone to a small child and soothing. She tried to copy her sisters and mouth the words, even Katie knew the mass by rote, but Annie was struggling with the unfamiliar Latin and it would take another year or so before she too would be word perfect.

Sal longed for the mass to end, she wanted to be outside in the fresh air; the smell of incense was pervading her nostrils and making her feel sick. She felt uncomfortable, as if eyes were boring into the back of her head. She turned round. An old lady sat behind her, her eyes were tightly shut, it could not be her. Sal turned to the front, conscious that her mother had noticed her fidgeting and was looking sternly at her from the left hand side of the pew. Still she felt under scrutiny, but did not dare turn round again and risk the wrath of her mother. She began to daydream. As her mother was helping father again today, it would be just an evening meal, so that meant that Sal could go spend a little time dawdling the back roads around the cathedral, where a few enterprising traders (not of the faith) kept stalls for the passing after-mass throng. This definitely would not be approved of, and so discretion was best and she was expected to return home promptly to cook.

At moments like this, she felt surges of resentment for those sitting slightly further to the front, such as the Lynch family who had their servant sitting with them. They did not expect their eldest daughter to do everything, they had it done for them. It was not as if her father could not afford a servant: he was making as much money, if not more than Mr Lynch who was a provisions merchant. Being so much older than her sisters all of the workload seemed to fall on her shoulders, the best she could hope for was marriage as a means of escape, but she knew that would just mean the same, more work, more drudgery. She wished she had the mettle to confront her parents and put her case for help, but she knew the reply would just involve mockery: 'why should they?', 'she hadn't got that much to do', 'Jeanie and Katie were doing more everyday'. It was best to say nothing, just enjoy the moments of freedom she could get, while she could get them and not wish her life away for more work and a loveless marriage.

The relief was palpable as she stepped down the steps of the cathedral into the sunshine of the spring morning. Annie was fit to burst, having bottled her natural enthusiasm up for such a long time, and everything was coming out in a complete rush.

"Are we going shopping now, Sal? Are we going to the market? Are we buying some tea? Is Mama coming? Where is James?.." The questions were coming so fast that Sal had given up trying to answer each one individually, she just said yes to everything and ignored those questions that required more specific explanations.

Her mother and brothers had waited to talk to the priest before leaving, and she had made her excuses of how much she had to do and she left with her sisters. Jeanie and Katie walked perfectly behind their elder sister, who had the hard work of Annie to deal with. She ambled into the backstreets near the St Andrews, following the slow process of Irish folk tarrying at the stalls they passed. Although this was not the grand enterprise of the Barras (Paddy's market as it was known because it was mainly Irish immigrants who had established it and consequently were the customers) it was still a social opportunity, an extension of the morning's gathering in their various places of worship, a chance for relaxing without the restrictions; it allowed for rowdiness and raucous behaviours after the pent-up observance of the morning.

All the time as she followed the stream steadily making its way north and east, she felt that same feeling of surveillance and scrutiny; she was not sure why, but she had a suspicion that she may know the culprit; she was not going to turn to look to confirm her suspicions. Eventually she faced number 10 once more, Annie Theresa in full voice, Jeanie and Katie looking tired; Sal made her way to her kitchen scullery, the excitement of the previous afternoon had faded like the sun in the grey sky, she just had her mundane tasks and mundane existence to look forward too.

Sal went to work on Monday and Tuesday and both days passed uneventfully, she had begun to relax. Nellie had made some comment about John's attentiveness on the Saturday last, but Sal dismissed it all as a non-event. It was on the Wednesday evening, when Sal had laid out the meal and taken her place that her stern, normally very silent father, made a comment that would set her course.

"You have been seen consorting with a young man... is this true, young lady?"

Sal was completely taken aback and speechless, even Bridget had no knowledge of what her husband was claiming and sat with her mouth agape. All others sat with their eyes downwards in uncomfortable silence all except Annie, that was, who suddenly remembered her introduction.

"John Flynn, John Flynn, John Flynn..." she repeated over and over, like small children do, almost singing his name. Bridget's hand came down hard on the table.

"Enough, Annie Theresa!" Annie gulped and hushed immediately.

Bridget started at Sal.

"Well, girl?... Your father has asked you a question, what have you to say for yourself?"

Sal was caught not knowing what to do, she felt guilty though of what she was not sure, she had not done anything.

She stuttered and tried to pull a suitable reply together for her parents whose facial expressions were like thunder.

"I... I... I... don... don't... know what you mean? I mean I met Nellie in the market, an... and her friend came by... and helped us while we did the buying... I haven't been seeing any young man... I wouldn't." She looked at both of them as appealingly as she could. Peter continued with his stern expression, and Bridget broke the silence.

"If that is all, then why do others say that you have been cavorting... now we want the truth, my girl... you must not lie to us!"

"Honestly mother... I am not lying... his name is John Flynn..."

Her mother made a hasty interruption.

"Not the boot-maker's family from the Gallowgate?"

"I believe so mother, but they are very nice people... I mean he is a very nice... well-mannered person. He is acquainted socially with Nell, and we bumped into him in the market, and all he did was help me with the parcels... that was all."

Bridget looked at her husband who nodded 'very well' and proceeded to eat the now tepid food, a signal to his assembled family to start, but Bridget's hand came up and all stopped again.

"We will take you at your word, young lady... but let me make this perfectly clear, if you meet someone, and if we approve, we are to be fully consulted before you start courting... have I made myself clear?"

Sal mumbled a downtrodden, "Yes," and stared in abject misery at her plate. This was 1901, not 1880; her brothers could laugh and have fun, talk to girls, go anywhere, see anyone. Even Nell had more freedom, she had to be careful for her reputation, but she could pass the time of day with a young man if she so chose and not become the subject of a family inquisition. After all, she was not even sure if she liked him, he was very nice, but she had not dreamt of going against her parents, well… until she had been told that she must not do this that and the other.

As soon as the meal had been consumed, Sal, her mother and the girls had cleared all to the scullery and washed up in silence. Sal took her sisters up to bed to settle them. Annie went to sleep immediately, but Jeanie and Katie were not as weary and very concerned for the plight of their older sister. The normally mousey-quiet Katie who would not say 'boo' to a goose was quite forceful.

"Well, I think that John is very nice… and I don't care what Mama says… I like him!"

Jeanie chimed in so as not to be left out, "So do I!"

Sal passed a very fitful night. Her dreams were full of illicit meetings with a young man and a piece of brisket and a beating from her mother with the stick she used to use when Sal was small. She did not speak of it again to anyone, and went through the following Sunday's mass, shrinking as low as she could in the pew so as to attract minimal attention; unfortunately her mother was keeping her under tight surveillance sitting next to her, and did not approve of her slouching and kept poking her to sit upright. The whole family processed back, there was no dawdling around the stalls today, or the following Sunday, despite Nell's persistent requests to the contrary.

The following Tuesday the two girls left work early evening and were making their way down Cowcaddens when a tall figure stepped out of a doorway.

"Good evening ladies," John announced, looking at Nell and smiling while she returned his smile and greeting.

"It is lovely to see you Miss McBride, I have missed you at the market."

Sal found herself struggling for words again, and was very conscious of all the onlookers, all the possible spies which was making her even more nervous.

"I... err... I... err... don't go very often... I mean I dinna need to go that often... my brother James is a grocer... I mean."

"Still it would be nice to pass the time of day, don't you think... together... a walk perhaps?"

"No, I don't think... and if you really don't mind, I have to go." And with that she strode on, leaving Nell to make apologies and catch her up.

Nellie was somewhat surprised by her normally mild-mannered friend's display of rudeness and quizzed Sal extensively on why she behaved like that. Sal was very emotional as she recounted what had occurred the fortnight before at supper, and she complained bitterly about her parents' draconian attitudes, but that she feared strong sanctions if she were seen again, even if it were innocent. She also told Nellie how used she had been feeling and how she wished she could just be her own person sometimes, or a little girl like Annie with no cares or responsibilities. Having confided all in her friend, Sal felt an enormous sense of relief, which raised her spirits immensely; Nellie, having listened attentively, wished Sal well till the next day.

Another week passed and a rather strange occurrence at work late one afternoon caused the normal pattern of Sal's day to change dramatically. While operating a spinner, Nellie – normally so careful – had managed to trap her fingers in the belt, leaving her with a very swollen hand and unable to help for the rest of the day. It was suggested that as she felt faint, that Sal should accompany her home, but rather than turning left out of the gates as they always did, Nellie beckoned Sal to follow her to the right and to the rear of the factory three or four streets away, where who should be waiting but John Flynn. Sal could see him waiting and asked Nellie to explain herself, realising that the whole accident had been staged as a rouse for a secret assignation.

"Please dinna be angry, Sal... the poor boy begged me... and he was sad... and you have had all these problems. I have explained to him about yer folks... he does ken you have to be careful... respectfully like... but please just hear the poor lad out... I cannae hae you both greetin' the way you are... and bugger me, my fingers are hurtin', what a friend I am to you."

Sal walked on up the street to John, who stood hopefully waiting.

"You have a real friend there, I hope you know that, lassie?"

"Yes I know... and a very stupid one... well, I think you had better explain yourself..."

"Sal... I like you... I mean, I have liked you for a long time... I have watched out for you but you have never noticed... you are always with your mother and family... and Nellie has explained... so I realise how difficult... how particular they are. Sal, I would like to go a-courting with you if you want to? I know this has to be done right and I will make sure I do this all the right way... but... but... I mean I don't want to do this unless you really want to... so, Sal, will you walk out with me?"

Sal looked into the two deep pools of blue that stared down at her like a love-sick puppy. He was even wearing his 'Sunday best' again, she thought, just to wait on a street corner, just in case she might say yes to walking out with him, she could have said no. Then there was poor Nellie with some very sore fingers, the subterfuge which she had gone to engineer this meeting, to match-make between her friend and the young man that she was actually sweet on. And then there was her mother and father, immediately disapproving and they had not even met him, or given him a chance... that was it... that made her mind up...

"Yes John Flynn, I will walk out with you."

Chapter 3 –

Making Time

Sal knew that the first thing to be done was to attempt to broach the subject with her parents, her mother at least. For a few days she made several valiant attempts to talk to Bridget, but each time her courage failed her as her mother did not seem in a particularly receptive mood. Sal had reached the end of her tether and was very close to giving up; Bridget must have detect the unsettled mood of her daughter, for that evening while they were clearing to the scullery she confronted Sal.

"Well, girl, spit it out… what have you been trying to say for the last few days?"

Sal was caught by surprise and very unprepared, but this was probably for the best as all she could do was to say what it was without dressing it up.

"I have been asked to walk out with someone… and I want to… and you already know who he is… it's John Flynn, the boot-maker's son."

"Of the Gallowgate?" Bridget looked sternly at her daughter. Sal lowered her eyes and nodded her head, knowing that she was going to get a negative response to her request.

"Your father and I have worked very hard to get this family where we are now, and you want to walk out with a Irishman from the Gallowgate?"

Sal continued looking downward, feeling her mother's reprimand singeing her hair.

"Is it not enough that we have placed a good roof over your head and opened up a world of opportunities to you? You could do so much better for yourself… you're bright and intelligent, and very well presented…"

Sal felt her temper rise and this time she was unable to contain her anger.

"What opportunities?… If I am not working my fingers to the bone in factory, I am here caring for the wee ones and cooking… I have to ask permission to go out to the market, whereas other girls my age have the freedom to come and go…"

Bridget interrupted. "Other girls have the reputations that come with loose rules, and loose morals, and loose living! That is not what we want for our daughter!"

"Yes mother… and which beau am I going to meet who is so suitable while I am chained to the scullery… you treat me like an unpaid servant, and that is all I am seen as, do you really think that any man from the class you find suitable is going to court a maid?"

Sal's last rebuke stunned Bridget into silence, not something that would happen many times in her life. For the first time, Bridget became aware of how much her daughter despised her lowly position and how little she felt of value to her family. But Bridget was not one to make rash decisions in the heat of the moment; she gathered her black Victorian skirts and headed out of the scullery away from her daughter.

Sal felt drained and nervous, she had never spoken to her mother in such a disrespectful tone, she would not have dared too. A few years before she would have received a caning from her mother for much more minor indiscretions, but all of sudden she could no longer contain herself from exploding like a bottle of soda water. It had brought an enormous sense of relief to her, as if this release of tensions and emotions had had to come out for the good of her own health, but she also felt remorse for seeming so ungrateful. She knew that if it were not for the hard work and good aspirations of her parents she could be living a very different life in the Gallowgate, with the lice, fleas and rats. Their rules, their diligence had got the family where they were now and would no doubt get them on further. Sal's only real misfortune was to be born the eldest daughter, with too many years between her and her next female sibling, leaving most of the toil on her shoulders.

Sal passed a fitful night and an uncomfortable silence at breakfast. She felt tense and nervous while she worked that day and was unable to reveal to Nellie why; she felt that it would be an act of betrayal, she wasn't sure who to, but confiding was not the right thing to do. She came home to George Street to take on her responsibilities to find the girls in somewhat of a silent mood in the back parlour; even Annie had little to say for herself. She gave them their tea while making preparations for the family meal, and it was then that her mother made her appearance.

Bridget slipped into the kitchen without acknowledging her younger daughters who sat quietly at the table eating.

"Your father and I have discussed your request... I must say now that neither of us are happy at the prospect... but we must not let our prejudice colour our judgement, after all we were the poor Irish from that Gallowgate once, and we worked our way out of it... what does he do?"

"He… he works on the railway…"

"Is he a ticket collector like Mr Dolan upstairs, or a shunter like Mr Morris?" There was a note of hopeful enthusiasm in Bridget's voice. Sal knew the answer would not be well met.

"Neither…"

"Oh."

"No, he is a labourer at the moment… but he has prospects…"

"Oh…" Bridget remained thoughtful and measured with her reply.

"Well, at least he is a Catholic… He is a Catholic is he not?…" A note of genuine concern.

"Oh yes… he attends St Andrews for mass every Sunday."

"Good. That gives me an opportunity to be introduced, and to make this a more formal arrangement. But you are to conduct yourself with absolute decorum, just in case you make a decision not to pursue this friendship further, then at least your reputation will still be intact. I want no disreputable behaviour, remember it is not just you that will be affected, you have your wee sisters to think of too…" Bridget made her move to leave and then, "By the way… we have decided that if and when the time arises, and if the girls are still too wee, that we will get some help in the house." With that, and without a chance to reply or thank her, Sal found herself alone as her mother left the kitchen. Sal smiled to herself, not quite believing her good fortune, her parents had actually agreed to her walking out with a young man, a young man she found very acceptable. But she knew that while she remained under their roof that they had made it very clear that she was still to skivvy as required; her father was determined not to part with his money foolishly, not when he had four daughters and wife.

Sunday brought about a very staid meeting of Bridget and John at the end of mass. Bridget looked him up and down as if choosing a horse in the Curragh market, she eyed him carefully, weighing up his appearance in an effort to judge his character. John felt distinctly uncomfortable by this silent scrutiny, a normally tall and confident young man had been reduced by the clinical stares from this diminutive woman. He tried to break the tension.

"Good day Mrs McBride, I am John Flynn."

Bridget fixed his gaze with her piercing eyes, and held him fast to the spot. "Well, Mr Flynn, I believe that you want to walk out with my daughter?"

"Yes ma'am, I wish to make a serious commitment towards Sarah, if she will have me?"

"Indeed... Mr McBride and I have discussed the matter and have given it great thought... just because your family live in lesser circumstances is not a reason to discount your worthiness... I am sure you are a hard worker?..."

"Yes ma'am. I intend to get on, just as Mr McBride has."

"There will be strict rules laid down, our daughter will retain her good character and be able to hold her head high, if this does not continue... do you understand me, Mr Flynn?"

"Certainly I do Mrs McBride, I can assure you I only have honourable intentions towards Sarah, and whatever conditions are placed on our meetings I will abide by them... ma'am..."

Bridget studied him closely once more, and paused for reflection. Sarah had stood by, willing her mother on, Annie had started to mither.

"Can we go now, Sal? I want to go hame now, Sal..."

Bridget was resolved. "Next Sunday afternoon at two o'clock... I will want my daughter home by half past four...

make sure that she is not late." She swept past him, barely acknowledging his grateful 'thank you's. Sal smiled broadly as she hurried past him, chasing her mother, with all of her sisters in tow.

The following week neither hurried nor dragged for Sal. She was not in love with John Flynn, she barely knew him; she was more determined to gain her freedom which she so desperately needed. Walking out with John was granting her that freedom, she was able to do the things that many other girls did without permission being required from their parents. It was not that she had fallen for him, or thought of him as her ideal husband; she really did not know what to think. He was very personable and reasonably good looking, but she knew no more than that. There was no school girl excitement building inside her, she did not feel the romance of the situation, just the excitement of doing something different with her life, a brightening of her existence.

Sunday came again. She felt that now familiar sensation of eyes that watched her from close by, his eyes. It was not an unpleasant experience, in fact she was feeling very flattered that someone, a young man, should be paying her that much careful attention. As she rose to leave with her family, she caught his eye; he was sitting six pews behind her, he smiled at her and winked. She was slightly taken back by this over-familiarity initially, she felt herself colouring up and then she smiled back quickly before returning her eyes forward to leave the cathedral. All the way back to George Street she smiled discreetly as she thought of that cheeky, very forward wink; maybe this afternoon was going to be better than she had expected.

But her joyful enthusiasm was to be short lived. After a more hurried than normal Sunday lunch, Sal was summoned into the back parlour by her mother and while the whole of her family looked on, Bridget proceeded to issue her daughter with a series of instructions as to her expected conduct for that afternoon.

"I don't want to hear from anyone that you were seen to be too familiar with this young man, I draw the line at you walking down the street holding hands, or even sitting holding hands. You are not to be heard to shout like a fishwife, you are to behave in an impeccable manner. You are to stay publically visible at all times, not scooting off down the side alleys or into the wooded areas on Glasgow Green. It is not just your reputation now and in the future that you have to consider, it is the reputation of the whole of this family, your sisters would be affected by any inappropriate behaviour on your part, as would your father's business…"

Peter nodded from the end of the table with his typical stern stare and a, "Quite right." Sal was feeling the whole weight of her future indiscretions, none of which she planned or dreamed of making; she was a Catholic girl, always feeling a sense of guilt even when there was none to feel. All the time, Hugh and Peter sat and grinned at her, making her feel very annoyed that they should be witness to – and party to – her public humiliation. Her mother offered her final coup de grace.

"In my day you were chaperoned when you went out with a young man, although your father and I were not fortunate enough to come from that sort of society…"

Sal began to curl her toes in her boots in horror, her knuckles turned white behind her back as she clenched her fists so tightly; *oh please no*, she thought to herself, not her mother walking out with them.

"I realise you modern girls do not need that sort of embarrassment, so we will employ the same method my mother used with me..." From the small occasional table that was next to her and hidden by her voluminous black skirt, Bridget revealed two knitting needles and a cable needle with some dark plum coloured wool. She had appeared to have started something which Sal could barely make out from where she stood.

"Here..." Her mother handed her the bundle triumphantly, as if she had achieved some major victory in preserving common decency for the McBride clan.

"I have started it for you myself..."

Sal stared in stunned confusion at the bundle of pins and wool that she now clutched in her right hand.

"It's a sock! You are to knit six rows every hour that you meet with your young man..." Bridget beamed in her cleverness. There was a collective intake of breath from each that sat at the table except Mr McBride senior, who was obviously party to the hatched plan that Sal's mother had just unleashed to her. Sal's mouth was agape; she did not know what to do, she would be the object of ridicule from all that saw her, never mind what John Flynn would say. She had no desire to walk out with him, she had no desire to walk out with anyone, not if it meant such a shaming. Bridget sensed her daughter was not fully committed to the idea, and interjected before Sal had a chance to respond.

"How much of this freedom do you want my girl?... At least you will be able to demonstrate a more suitable skill that those demonstrated by other more immoral girls of your generation... he will be able to see how clever you are at making a home."

Silenced gripped the room, the tension was palpable. Sal was close to tears. James felt pity for his younger sister's plight and tried to raise her spirits.

"Sal it is just a sock, I would be proud to go out with such an industrious young lady, I am sure John will feel the same."

Sal stared at the alien article in her hand. She knew it was pointless to protest, she would find herself having to knit nine, or even, twelve rows if she did. James was right: it was just a sock, and six rows in an hour was very little, if they sat somewhere for half an hour she would have all, six… twelve… fifteen done, yes that was right, fifteen. Two and half hours, that was fifteen rows; that was probably more than she needed to do, but she would show her mother that she was not going to be put off, for she knew in her heart that was why this task had been imposed on her, if she was not determined to pursue her relationship – for Sal, her freedom – she would not subject herself to such a humiliation. But Bridget had misread Sal's tenacity to have some life that did not exist around the kitchen and scullery of George Street.

At five minutes to two, she was waiting in the front parlour with her father and mother; they were all seated. Sal had already donned her hat and coat and sat with a small carpet bag concealing the offending knitting inside. How was she going to broach this subject with him? What was she going to say? But she need not have worried about the details, her mother's planned humiliation was to be played in two acts; the second act commenced when John was shown into the parlour by James. He looked terrified as Peter looked at him, without any change of expression or acknowledgement on his face, remaining seated to enforce his seniority.

"Good day Mr and Mrs McBride, good day Sal." He summoned up all of the courage he could to force his greetings out. Sal looked at her knees in embarrassed silence. Peter's expressions remained unchanged, Bridget smiled unnervingly.

"Good day Mr Flynn, punctual I see. Make sure you are as punctual when you return our daughter to us, half past four remember?..."

"Yes ma'am."

"And just so neither of you has the need to find distractions other than talking..."

Sal froze in the seat, realising her mother was taking this opportunity to cause her further embarrassment.

"... She has a wee task to do, to keep her occupied... mind that she does what is required please? Otherwise she will not be walking out with you again..."

Sal was mortified, she just wanted the seat to swallow her up, to wake up and realise that she was in some gruesome nightmare and that it was Sunday morning before mass, but alas it was all too real.

"... Away you go lass... and mind you do as you have been told." With that, Bridget and Peter stood in unison. With that signal Sal and John were dismissed and left, Sal wondering exactly what he would say or do. Would he laugh at her? Would he walk away and be too embarrassed to be with her? John was wondering just what little task could possibly be concealed in a carpet bag? And what was the nature of this task? He was not a little curious; in fact, he was quite intrigued. They walked in silence towards the Green.

Glasgow Green was where all Glaswegians headed for on their day of rest; all, that was, except Sal's family, who were not allowed to indulge in such unseemly activities as a family day out. It was a central area of semi-rural bliss just on the North bank of the Clyde as it bends its knee towards the east. It was land that was given to the city, and the oldest park. Everybody would congregate there whatever the weather, and it was invariably dreich and dreary, but that never seemed to dampen the enthusiasm to take in the fresher air. There were meandering paths where one could wander, or park side benches to sit and pass the time of day. Occasionally, there was an event or market, the circus arriving or the Glasgow Fair, but even if it was just a Sunday afternoon stroll, that could have a surprisingly good effect on the spirits of facing another working week in the city.

Neither knew quite what to say to the other, it was a discomfort caused by uncertainty. Sal feared that when her beau knew of the old-fashioned methods that her mother had employed to keep her reputation intact, that he would either subject her to humiliation or that this would be their first and last meeting. Maybe that was her mother's strategy all along, she thought, maybe she was testing the strength of his resolve and having already got his measure at mass, Bridget had decided this was the easiest way to see him off. John was secretly terrified; it had taken considerable courage and some very creative strategy to get to this moment. This moment; he could not believe his luck, she was the prettiest and the cleverest girl in Glasgow and in a league above and she was walking next to him. He worried that she did not want to be with him at all, that she was just tolerating him; she barely spoke to him normally and now she seemed cold and withdrawn, she had obviously had second thoughts since he had finally managed to engineer their meeting and steel himself to ask to court her. Just before they stepped into the Green he stopped in his tracks, which caused Sal to stop. He could no longer contain his curiosity, he had to know, he had to save them both from further embarrassment.

"Sal... I realise that you may have changed your mind... I will understand if you have had second thoughts... I mean it is not as if there is anything between us at the moment...

so if you want to go back, we can… I mean I will take you home… if that's what you want…"

Sal was still in a state of shock from all that her mother had imposed on her just before leaving home; now she was suddenly confounded by John's admission. Fear overcame her, he thought she did not want to be with him; he had no idea that her silence was not caused by him, but the bundle she carried. She did not know him, but she did like him, he was a nice young man, and it was her sense of true freedom, she must do something to rectify his misunderstanding of her manner.

"No… I mean, no I don't… I don't want to go back I mean… It's not you, it's my mother… I mean it's this…" She held up the bag open to John; he peered inside, not a little confused by what he saw there.

"A bundle of knitting? Why?" He looked at her, puzzled, waiting for her explanation. It all came out in a garbled rush: her mother's particular nature, her feelings regarding reputations, the strict home life that she had.

"… and I must do fifteen rows before I go back or she will think I have behaved disreputably."

John stood amazed and silent, then a smile broadened across his face, then he grinned as the smile grew wider, then he burst into fits of laughter. Sal was offended and annoyed.

"Well, thank you! I knew you would laugh, I knew you would make fun of me… it's not my fault!" She spun on her heels to leave for the route home. John managed to contain himself and grab her arm all in a split second.

"No… sorry, I am not laughing at you… honestly… I am laughing at the situation… I thought you had second thoughts and changed your mind… I had no idea you were worried about your knitting… Look, there is a bench over there…" He manoeuvred her gently but firmly towards the bench; he was not going to let her go again.

"How fast can you knit?... Come on, you had better get those rows knitted so we can talk and walk later."

Sal smiled; this was not going to be a bad day after all, in fact it looked like she was going to enjoy the rest of the afternoon, despite everything that had conspired against her. She got out the bundle, arranged the pins and the wool. Soon she was clicking away, while they chatted and passed the time; every now and then they laughed as they watched the sock begin to grow.

Chapter 4 –

The Planting of the Seeds

As time went on, John and Sarah had regular outings; much to the chagrin of Bridget, it seemed all of her clever machinations to scupper the relationship had come to nought. Sal's feelings for John grew as the sock grew, she found him charming and funny and very intelligent; he obviously had much more about him then she would have ever suspected by just looking at him. The characteristic that most drew her to him was his determination. It was a trait that she knew well in her mother, and she presumed her father, though she was never close enough to her father to know his level of tenacity to succeed. Many a time John would reveal his future plans to her, he had one dream which he held most dear in his heart.

"Sal... one day I am going to make things grow... just like my grandfather and his father before... I am going to kick up the dust of the city and find some green fields in the shelter of a valley... and I am going to plant seeds and grow things... not just potatoes, I am not like the failing Irish... no, grow all sorts of vegetables and things that people want... I will keep some cows and sheep and hens... and then I will take it all to market and make money from all my hard work and then do it all again… I don't think there is anything more satisfying or fulfilling in the world."

Whenever he spoke in such a way Sal would see the glint in his eyes, as he seemed to smile from the inside out with happiness; it was an idea that he really wanted, a dream that he was going to make happen come what may, and she felt that drive and determination exude from every pore of his skin, every cell of his being. She knew he was going to do it and she felt proud that she was with such a young man, that he wanted to spend time with her so much. Gradually, that pride turned to a deep affection and she took comfort in his company. The sock soon became a stocking, and the aubergine coloured wool had long since run out; a thicker gunmetal grey had been joined on. Bridget knew that it was no longer possible to ignore the direction that this relationship was taking, and that the two young people had been together too long to allow them to discontinue; it was now time to make a public display that this was an accepted state of affairs and John Flynn was the 'intended' of her daughter Sarah. John was encouraged to call often, rather than the knitting walks. These visits were often quite uncomfortable as initially they took place in the controlled atmosphere of the front parlour with both parents as silent spectators. After a while, and with some encouragement from James, John was welcomed into the more informal setting of the back parlour, where he could chat with James and the younger brothers, while Annie nagged him constantly.

The more he called the more he was noticed by others in the street, particularly the neighbours, and the lodgers who both worked for the rail too. They went from nodding terms, to greeting each other until one day Mr Morris mentioned that he knew of some better positions going at the railway and he would put a good word in for him. Although it was not John's ambition to work for the railway, he knew that it was a means to get on and it could also make his serious intentions towards Sal more acceptable to her parents, so he gratefully thanked Mr Morris for any assistance he could give.

After two years of courting, Sal had begun to accept that this sweet and dedicated young man was her way through life; she felt comfortable when she was with him, not swept off her feet in the frame of a Victorian melodrama, but comfortable. He was caring and considerate, he had a witty sense of humour, he was earnest in his intentions towards her, and she had no doubt that his feelings for her were deep and true. She considered that, as she had grown into the relationship, one day she would grow into that same depth of feeling, it would just take time, after all not everyone could feel the same powerful expressions of feeling for one another all at the same time, could they?

That was a question that had kept her awake on more than one night, and she worried that she might never feel as truly in love as some, but then she would reflect on her own parents' marriage. In her eyes there was no love lost there: how could her mother, so outgoing, so determined, love someone like her father, who was so conservative and uncommunicative? What had they possibly got in common? They had obviously just married out of a sense of needing to, there was no grand passion between them. Yes, Bridget had done her duty with producing a collection of living chil-dren, but that was because she was a good Catholic and it was expected of her by her priest. In Sal's naivety that was all she could possibly believe, and if her parents could com-mit to such a marriage of mere convenience – he for his supportive driven wife, her for the social standing that his hard work and determination had granted her – then surely Sal could marry John and it would be a much happier state of affairs, for at least there was some affection that passed between them; admittedly more from his direction towards her, but she considered that she would grow into that once they were married.

It was in a similar frame of mind that she had finally made a half-hearted acceptance of one of the many proposals that he had made in the last year of their courtship. She had never directly rejected him on any of the previous occasions, just politely ignored his entreaties by declining to answer either way. But having passed her nineteenth birthday in December of 1903 she was becoming acutely aware that she must make a commitment to him, as it was unlikely anyone else was going to sweep her off her feet, especially as she was known to be courting, and she had begun to feel too old to be a bride.

She was becoming tired of her work situation and Nellie had long since gone, having been asked by a second cousin who was a farmer in Bute to marry him. She had not taken a second thought, and had decided that it would be the best for her, having her own home and a good income, and he was a rather nice man; a little round and chubby, but the two were well suited. Sal had found herself one of the older girls in the factory now, as most would leave before they were eighteen for the marriage market. She did not live near any of the others and was considered stuck-up because of her George Street address. At home life had changed little, apart from her sisters Katie and Jeanie taking a greater share of work; Bridget was insisting that her other daughters did more as she was acutely aware that Sal would be gone soon. Even little Annie was doing her bit in the scullery, cheerfully chatting away as she undertook every task, if a little clumsily. Bridget's daily admonishment of her youngest daughter could be heard echoing around the parlour.

"Goodness gracious Annie Theresa, keep your mind on what you are doing girl... that's the third thing you have dropped today... less chattering, more working please!"

When John had asked her again in January while she was quietly reading in the back parlour, quite expecting her reaction of polite ignorance yet again, he was quite surprised when she replied: "I think I will." And then she returned to her reading.

John was delighted that she had finally agreed, and found it very difficult to contain his initial excitement; Sal carried on in a nonchalant manner, but smiled discreetly at his boyish enthusiasm. However, it dawned on him quite quickly that he now had a much more challenging situation to deal with and a far more difficult conversation to have. He knew he now had to approach Peter formally. Despite John's affability and good humour, he had never been able to cross that cavern of space between himself and Sal's father. Peter barely spoke to John; mind you he barely spoke to anyone in his family, and he had never shown any warmth towards his daughter's prospective husband. John thought it was best to approach Sal's mother in the first instance, for her to arrange an opportunity; that had been a daunting discussion to have.

Bridget was quite abrasive when John had finally summoned up his nerve to seek her assistance. She was preoccupied and busy with other things, her lack of patience being made apparent in her shortness towards him.

"I have other things to do, lad... can this wait?"

He was suddenly struck dumb; he did not want to jeopardise his chances by not eliciting her support at this time, what did he do?

"Well, speak up, John, I must get on!"

He bit the bullet, if the worst came to the worst, he would have to wait, he knew that; and he would rather wait for Sal a few more years than face running the gauntlet of Peter McBride.

"I want to marry Sarah... I would like to speak to her father."

"You have taken your time, we were beginning to think that you would never ask." Bridget's tone was quite cheerful, something that he had not expected.

"And you want me to smooth the waters so that you can ask her father?"

"... Err... yes... yes, if you would not mind."

"Well, he is the front parlour now... let's ask now..."

John panicked; he had thought at least a day or so, or a week.

"Er... I don't want to disturb him on a Sunday... I can wait, it is no trouble..."

His pleas for a reprieve were falling on deaf ears. Despite her diminutive size compared to his vastness, Bridget has successfully cornered him in the hallway like a sheep dog working her flock; she skilfully circled him round and had ushered him into the front parlour, where a somewhat taken aback Peter sat, having been disturbed by this untimely and unannounced intrusion into his quiet Sunday pastimes. He dropped his spectacles into his paper on his lap and looked sternly at his wife.

"Mr McBride, John would like a word with you." Bridget gave John an encouraging shove further into the centre of the room. Peter's blue eyes fixed John to the spot; he did not have to say anything, his look spoke loudly. This young man had dared to disturb his quiet enterprise which he valued greatly, he had better have something very important to say. John swallowed hard, his throat was dry; he feared that when he opened his mouth that no sound would come out, rendering his attempt to appear to be a strong suitor for Sal invalid. He felt his heart hammering in his chest, he hoped that neither of his prospective in-laws could hear it, or indeed smell his fear. He felt like a prey animal having accidently strayed into a wolves' lair and waiting for the inevitable gruesome ending.

"Mr McBride… you know that I am very fond of your daughter… I am very fond of Sarah… and I have made improvements to my employment. I am working as a shunter now… I know that is not the best but I am a hard worker… I have plans… I would like to farm one day… or I will turn my hand to anything. I am sure I can look after Sal… sorry Sarah… and I intend to be a good husband and one day a good father… that's if of course… you would give your consent to our marrying?"

John waited for the inquisition to follow, he knew he would be dissected in finite detail by Mr McBride senior; he was known for running his business transactions with the exact same precision. He tried to think of all of the possibly responses to what questions may come in a split second, well aware he was not prepared for any. Peter continued with his stern stare. He picked up his spectacles and cast his face downwards while placing the spectacles on his nose, and in the same nonchalant manner that his daughter had displayed less than an hour previously, grunted, "Agreed," while returning to his reading. John was caught out for a second time, not sure what to do; whether to shake him by the hand, or whoop for joy or just say thank you. He stood hopping from one foot to the other in the centre of the room. He thought that he had better add hastily, "Of course, I would like to marry Sarah this summer?"

Peter did not look up, simply nodded. Bridget had already taken the cue to usher her prospective son-in-law out of the room and was busying herself in that pursuit while uttering, "We shall sort out these details in good time."

John was elated as he walked towards his parents' home in Gallowgate to break the good news to his father and mother, who being simple souls were ecstatic in their celebrations, and his younger brother and sisters and friends joined in the makeshift party that assembled that evening. He was in a fog of elations as he left for his digs, how opposite the reactions had been of the two families; his parents so joyful and excited, her parents so restricted and contained. What worried him more was Sarah's reticence, he had hoped at least for a hug or even a smile, but she had barely acknowledged his proposal and had seemed almost to have dismissed it all after he had returned victorious from the spontaneously arranged interview in the wolves' lair. Maybe it was just her way of teasing him, he thought, as he rounded another darkened corner shivering against the cold; maybe she would get excited and start to plan their lives together, the way he had been dreaming.

From time to time over the ensuing months, Sal would have her moments when they would discuss their future and John would try to inspire her with talk of their farm. They would have a pretty little house with a little kitchen which was always warm, and she could bring their bairns up while he worked the land, and sold his crops and livestock at the market. Sal would get very animated with the thought of her own kitchen and the prospect of being responsible for her own life, she had every confidence that John would do all that he said and much more; she felt a greater reliance on him, and she knew that once they were married their lives would change so much for the better. She would be able to face her mother as her equal and not as a subordinate daughter, and she would have to come into *her* house and sit at *her* table, in *her* kitchen. Yes, life would be complete and perfect.

When he told her one evening that he loved her, she was a little reluctant to reply; she did not know what love was, but it must be this safe comfort that she was feeling when she was with him, it must be the way he could make her laugh, that must be what love was. She decided that she had kept him at an emotional distance for long enough, so she replied in a matter-of-fact tone that she loved him too. John was content with this, he put her dismissive tone down to girlish shyness and he felt that he would be able to win a more passionate response from her once they were married.

Which happened so soon! It only seemed like yesterday he had stumbled over his words to a stern-faced Peter in the front parlour of George Street. All of a sudden it was 6th July and he was standing at the altar of St Andrews marrying the girl he adored. She was looking beautiful in a blue woollen skirt suit with a white blouse, she carried a small posy of carnations in her hand, and the whole ensemble was crowned by a navy-blue felt hat and veil with a diamante hat pin. He had borrowed a dark suit probably used for funerals from one of the ticket collectors, who was a little shorter in the leg than he was, but it fitted well in the frame. His younger brother Thomas stood up for him that day, and all the little Flynn girls – Bridget thought that they were too numerous to count – sat giggling in the pews, next to their parents.

Bridget had actually smiled once or twice that morning and her younger daughters dressed up in their finery were cock-a-hoop at their elder sister's big day. Peter McBride remained stony silent; he had barely grunted greetings to John's father and mother, who were most proud of their son as he stood with his new wife on the steps of the cathedral afterwards, and even the sudden thunderstorm failed to dampen their spirits. As the younger members of the families who could indulge in a celebration sat in the back parlour chatting and feasting into the small hours of that evening, John took his young bride to their honeymoon suite, which had been the room that all the girls used; the others were temporarily situated in the front parlour for a few evenings until John and Sal would move to their lodgings. All seemed fresh and new, the pages of their lives had turned to a new chapter.

Chapter 5 –

Hard Cold Realities

Sal lay on the bed, gripped by another pain. The pain felt as though the whole of her body would explode, she was so exhausted; for hours and hours she had been wracked and contorted by vicious spasms. She just wished that it would all stop, just all go away, and how she wished she could just sleep.

Where had all the magic gone? Where had all those dreams and plans disappeared to? This was not the way it was supposed to be. After they were married it was meant be the start of a better time, the best of times? For hours and hours she had worked so hard, she had tried not to scream, but it was so difficult not to; this was the worst thing that she had ever felt in her life, and her mother had been so dismissive of her predicament.

"I have had thirteen children and I have never carried on like this! Sarah Flynn, you are not the first woman in the world to have a baby, you know!"

When her mother had said those words to her some four hours ago, it had made her angry, more determined, and as the wifey helped her the best she could, Sal had tried to breathe her way through each powerful contraction that had seemed to bisect her, like a butcher taking a meat cleaver to a carcass. Her mother had gone very quiet and had long since sent John to get the doctor; the doctor, she had insisted would not be needed because, "Sal is my daughter, and I practically delivered all my bairns myself, she'll manage."

But she was not managing, even Bridget had realised that this was now going on far too long, and Sal seemed far too tired to go much further; it was like she had given up and she had lost the energy to do any more. Bridget's manner had softened towards her daughter, she had fussed around for hot water, and intermittently mopped her daughter's pale and wan forehead and face; her eyes were rolling and a grateful, "Thank you Mama," would come every now and then, but all of her effort was gone.

Finally, a young doctor arrived and attended Sal directly. He left her to speak to Bridget out on the landing, Sal could barely make out the hushed voices in her almost delirious state.

"This is very serious Mrs McBride, the bairn is not progressing; it appears to be stuck, if I don't do something soon we could lose one or the other, or maybe both." His earnest expression evoked a sudden rush of genuine fear in Bridget.

"Surely you dinna' mean I could lose my daughter, doctor?... And the wee one?"

"Yes I am afraid I do madam, she has very little strength left, and it appears that her body is giving up the battle... I can barely hear the baby's heartbeat... I am going to try and extract the child... I think we are too late for a caesarean and it would be far too dangerous in these circumstances... if you had fetched me sooner?"

Bridget hung her head, only too aware it was her stupid pride and stubbornness that had brought her daughter and grandchild to harm; she had been determined for the last seven months that no interference or meddling was necessary and that is what she had continued to insist to her daughter.

"There is no need for hospital and doctors, women have been doing this forever… your body will know what to do when the time comes, you won't need any of those medicos getting in the way… it is not a man's place… it is women's work!"

The more Sal had spoken to other young mothers and neighbours, the more she had been concerned that her mother's entrenched attitudes may well be wrong. She had heard so many horror stories of how childbirth had gone wrong, and how visiting these hospitals was sometimes better, after all not all of her own mother's pregnancies had gone according to plan. But as ever, the will of Bridget McBride was all consuming and all powerful; despite Sal's plans to break free from her mother's influence, it had seemed that every knock she had suffered, that they had suffered, had caused her to be drawn back into her mother's web still tighter. John was weak when it came to his in-laws, he could have very little influence against a family that had intimidated him since the first day they had met. His parents were unable to get involved as it had been made very clear that Sal was not their daughter, and they had, "Far too many of their own to concern themselves with." John knew better than to protest, he had been wrong so often already; he had watched his young wife grow less and less dependent on him and turn more to her own kin. What could he do but watch?

That first night together nearly nine months ago was the closest that he had felt to her. When they had lain together that first time, and he taken to heart all that his father had told him: being gentle and tender, remembering he was so much bigger and stronger than she, and to take his time. He did try to remember all these things. The first awkward moments of climbing into a bed, when the house was erupting with noise and raised voices, and both feeling the cold through their night shirts dissipate as they lay close and chatted about the funnier moments of the day. Then he had reached for her with his left hand under the blankets, his hand had met calico, which he began to tug gently, pulling it up towards him. He reached over with his right hand to touch her.

He felt the softness of skin and downy hair, and he felt himself grow painfully hard; the more he felt, the more he needed. She had all of a sudden gone quiet and rigid, her muscles had tightened. His urges were overcoming him. He forced her maidenhead open with probing fingers, seeking the warmth and wetness; she was warm but not wet or even damp. He began to finger her, forcing her legs apart with the breadth of his strong hand, while at the same time twisting his body over hers, as he felt his penis, so painfully hard that it might burst, brush against the top of her thigh as he tried to force his body between her legs. Just for a second in the candlelight he caught her expression in his view, her eyes were screwed tightly shut and she had gritted her teeth, but that was no matter: he had something to do, something that had completely overtaken all of his sensibilities and sensitivities.

He had forced his right leg between hers and used his strength to widen the gap, while he lowered his body on to his elbow. His right hand still fumbled clumsily around her clitoris, he had managed to get two of his fingers inside her vagina, she felt dry but he had not got the time to worry; the pain that he felt from his throbbing member was nagging him to get on with it before it was too late. He probed with his penis towards his hand, and grabbing the hood with his thumb and forefinger, he began to force himself into where his fingers currently were.

He felt her turn to stone, still beneath him, and clench all of her muscles. He removed his fingers, all the time trying to force himself in. She was too dry and she was making noises of pain, but he had not got the time to worry, he was not inside her, he was only just in the neck of her vagina, he pushed, no good, he pushed again, a little further, God that felt good. He pushed again; she was tight, she was rigid, wincing in pain. He pushed, he had to get inside properly, but push, he felt himself overwhelmed and nauseous all at once, his head was spinning, his body exploding, his penis throbbed rhythmically.

He had released everything, his member throbbed just inside her and was spilling seed all over the inside of her thighs and the sheets and nightgowns; his legs had turned to jelly, he collapsed onto his elbows, his weight bearing down on her on the bed, she was still absolutely rigid, she had made no noise and very little reaction. He felt his penis growing flaccid and slipping out of her; he felt relieved but not completely satisfied. He rolled off her onto his back and lay there, slightly comatose with sudden drowsiness, his member lying cold and wet still throbbing against his leg. He pulled his gown over himself; he felt shame.

She lay there for what seemed like hours, listening to the heaviness of his breathing as he lay in a postcoital stupor. She felt sore, cold and uncomfortable. Sore from the vigorous rubbing and fumbling that had been employed. She was lying in total wetness, just as when Katie had wet the bed a couple of years ago in the night, and Sal had woken up in the coldness hours later. She did not want to move in case he woke, yet she just wanted to run away and scrub herself. It was not meant to be like this, not that she really knew what it was meant to be like; it was only ever stories that she had heard from nice girls.

These were the sort of girls who had learnt from their elder sisters, but had not yet gained their own knowledge because they would be virgins until the day they married.

Nellie had told her that it would be romantic and gentle, and that she would hear birds singing and all the best feelings in the world, as he had slipped himself inside her to make her a woman. He certainly had not slipped inside her, and she felt anything but joyous; she would be quite grateful if she never had to do that again. They had had such a nice day up until that point, she had felt closer to him, he was more in her heart than he had been, and she felt proud showing off her tall, good-looking husband as they had walked arm-in-arm back from the Cathedral. She had witnessed all those younger girls that she knew laughing and giggling coquettishly as John had passed them. Sal had not realised the effect that he had on other girls; well Nellie of course, but that was just Nellie. Now Sal could see that many of the young ladies found her man attractive, and she felt in control as she hooked his arm tightly with her own, and showed her ownership and marked territory. And during their meal at George Street, where twenty bodies had crammed themselves into the back parlour as two families mingled in celebration, for the last time as far as Bridget was concerned, Sal had felt grown up for the first time; even her father had smiled a little and passed the odd comment. She had admired John across the room and thought how lucky she was to be with him, but now she lay there, feeling very relieved that close association was all over.

All of a sudden Sal was brought back to consciousness; there was a young man leaning over her, she felt an enormous sensation of ripping and coldness. She tried to move her legs but she felt them gripped at the ankles by human hands, and she could just discern her mother's voice.

"There there, Sal, the doctor is going to help you get the wee one out... try not to cry."

Cry? Why? Owww! What is that?

She felt an ice cold metal contraception being forced inside her. The doctor was unaware that she was almost conscious.

"I can see the bairn's head, if I can just... get... this..."

She wanted to die; she was too tired to scream, too tired to cry, what was he doing? Why was this happening? She wished she had not been with John that night, she wished she had never met John at all. She had only been with him just that night, because it was so awful she had not wanted to do it ever again, despite him nagging at her insistently week after week.

And by September she was being violently sick every morning, living in awful digs; one room with rats and cockroaches, no fire, no water inside, only an unsanitary toilet in a shared yard. John had promised better, but every place that they had gone to find rooms, they could only get that standard on his wages, and she could not work because most were operating a marriage bar against married women. They had tried to rent rooms in someone's home like many had in George Street, but good families generally would not take newly-married couples, because that usually meant sex and babies under their roof. Sal had become totally miserable; she spent the days when she was not being sick every five minutes walking the streets even when it was excruciatingly cold. Anything was better than being in that awful room. It was on one of those strolls that she wandered into George Street to seek support.

As she entered the back parlour, the rush of warmth of the range in the kitchen met her, smothering her in familiarity; it was nice to be home. Her mother beckoned her to sit at the table, while dismissing the wee girls, who were very excited to see their elder sister, away to the scullery; this they did reluctantly, especially wee Annie, who had to be told more than twice to go. Bridget looked at her thin daughter, who was very skeletal; a combination of sickness and lack of food had wreaked havoc, her clothes were less than clean, and her general appearance had slipped.

"Being a wife is not such a fairy story, is it now?"

Sal looked down into her lap, she felt the hot moisture welling up in her eyes; she was so tired, she was so hungry, but she felt so sick and terrible.

"Mama, I am going to have a baby."

"Goodness gracious, could you not have waited, girl? I know you two are living in a terrible place, you could have least have waited until you had somewhere decent, think of the bairn."

Sal felt dreadfully unhappy, as if she had any control over her predicament? Her mother most realise surely that it was not her fault? She did not even like getting intimate, it had been a humiliating experience. A hot trickle burst down her cheek, one that Bridget's hawk eyes saw immediately.

"Don't start your greetin', you should have thought of this when you and him were getting silly and messing around without thinking about the consequences… well, it's too late now, you have the consequences inside you, now you will find out what being grown up's about… when is it due?"

"I don't know."

"What do you mean you don't know?… You know enough to judge… when was the last time you had to stop washing rags out?"

"In August."

Bridget's facial expression froze in anger.

"You bad girl! You could not wait until you married, could you? The shame of all this."

"No Mama, that is not true! I have only been with John once on our wedding night, I haven't done it before and I haven't done it since!"

Bridget was taken aback by Sal's honest outburst, a little too honest for Bridget's conservative nature, but then it dawned on her that Sal had been caught out and had not planned any of this.

"Just the once then?... Aye, that's all it takes... many a lassie has been caught exactly the same... well, there is no good crying over it, you've got to get on with it now, no one can do that for you... But I won't have my first grandchild coming into the world in such a terrible place! I am going to find you somewhere better. It is what your husband should be doing for you, if he could be bothered..."

Sal felt immediately defensive. "He would! He has been trying, but he does have to work!"

"Aye... that he has... still a shunter, is he?... Your father had already started his enterprises by the time we married... but he is a different sort of man. And James, look at him... well-established in retail, a lovely lass in his life and to marry next June. I know he won't be struggling to give her a good home and a good life, and she was just a servant too, so you could have found someone better, if you had nae' been so foolish and stubborn... No matter, it is more important that my grandchild comes into the world in a better place than the one you are in now."

But on this Bridget was not quite going to get her own way, for – fortunately for John – he had found better digs for his expectant young wife in David Street, just off the Gallowgate. It was not a palace, and it certainly was not what

Bridget wanted or expected, but it was as clean as it could be. An old couple, the Andersons, lived downstairs in this small terraced house, and there were two rooms upstairs. Sal could share the basic kitchen scullery, for which, although it did not have running water, the pump for the shared court was just outside the back door. The range was serviceable enough and old Mrs Anderson always kept a good supply of water simmering on top. From time to time, she would share the meagre broth that she would prepare daily for her and her husband with John and Sal, and Sal would return her hospitality by making a stew or some bread.

The two rooms that they rented were very basic and were ostensibly both bedrooms, but by moving the bed in the second room to the wall and adding two old armchairs that were found in a junk shop, the young couple had managed to model themselves a small sitting room, which at least gave Sal a warm escape to save her walking the streets. By the time she had reached Christmas her sickness had settled, and she had let her skirts out to accommodate her growing child inside her. She was also putting her innate needlecraft skills – probably inherited from her mother – to good use, and was busying herself with making simple baby gowns and bonnets, from whatever scraps of cloth that she could get from her parents; Peter was a businessman first and foremost and good cloth made him money, he was a little reluctant to give his profits away to his daughter, but was eventually persuaded by his ever-persistent wife. The bottom drawer of Sal's chest of drawers had been reserved as a makeshift cot, for the young infant once it arrived, and sheets and blankets had been cut down to provide warmth and comfort.

Mrs Anderson had had many children, and like Sal's mother only a few had made it through infancy; unfortunately none were now alive. She became very maternal towards Sal, and took on herself to provide whatever she could to help the young mother-to-be; besides setting about knitting booties and mittens, she had found some old towelling to make into nappies. The finished articles were very grey and discoloured, but Sal knew that it had been a labour of love for the old lady, and to refuse or decline such a thing would be a terrible insult, and she received them with genuine gratitude.

Bridget, who was already feeling quite put out that her plans to draw her daughter back within her control had been somewhat thwarted by her son-in-law's tenacity, was now feeling doubly so by the interference of this old inter-loper. This had benefits for Sal: for the first month or so Bridget hardly made an appearance, giving Sal a chance to have some time to settle in and make new routines for living. Then Bridget armed herself with determination to re-estab-lish her maternal authority of the old woman, by appearing daily with more offerings for her daughter's layette. By the time the baby was due there was such a pile, Sal could not believe she would use half of it, but she had never had a baby before; she would soon realise how needed it all was, especially with the huge copper she had to boil on washday.

John had remained quietly by. He knew not to push Sal who had made her feelings clear for many months that his close attentions were not desired, and his mother had coun-selled him that a young first-time mother needed to get used to much; he had listened and respected this. He had felt very proud of himself when he had managed to improve their liv-ing circumstances just in the nick of time, and had watched his mother-in-law squirm, unable to interfere or influence further. But he knew that this situation was far from satis-factory, and was not what he had wished for his young wife, and now his young family. He pushed continually at the railway yard to try and find a better position, at least one that would not elicit sneers from Bridget every time his occupation was mentioned. Usually this profound humiliation had taken place at the end of Sunday Mass, when some interested neighbour or client of Peter's had made an unsuspecting enquiry of the progress of the young couple, and been met with Bridget's rising snobbery.

Whenever things became too difficult for John, either from his young wife's erratic temperament, or because her mother was visiting imminently, he was able to give a plausible excuse that he needed to nip round the corner to see his parents. Consequently, he had found himself spending more and more time with his parents and less and less with Sal. Neither seemed particularly bothered; at least Sal made no commentary, and John's mother knew better than to criticise his young wife openly, but she was quietly concerned for the emotional state of her son. John just felt safe within the bosom of his kin, and not lonely.

Unfortunately, these convenient absences which had coincided with Bridget's visits, and unbeknown to her quite intentionally, had drawn even greater criticism from her towards the young man that she had already viewed as feckless.

"And where's yer man this time? It is not right leaving you all alone all the time. If he was my husband I would have one or two things I would say to him."

Sal did as she was getting very used to doing now, and whenever these onslaughts came she switched off. She felt her nesting instinct very strongly and her baby kick inside her; these were the only things that mattered to her, and her mother as much as her husband was just an annoying irritation which she had to live with.

On the day that the pains had come, John had already slipped away fearing an impending visit. Sal had been up early and had black-leaded the grate and scrubbed the scullery. She had just taken a bowl of scorching hot water to the stairs and was on her hands and knees vigorously scrubbing when the knife had ripped in to her guts and caused her to scream loudly. Mrs Anderson, having already observed the signs of scrubbing and washing in the proceeding few days, knew exactly why her young neighbour was crying out and made her arthritic way to aid her. Just as she got to the stairs, Sal, who was on all fours, screamed again just as her waters broke, gushing down the stairs like a waterfall, and soaking her skirts.

"Oh dearie, dearie, dinna you worry yersel' lassie… let's get you to yer bed… Thomas!" Mrs Anderson shouted back to her husband. "Thomas!... get some water from the copper… the lassie's having her bairn."

By the time Bridget had arrived, Sal had been put to her bed and seemed to be in the grip of what all had hoped would be a quick, intense labour.

Chapter 6 –

New Life and New Hope

Sal drifted in and out of the world. The painful intrusion of the doctor had ceased, and she was most thankful of that. All had gone quiet in the room and she felt so sleepy and strangely at ease, half of her was in dream, half within the room where she lay.

She felt at peace, like the lazy sunny days of summer, lying on the grass of Glasgow Green as a child, on the rare Sunday afternoon picnic. She felt a glow of warmth and nothing seemed to matter anymore, not the squalid room she was lying in, her nagging mother, the regret of the life she had chosen in an effort to free herself from the unacknowledged slavery of being the eldest girl in a poor home. She could hear voices, but they felt strangely distant and indiscernible as speech, they were just there. A man's voice, low and serious, and a woman's voice, troubled and anxious, somehow distant but somehow familiar. Nothing mattered anymore: Sal was slipping away, somewhere where nothing and no one could trouble her in anymore. *But what about the baby?*

Was that a voice in her head? She could not discern voice from dream. Was that her mother's anxious tone? Was it her own soul crying out to her to remember what she was at, what she was there to do? But it did not matter, she slipped back into her warm glow of release, feeling the dream-like state taking control of her more and more.

The voices around her grew more insistent and troubled. Were they talking to her, or talking amongst themselves? She knew not, and cared little. She wanted to be a little girl again, untroubled and carefree, feeling loved and safe in the heart of her little world.

In the far corner of the room a diminutive fearful woman listened to the grave concerns of a doctor whose skill had failed him.

"Mrs McBride... the baby is too high... and Mrs Flynn is no longer with us. Her contractions are lessening all the time... I cannae' reach the bairn's head with the forceps, and without her working with me there is very little I can do to deliver this child... I think it is best to make her comfortable... I would call for the priest... though I doubt he would be here in time... You have to prepare yourself, Mrs McBride... your daughter is dying..."

Dying? Me? What about the baby? Sal could hear herself inside, but she could not make the words come out; she was so far beyond the real world, as in a dream from which she could not wake. She could hear her mother's voice, overwhelmed with emotion, close by her bed.

"Ave Maria, gratia plena, Dominus tecum. Benedicta tu in mulieribus, et benedictus fructus ventris tui, Iesus..."

Sal could hear the incantation of the rosary, her mother was praying over her. *Why was she doing this?* Somewhere inside her drifting mind, the acknowledgment of her near-death state gripped her: she was dying! *I cannot die! I must live! For the baby!* As she formed this thought, she was rocked into consciousness by a profound sensation of intense pain; she screamed in intensity, her eyes wide open. She was back from the other world.

"Mama!" she screamed.

"Doctor, please try?" Bridget pleaded with the doctor, who had been slowly returning his implements to his case. He spun round and dashed to Sal's bedside.

"Mrs Flynn, I need you to help me... for the sake of your child."

He began once again with his intrusions. Sal was overcome with a need to push, to rid herself of this pain, to bring forth the other life that she had tried to abandon with her own. All at once, metal was on flesh, cold and intensely painful, her urges to free herself from all that was invading her was overwhelming, the struggle to survive, the fight to save her child. All came to a crescendo in extreme haste, and desperate pain. First a head, misshapen and blue, then the shoulders and body, blue and wet, all came at once. Sal, in one final desperate burst of energy, her chin on her chest, forced the unborn infant out into the unforgiving environment, and with that effort threw herself back on the pillow, completely exhausted.

Then there were those terrible moments of silence, which seemed to last forever. The poor child, having suffered such a delay at a time when it should have come into the world, was starved of all it needed, constrained, unable to fight for life. As much as the mother had allowed herself to slip away, so too her child had begun to leave with her. The baby was blue, floppy, now cold. The doctor worked feverishly in those first few seconds to clear the mouth, the nose, rubbing vigorously, still nothing. Then gently, with the utmost care, he blew warm breath into the small floppy doll's mouth.

A sharp intake of breath, a cry of resentment and anguish, a penetrating scream, as the first painful breath was drawn. Swaddled quickly, and passed to Bridget, announcing,

"Mrs McBride, you have a grandson! A very lucky little boy."

Bridget's eyes welled up with emotion, as she held the bawling infant. His face was pinched, but now red, bruising now beginning to form around the places that unforgiving metal had gripped him in the desperation to pull him into the world. Bridget scrutinised him carefully. His black hair, tiny frame. He was not the strongest baby that she had held, but he was there: he was alive. She bit back her emotions and looked towards where her daughter lay, now being attended by the doctor in the last moments of labour. This birth had nearly killed her, nearly killed the little boy that she now clutched protectively. In Bridget's head, it was not her own actions that she blamed. Not her need to make her daughter face up to her consequences, and do all as she herself had done, alone, without medical intervention. In her mind, she knew where the blame lay for this near calamity.

Sal lay still, her last burst of effort had left her totally drained and unable to focus on anything. Most protective female relatives at this time would be in the state of utmost concern, and be considering the need to be gentle and kind. This was not the McBride way, not Bridget's way. She placed the small swaddled bundle in the crook of a limp arm.

"Well, here is your son, my girl. He is a bonnie wee thing... a bit small and no doubt sickly, but he is here, and you are his mother, you have a job to do."

Sal craned her neck to one side to try and glimpse the little boy who now lay quieter, staring, unable to focus. She could not even raise her head, never mind contemplate all that she must now do to take her place in the union of motherhood. Bridget continued.

"Be grateful he is a boy, he will never have to go through what you have just endured, he will never know. Just like his father, a moment of pleasure and he will not be around when needed."

Sal was unable to answer, unable to even acknowledge that last cruel slight against John. She had always known that her mother had disapproved of her match, and found him lacking, but for the first time her tone held a perceptible note of bitterness; she was despising John Flynn and all that he was.

Poor John! All this time he had been confined to the scullery with the older folks. He had been sent to fetch the doctor and then ushered away. "It's no place for you," had been the final snipe from his mother-in-law. He had grasped the gravity of the situation. The very fact that the doctor had been summoned had made him only too aware that his wife was struggling and he was also of the view that the interferences of Bridget had probably added to her distress.

He had sat the last four hours, first witness to awful agonies through her screams as she endured, but those had grown less and less. He had hoped for that first cry of a newborn, anything that would have signalled that all was well and the worry had passed. Then there was the hour of silence and the hushed voices. Mrs Anderson tried her best to distract him, offering words of reassurance.

"It'll be alright, hen… she is strong, she will do this." Mr Anderson had just sat nodding, having witnessed this many times. But no amount of reassurance could settle him. He desperately wanted to know what was about, but he knew that he had been dismissed and that Bridget was going to exclude him from all further involvement, because she could. She would not consider his feelings or concerns, not for an instant.

Then had come that blistering scream, as Sal had burst back to life. He had gripped the arm of the wooden chair that he was sat in by the scullery fire, he had felt his nails sink into the hard wood and his knuckles had turned white. His poor lass! What had he done! He was beside himself, but he knew as all men had to, that he must contain his emotions, it was not 'done' to let go. As much as he had developed a friendship with these old people, who now sat carefully by, they were not his kith and kin. He would not have cried in front of his own family, he could certainly not display weakness to people that he barely knew.

Then the sound he had desperately hoped for, the cry of his child. The relief in the scullery was palpable, as Mr Anderson struggled to his feet to congratulate John, Mrs Anderson chiming in.

"There there, laddie… all is well with the bairn."

His surge of adrenalin began to wane when a half an hour later he still waited for news, still waited to know if the girl of his life was doing fine too. Too unnerved by Bridget's dismissal to be demonstrative enough to climb the stairs and knock on the door, too inexperienced to know whether his intrusion in such a private place would be welcomed. That was the point where Bridget had lain the young infant in the crook of his desperately tired mother's arm, and had made her statements of reproach about his father to Sal. She then spun round in her boots and made for the door: Sal knew what that meant, but had no energy to protest or shield John from the coming onslaught.

The door opened and the clack of hurried heels scuttled down the steep flight of stairs. John's frame appeared in the scullery doorway, his anxious drawn face, in anticipation of the long awaited news. He had no time to ask; Bridget marched towards him, her anger obvious.

"Well, man? Don't you want to know about your wife and child? I can see you have taken very little interest all these months in the state of my girl, and you are set to continue obviously. Well let me tell you, she has not had an easy time of any of it, we were calling for the priest not long ago, and but for her spirit, you would be burying them both tomorrow. I have said it to her and I will say the same to you, you are parents now, too late to change any of this, you had better do your duty by your wife and son, or I will have a thing or two to tell you. If she comes to her senses she'll have a home with us, her and the bairn. Until then, it is your job, and you mark my words and do it well."

John stood completely speechless, a mixture of emotions swirling in his brain. He was a father! He had a wee boy! He felt hurt and angry at the attack that he had been unable to defend himself against and it was too late to come back now, she had already got her hat and coat and was heading for the front door in high dudgeon, accompanied by a very confused old man. Meanwhile, Mrs Anderson was pushing him to hurry up the stairs.

"Go see yer wee boy, sonnie… go see yer wife."

He wasted no time and raced up two steps at a time just to encounter the doctor coming out the room.

"Aye, slow down Mr Flynn. Take a breath." And then looking around questioningly, "Is Mrs McBride not here to help you with Mrs Flynn?"

John was somewhat flustered and confused and stuttered, "N-o-o…?"

The doctor, obviously in the same hurry to leave, and with little concern for aftercare, said, "Aye, well… no matter.

Your wife is going to need some care and help the next few days, she's very weak, you know? Make sure she gets plenty of rest. And the wee boy... well he's made it this far, I hope he keeps going." With these comments he shook John's hand firmly and headed down to bottom of the stairs, where an old lady listened, concerned.

John had barely taken any of this in. He knocked the door tentatively, a faint voice answered.

"Come in."

The picture that greeted him was one of a war scene; having had no female relatives in attendance other than her mother, blood-stained swaddling lay in a crumpled heap on the floor, next to slopped out buckets of now very tepid blood-stained water.

Sarah looked completely ashen, black circles around her eyes. He could see she was unable to even raise her hand, and a bundle next to her was beginning to wriggle frantical-ly, making small pathetic whimpers, rather than lusty cries. Sal looked at John, tears in her eyes; faintly she said, "You'll have to help me John, I need to get out of bed. Mama says that I must get on with it." With that she made a desperate effort to raise her head and neck. John protested, the door still ajar.

"No you must not, the doctor said. Just stay there, I will get help for you, I promise." No sooner had he said those words than poor arthritic Mrs Anderson had appeared and was doing her best to begin to clear the mess, not that she could have done much good, but what she had to say did.

"Now dinna you two fret, I have sent my Tam to the Gal-lowgate, to yer kin, laddie, he may tak' a wee while, he's not quick these days, but in the meantime, just you wait on them and comfort that poor girl and best rock yer bairn."

John reached for the small bundle; compared to his father's grand frame the little baby was almost lost in his arms. He delicately collected the tiny child and his ever-loosening swaddling, and scooped it all up into his arm. He knew how to hold a tiny baby, having always been the eldest in his family. His enormous hands, cupped the small, bruised head into the palm of his hand. For a time the wriggling stopped, as father stared at son, and son wrinkled his nose and face against the light. Eyes met eyes, and John was immediately smitten. He had made this small life, he was his son. As tears began to flow down his cheeks, a broad smile extended across his face. Every emotion that had been concentrated in that few minutes now completely overwhelmed him, and he could no longer contain himself.

Sal watched as her husband and son came to know one another, she was very touched by John's loss of control; she felt a wave of compassion for the man she had treated so harshly these past nine months. In her own thoughts she checked herself suddenly; she felt something for John, but she had no feelings for the bundle he was admiring so tenderly. Even though for a few months she had been so physically close to the wriggling and squirming and the movement inside her, and even highly maternal at times, now she felt nothing! Why, why did she feel nothing? This disturbed her. Then there was huge discomfort and pain that she still had, she felt damaged and abused, and messy. But she smiled a faint smile back at her man, holding her child, for she knew that is what she had to do.

The next days passed in a blur of fever and sickness for Sarah. The first night John's mother Maggie came to stay and sent John back to the Gallowgate as there was little he could do to help. However, when she realised how unwell

Sal had become, and concerned for the struggling little boy, she decided that they would all be better off in her meagre home. She organised a handcart and moved the frail pair. Over the next week, she carefully nursed Sal, trying to encourage her to feed the baby whenever possible. She made weak broths, for that was all that Sal could stomach, and woke all through the night to calm the little lad who was becoming quite fretful. By the end of that week, Sal was able to sit up in bed and do more to look after the bairn.

John did what he could, just little things; picking a bunch of spring flowers, holding the little boy whenever he had the time, reading to his wife. They had peace from Bridget, as she had not return to David Street to check on her daughter or grandson, and was completely unaware that her strategy to force her daughter on her feet had been completely foolish, even life threatening. By the end of that week Sal was beginning to take to her feet, and eating a little more. She did her duty by the little lad, feeding and changing him, waking in the night and being ever-attendant on his needs, but her feelings were detached. It was as if a link had been broken at birth, that was deeper than the umbilical cord. She knew that she must feel something more than concern and care for him, but she looked at him and just saw a small fragile baby, not her son.

While John was at the railway the following day, the dreaded knock came at the door. Both Maggie and Sal knew that this would be inevitable, and although they could see to the street from that front parlour, they both knew that Bridget stood the other side of the closed door.

Maggie Flynn steeled herself to face her foe, and on opening the door greeted Bridget with the utmost courtesy, only to have Bridget barge past demanding to see her daughter.

The baby's cries gave her location to her mother and she marched into the parlour, followed by a protective Maggie. Bridget let fly, before checking her facts.

"Well, my girl? What do you call this? Visiting your in-laws yet you have made no effort to see your own kin. What is the meaning of this? I have been round to David Street to see where you were and Mrs Anderson informed me that you were here. And bringing a child to this place!"

At that comment, Maggie rounded on her. The normally mild mannered Margaret Flynn was not one to create scenes, but she prided herself on the fact that she would make do, no matter how little she had, and she always kept a clean home.

"Now Mrs McBride, you really have gone too far! Do you not have any concern for your daughter and our grandson? Do you have any idea how ill Sal was when you took off? Never mind the state that everything was left there. Your daughter has just got over a fever that would have probably taken most, never mind a woman who has just come through hard labour. We were lucky the wee man did not get it. And you do not come here casting your bad eyes and mouth on the way we live! I keep a clean house here and don't you forget it!"

Sal was stunned. Someone had taken her mother on and quite literally left her speechless. It was all that Sal could do to suppress the smirk that she felt come over her face at her mother's dressing down by another woman. Maggie had shocked herself too, and was hoping that was the end of the matter.

Bridget was never a fool, and she realised then and there that she had been wrong-footed; she had spoken in haste and was paying dearly, but always the one to make the last word, "Well if someone had had the decency to come and tell her family, we would not have been the last to know, or is that something else that your son fails in, manners?"

That was enough for Maggie. She pursed her lips, and firmly replied, "You have said quite enough Mrs McBride, my John is a good lad, and always has impeccable manners. Maybe if you had not spent so much of your time interfering since these poor young people were married, and had a little more support and not so much criticism, he may well have tried to match up to your insensitive expectations. He does his best, Johnny boy, and I will not hear another bad word against him. Until you have a more civil tongue in your head I do not want you here, and I must ask that you leave now."

The final statement was uttered with such firmness that Bridget had no choice but to obey, without another word she left the house and Maggie shut the door behind her. Back in the parlour, there was a minute of shock, as one sat and one stood, both in disbelief as to how Bridget McBride had been put in her place, the silence gave way to a fit of laughter from both women; not a remark against Bridget, just a release of tension with humour. Sal's spirits began to lift.

Chapter 7 –

A Time of Calm

The Flynns' home was very hectic, but happy. The weeks that Sal spent there were exactly what she needed. There were the three younger girls still living there; Kate, now 16, Mary a sweet 11, and baby Lizzie, just toddling. John's next sibling was his sister Annie, now married and a content housewife. The next girl Margaret was in service, but had a beau, and was considering the next step in her life. The only other son that the Flynns had been blessed with was Thomas, very quiet and scholarly; he was working for an engine fitter as he had to earn a living; he had moved into digs ten doors down on the Gallowgate.

John senior was a cheerful soul with a head full of stories. Maggie and he had married while he had been serving in the British Army and he took her with him to India. There she had given birth to both John and Annie. Then returning to an English camp for a while, the family had grown with Thomas and Katie. Having completed his time in the service of his Queen (which was a strange sentiment for a catholic Irishman) the decision was taken to move north of the border to Glasgow; John turned his hand to boots and shoes. He was a hard worker and he kept a roof, albeit a simple one, over the heads of his family and they never went hungry. The Flynns were like many of the simple people that kept Glasgow thriving; they never asked for much, and always did their duty.

Bridget did not return to the Gallowgate since the events that had so shamed her; she knew better than to be embarrassed this way again. She waited on her daughter to visit, and in her haughty manner, expected it. Sal and John knew that they had to do the decent thing, and once a week, usually on a Sunday in the afternoon, they made the walk, with their young son – in a pram that had seen better days – round to George Street.

There they were always greeted cordially, but the atmosphere was frosty and far from homely. Sal reflected to herself how different this place seemed to that of the Flynns. It had changed in many ways in the last year, with Peter and Hugh having flown the nest finally, and James was preparing to leave soon to be married to the perfect Mary Ann Gunn. It was just her parents now and the three girls. Katie had always seemed frail, but now at the age of 8, she was smaller in stature than her peers and forever with a cold or a cough. Jeanie was quiet and withdrawn, in fact they both were. It was only Annie Theresa who seemed remarkably untouched; still chatty, but she had learnt there was a time and a place to talk. Jeanie and Katie shared the chores which Sal had been tasked with previously, but now that there were few in the house the burden was much less than had been the case for Sal.

The hour or two they would spend there always seemed to last too long. Conversation was stilted, and usually comprised the same topics. How well James and Hugh were doing, and that Peter junior had excellent expectations; this was the sideways dig at John. Then it would be the same old discussion about moving to the country; how bad it was for young children to live in the city, but it must be difficult to do that when your work is in the heart of the city? Another dig at John. What was most marked about the conversation was the fact that Bridget always refused to use her grandson's name, she would refer to the 'little lad', 'the bairn', but refrained from naming him.

Sal had made another revolutionary decision to call her son John. She knew that it would cause some distaste with her mother; having all the other male names on her side to choose from, and obviously deliberately calling him after his father. A man that Bridget considered so feckless and good for nothing, that naming the first child likewise, in her eyes, had immediately condemned the baby to a hopeless life. This was John's opportunity to rub it in with his mother-in-law, and he would pepper every conversation with as many references to his son's name as he could; 'John John', 'little Johnny', 'Johnny boy'. Bridget would remain stoney-faced throughout, but all knew that she was squirming inside.

When the time came to leave, it was always such a relief to the young couple; they would feel like the weight of the world had been lifted from their shoulders. The events of the birth and the time after with Bridget had brought the couple closer together, and it was spring. They had moved back to David Street and had a comfortable retreat from the world. Little Johnny had settled into a routine, and Sal was finding the whole experience of motherhood better than she had hoped for. The initial feelings of disconnection from the infant were leaving her gradually, as he was such a good baby and so easy to serve that the love began to grow between mother and child. As the first smile arrived on the infant's face, so the happiness in her grew. John knew that all things would take time, and he had listened to his mother's counsel to leave Sal and little John to become acquainted, and not to try and rush her towards 'anything else'. This non-specific reference John knew meant any physical closeness with him. But on the other hand, with working such long days in very physical manual work of shunting trains, to then experience the considerable sleep deprivation of a bawling baby, in two rooms, the inclination towards anything of a carnal nature had somewhat left him.

Sal's feelings towards her husband had begun to mellow. She was beginning to appreciate his kindness, his consideration. On the rare moments that she could steal for reflection, in between feeding and changing the baby, and trying to maintain her modest home for her husband, she was realising just how hard she had been on him. She knew her defiance had sprung from her resentment in her previous life, she also knew that she had made a marriage of convenience with all the wrong notions. *It was not his fault*; he had always expressed genuine feelings and motivations for wanting to be with her. She, on the other hand, had not been so open or 'real' in what she was out to do, or what she felt for him.

As her self-awareness grew, so began the first seeds of real affection for her man. It was imperceptible at first, a returned smile, a sweet act of care – polishing his boots for Sunday, cooking what she knew he liked. The latter had been in consultation with Maggie, whom she had made efforts to go and see most days, and that attention too had brought rewards for Sal, with additional food and, "I'll watch the bairn while you take a while for a wee sleep hen."

Sal's attentions towards John became more demonstrative as the weeks passed. Then, one morning just as he was about to leave for the railway yard, came the moment he had long hoped for. It was not ridiculously romantic, that was not Sal's style, and neither was it overly done. She kissed him – quickly and politely, but she kissed him. She had made the approach, and then carried out the action. He had not been dismissed with a turned head, or a coldness as he had so many times before. He felt a moment of pure joy and absolute elation. For him it was marking a turning point in their relationship. The depression post the marriage that had been long holding a cloud over him raised, and real hope was manifested that for the first time things were really looking up.

Bridget was markedly not happy. Not only was she contending with being frozen out of her first grandson's life, and being marginalised in preference for a family that she considered to be in every way socially and intellectually beneath her, but her own home life had taken a turn for the worse. Katie's various coughs and colds had developed into breathing difficulties, and there were some nights where she had sat with her daughter all night concerned that she may not see the next morning. The doctor seemed unable to suggest any type of remedy, other than steaming bowls of infusions, and hot towels applied to her chest. This, added to her already frail frame and poor appetite, meant that she did very little to help poor Jeanie in her endeavour to keep on top of the domestic tasks; thankfully with all but the three girls and the parents there, it was considerably less of a trial for her than it had been for her older sister. Bridget was not a young woman by any standard being in her late forties, and although her dynamic ambitions kept her going, she was finding that the tribulations of her age and much child-bearing had taken a toll on her physical energies. She had always been such an intensely hardworking woman, and had driven her family to the same industrious endeavours, which had taken some of her energies too. Now she was feeling the pressure of the care of Katie, combined with the strains of separation from the one thing that she – albeit secretly – coveted: her grandson.

She was at a loss as to what exactly to do about it, and she had not got the time or the energies to try. She was certainly not going to bend at the knee and make any sort of humble gesture of conciliation or humility. If that's the way things are, they were best left until they sorted themselves out. And one day that silly girl would need her; she may have been foiled in her attempts this time, but there would come a day, of that she was sure, she just had to bide her time and wait.

The weeks and months tumbled into one another. Before anyone had a chance to think it was March 1906, and little John was going to be one year old. Katie had rallied from her problems of nine months earlier, but a stern warning had come from the doctor that she should avoid draughts and chills, and any others with infections; effectively Bridget had been told that her daughter was never going to be strong and able, she would be an invalid for the rest of her life; and on that she was not expected to make 'old bones'.

John had come good though. Whether it was because of his new found enthusiasm for life now that relations had warmed between man and wife, or because he had finally been recognised for the promise that he possessed, he had been promoted to become a Railway Goods Guard. Not much of a rise in

Bridget's determination, but no one could deny that it was an elevation from his lowly status as a shunter.

Little John had just started to walk, and his speech, though not as precocious as his slightly older aunt – Annie Theresa – was admirable for a toddler. It was helped by the continual contact of his mother, who had taken in home work rather than trying to get an occupation elsewhere. She was an accomplished seamstress and was making baby clothes for local businessmen known to her father.

As much as Peter McBride recycled the cloth detritus collected from others and made money, there were others who had cloth garments to sell made by many others that they employed around the city. It was sweated labour, for the women who applied themselves to the task were like Sal, young mothers who had to be with their young children, or much older women who could no longer get work elsewhere. As long as their eyes could still focus, and they were still manually dexterous they could be employed. But there were many hundreds of such women; as such the middle men (and women) who went around collecting the finished garments could take quite a cut from the profits as their payment, leaving the hard working souls with very little for their efforts. It was pin money; this was the price for home-working, this was the price for being a woman.

It helped to buy the food and household needs, and allowed John's wage to stretch a little further. Sal tried to keep a jar of rainy-day money too, she knew how quickly they could struggle if things did not go right. She might get sick and be unable to work for a few days, and god forbid, John could have an accident. They had to keep a weather-eye on paying doctors' fees or just keeping the roof over their head and the rent paid. Her father made the odd contribution in clothing. Peter was never a great one to show emotion or connection to anything, but he was a rising businessman, conscious now that all that his family did, and how they were viewed by the world, reflected back on him. He had a grandson, who needed to look 'well taken care of' by his daughter and her husband. As much as he was none too impressed with the little that had been achieved through that union; he had to make sure that they looked better than they did, especially when they were still viewed to all outside as part of the family; part of the clan. Whenever he got some semi-reasonable clothes (not the best, for those were the items that kept him turning a profit), for a small child, young woman, or a tall man, he would send them (via Bridget) to David Street. He was not going to breed over-familiarity with the young family, he maintained a detached discontentment.

Bridget's calls on her daughter had increased in frequency. She was arriving, usually unplanned, at least once but sometimes twice a week. It was actually complicating Sal's movements, for in the little free time that she actually allowed herself, in between her sewing occupations and administering to her son's needs and household chores, she would have liked to have taken a walk in the fresh air or visit Maggie. But with her mother's sudden attentions, and not knowing when she would call, and dreading the offence it might cause if for some reason she had left, she had found herself tethered to David Street, as an unintended prisoner.

Bridget had her agenda, to re-establish her authority with her daughter over that of the Flynns. As much as her time was complicated by Katie's health problems which would come and go, and her need to support Peter, she made herself find afternoons to visit Sarah. She knew full well that her daughter was using all of the other moments to keep body and soul together earning her pin money, and she also realised if she were there in her daughter's company, then Sal would find it completely impossible to be elsewhere. So she had made up her mind, to be extremely attentive and nice. So much so that even John experienced some cordiality from him the few times that he had returned from work to find her still there.

She would turn up bearing some sort of gift or so. A package of clothing from Peter, a scrag-end of meat to make a stew, some soap for the continual round of washing that Sal had to endure as the mother of a small child. It just so happened that little John's birthday fell on a Thursday in this year; as it was a working day, John had suggested a visit to Glasgow Green might be in order on the Sunday following to allow the 'little lad to run a bit', before making their expected visit to George Street. No fuss was going to be made on the day itself; as such, Sal expected none. None, that was, until her mother made yet another of her unannounced visits, carrying a tin. Mrs Anderson let her in as normal, and ushered her up towards Sal – Mrs Anderson had stopped being social to Bridget since she had abandoned her daughter after her traumatic labour. Bridget knocked at the door of the upstairs landing, and Sal, musingly, let her in.

"I have brought a wee something for the bonnie bairn."

There may have been somewhat of a transformation in Bridget's character, but she still could not bring herself to use her grandson's name as yet.

She handed Sal the biscuit tin, and she tentatively opened it to find eight scones, filled with blackberry jam. She knew this had not been Bridget's doing, she had never had time for such motherly pastimes, or the money to waste. Bridget qualified the gift.

"Katie and Jeanie thought it would be nice to give the wee man something for his birthday. Katie made the scones, and Jeanie had made a wee bit of jam last summer from the fruit that she had got when we went for a picnic..." She searched for a reaction from Sal, who was somewhat stunned by this turn of events.

"...We hope that you like them?"

"Yes, Mama. What a wonderful thought and so nice of the girls to take the time... why didn't they come?"

"Oh well... Jeanie is at school of course... and Katie has a cold again... we thought it best for the little one that she didn't come, I mean that you never know with these things... I often wonder if that is why Katie is in such frail health now... I mean living in the city and the smoke and the fumes." She stopped and looked a little unsteady. Sal suddenly felt a wave of concern toward her mother; she had been so taken aback that she had not even offered her seat, never mind a cup of tea.

"Mama, here, sit." She quickly ushered her to the only other wooden chair in the room, next to the rickety table. Bridget moved reluctantly and sat firmly, breathing heavily as she did so.

"Are you unwell?"

"Nae... just a little weary... Katie needed sitting with last night."

"Shouldn't you be resting, Mama? I mean it is really lovely what you have done bringing this for Johnny, but you mustn't make yourself ill."

Bridget bristled with the sudden acknowledgement of her own frailty.

"I am not at death's door, girl…" She checked herself, realising that her tone was probably too sharp, and Sal's face had frozen.

"I mean it will tak' mair than one night without rest ta' knock me off my feet."

The sudden switch in her accent to her more broad former self was a signal to Sal that her mother had become somewhat flustered by her reactions, and was trying to talk her way out of a difficult situation. That too refigured itself in Sal's reflections, this 'nice-ness' which had greeted her was as false as everything else; she was merely trying to ingratiate herself back into her daughter's reluctant affections, and there was probably another motive, which as yet had not been made clear. Sal decided to keep herself more contained and wait on the revelation that may, or may not, follow.

"Well you look tired Mama, you have obviously been overdoing everything, you need to think on your own health or you will be no good for father or Katie."

Bridget mused for a moment and then, "Well, a cup of tea might help… and you can give this wee man a scone."

Shortly tea had been set on the rickety table, while little Johnny cruised around the room's meagre furnishings, carefully attended by his mother, just in case his attentions turned to the scalding hot teapot at the side of his grandmother. Every now and then he would make tentative free steps back to middle of the room, to find the half eaten, but discarded sweet treat; that he liked but found a little dry, and there were much more interesting things to do, attempting to walk was one.

Bridget watched for a while and then remarked,

"He is a busy wee boy… you shouldn't follow him so… he will get too used to having all your attentions… that's the way to spoil a child, you know?"

Sal was none to pleased at this barbed criticism, but knew better than to react. She replied, "I don't 'normally' follow him like this, but I don't 'normally' have a hot teapot near him... I am usually working and he gets on with it."

"Well, there was no need to have troubled yourself on my account, you only had to say and I would have waited until I had got home."

Again Sal chose not to take the bait, and carried on keeping Johnny under surveillance. Bridget continued.

"Well there is something you need to know... Your father and I have been talking and have decided it is better for the girls, particularly Katie, if we move out to country sooner than we thought."

For the second time in an hour, Sal was disarmed; she could not quite take it in, but this statement had been made so often it could just be a whim that would come to nothing. But that was not what Bridget was about and there was more to come.

"Of course, we will move to the east, the houses the other way are too expensive to rent, but we think we can find a nice little villa with a garden... good, healthy fresh air, excellent for Katie. Your father will stay in Glasgow during the week, he has made himself a little flat above the warehouse he has now, he will come in at weekends..."

Still Sal sat; she knew this was not the end of this pronouncement.

"Of course, now there is only me and the girls, there would be plenty of room..."

Just for a moment Sal's heart leapt - she was going to offer to allow her to live there with John and Johnny; *of course, John would not be happy with the arrangement, but he would get used to it–* Her thoughts were stopped in their tracks by Bridget's final statement.

"It would be a lovely place for the wee one and yourself... but of course, you would have to come alone."

Sal could not believe the audacity of her mother, to arrive under the auspices of gift-giving to her grandson, when in fact her intention had been all along to break the family up. She quickly swept John up in her arms and stood over where her mother was sitting.

"I would like you leave now, please?"

"Sorry, I do not understand, I have offered a decent home for you and my grandson."

Sal's anger rose, and not for the first time her defiance came crashing in.

"No, mother! My son and I are staying with his father, who is doing alright by us, mark you. Despite all that you have said. This may not be a palace, but we are happy and we make our way. We do not owe money, and what we cannot afford, we do not buy. You have never taken to John, and you have tried everything, even before this little boy was born, to separate us. Well it is just not going to happen now, I tell you! Now I would like you to leave!"

Sal stood still and waited for the reaction that her mother had tried so hard to contain earlier.

Bridget rose to her feet, holding her daughter with a fixed stare.

"You will never know when you have a good offer. You are determined to carry on with this charade of a happy home and a happy family. How can you live like this when there is so much more for you out there? You mark my words young lady, once the next bairn comes, and you are both too stupid not to stop with this one... once the next bairn comes life will not be so easy and you will rue the day that you turned down such a good offer. I will not make it again, you will have to ask next time!"

With that, Bridget flounced towards the door, and not for the first time marched out of the David Street house, leaving poor old Mrs Anderson spinning with the speed of her exit.

Chapter 8 –

May All Your Problems Be Wee Ones

An uncomfortable few months of Sunday visits to George Street ensued, with the atmosphere more tense that it had ever been. The only lightness in an otherwise terse situation had been little Johnny, who had turned into quite a character. The attentions of his three aunties: Jeanie, Katie and Annie Theresa appealed to his comedic nature, and whenever he could he played to the gallery.

Sal's resentment for her perfect brother and his 'oh so perfect wife' grew as the marriage had become established. Now living in Coatbridge, they had just welcomed the birth of their first son, and had called him Peter in deference to the great, stern patriarch of the family. It seemed that they could do no wrong and were constantly used as a way to highlight her own husband's short-comings, whenever her mother found that the opportunity had arisen. Sal had made little effort to visit or befriend Mary Ann, not that she had the time to do so, even if she had felt the obligation.

Active searching for a place out of town had been maintained apace by Bridget. By the end of the summer the announcement came that a small cottage – Mary Lea – had been found out in Shettleston. Sal was quite relieved that it was so far away, it meant there could be no expectation of frequent or even regular visits from the family, as it was a good walk, and the train journey was not an affordable option often. John was not so content, for he knew that Bridget had made the rash offer that she had and that Sal had very rejected it, but somewhere at the back of his mind was a discomfort with the distance away. It was not for him a relief, it was a danger. If ever there were any problems, or any reason for Sal to have to go there, she may be too far – both physically and emotionally – to ever return. He treated the whole concept of the impending change with dread, but this was never articulated to Sal.

The move was scheduled for early November, and unbeknownst to Bridget, it coincided with Sal suspecting that she was – as her mother had predicted – pregnant for the second time. She knew better than to alert her mother to this prospect, she could hear the bitter commentary in her head; more criticism of her stupidity, more criticism of her husband's fecklessness. Sal was very worried herself about exactly how they were going to manage with one wage, Johnny growing faster than she could keep up, and needing bigger clothes, at a greater rate than her father could supply second-hand. Then there was David Street, it had served them well as a small home, and even with the arrival of Johnny they had managed, but with two babies there? It would be too difficult, it was hard enough watching her little monkey of a toddler without trying to mind a small baby in such a confined space. They would have to move, but where? And how could they possibly afford it? These were all problems that she would face later; for now, she was going to enjoy the lifting of the oppressive cloud that had overshadowed her for so long. She felt her spirits rise noticeably as her family's day for moving eastward came, she knew that every mile they travelled was a mark of Bridget's waning control over her life and that of her family's.

A noticeable sense of peace descended over the small family in David Street, and although Sal was consumed with her worries, for a week or so she felt so free and at ease, she had not yet revealed her condition to John – she was hoping that she may be wrong, or as often happened in early pregnancy that it might not stay. John was a changed man, the pressures of his ever-critical in-laws had lifted from his shoulders, he was settled with his wife and child in their modest home, and now with a job with prospects, all in his life seemed good for the first time since he had taken his marriage vows.

Sal's sickness came once more, with as great an effect as the previous time; the only difference now was the demands of a toddler, who was now needing constant attention. She could not take to her bed this time, when things became just too difficult she had to keep going. Unable to hold anything down at all during most of the day, it was not long before the over-whelming tiredness of malnutrition consumed her, and with that the depression and hopelessness. She could no longer ignore her condition, and John recognised the signs, so that when she did reveal her secret, he was somewhat prepared.

"Sal that is wonderful, another wee bairn on the way..."

Sal burst into tears, she had thought about their prospects again and again, she felt dreadful and could not see any way that they could possibly manage. She blurted all out in fits of sobs, what were they going to do? There was not enough money to manage now, never mind how they were going to accommodate a second baby in such confined conditions?

And she knew that her mother would exploit this against them again, and do her best to destroy what they had.

John quietly listened to her concerns, knowing that it was best not to try and approach her with physical comfort while she was letting all of her worries come to the surface, he had learnt it was best to let her express herself and then answer her concerns with care. He too had been considering their prospects and thought that he may have a solution; quietly and calmly he responded.

"I know you are worried, and watching you the last week or so, I had suspected that you had news to share. Now listen Sal, there is nothing that we cannae' get through… look at what we have been through till now… Yes, we have nae' got a lot, but we have each other, and my family will help you know that… My ma thinks you are wonderful, and she will do whatever she can to support us, you know that…"

Sal calmed and looked into his eyes, she saw his love and devotion reflect in those blue pools.

"…And space, I think we can do something about that, and now I know I shall find out if that is possible… we can get through this… trust me. Now you go and rest, I will take Johnny and put him to bed, you have another one to worry about."

Sal was too exhausted and hopeless to protest, she knew that she had no answers, and anything that could be done would be a step forward, she just had no ideas how to do it. John acted quickly, he knew that Sal was unwell and that her pre-disposition to depression was a slippery slope; unless he could find a way to put her mind at peace, he might not be able to recover her from a deep descent. Bridget was ever-present in his thoughts, especially her last attempts to manipulate Sal and Johnny away to Shettleston and out of his life. He was not going to grant her a second opportunity to exploit Sal's weak physical and mental state to her own advantage and he knew that as soon as she knew their expectation, she would.

The next evening when he arrived home from work, he delayed his ascent to his rooms, and stopped in to see Mrs Anderson. Sal, expecting him through their door at any moment waited a while, and was just going down to find out where he was, when he bounded up the staircase with a broad smile on his face. He bubbled with enthusiasm, as he moved her gently back through the door, closing it for privacy behind him, he ushered her to sit, concerned about her obvious tiredness.

"I have got good news, my love! I have spoken to Mrs Anderson, she is thrilled with our news; I have had to tell her because I have asked if we can have a little more space. She is more than happy to vacate her parlour, so that we can make both these rooms for sleeping, is that not the best news?"

Sal was overwhelmed by the suggestion, and her concerns mounted.

"But John, Mr and Mrs Anderson have already done so much for us, they are old, they need their space too, and how can we pay for the extra room, we can't take it for nothing... it's not right."

John was somewhat taken aback, but quickly recovered himself, knowing that what Sal needed now was strength of purpose and strength of mind, not doubt.

"I have raised all this with Mr Anderson, she won't hear of us paying her more money, she knows that we are struggling, and she would rather have us here, than new tenants that she does not know. She says that she rarely uses the parlour now, her and Mr Anderson prefer to sit in their kitchen in the evenings and it is getting too much for her to manage her housework with the extra room, she would prefer not to worry about it... Don't you see it is a gift for us, and it helps her?"

"Yes, but it is down a flight of stairs, what about Johnny, what about the new baby?"

"Now Sal, you are just creating problems, many families have their sleeping rooms above their living quarters, and the bairns will adjust... and thinks of the space that you will have in the parlour. It is much easier for you to do the work that you do, and the wee ones can be with you during the day, it is just at nights... it is much nearer the kitchen... and Mrs Anderson is more than happy for you to share her range, it will be much easier all round... We can sleep in this room and the bairns in the other."

Sal realised that John had solved the problem well, better than she could have ever imagined, she knew too that Mrs Anderson was a genuinely kind person, who had always shown them the greatest consideration and she would have made this offer willingly. She had to accept that this was the answer, after all beggars can't be choosers, but that was her problem, having to admit that only by falling on the charitable acts of others had they any hope of getting through. Unfortunately for Sal, the years of having had the moral values of her parents imposed on her had left her with an acute sense of pride, of never having to ask for help from strangers.

By the turn of New Year, Sal was resigned to the changes that were going to take place in her life; it was February, and she was still not showing, this was much due to her extreme morning sickness, which as with Johnny's pregnancy persisted most of the day. It had been a blessing over the Christmas and Hogmanay time, when her family insisted that she and her small family made a visit; although she was under the weather, she was able to disguise her predicament from her mother. Bridget had been so preoccupied with showing off her elevated living conditions to Sal, and crowing about how lovely and quiet it was living in the country, that it had escaped her to suspect that things might not be quite well with her daughter.

Sal had been shocked at the frailty of her younger sister Katie, who seemed so thin and fragile that a good gust of wind might take her away. Bridget insisted that Katie was much better than she had ever been living in the conditions of industrial Glasgow and the fresh air was doing her the world of good. As usual Peter had been aloof and non-communicative; he was spending more time in the city in the flat above the warehouse than had been initially envisaged, and despite the fact that he had been quite close by to his daughter and son-in-law this was the first time that he had been seen in the few months since they had moved.

James, too, had been wrapped up in his business interests in the city and rumours of an intention to make his own way as a grocer. He had visited with Mary Ann and Peter briefly, and made their excuses to return to the city as soon as they could. For Sal, this was a relief not to have the visible comparison of how little progress that they had made against her ever-successful brother. It was only her three sisters and her parents that she had to contend with. Jeanie and Annie Theresa were still chalk and cheese, Jeanie liking her own company and quiet solitude, Annie Theresa insisting on being the centre of attention, but always in a humorous way. Little Johnny had thrived on the attentions of his young aunts, and was the only one reluctant to leave; Sarah and John had done their duty and needed to get away.

However, John had been unable to contain his good news with his own kith and kin. Maggie and John senior were thrilled with the prospect, but were asked to keep it all quiet until Sal had told her family, and this they duly did. John's sister Margaret had news to share that she was to marry a young man from Coatbridge, which had been enough cause for celebration amongst the Flynns. Sal felt more at home with John's family than she had done with her own, and being so local to their own lodgings it had been easier to come and go and take her rest when needed. Maggie had been a calm voice of reassurance, telling her that they would manage and that a new baby was a blessing from god, that they would have great joy from.

Eventually in April, Bridget came again to visit her daughter. By then John and Sarah had begun to occupy the downstairs parlour, that and the obvious weight gain alerted Bridget immediately to the impending arrival as she sat in the parlour, scrutinising Sal closely.

"Aye you're expecting again, no surprises there... when's it due?"

"The summer." Sal had decided to keep her responses short, she had no desire to be sucked into yet another pointless discussion about her reduced circumstances.

"Well, at least you have more room, that shows he is making a better living than before, though I am surprised you have not taken a new place rather than staying here?"

Sal was not going to divulge that nothing had improved, and but for an act of kindness by too lovely old people they would probably not have a roof over their heads.

"We thought it was better to stay here for now, rather than unsettling Johnny, with everything changing and the new baby..." She decided to try and change the subject. "John's sister Margaret has married, isn't that good news?"

"Mmm… another feckless marriage for the Flynns no doubt, mind you she is girl as long as she has a good man."

Sal checked her anger. "She has married a hard working man like John, and they are living in Coatbridge."

"Aye well… there is hope for them, then. I bet she waits a while before having a bairn."

Sal ignored this, she knew that Margaret had no intention of waiting, and that she had hoped for her own children as soon as possible. Bridget broke the silence.

"Still working your fingers to the bone, I see?" She surveyed the cut-out pieces of linen, and the pin ball. "I never expected a daughter of mine having to take such work to make ends meet."

Sal lied: "Actually Mama, I making a gown for this one…" She touched the top of her waistband gently. "After all, you would want a good show at the christening, I am sure."

"Be as it is, you do not look well again… You should be taking more care… And I am too far away to help with this one, but I am sure you have made arrangements with his family?"

"I am sure when the time comes, all will be fine… If I am worried I shall see about going to a hospital, I know what I need to do this time… Maggie will take Johnny and John for a while, she has never had any problems with stepping in when she is needed." She said this with some relish, knowing that it was a deliberate snub to any interference that her mother was trying to impose.

Bridget bristled in her seat, and with her steely gaze pinned Sal to her seat. "We have never exchanged much in the way of pleasantries… maybe I am responsible, always having to work when you were small, having you as my daughter first, expecting you to behave with the same dutiful spirit that I had to my own parents… At least the wee girls have a better relationship with me and do not always view me as their enemy... but if this poor unfortunate that you are carrying happens to be a daughter, and you have to struggle the little that I did – and I think that you will struggle more – maybe one day you will consider how difficult it was for your own mother to do the right thing by everyone."

She rose from the chair, and made her way out as she had on other occasions. Sal did not rise and remained staring at the empty chair, which still held the indent of her mother's form. She stayed like this for what seemed like an eternity, angry and unsettled by her mother's words. She was angry that yet again, she had been dissected by her mother's tongue, but she was uncomfortable with the truth telling. Had she really been so selfish not to consider her own mother's experience? Was it her at fault? After all this time of being so sure of her motives and actions, doubt of her own integrity had begun to creep in.

She was suddenly shaken out of her deep reflections by a crash in the house. She had left Johnny in his bed upstairs for his afternoon nap. Panic gripped her that he had awoken and taken a tumble, maybe down the stairs as her own brother had. She dashed to the door of the parlour and was greeted by a heartbreaking sight. It was not her wee son who lay at the bottom of the stairs, but old Mrs Anderson, an overturned pale of water by her side, a scrubbing brush still tightly gripped in her hand. The water oozed around her frame in all directions, her skirts were soaking up the excess, her hair bun had come loose, with her white hair drifting around her head in the pool, like an angel's halo.

Sal feared the worst. There was something about the strange pallor on her face, and even in half light she could see that her lips were tinged with blue, and her expression was peaceful. Sal bent slowly to her knees on the wet floor, and placed her cheek near to the old woman's mouth and nose. There was no sound, no heat of breath; she was gone. Sal felt a sharp ache in her stomach and gripped her midriff, at the same time from deep within her a wail came. She had felt a great affection for this soul, a soul now gone from her, who had shown her greater kindness than she had ever shared from her own mother.

The following weeks passed in a complete blur. From the moments that old Mr Anderson had struggled from his chair in the kitchen, unable to contain his own grief, and the neighbours had dashed in to help with all that needed to be done, to when she and her small family had found themselves without a roof over their heads. Mr and Mrs Anderson had rented their home from another landlord and then sublet their rooms to Sal and John. Of course with his wife now gone, old Mr Anderson, who had been invalided for many years, was unable to look after himself and the money was gone, much probably to help the young couple who had shared their rooms.

As was often that way in the Glasgow of this time, neighbour helped neighbour, and Mr Anderson was taken in; he was not considered to be long for this world and his grief at losing his long-loved wife was so extreme, it was to hasten his inevitable end. However, John and Sal were not in any position to take on the whole rent, or even a true portion. Temporarily they moved in with Maggie and John senior; this was never going to be the best solution, as their space was far too restricted for the family to join them, but they made do for a while. Sal and John had resolved not to ask Bridget for help and had made it clear to her, when she had heard the news, that they would manage. Sal knew that the only offer she would have received from her mother would be one that would not include her husband, and there was no way that she was going to let her mother have her way of destroying her marriage.

Sal was near her time. John's sister Margaret came to the rescue: she took Sal and Johnny to her new home in Coatbridge, John remained with his parents. Sal was now in her confinement, it was not long until she had a show, and knew that the birth was imminent. Maggie and Margaret sat with her each day and took care of little Johnny. The pains came. It was hard, the second labour, but not as extreme as the first. Maggie was a good help, she knew exactly what to say and the right moments to intervene, she told Sal when to breathe and pant, as she discussed with her the days before. Sal listened to the voice of calm in her pain, but she was not as distressed and out of control as she had been with little Johnny. It was a lovely June day, the sun shone, the labour progressed well and by the following early morning as the sun rose again, she was holding another wee baby boy in her arms. He had a mop of dark hair, just like his father's, and when his eyes briefly squinted she could see that they were as blue as John's. She felt one with him, and as Maggie and Margaret looked on with joy, she announced, "This is your grandma and your aunty, and this is Edward Christopher Flynn, my bonny wee boy."

Chapter 9 –

The Luck of the Irish

John was so excited to see his new son, but as always, careful to make sure that Johnny was involved and would love his baby brother. Margaret and Maggie made Sal comfortable and placed Edward in her arms. By the time father and son were allowed to see the new arrival, the picture that greeted them was one of pure contentment. Sal was sitting propped up in the bed, little Edward swaddled in a knitted cream shawl and in the crook of her arm; she was gazing at him, taking in every aspect of his face, which was still slightly wrinkled and red as a new born is, and sleeping peacefully. John approached quietly, clutching little Johnny's hand and placing his index finger over his lips to encourage his little boy to be as quiet as a mouse. He lifted Johnny up so that he might see better.

"See, Johnny... this is your new baby brother... Edward... Say hello to Edward."

Johnny had a broad smile on his face. "Baby..." he said, looking back at his father's face, then looking down once more.

"Ed... ward."

"That's right, my wee man, this is Edward."

"Baby with Mama," Johnny replied gleefully, waiting for the praise. This time both parents responded in unison.

"Baby Edward."

Silence fell as all sank into the calmness of the room. Sal looked up at John's face, his smile stretched from ear to ear, love shining from his eyes.

"He has your hair and eyes," she said.

"Oh but he has your face and beautiful skin... he is a bonny wee man."

By now Johnny had become restless, and was allowed to run out to his grandma and auntie. John sat on the bed, alternately stroking mother's hair and baby's cheek. After a while, he broke the silence.

"I have some news for you, lassie..."

Sal looked quizzically at him.

"James and Mary have asked to pop by in a day or so to see you both... that's alright, isn't it?"

Sal tried to appear enthusiastic, but John could see she was more than a little reluctant and far from pleased.

"What has happened between you and James? You always said that he was your favourite brother, but you never want to see him, he is very happy for us, you know?"

"I know... and he is, I am sure... but..." she paused trying to find the words to say that would not seem like she was resentful or jealous, which of course she was.

"It's just... it's just..." She paused again.

"Everything is so perfect for him... He has everything... A home... a steady job, an income... and a perfect wife..." Those words came with a slight edge in her voice. "He does not know what struggle is... I just don't know what to say to them... and why is everything right for them? And why can we not get things right?"

John interrupted. "Now listen Sal... I know things have nae' been easy for us, but we keep going... don't we? We just need some luck, that's all... Things will start going our way, I am sure... after all we have had more than our fair share of the hard times... but I do have a better job now... and I will find us somewhere to live, I am looking now... It won't be long until we and our two wee bairns have a home and we can start making our way forward and then all will be fine... won't it?"

"But John, we always seem to struggle... it's like someone is punishing us... for what I don't know... it just does not seem fair, that no matter what we do, things keep going wrong."

"Nothing has really gone wrong Sal, you are looking too deep again... You could even say that we have had plenty of luck already... After all, who would have ever thought your parents would have let us marry in the first place?... And we are lucky that the Andersons took us in and gave us a good safe place to start our lives together... and yes things change, but we will cope... And I consider myself very lucky every day, especially today... I have my health and a wonderful family... and I have the most beautiful and kind wife and two lovely boys... And had it not been good luck that you and Johnny survived, I would nae' have half of that, and without you I would nae' want any of it..."

Sal was brought to book. Yes he was absolutely right, she had been very fortunate, she knew she should stop this feeling sorry for herself, she was alive, wasn't she? She had two little boys who were a blessing with every smile, she had a very loving man, who kept trying so hard to make a life for them all. She may not have everything yet, but one day they might have enough, and what did she really want, and what did she really want to be? Did she want to be like her mother, never satisfied and forever aspiring to the perfect life, or like Maggie content to have a hearth and home, love of a good man, and a happy family? And did she want her boys to grow up with a father who was unapproachable and cold, never home because of the drive to make more, or did she want her sons to have a kind and loving father who put them first and always tried his best?

"I know you are right, John... and I know I am being very silly, but..."

"Go on."

"But... Mary Ann just makes me angry... I just don't know what to say to her... She just has everything now and I feel so much less than her..."

John smiled, and chortled slightly.

"You know your problem, Sarah?" He never used her full name except when he was going to make a point in jest.

"You are just jealous."

"No!"

"Now don't get upset... you are... it's obvious...and do you know what? You have absolutely nothing to be jealous about... She is not as clever as you are... She is not as beautiful as you are... She does not have two bonny boys as you do... And please give her a chance, you must try to get her know her better... She is a nice person, you know... if you would just give her a chance."

The following Sunday, while the little family remained at Margaret's home in Coatbridge, James and Mary Ann came to call. Sal was seated in the parlour with the young infant asleep in a little bassinette that Maggie had begged from a kind neighbour and placed on a low table next to Sal. John greeted them both at the door, little Johnny exploding with happiness running towards them.

"Uncle James! Uncle James! Look Mama, Uncle James!"

James bent down and gave him an encouraging pat on the head. "Well haven't you grown, little man... And look at you, lassie..."

He moved over to admire his new nephew contently sleeping.

"He is a little man... another little man for my bonny sister."

Sal smiled at her brother with genuine pleasure. Mary hung back behind, not wanting to spoil the reunion; she had always detected an aloofness from her sister-in-law. Sal looked at John and broke the ice.

"It's lovely to see you both... come, Mary, take a seat... come and see Edward."

Mary smiled and moved to the chair closest. John took this as a signal.

"James, I had been meaning to come and see you, I wanted to ask your advice about something, can we just move to the scullery and help Margaret make some tea, and find a bun for Johnny?"

There was an awkward silence momentarily as the two men and the toddler moved out of the small parlour and left the women alone.

"How is Peter?... He is not with you?"

"Aye he's fine... He was coming down with another cold and we thought it was best not to bring him... After all, little Edward does not need that does he?... He is beautiful Sal... and what a content little boy?"

"Don't let appearances fool you Mary... He lets me know when he needs something... very loudly... He is just sleeping now because he has been fed, I made sure of that."

The two women laughed; the shared knowledge of infant demands was common to both.

"Aye… I know what that is like… Peter is just the same… Less so now obviously, he is nearly a year old, but he still has his moments… Still, they say it is better with the second one? I mean you know more and it is better, isn't it?"

"I don't know about that Mary, it is still too soon to say and I am not living without help at the moment… Margaret and Maggie have been so good to us… I am sure once we are on our own it will be a lot harder, but yes you are probably right it must be easier with the second one."

Mary looked relieved to have this news, and sat back in her chair; Sal detected that the question had been more for gaining reassurance than small talk and suddenly the penny dropped.

"Why are you so concerned, Mary?" She examined Mary's face and knew that she had look about her, the look of a women with a secret not told. "Are you expecting again too?"

"Oh… Please don't say anything… I have nae' even told your brother yet. It's very early, but yes I think I am."

"I am so pleased for you… both of you… are you happy?"

"I am not sure… I mean Peter is still not out of nappies and they seem so close in age… I am a little worried that I won't cope… But I look at you there and that gives me hope."

"It's funny… I always thought that you coped so well with everything… I thought that you feared nothing… I mean, you always seem so confident?"

"Quiet, Sal… Never confident… Just quiet…" She paused.

"And I have to be like that because your brother is always like that… And then there is your mother, of course…"

A knowing look passed between them. Yes of course, Sal thought, poor Mary would have experienced the same intense scrutiny that John had been subjected to, probably much more exacting because she was a woman and marrying the precious eldest son. She had misjudged her terribly, it must have been so difficult for her being inducted in the McBride household, and Sal had not supported her as she should. It was at that very moment Sal made up her mind to be different towards her, to show her the kindness that she deserved.

Just then the men reappeared, clutching tea trays and cakes, and very soon all were seated in a congested parlour, laughing and smiling, consuming buns and drinking tea. When it was time to leave, Sal rose from the chair, to hug Mary and offer her a fond farewell, John showed her to the door, while James hung back a little.

"I am so pleased that you and Mary are getting along again… She needs a friend, Sal, you more than most know how difficult things can be, she tries very hard for Mama, but she does nae' find her easy."

He hugged Sal; her small diminutive frame sank into his brotherly embrace, she had not done this in so long, she had forgotten that safeness of the unconditional, familial affection that he had for her. She broke the embrace and looked up at him.

"Yes I will James, don't you worry… And look after her, she needs you to look after her."

A few days later, John returned bubbling with good news and a letter from James. Sarah had ominous feelings about the note he had clutched in his hand and grabbed at it before he had a chance to tell her what he had done. She tore it open, there was another smaller envelope inside; ignoring her brother's brief script and recognising her mother's handwriting she opened it, keeping silent as she read. Bridget had apologised briefly for not coming to visit and made the excuse that Katie had once more taken a bad turn. But with her normal negative qualification she had quipped that while Sal remained in such a congested home with her in-laws, she did not feel it appropriate to visit now. Sal's face froze.

"Well that's it then, she can't even be bothered to come and see her new grandson…" She looked again at the envelope that had contained her mother's note, then at the larger note and envelope with James's brief letter, explaining that mother had been with this letter…

"She has been to see them just up the road, yet she could not make the trip the trip to see us… god damn the woman!"

John was shocked by Sal's sudden exclamation, she was not one for profanity and this was her strength of feeling exhibited.

"Sal, you knew she would not come to any house again where my mother might be… are you really so surprised?"

"I know… I just thought she might and for god's sake John… James only lives a few roads from us… god knows how embarrassed he must be having to act as postman… and why did he not bring it to me in person?"

"Hold on Sal, dinnae' go down that road again… James probably would have brought himself, but he knew that I was stopping by to see him this evening… he probably thought it may be better to hand it to me… I know that James does feel very angry about this. He said she fetched up yesterday, supposedly to see Mary, yet spent the whole time questioning her about us and Edward… She seemed, in Mary's words, quite disappointed that everything had gone so well…"

"No surprises there then… she would have loved it if I had repeated the last terrible birth, she would have made great mileage out of that…" She paused, looking questioningly at John.

"Anyway, why are you seeing my brother? You didn't tell me you would be stopping by?"

"I did not want to raise your hopes, Sal… and I wanted to make sure all was settled… and…"

"Go on…"

"It's excellent news and thanks to James it is all going to happen! There are some nice places going near the railway, in Comely Park, really nice! But we needed a reference from someone respectable… James has been magnificent… As he has just become his own man as a grocer I mean, he has written a wonderful reference and been to see the landlord on our behalf… It was all confirmed today, we can move in next week!"

"Oh John! That's wonderful news! What's it like? Is it big enough? Is it clean?"

"Hang on, I had to take what was going, they are rented out very quickly, I had seen one but that's gone, but they're all about the same, I am sure this one will be fine… I know there are two bedrooms, a parlour and a scullery and a shared yard with a wash house… but everyone I know that rents there never complains and there are quite a few of the railway workers there, you know."

Sal was happy, but worried. She had not seen this new place that would be home, and neither had he, it could be rat-infested and flea-ridden, as many places were off the Gallowgate; they had been quite lucky with David Street and the Andersons', she never underestimated how fortunate they had been there. John could sense her reticence and tried to reassure her further.

"Sal, I am sure it will be lovely… and it is much further east than you think… it's almost a village, it will be just like living here… And I have more news, James is looking to move back to the city too... At least we will have him close by, that should make it seem all the more better, don't you think?"

A week later, all their belongings on a handcart, they moved what few possessions that they had stored at the Flynns' to their new home. Sal had been full of trepidation, but Maggie had done her best to enthuse her with the prospect of a new home, their own home. The place was a bit damp, because it had been vacant a few months, but to Sal's pleasant surprise clean, and much roomier than she had expected. It was on the dark side, as it was on the ground floor on the inner part of the court. The scullery opened onto the yard, which was actually more convenient for washdays, with the laundry at the far side of the court. And unlike many of these communal dwellings in the city, the court was kept relatively clean and free of rubbish, so fewer rats and strays. There was cold water into the scullery and a good size range; once lit, the warmth began to fill the room well. There was a small parlour to the rear, with a fireplace, and two small bedrooms above.

John senior and Maggie had managed to find an old bedstead and a reasonable mattress for Sal and John. A small day bed had been found for Johnny that would do for now, and the bassinette that Margaret had begged from her neighbour for Edward; Sal thought it would last him a few months until a proper bed could be found for the little boys to share. A few chairs and two side tables took their place in the parlour, and the scullery already had a good-sized wooden table and a few chairs.

Sal set about making her kitchen her own. Filling the few wooden cupboards with the pots and pans that she had acquired in David Street, and the few provisions of meat, butter and bread in the meat safe. Maggie rushed round trying to do all that she could, knowing that Sal would do far too much if she let her and she had only just had a baby. Little Edward slept beautifully, Johnny ran round excitedly helping grandma and Papa. Not before too long, most was organised and a stew bubbled invitingly on the range. Maggie made her way to leave. John, Sal and Johnny sat to eat.

"Well, my wife... Is this better than you expected?"

"John, it is marvellous... So much better than I thought it would be... I really feel at home here already... I think things are finally looking up for us... Our luck is going our way."

Chapter 10 –

Clouds Over Comely Park Place

News of their move reached Shettleston and it was not long before a visitation from Bridget took place. It was a very cloudy day in July, and the greyness of the sky only added to Sal's ominous feelings as she greeted her mother at the scullery door and showed her into their makeshift, humble parlour.

"I am sorry Mama, if I had known that you were intending to visit I would have lit the fire, normally I work in the kitchen because the range is on and it is easier to watch over Johnny and Edward."

Bridget sniffed dismissively as she bent over to feel the dampness of the chair.

"I think I shall come in there then, this room is not fit for company. And where are my grandsons?" Her tone was terse and suspicious, as she turned on her heels back into the warm kitchen.

"Edward is just having a nap upstairs, he will be awake just now… And Johnny is with Maggie…"

"Oh."

"She takes him out most afternoons… it gives me a chance to do some work and look after Eddie."

Bridget scowled at the thought of Johnny so much in the clutches of the other family. "And this is your home now?" Again there was a question preloaded with the impending criticism. Sal decided to face it all head on.

"Yes, we have been very lucky… James has been very supportive, and if had not been for him we would not have such a nice place, and it is much closer to the goods yard for John."

"Indeed, if your brother had not intervened god knows where you would be now… You have a great deal to thank James for, I cannot imagine that John would have found anything and you cannot keep falling on the charity and goodwill of others."

"Actually Mama, John did find this place, through the people he works with, James wrote the reference for us and spoke up on our behalf… So it is entirely due to John's efforts that we have a roof at all… And I am very happy with what we have."

"Well it will do I suppose… While you get yourselves back on your feet… It's a bit too close to the Gallowgate for my liking."

"You and father lived in a few places on and off the Gallowgate before we moved to George Street as I remember… It did not do us any harm. At least people look after each other round here."

"And keep you here if they can. No matter, how is your man, still working on the railway then, as a goods guard?… I hope he intends to rise from that, you might afford a less damp place to live, after all it cannot be good for the boys. I still think that if Katie had left the city sooner she would not be as frail as she is…"

Sal was quick to enquire after Katie, before she was accused of selfishness. "She's a great deal better than she was, she will never be strong, but we hope that she may improve in time... Your father feels that she benefits from being in the fresh air, and encourages her to walk and keeps the windows open at nights, he thinks it helps, I am inclined to agree. At least we can live in Shettleston without fear of being molested in our beds." Just then small cries began to come from above; Edward had woken. Sal went to fetch him, changing him to make him slightly more fragrant before presenting him to his pernickety grandmother.

"I cannot hold him dear, show him to me so I might get a better look... Well, well, he is a McBride then, dark hair, strong features, he is going to be a handsome lad... He is sturdy, far more so than John... I suppose you named him after the king?"

"Yes... And his second name is Christopher like his father."

"No McBride names then this time, what a shame... Never mind, at least James named his after his father, and Peter is a little chap, the apple did not fall far from the tree there, his grandfather finds him a very nice little boy."

"Just like Johnny," Sal interjected shortly.

"He sees a great deal more of wee Peter than he does of John, it is very hard to make that judgement."

This game of comment and counter comment continued for an hour, until Bridget made her excuses of tiredness to leave. Sal felt the enormous relief as she rose from the chair, towards the door, to be confronted by Maggie holding Johnny's hand about to knock.

"Oh Mrs McBride, I wasn't expecting you... Say hello to your other grandma, Johnny."

Johnny sheepishly looked up at the woman that he hardly knew and who hardly knew him.

"Hell-o..." he said slowly, clinging tightly to Maggie's hand, then catching sight of his mother, running hastily passed and hiding behind her.

"Strange little boy," Bridget muttered. "Still, if he hardly sees us, we cannot be surprised. Good day, Mrs Flynn."

Maggie sat nursing Eddie in the kitchen and entertaining Johnny, while Sal set to making supper for her small family. They discussed how the visit had been, Sal expressed her relief at her mother having left and how she could not abide the constant picking apart of her life by her non accepting mother.

"Now, Sal... as much as I find her difficult, she is your mother and the only one that you will ever have... and I have to say, she and your father have worked very hard and got on... I am happy with my lot in life, but I have lived in some very different places, and it makes you glad just to have a roof over your head and a loving family... but she has made a good life for hers... but she has had to be the way she is... You are never going to change her... but your little boys should know their families and where they come from, that is very important... Don't let your feelings come between them, you have to rise above all this, for the sake of the wee ones."

A few weeks past. Sal knew that Maggie was right, and determined to make the necessary effort to participate in the life in Shettleston, in the same way that she had drawn a line under her petty jealousies towards Mary. She and John resumed their regular Sunday visits to her family's home; it was, as always, strained and short for the parents, but much fun for Johnny with his aunties, who instantly fell in love with their new baby nephew. Bridget gave the news on one such visit, that Mary was expecting again, expecting a disgruntled response from Sal.

"I already knew," she said cheerfully. "Mary told me her good news when she first came to see Eddie, I am so pleased for her."

"She told you then!" Bridget was horrified. Sal realised that she had created difficulty for Mary and James and quickly recovered the situation before it escalated further.

"It was very early on... She was not sure... She hadn't even told James... I think that she thought it was too soon... I understand, surely you do, Mama?"

Bridget grunted. Sal continued, "Do you know when she is having the baby?"

"Early in the new year, I believe."

"Well then, I was right... After all, it was early June when she told me... She was right to wait rather than raise everyone's hopes."

Sal made sure to visit Mary the following week and explain what had happened before any commentary was made. Mary laughed, "Sal, dinnae' worry lassie... Your Mama has just had her thunder stolen... She'll get over it... and there is nothing that she can say to me... she does not like getting on the wrong side of your brother, he knows too many people now and he is beginning to have a good circle... She wants to make sure she stays in with us."

Life settled at Comely Park Place. John's routine was a simple one, up early in the morning, a brief breakfast then off to the goods yard to attend to his daily duties, before taking a train here and there and managing the loading and offloading of various wares and products, valuables and consumables. He sometimes stayed at the corner of the court briefly to chat to friends in the evening, before returning home to help Sal getting the boys settled for bed. Johnny was now a strong little boy, always happy and chatty, always smiling. Eddie too had a fine disposition, never crying when he woke up from a sleep, very easy as a baby, which Sal was very grateful for as she was able to resume her homework for the little bit of pin money to help. They were not struggling as they had, rent was always paid on time, they ate simply but well, and clothes were always found; and thanks to Sal's skills, patched and mended as required.

One evening, John was approached by a nodding acquaintance, a man he thought worked on the rail somewhere as most did round there.

"Er... Mr Flynn, isn't it? I thought I recognised you..."

"Yes... Mr..."

"Jim... just Jim... I wonder if I might have a word?"

"Yes, what can I do for you?"

"You work on the goods trains, don't you?... My friend tells me that you work on some good ones?"

"Er, yes... Why, are you looking for work? I am not sure I can help you, but I can have a word with the foreman."

"That's very kind of you... John... it is John, isn't it?" John nodded.

"My friends and me were just wondering if you wanted to make a bit extra... I mean you have a young family... Every little bit helps, doesn't it? We can all help each other... That's how to get on... A bit here and a bit there..."

John felt the hair on the back of his neck bristle; there was something about this man that was making him feel uncomfortable, and the more he thought about it, he had never actually seen him with any of his workmates, he was always having aside discussions with some, and generally dismissed. John did not like what he was saying, or what he was trying to imply; he thought it best to extricate himself from this situation, as nicely but as firmly as he could.

"Er, Jim... I am not sure what you are asking or wanting... But I am not sure I can help you... Sorry, but I am perfectly fine, best you ask somebody else."

"Ah well, Mr Flynn, if that's the way you feel... No offence like... let's just keep this between ourselves." And with that he turned and walked away, leaving John slightly confused, but greatly relieved that he had not involved himself. He returned home without considering it further and he certainly was not going to burden Sal with it, after all there was always someone on the make round that part of the city.

Sal's life, too, had established a rhythm of homemaker and mother, with all of the associated tasks and responsibilities. Apart from the weekly trial of Shettleston, there was not much that troubled her. Once a week she would take the two boys to visit Mary in Cathcart; this was great fun for Johnny who had taken to his cousin Peter and they would play happily. Meanwhile, the women would pass the time talking of her pregnancy and the growing Eddie, who could sit happily on the kitchen floor and play with a pot and spoon to his heart's content. Mary said that she hoped for a girl this time, but like Sal would be glad of another son, as she was used to little boys now.

"And little boys grow into strong sons... And we need strong men in our lives, Sal," she used to say.

In the court, Sal had made friends with the neighbour Annie Gillespie; she was about ten years older than Sal, and had a hard life. She had one daughter, Ellie, a plain little dumpy girl of thirteen; she was Annie's little angel, the only highlight of a bad first marriage; one that had been punctuated by regular beatings until he had died as a drunk in some backstreet in the city. Annie had taken up with a nice kindly man, much older than herself, she had taken his name, yet Sal suspected that was all they had done to keep up the appearance of a marriage that had not actually occurred. Ellie had a lovely disposition and would always pop in and help Sal with the boys; not having any siblings herself, she had almost adopted the boys as her own brothers. Her marriage prospects were a long way off, if obtainable; she was very homely but painfully shy, and working in a factory was all that she could aspire to once she finished school at fourteen. Thanks to Ellie, Sal was able to fit all the things in that she had to do in her increasingly busy days. Whenever Sal needed the boys watching so that she could go and get fabrics, pins and threads for her work, Ellie would do this gladly. She would return the kindness to Annie by making pies and preserves to supplement her kitchen. Sal had had plenty of experience of cooking, and now that it was for her home it was less of a chore and more of a joy; whenever she managed to afford the ingredients to make a bit extra she would take to the market in a wicker basket to sell. She kept a jar of pennies under her mattress; she saw this as money for the boys, for small treats.

Months passed and this blissful time of peace culminated in Eddie's first Christmas. This time was shared with James and Mary; there were no challenges to this arrangement from Bridget, who understood that Mary – who by now was heavily pregnant – was not up to the journey to Shettleston and Peter was an ebullient little boy, who desperately needed the company of his playmate cousin. The grown-ups shared a simple Christmas meal together, thankful to James for as a grocer, he had saved the best cuts of meat that he could get from his butcher neighbour, and in turn, James had given the butcher a fine selection of vegetables and treats. The Christmas afternoon was spent playing charades and card games.

Hogmanay was at home in the court. Annie 'first-footed' Sal at midnight with the statutory lump of coal, freshly baked bread and a handful of salt.

"May your pocket nae' be empty henny, your hearth be warm, and yer bairns' bellies be full," she cheerfully chimed as she entered the small kitchen with Ellie for a wee dram. Sal, Ellie and John toasted the new year 1908, with all the hope and expectation which had been their happiness to know during the last six months.

They then made their progress the next day to Mary Lea Cottage. Bridget was remarkably warm and even made an effort to smile, more at little Johnny than his parents. Peter was his normal aloof self, not enquiring after their health or lives – he had eyes and ears everywhere in the city, there was not much he did not know. Katie seemed well, and Jeanie, now a rising 13, was blossoming into a very attractive young woman, with expectations to start work sometime in the next year. Sal asked her where she was planning to look for a job, expecting her to go into the trade as she and Bridget had.

"No Sal, it's Katie that likes to make things… there are plenty of good jobs in the shops that will pay better than the rag trade, I might look in Shettleston and see if there are some opportunities there, but I have a while to wait yet, I cannae' leave school till the summer."

Sal noticed how easy it was for the girls, compared to all that she had had to do. With none of the brothers there, and Peter very rarely home, it was just Bridget, Jeanie, Katie and Annie Theresa, and Katie ate like a sparrow at the best of times. Annie Theresa was not quite as loud as she used to be, but what she lost in volume she had increased in chatti ness; her latest excited topic was the impending arriv another niece or nephew.

"I am so excited Sal, we will have girl visiting soon that will mean I a. think that is amazing, don't you? I m four times? My friends think I am real.

"Goodness gracious Annie Theresa, slow down, what have I told you?" Bridget interjected sternly. "You have far too much to say for yourself."

Annie sat back, admonished once more by her mother.

Then came the new arrival. It was early afternoon on the eighth of January, in their home at Whitehall Terrace in Cathcart, that James and Mary welcome Ernest into the world. Sal was amazed at the choice of name, and enquired of her brother where it had come from.

"Aye, the butcher's that Mama uses in Shettleston has a really nice young man working for him, his name is Ernest. Mary and I were really taken with him, and thought it would be a nice name if we had another wee laddie."

He was a small baby, which had meant a relatively trouble-free birth for Mary. Sal brought over a few pies that she had made to help with the meals, and took turns with Mary's mother to help get her daughter back on her feet and coping again with two little boys. Mary was thrilled to have another son, and looked to the future.

"Oh Sal, four little cousins, all boys, won't they have a fine time together? It is so nice to see how Johnny and Peter have taken to one another... Now Eddie and Ernest can do the same."

And indeed, for the coming months, the families grew closer, and used any times they could to be together. Sundays were not always in Shettleston now, and it was hard for Bridget to upset the applecart as she wanted to maintain her good relationship with her son. Often the two families would meet at Glasgow Green, which was a short train ride for James and Mary. There they would walk, or on fine days ave a picnic; while Johnny and Peter got into mischief, Eddie stigated his growing world, and Ernest slept in his pram.

Sal and John had now passed a whole year; everything seemed settled and calm. They had carved a simple but happy existence. They had friends and good neighbours, and they had learned how to manage the intrusions from Bridget that had marred so much of their first years together. John was very optimistic that he had made his mark with the rail guard foreman, and that it would not be long before he would have a small promotion; a little more could go a long way.

Chapter 11 –

Turn and Turn Again

John was right. By the end of the summer he had been given greater responsibility; he was now trusted to supervise the loading and unloading of goods on some of the larger commercial goods trains. He had a junior guard Alfie, who would work alongside John, and eventually John would train him up to take his role when he moved on. Alfie was newly married, and as keen as mustard to learn, he took his responsibilities and his duties to railway extremely seriously.

The yard was always full of commercial freight during the evenings, with trains having arrived from the ports with goods to unload, to be sent on by wagons to the many factories and outlets across the city, there were many men busying themselves with the various collections, which meant lists, dockets, manifests and receipts to be administered. Alfie would watch over what was to be taken off and which wagon was to receive, while John checked the lists and signed off the consignments.

It was a busy evening in late November, one train had arrived earlier than expected and the next was late to arrive. Some of the merchants' wagons had not arrived to collect their goods, and John and Alfie waited on a half empty rail car for the late wagon arrivals. Twenty or so others bustled around on the platform moving trollies and chatting. Alfie asked if he could just pop round the back to relieve himself as he had not had a chance since the morning. John nodded and stayed by his post. Then he saw a figure that he recognised that made him feel uncomfortable.

He was standing to one side on the platform talking to another roughly dressed character. He could see it was Jim, who had stopped him by the court those many months ago. John was very concerned that he should not be there; he had already made up his mind that this man was up to no good from the approach that he had made to John. He stepped off the train and walked towards the pair. Jim smiled and called, "Hey if it isn't John Flynn… How are you, Mr Flynn?"

"You should not be here, I think you know that?"

"Now Mr Flynn, dinnae' be so inhospitable… Now I was just telling my friend here, wasn't I, what a nice man you are…"

"I will say it again Jim, you shouldn't be on the yard, I will have to report you to the foreman if you don't leave."

"Well that's not a nice way to treat a friend… and I had heard you were such a nice chap… We are not doing any harm, we are just standing here passing the time of day… there's no harm in that is there?" All the time Jim smiled as if he had known John all of his life, but made no attempt to introduce John to his colleague, who looked John up and down suspiciously.

"I am not going to say it again… Leave, please… or you will be reported, no unauthorised personnel should be on the yard… Now go."

"OK Mr Flynn… We will leave…" He turned to walk away, and then turned back. "Oh, and thank you for all that you have done."

John stood stunned for a second; he did not understand the cheeriness and the thanks. He turned back towards the train, Alfie had stepped back on and was looking in his direction.

"Who was that?"

"Oh just some chancers, I have sent them away... if you ever see them, Alfie, you should do the same."

Just then a drayman pulled in to collect his load for the local spirits merchant. Alfie unloaded the crates of whisky, and counted them off. He stopped.

"We are four short, John?... There were twenty, I know because I counted them before I went round the back... we are four short!"

"We can't be!" John was alarmed. What had happened? He didn't understand it, he had only stepped off the train for a second...

The penny dropped... No wonder Jim had been so nice and tried to engage him in conversation... He had been so stupid! He had been scammed! While his back was turned and Alfie was off the train, Jim had more friends lying in wait for him to be distracted and they had taken the whisky! The colour drained from his face.

"Oh my god! You wait here!" he garbled as he shot off the train, running down the platform, desperately seeking the thieves with the missing goods; the drayman complaining that he would be in for it, if he had not got the full consignment. Frantically he searched up and down, there was no sign of anyone, Jim – if that had even been his name – and his suspicious friend were nowhere in sight, and there was no sign of others carrying the crates of missing whisky. By the time he had returned to the rail car, an angry drayman was venting his steam at the foreman who looked none too happy, and was trying to get an explanation from Alfie.

"What do you mean you left the train, sonny? You never leave the train, you know that?"

"But... but..." Alfie stuttered, trying to get his words out.

"It was my fault, Mr O'Brian." John made his shame-faced excuse. "I was conned, sir... There were two men who shouldn't have been here, and I stepped off to challenge them, I had no idea they had others waiting..."

"How did you know they shouldn't be here? And you should not leave the train." Mr O'Brian, the foreman, was visibly furious, the drayman continued to rant, Alfie felt uncomfortable.

"I had seen one of them before a while ago, he tried to get me to help him... I told him no," John pleaded. Alfie shifted foot to foot, still feeling amiss.

"You are both idiots! And I expected much better of you John, if it wasn't for all the good work you have done, you would be dismissed instantly, you know that... As it is this has got to be paid for!" To the drayman, "I will make sure that you have full payment to give to the merchant. Come to my office," To John and Alfie, "And you two can make good out of your wages."

Alfie protested, "But..."

"No buts, sonny... think yourself lucky you still have a job!" With that the drayman and O'Brian headed to the rail yard office. John was crestfallen.

"I am so sorry Alfie... I really am..."

Alfie was disgruntled. "This is not fair... you let me go off and now I am in trouble... I will never get a promotion now! If you hadn't let me go, it would not have happened!"

"I am sorry Alfie... I was taken in, honestly."

"Let's just get this wagon unloaded... I'm away hame!"

Two days later, Mary opened her door to see Sal on the doorstep.

"Oh how lovely to see you... This was unexpected... Where are the boys?" Sal promptly burst into tears.

"Oh my goodness Sal... Come on in... what is wrong?"

It took a while for Mary to settle Sal and calm her down enough to make sense of her garbled sobs. Sal tried to explain what had occurred the other evening at the rail yard, the turn of events with the two characters; one John had met before, but not liked and the other he did not know at all. Then she explained that John had let Alfie leave to go to the toilet and he had stupidly left the car to confront the men. Then the crates of whisky had gone missing, and John had realised his error. He had come home, none too happy, but after they had done their sums they had thought they could just about manage to make ends meet as Alfie was to pay half, and the foreman had been quite fair and given them a month or two to pay all off.

"Then..." sniff, "...he went in yesterday..." Sniff, sniff, "...and Mr O'Brian took him into the office and asked for his uniform, he was sacking him!"

"Oh my goodness... Why? It was nae' his fault?..."

"That's it... it wasn't! But Alfie had said, he had seen John being 'friendly' with the two on the platform... Alfie insisted to foreman that he had nothing to with it, John had sent him off the train... he thought that John was involved! He told the foreman, that he thinks John helped them and turned a blind eye to let the steal the whisky!"

"Oh no, Sal, that is terrible!... Did John not try to explain?"

"Of course he did! But O'Brian would not listen, as far as he was concerned; the evidence against John was too strong and he must be dismissed..." she sobs, "...And he told John he was lucky he wasn't up before a judge. He said, if ever he hears of him getting any money or handling any whisky he will be!"

"Oh dear... oh Sal... I know times have been tough for you, but I know John would never have done anything like this... You must do too?"

"I must admit, Mary... when I first heard the story... of this man talking to John... I was a little bit suspicious, because he never told me about it... but no... I don't think he was involved." Sal sobbed again inconsolably. "Ellie has the boys... John is out looking for work... I just don't know what we are going to do now... and I know my father will know, he knows everything! What are we going to do?"

"Oh Sal... I just don't know... and things had been going so well... maybe if John can find this man, Jim you said? Maybe if he can find him, then he can get the police involved and he can prove he was innocent?"

"John says that he has only seen him a few times talking to others around... and most of them won't talk to John now, because they either think he did it, or don't want to be associated with him in case O'Brian thinks they are in on it... One man did talk to John, and he said this man has tried asking others, and there are a few bad men from the city who come and do the same thing. But he does not know who he is, where he comes from, and as John now suspects, he is not called Jim..."

"Oh dear, oh dear... Look Sal, John's a hard worker... he'll find something I am sure... and we will help you if we can... It will not be easy, but you will manage... the boys are bigger, you can do some work, or something?"

"No, Mary, I can't..."

"Why not?"

"The worst of possible news... I am expecting again..."

Christmas 1908 was very bleak, not what the happy couple from the year before had ever expected. There was no family meal, or shared joys. John had only found labouring work and that was not regular; he mended roads, he helped build walls, he did get offered a job building houses, until the gaffer heard of his misfortune and began to doubt his honesty, so retracted the offer. Sal was experiencing the same sickness and tiredness she had with her previous two pregnancies, and there was never enough food to go around. She would make sure that John got the lion's share to keep him going, working or looking for work, and the boys came next. There were a few days she didn't eat at all, and she was always grateful when Annie or Ellie stopped by with their leftovers, expecting Sal to eat it, which she always promised she would, but as soon as they left she would add it to the meagre scrapings for John and the boys. Lack of food and nourishment increased her nausea tenfold, and she was weak and tearful, struggling to manage with a little boy and a toddler.

She had been correct in her assessment of her father's tentacles of information. He had been made aware of his son-in-law's sacking for dishonesty within a day. Bridget had been incandescent with rage and the perceived shame that he had brought on her family, and most particularly her husband, who was a most honest businessman. The only blessing was that she had refused to see them and had sent a verbal message through James not to visit at Shettleston for a while; they were just not welcome. James and Mary stood by John and Sal, and tried desperately to intercede with the ragings of the McBride matriarch, all to no avail. James counselled that time would heal all, one way or another, and it was probably safe just to let everyone calm down. Sal was glad that she had not got to endure what would be to come when she eventually was faced with her mother's wrath, even more so now that she knew she was pregnant, and thankfully – due to James and Mary's discretion – her mother did not.

Maggie came to the rescue as much as she could. She knew and believed absolutely in her son's honesty and was pitifully sorry for the turn of events that had happened for the poor young family. She could see that Sal was pregnant again, but was desperate to do some sort of work while she still could, just to bring the much needed pennies in. Maggie took the boys from Sal on a couple of mornings a week, to allow her to go and clean in a big villa in West George Street – the household there had been hit by staff sickness, and they were desperate for any help, with or without references. Sal knew the work would only be for a few weeks or so, and she would be showing soon; she could not continue too far, maybe just to the end of January. But while she was there she was warm and the cook would always give her a cup of beef tea, before she would set to cleaning and leading the grates in each of the rooms.

This modest villa was a mansion in comparison to anything that Sal had ever known, with vast rooms bedecked with velvet curtains and plush carpets on highly polished wooden floors. It was well-furnished and normally boasted a cook, a house maid, and housekeeper. All this was for a man and wife in their mid-thirties, who had a young son about Johnny's age. The man of the house was the son of a well-to-do and worked in a bank, and the wife was the daughter of a wealthy family of tobacco merchants. It seemed so unfair to Sal that these two were just lucky, because they were born to the right family, and had so much for so few of them; they could rattle around these large rooms and did not need half of them. The housemaid had been taken ill before Christmas and it was her absence that Sal was filling in for, although the housekeeper did not want Sal to perform any of the familial duties, just the heavy duty cleaning. She was not considered well-polished enough to wait on the family and most of the time she was kept away, never seen. The only exception was when she had to clean out and remake the fire in the little boys' room.

He had taken ill at the same time as the maid, and was visited daily by the doctor. Sal was not sure what was wrong with him. She could see he had a fever and was slightly flushed, and he had a persistent hacking cough, but whenever she was in there too long, she was shooed away by the housekeeper, who was attending to the little boys' needs, with various embrocations and inhalations. By the third week of January, she reported to work to be told by the housekeeper that the regular maid had returned and she was no longer required. She was paid for her trouble and the cook kindly made another beef tea.

Sal decided to collect the boys from Maggie and take them for a treat, they had had so little recently. On arriving at the Flynns', she was greeted by a very worried Maggie.

"Oh Sal... I have sent my John to find yours... I was nae' sure which house you were at..."

"What's wrong, Maggie?"

"It's little Johnny, henny... He has a fever... We must get the doctor to him."

Sal rushed in. Johnny lay listlessly on the couch. He was pale and drawn and his skin was clammy to the touch, and he was starting to cough every now and then; he opened his eyes.

"Mammy," he whimpered. "I dinnae' feel good."

"Oh my little lad, don't worry sweetheart, we will get the doctor and he will make you all well. Grandpa has gone to find Papa, and we all be with you... Mama's here now... don't you worry."

Maggie had brought in a flannel to try and reduce Johnny's temperature, Sal looked at her pleadingly.

"Dinnae' worry Sal... he is a tough little one, he will get through this... Eddie is fine... It's probably best we keep him here, while you nurse Johnny... We don't want them both getting sick now, do we?"

Chapter 12 –

No More Valentines

The doctor came and diagnosed scarlet fever. He instructed Sal to break the fever the best she could by cooling him down with flannels, and he too thought it was best to keep him away from the baby, who was far more vulnerable. John had been found, and came rushing back. Together they took the decision to take little Johnny back to their home and nurse him there. As they carried their sick little boy home on that bitterly cold day at the end of January, Sal mithered: had she brought this on him? The house where she had worked with the little lad with the same symptoms? She did it all to earn extra money to help her family, and now it seems she had brought greater problems on everyone.

John clutched his son, wrapped tightly in a blanket, barely conscious.

"Now Sal, you weren't to know... You did what you thought was best... It might not have been there that you picked up the infection, there is plenty in the city... You heard the doctor, this is the season for it."

Little Johnny was laid on a mattress in the parlour; it was close enough to the scullery to keep a good watch on him, and the room was cooler to try and break the fever. Sal and John took it in turns to sit up with him that night and the following to nurse him. By the third day, Sal was more concerned that John found work to pay for food and rent and insisted that he must sleep and go out to seek any labouring he could get. Then she took over all of the care for their son. Ellie and Annie came by each day, trying to get her to take a break and most importantly eat something; in all this commotion she had almost forgotten that she was pregnant. She was over five months gone by now, yet barely showing as she was so undernourished. The more that they tried to share the burden, the more that Sal insisted that she could not leave him. Her sense of guilt for having brought this crisis on her family grew inside her and she would not leave his side for more than a few minutes at a time.

Maggie stayed away; the risk of transmission to little Eddie was too great. John had been to see James and Mary warning them not to visit, Ernest was far too small and Peter had never been a very strong child. It was unlike Johnny, who had always seemed feisty and sturdy; now he just lay motionless, flushed and drawn, his eyes staring madly. In his moments of reality, he would cry and plead to his Mama to make him feel better. Sal felt completely helpless, and wished that there was something that she could do, something more than cold flannels that she could administer to ease his suffering and break his fever. Annie tried to counsel her.

"He looks better, Sal... I am sure in a day or so we will be able to get some broth into him, then he will get better... You just have to give his body a chance to fight this... Once the fever has broken he will be fine... Look at you henny, you don't look well and you have another to think of..."

Sal looked up at Annie, her eyes moist with tears, sunken by tiredness.

"Annie... I just want my little Johnny well... I don't care about this one." She patted her midriff. "... I wish I wasn't pregnant again... I just want this little man to get well, I would give anything for him to be well."

"Now Sal... You know you don't mean that... Of course you must care for the new baby... don't say things like that, don't wish ill on the new life that you have."

"But don't you see... I was not close to Johnny when he was born because it was such a terrible time... I think god is punishing me for not wanting him... I wish I could take it all back... I really wish I could make him well... have the medicines that housekeeper had in West George Street... but we can't even afford food for the table now, never mind medicines."

"You mustn't think like that, Sal... it won't help anyone... You must stay positive... you've just had more than your share of bad luck recently... It will all get better, I am sure."

Three more days passed, and the fever finally broke. They managed between them to begin to feed Johnny with a weak broth. For a day or so he seemed to rally and improve; Sal thought the worst had passed and began to plan to bring Eddie back, and then the cough came. At first it was a little hack of a cough, like the one she had heard in the boy's bedroom at the grand villa, then it began to manifest with the distinctive whoop, whoop. She knew he had now developed whooping cough. Annie and Ellie kept the copper boiling with plenty of hot water and Sal sat with Johnny on her lap in the scullery with a bowl of steam trying desperately to ease his breathing, to give his body a chance to fight this second new infection.

John had worked for three days, but now could not find anything, yet did not know what to do at home, so he would go out every day walking the streets aimlessly in the hope of just finding something, anything to do. He had hit the bottom; he was feeling like a complete failure. In his mind, he was neither a husband or a father; he could not support his family, because his stupidity had caused him to lose his job – a good job with real prospects. Now he had absolutely no hope of getting anything long term, his character had been blemished, yet he was innocent, but no one would accept that; he had been tarnished as a thief at worse, and inept at best. His mother-in-law had been right about him, he was feckless and useless. Now his son lay desperately ill, and he could not face that either; he would rather walk through his shoe leather than stay and be of use.

Just then, while in the Trongate, he saw a poster casually nailed to a door; he had probably passed it a thousand times, yet it had never caught his eye before. The line 'Homes for millions' caught his eye and he read the headline 'Canada – The Last Best West'. The poster was part of the Canadian government's campaign to encourage immigrants world-wide to come and break the land. Most of Canada towards the west at that time remained wild and unpopulated, the land was hard and unbroken, but the government feared that with the drive across the border in the United States to find land, that there might be a land grab, and that had led to an appeal to other parts of the Empire and beyond for people to come and help cultivate the provinces, in a hope of stopping the land being reacquired by stealth. The poster was offering parcels of land to anyone willing to break it; all they had to do was to register and make the commitment and their passage would be paid.

John knew this was what he had to do; he had no other choice. What could he offer his wife and children here, with no job and no hope of one? Bridget was just waiting for him to fail, so that she could wrestle all from him, at least this way he could make a real go of things, he could have land, his land. He could build a home and be his own man, not answerable to a foreman, or parents, not answerable to anyone. He was elated, full of enthusiasm, this was the answer to all of their problems; this was the answer to his prayers. He was full of the good news when he returned to Comely Park Place, but when entering the door, his mood changed as he was greeted by an anxious Annie; Sal was back in the parlour, the unmistakeable hacking and whooping sounding around the house.

"Oh John... yer bairn is taken bad! Sal does nae' know what to do... I dinnae' know either... I have some pennies for you laddie... I think ye best fetch the doctor to him again."

The doctor's face was grave. Having fought one bad infection, Johnny's immunity had been badly compromised; he could barely fight anything and this new infection coming on top of the first was not good. There was not much he could do, so he told the parents to keep him as comfortable as they could and to try and ease his breathing, all that Sal had been doing anyway; however, he stressed that if he took a turn for the worse that it was best to take him straight to the Belvidere Infectious Diseases hospital.

"At least they can help his breathing with oxygen there if needed."

Sal looked helplessly at her little boy, John forgot all of his elation and came back to the hard cold reality of the here and now and not fanciful pipedreams.

Another two days passed, and Johnny's condition worsened considerably. He coughed almost continually and struggled to breathe, he could no longer lie down, and all, including Annie and Ellie, took it in turns to sit with him on their laps, allowing him to sleep sitting up when he could, exhausted from all of the coughing. Sal grabbed some sleep, and barely ate, her face looked skeletal and the black circles around her eyes heightened the sunken cheeks further. It was now the twelfth of February. That morning had followed a day of vomiting and coughing; the parents could take his suffering no more. John borrowed a handcart from a neighbour and pushed his sick little boy and his wife, who could barely stand, let alone walk, the mile to the hospital.

There they sat and waited, while nurses swept the boy up into an isolation ward and a doctor was found to examine him. Sal clung tightly to John's hand; he sat and stared at the opposite wall. They said nothing, each lost in their own hopeless state, making silent prayers for the life of their child. The doctor came to them.

"Mr and Mrs Flynn, your son is very sick… It is much worse than we feared, he is full of infection… his blood is full of infection…"

John stood and looked at the doctor appealingly. "What are you saying, doctor? You can help him can't you, you can make him better?"

"No, Mr Flynn… There is nothing we can do… I don't think he can fight this, he has no strength left… all we can do is make him comfortable…"

Sal gasped and collapsed on the chair in a dead faint. The doctor rushed to her. "Mrs Flynn… Mrs Flynn? Is she unwell?"

"She's expecting doctor, about five and half months… but she is not eating or sleeping…"

The doctor waved some smelling salts under her nose, which brought her back. Tears began to roll down her face, it was all too much to take in, she had fought so hard for her son, she sobbed. "But… but… he might… with god's help come through… he might? He could?…"

"Well... It is in god's hands now... Why don't you come and sit with him... It may help..."

Sal leant on John as she was led to Johnny's bedside. He looked so small, in the giant hospital bed; the hospital was much lighter than their dark little home, she could see purple blotches were now appearing over his face and body. She looked back at the doctor, alarmed by what she saw.

"It's the infection in his blood, Mrs Flynn... If he can fight it, these marks will go... At least he is unconscious now, and his body is resting a little... the next twenty four hours will be the telling time."

For two days and two nights, Sal remained by his bed. John was sent to tell everyone the news and to warn all to stay away from the hospital. Mary and James were devastated by the turn of events and set out to see Bridget and Peter. Maggie tried to get John to stay and eat a meal, but he was too desperate to get back to Sal, who he knew was completely exhausted, but still unwilling to face the inevitable.

That morning at about six o'clock, Johnny's eyes fluttered open. Sal, who had been watching over him, took it as a good sign and called for the nurse. Sal held his little hand in hers.

"My wee man... Mama's here..."

All he said was, "Mama." Then he closed his eyes again. The nurse came and felt for his pulse.

"It's very weak... I am afraid he is leaving you."

Sal froze, listening for his diminishing breath; soon all was silent.

"He is at peace now... god rest his soul." The nurse placed her hand on Sal's shoulder, as the silent tears fell like rain down her face. John, who had been sitting nearby, began to shake with silent sobs, and came and knelt by his bedside, an arm around Sal. She moved her face into his broad shoulder and let her grief go. It was St Valentine's Day and his little soul had gone.

Sal was completely shattered physically and emotionally. It was considered by everyone that she was in no fit state to care for a toddler and Eddie should remain with his grandparents for the time being. Mary and James took Sal in, to try and bring her out of the depression that now engulfed her absolutely. John would pass between the two homes, trying to help with his sick wife when she would let him, and keep his other little boy from fretting at the lack of contact from his mother. Mary sat with Sal and comforted her.

"He is at peace now, Sal... you did everything that you could... you could have done no more..."

Tired and mournful, Sal replied, "I blame myself... if I had not worked at that house... if I had just let John do what he could to bring the money in this would not have happened... I have lost my little boy, because I tried to get more... just like my mother, I wasn't content just to settle for what I had..."

"You can't blame yourself, he could have caught this from anyone, from anywhere. You don't know that it was your fault... and you were just trying to do your best, Sal..." Mary paused, thinking how to phrase her next statement. "Just like your mother has already tried to do her best..." She paused again, waiting for a reaction, but none came. "She has asked if you would allow her to visit you... here. She wants to give her condolences in person..." She paused again apprehensively. "Will you see her?"

Sal sat, stone faced. Inside she was in a maelstrom of emotions, deep grief at the loss of her beloved little boy that she had fought so hard to keep alive; critical of herself for what she saw as her own fault; angry that the first time her mother had shown interest during all of their misfortunes was the death of her first grandson.

Mary continued, "Sal... sometimes it takes something like this to change people... I do think your mother is genuinely sorry and really does want to make her peace with you... I do think that you ought to give her a chance to try... Will you see her, please? If you don't you will never know, and worse than that, the wounds may never heal."

Sal reluctantly agreed. She knew that Mary was right in her assessment of the situation, although naïve to expect too much. Sal knew her mother; Mary only ever saw the good in people. What Sal feared most was that the person that she disliked the most was in fact more like herself than anyone else; she was very much her mother's daughter.

A week or two passed. Sal was stronger, she had eaten and slept and although now in her third trimester, still barely showing, she knew her mother had already been told. She sat and waited in Mary's parlour while Bridget was shown in by Mary and then the two women were left alone. Sal did not rise to greet her, and barely acknowledged her as she took the seat opposite. Bridget was visibly shocked by the appearance of her daughter, and she had not seen her the weeks before now she was emaciated.

"I am dreadfully sorry for your loss... he was a lovely wee boy... your father, too, has asked me to pass on his condolences, he would have come, but James said that you weren't up to having visitors... I can see..." Bridget waited for a reply. Sal stayed silent. Bridget moved uncomfortably in her chair, not sure what to say now; she stumbled over her words, trying not to appear insincere. "Er... and... we

are sorry to hear that things have not been going... well...
for you... and your... husband..." Still Sal sat silently staring. Bridget continued. "It was unfortunate that he lost
his job..." Sal's eyes flashed. Bridget made an attempt to
recover her position. "And I hear you are carrying another
child?"

Sal pulled herself up in her chair and leaned forward,
almost menacingly. She began, "Mother... If you have come
here to be genuine and mourn your poor wee grandson,
that is one thing... I am not myself at the moment and it is
very hard not to be emotional, something I know you see as
weakness... but if you have come to criticise or accuse John
of dishonesty or fecklessness, you can leave now. We have
been through enough and you made it all very clear that we
were not welcome, and had brought shame of you and your
family. John is neither feckless or dishonest... We have had
more than our share of difficulties and losing Johnny has left
us both desperately in grief... We have little or no money,
John is struggling to get work... and yes mother, I am carrying another child, and like you did, I will probably have
another and another... One day I hope that you accept me
as a daughter and that you will accept John as my husband,
but until that day, I have neither wish nor desire to pass
meaningless discussions with you about how we should or
should not run our lives... As you have already pointed out
to us on numerous occasions, we have made our own beds...
Now I thank you for your condolences, not that any words
will ever take away this pain that I feel... but I respectfully
ask that you leave now, I am tired... When the baby is born
I will let you know."

Bridget knew better than to react; she could see her
daughter's mind was determined and that there were no

words that could make her rise or react, or forgive. Whatever Bridget's intentions had been that day – and she was not sure herself whether she had come to heal or pour scorn – had failed. She left for Shettleston, deeply sorry for the tragedy, but as stoic as ever.

Chapter 13 –

Beckoning
New Horizons

By the middle of March, Sal had returned to Comely Park Place to be a mother to Eddie and a wife to John. She believed that the baby would not be with her until the end of April, so there was time for preparation and adjustment. This was a hard time for their small family, with John only managing at best a couple of days of casual work in any one week, but this was the time that their friends, neighbours and family rallied round them. There was little or no money to buy food, yet there was always a meal on the table, donations from others around the court, and from Maggie's pantry. The rent could not be paid, so James and Mary took care of that. The money that they had, they used to make their home a little better for the impending arrival.

Sal, still deeply saddened by the death of her little son, did what she could to cheer Eddie, who was very happy to be with his Mama and Papa, but searched for his elder brother and in his infant vocabulary tried to make himself understood. "Johnny… where Johnny? Mammy, where Johnny?"

Every time she heard his childlike pleas her heart ached for that missing part of her, but then she would feel a sharp jab under her ribcage and remember she had not got time to think, she must be ready.

One evening in early April as John was returning from a hard day's labour, Sal doubled up over the range, whilst trying to prepare food. *It's too soon!* she thought. *Not now, it's too soon! It can't be coming now!* The sharp pain came again, much more fierce that before; at the same time she felt the strangling hold of her belly tighten in a wave, then another pain, so fierce she cried out, so intense she felt her legs buckle. Her instinct told her to squat immediately. As she did, there was a gush of liquid spilling all over the quarry tiled floor, her waters had broken! *It can't come now, it's too early!* She lifted her skirt and felt between her legs. She could feel a hard bulge pressing incessantly downwards; it was the baby's head. It was coming now and there was nothing she could do about it, she was feeling the violent urge to push. She was on her own; what was she going to do?

She remembered Maggie's advice to pant to delay pushing. She got herself onto all fours for comfort and panted like a dog, to take the strength out of the violent pains that were forcing her to push. Just at that moment, John arrived.

"Oh Sal! What's wrong? Have you fallen? Are you all right?"

"The baby's coming... No time for the wife... fetch Annie!" John raced around to the neighbour; within moments they were back, and Annie dashed to her side on the floor.

"There's no time..." Sal frantically screamed. "Annie, you'll have to help me!"

"I've never done this henny... What should I do?"

"Just catch the baby, it's coming now!"

Annie frantically pulled over Sal's skirts just in time to catch the baby as it slid out of her. Blue and silently. Within an instant, the shock and suddenness of the cold arrival turned the child pink as it made its first raging cry. John stood stock still, unable to move, horrified by the violence of what had just occurred, but mesmerised by the start of life all at the same time. Carefully, Sal turned and sat on the floor as Maggie held the still attached baby.

"Get a knife, Maggie... We have to cut and tie the cord."

By the time Ellie had arrived with another elderly woman from the court, who was often the wifey when in need, she was greeted by a scene of joy. Sal still sitting on the floor by the range, the very small infant raging lustily in her arms, Maggie and John both kneeling beside trying to get a better look. They had another little boy, from what they could tell his hair was fairer, maybe ginger; he was still blood smeared. He was tiny, or at least much smaller than other two had been, but what he lost in size he made up for in noise.

Sal was cleaned up and laid in her bed, as was the little boy. The old woman could see that Sal had concerns about his size.

"Dearie, I have delivered them all, big and small... I can tell you, there's nothing wrong with this wee one."

Sal could now see that his hair was red, and he had a small frame, he was never going to be a big man like his father, more like the build of the McBride men.

"What shall we call him, my love?" John asked as he leant to see him swaddled in the crook of her arm.

"If it's alright by you, I would like to call him after my brother James... after all, he has done so much to help us."

"Then James it is! Welcome, James."

In the days and weeks that followed James' sudden arrival, Sal barely had time to think of all of the tragedy which had preceded it. Once or twice she would feel a sudden twinge in her heart, especially when Eddie would be mischievous or funny, she would see a little of Johnny again. James and Mary were ecstatic with the arrival, and James was particularly proud that he had been given his name, he felt it was an honour for himself. Bridget did not attempt any more reunions, but did send a short letter to congratulate the parents and welcome baby James; having discussed this with her son and daughter-in-law, all thought that it was for the best to let matters lie for now.

John struggled day to day, as he tried most times unsuccessfully to find anything productive to do. There was always some labouring on roads, but he had found himself travelling further and further for this. It had meant getting up earlier and returning later; he was conscious he needed to be home to help Sal. More and more, he felt that there was no hope for him to stay in the city, word had got around and no matter how much he protested his innocence, good work or more permanent positions were always gone whenever he gave his name. All the time, the poster for Canada played on his mind. By chance one morning, while making his trek north through the city centre in another fruitless search for work, he passed a crowd gathered round an American-sounding man on a street corner, he was handing out something and answering questions; he was a Canadian land agent.

"That's right, sir... My government will pay your passage to come to Canada... you must oblige us by making your way westward and staking your claim to a section of land. You then have three years to break a proportion of that land for agricultural use... growing wheat, or herding cattle... and then you have further time to build a home... Once you have done this, sir, the land title is yours!"

Another question was mumbled, which John could not quite hear.

"Yes sir... It's a mile by one half mile... All yours, your own piece of Canada."

John stood and waited for the flyer to be thrust into his hand; he continued to listen. He could not believe it could be so easy. Get on a boat, passage paid, get over to the west, stake a claim, a good period of time to break so many acres of land, build a house and it would be all his. The man continued.

"And you don't have to stop with one section, as we call it... You can file another claim and break that too... then you can double your farm!"

John knew what a mile was in distance, he knew of no farms around the outskirts of the city that were anywhere on that scale; it was quite unbelievable to him that a man could be given that much land, and get even more if he was prepared to cultivate it. Just then, the piece of printed paper got handed to him from another in the crowd. It was a drawn and painted image of a fine looking man with a cowboy hat on, standing in front of a vast field of wheat in the background. It simply read:

'Canada – where dreams are made.'

The crowd were quite animated. A man next to him turned to John. "My cousin went out six years ago, he is doing so well now... He could barely meet the rent here... He has a fine wife and three children... he tried to get me ta' gaw', I was stupid... I wish I had... cannae' naw'... ma back's gone... A strong fella like you, yer ken, I'd be aff in a flash... yer dinnae' see if I dain't."

John stayed in his thoughts of a new life over the water. What had he got to lose? Sal and the boys would do so much better there out of the dirt and stench of the city. Good healthy clean air! Maybe if they had the chance to go a few years ago, Johnny would not have got sick and died. And if he went there, he would be anonymous, it would be a fresh start for him. No one would know him and know what he had been falsely accused of. He would not get sideways looks anymore, or be consider untrustworthy; it would be a completely clean slate. He made up his mind that he must talk to Sal, and convince her of the opportunities that were there for them both. He carefully folded the flyer and placed it in his inside jacket pocket and headed back to Comely Park Place.

When he arrived, Sal was full of news and unable to contain herself.

"I have solved our problems John... well, Mary may have done... it's not permanent but it will see us through... Mary has an elderly Uncle living out Troon way, he has a little money, but he is not good on his feet anymore. He is looking for a housekeeper to live in... Mary has asked him if he will consider me, but not living in... she has said that I am a fine worker and seamstress and an excellent cook... She thinks that there are plenty of small cottages close by where we can rent... if you watch the boys during the day, I could do this for as long as it lasts... what do you think?"

John was taken aback; he had never considered the prospect of his wife being the breadwinner. He was not entirely comfortable with that position, or being a man looking after the children. In his head he had always been brought up to support his wife and family, be the man of the family. Never mind the trouble that would be caused when Bridget found out about this. He could see that Sal had already decided that this was their best course of action, probably in her mind their only course of action. He carefully thought through his reply, in an effort to try and be as tactful as he could.

"Sal you shouldn't have to work with the bairns, that is my job to provide for you… I know that you think it is the only way, but I think I have a better idea… why don't we try for Canada!"

Sal was astonished. "John, you are not listening to me… I have a position, something that can pay our way… who cares if I work and you do not, it will pay for food, if the boys a good life by the seaside… Don't you see it is the best idea, and Mary has been so helpful to do this for us… and do I have to remind you, we can't even pay a tram ride, how do you expect us to get to Canada, try being sensible!"

"No Sal… we don't have to find any money; the Canadian government will pay for us to go, and give us land, all I have to do is make a farm and build a house—"

Sal cut him off mid-sentence. "All you have to do is make a farm! Do you hear yourself? You don't know the first thing about farming and as for building a house… John, just be reasonable, this does not make any sense whatsoever!"

"But it does, don't you see? We will have a home of our own, we will actually get ahead and make some money, everything that your mother has always said I couldnae' do… Sal, don't you remember when we first met, I told you this is what I always wanted… I do know enough about farming to get started, and what I don't know I can learn… and my god, I am good with a pick and shovel, I have had plenty of practice… I can go out and in a year or two you and the bairns can come out there and join me—"

Sal had listened to enough. "A year or two! And what do you expect me to do while you are off on your fantasy?

How do I keep the roof over the boys' heads? I won't be able to take this position, not with the children to look after as well, and Mary may be many things but she is not a saint, I cannot expect her or your mother to have the children full time while I work away in Troon. For god's sake John, all I am asking you to do is move to Troon, at least we would still be able to get to see family; you want us to go to the other side of the world! I can't be doing with this now, I have heard all I am going to here, you had better think long and hard whether we are going to take up this offer, we haven't got long to make up our minds, and I think we HAVE to take it."

A week passed, with neither really speaking to the other. Sal hoped that in the light of day, when he struggled to find work again, that John would come to his senses; John hoped that when his grand plan had a chance to properly manifest itself in his wife's mind that she would see the real opportunity that a fresh start in a new country may grant them, but neither relented. John knew that he was being forced down an avenue that he was neither comfortable with nor happy to do; he knew it was pointless trying to elicit the support of James and Mary, after all it had been Mary that had proposed the whole idea. It was then he decided to approach his mother to try and act as the voice of reason; he knew that she would not be thrilled with the idea of him leaving and going thousands of miles away, but she would be less pleased with the idea that he would live as a 'kept man'.

It was as he suspected with Maggie. She listened to his dilemma, and heard all he had to say about what he had managed to find out about this great opportunity. Her answer was considered and reasoned.

"Aye John, I can see you are not happy with Mary's scheme and I can understand why... Your father would never have been happy with a situation like that, and we did not bring you up to be that way, I am sure there will be something else come, if you just bide your time... but Canada... oh John, it is so far away... I can see why Sal is scared by the prospect.... All she has ever known with you, apart from the few short months last year, is struggle and hardship, and the only way she has got through and made things meet is through the help of loving friends and family, you know that..." She paused. John nodded, his eyes cast down in the shame and inadequacy that he felt, and she continued, "I would be scared. Anyone would with a history like that, and everything that you are asking her to do... I am not very happy with the idea of you going so far away, on your own... What if something happens? How could I get to you? How would I know that something had happened? I don't think either of you are being at all sensible about this, you really should be more patient... something will happen here, I am sure of it, people do have short memories... I am sure you will get something if you just bide your time."

John tried desperately to sell the prospect of his settling in Canada with Maggie, but the more he tried, the more she insisted it was foolish for both of them; there were too many problems that he not considered, not at least it would probably be the final break between Sal and her mother. Had he considered that? Had he considered that he would be held responsible if anything untoward happened to her or the children while they were out there? Equally, she considered that Sal's suggestion was unpalatable and quite fanciful, to move to Troon like this, with no real prospects; after all no one knew how long this old man would live for, they could get there to find that they had to move back a week later. The whole thing was completely unsatisfactory in her eyes, no matter how desperate they were. Maggie counselled that they should just stay put, that family and friends would help where they could and things would get better; they just had to wait and see, and yes, she would speak to Sal and dissuade her of her notion of being the breadwinner.

There were few times in Sal's knowledge that she had ever seen Maggie have a cross word for anyone; even the time that Bridget had challenged her after Johnny's birth she had remained controlled and peaceable. Sal had never known Maggie be angry with her at all, but this was the occasion that Maggie left her in no doubt of her strength of feeling. Maggie arrived at Comely Park Place bright and early the next morning, and making sure that John had left, sat Sal down in the scullery, and proceeded to tell her exactly how ill-considered she had thought that both their plans were, she made her points with some force, all the points that she had raised with John. Sal sat shell-shocked at Maggie's strength of feeling, and guilty that she had obviously caused this much upset to someone who she loved more than her own mother. Maggie rounded up her discussion with a simple statement.

"I will walk over hot coals before you make me stand by and see my son shamed in such away by you taking this position… I have told him and I will tell you, I will not respect you if you do this to him. Now it's best I go before I say something that you and I might regret."

Sal's head was still reeling with Maggie's outburst when she visited Mary that day to tell her that for the sake of family harmony, she really could not accept the position and her uncle had best find someone else. Mary was disappointed, but could see the points that Maggie had put to Sal and totally understood why she had felt so strongly against it.

"But what did John suggest to you that Maggie has taken against, Sal? You didn't make that clear."

"He wants us to emigrate, Maggie... make a new life on the other side of the world... he wants us to go to the west of Canada."

Chapter 14 –

Many Challenges to Come

Mary had gasped at the ludicrous idea. Canada? What was he thinking about? Leaving all of their family, when it was obvious that without the support that they had, they would never have made it this far. She was of one mind with Sal: this was too much, he should stay and wait out the bad times, things were bound to get better. Sal stressed that she did not want her mother to know, she could not face anymore criticism or interference. Mary agreed, this was far too sensitive a subject and would just lead to more disagreements and misunderstandings.

The summer passed uneventfully, although the tension between John and Sal increased. He tried on a few occasions to raise the prospect of Canada to her, to show her how serious he was, and each time she dismissed him without comment, refusing to acknowledge his pleas for discussion. Instead, she encouraged him to make the fruitless daily search for work. Eventually events turned, and as Maggie had predicted memories were short; John was able to start work on a building site in the centre of Glasgow, a new phase of slum clearance. He was not skilled in a trade such as carpentry, stonemasonry or the like, and was restricted to labouring for others. The work was hard and the money was low, but in Sal's eyes it was a regular income and the best that they could expect for now. She grew warmer to him, in an effort to settle his nomadic spirit.

Little James was a bright little baby, and although small, as strong as an ox. Eddie had assumed the position of the big brother, playing with James and encouraging him to talk. Mary visited regularly, still bringing contributions from her husband's shop to help maintain the household, which had survived on very little for a long time. By November she announced to Sal that she was expecting her third child. Sal was thrilled for her, with a bitter-sweet joy, missing her third and much-loved little boy. Mary said that the new baby was due in April; the women laughed that they would be able to share the birthdays of James and the new little one in years to come. Once again Mary thought it best to hold the news to herself for a while; her own relationship with Bridget was strained because of her own allegiance to Sal. Her husband was never one for confrontation with his mother and avoided it whenever possible.

John could not settle his mind. He knew that his plan was the best opportunity that he could ever offer his family. The more he talked to others who had family already there, or who wished that they could make the journey themselves, the more he knew he was right. To him the desire to own his own land, and become his own man, were all-consuming, especially as he now found himself no better than an apprentice in his late twenties; his prospects if he stayed were not good. He could never get back to where he had been working as a goods guard; he could not increase the money he could take home; they would always be poor if he stayed. It was then he decided to approach the one person he knew that could make a difference with his wife; it was a gamble, but it was the only option left open to him.

They had made a few, very short, visits to Shettleston; they had not been for a while, it was about time that they went again. Mary and James had decided to make a day of it, taking Peter and Ernest, and suggested to Sal that it might be the ideal opportunity for her to take the boys with John. That way Bridget would have other people to focus on, and less desire to create difficulty with her elder son there. The following Sunday all arrived at Mary Lea, and were greeted by Jeanie, who was by now a fine looking young lady, working in the local haberdashery and less withdrawn than she had been. Sal reflected how much she had changed, much as she had when she had ventured into the world of work and away from the maternal clutches.

Katie was a poor little thing, she was very thin and frail and seemed to have a permanent cold. She kept herself busy sewing, and was forever producing new things to decorate their home. She was very much a home body, and unlike Sal enjoyed the domestic role that she had assumed. She cooked and baked, and ordered Annie Theresa to do things as her assistant. Annie Theresa was not so domesticated, but knew that she was the youngest and in no position to refuse; although she did not find herself a natural housewife in the making, she would muddle through when given clear instructions by her elder sister.

Mary had made her condition public a week before and allowed the news to settle. Bridget was remarkably enthusiastic, using the opportunity of commenting to make a pointed remark of comparison.

"Well, no one can deny that you make good parents... You have two fine wee boys, and James does his very best by all of you."

Sal swallowed the jibe, she was so used to these pathetic remarks that they no longer had any great impact; besides which, the pain she was still suffering following Johnny's death had not dissipated, she just internalised her personal grief. John shifted in his seat uneasily; he was even more determined. Sal was conscious that Jeanie and Katie were preparing food on their own for many, Annie Theresa had assumed the role of child minder in the back parlour to the four little boys. Sal and Mary went to assist, while James chatted to his father cordially about business. John used this opportunity unobserved to make his approach.

"Mrs McBride, I wish to talk to you about something important, will you hear me?"

Bridget was somewhat taken aback by John's sudden display of confidence towards her. "What have you to say to me, John Flynn?"

"I have been looking in to a way to create a better life for my family… and I believe I have found a solution… I have decided that I should take a package to Canada… Saskatchewan… I can have piece of land to farm there and make a real home for my family…" He stopped. He could see that Bridget was visibly shocked at the prospect; had he made a miscalculation in his approach? He tried to recover his position quickly. "You are always saying that I should do more… as Mr McBride has… that I should be a better provider… Don't you see that this way I could actually make a real go of things… that Sal and I would finally get our lives in order?"

Bridget's initial reaction was annoyance that he should come out with such a rash proposal, but she had always been one to consider all possibilities, and this one could suit her well. She curbed her temper and enquired more of him.

"So you plan to go… all of you? When?"

"No it cannae' be done like that… I would have to go first and stake my claim, work the land, and build a small place… and then Sal and the boys could join me in a year or two."

Bridget considered this carefully. "A year or two, you say… they can join you then?"

"Aye… obviously Sal would have to stay elsewhere, she could not remain at Comely Park… I would not be here to support her… but if you would allow her stay here, maybe, with the boys… It would not be forever, just until I was established… a year or two?"

Bridget pondered for a moment, indeed this was better than she had hoped. He was making his wife come back to her, and once he had gone, once the distance had been created, she could make Sal see how foolish she was to remain with him. John was conscious that his wife would be back in the room with them shortly and asked for Bridget's support.

"The only problem is that Sal is not of my mind… she thinks that I should carry on working all the hours that I do for little money and no prospects… and others have supported her (He thought it best not to mention Mary by name, with her husband sitting in earshot)… But you must see the sense in what I am proposing… maybe you could help me convince her?"

Bridget was just about to answer when Mary came in summoning all to the parlour for lunch. John was left not knowing whether his mother-in-law would support his proposal, or use it during a family occasion as another stick to beat him with. Bridget saw an opportunity, one that she had never counted on: that he would leave and create the space that she needed, she knew she had to handle this situation with care unless she wanted it to backfire on her further. Nothing was said; John sat uncomfortably knowing that Bridget had him fixed with her blue eyes throughout the lunch. All the others – except Peter senior who had reverted to his normal silence – chatted informally throughout, unaware of the new tensions that had been created.

Before leaving, Bridget took John aside. "I will talk to my husband, and I will discuss with you when we have considered your plan."

Another two weeks passed, John was anticipating trouble once all had been considered by the McBrides; he felt lost and isolated. He found that he was unable to concentrate on much, not that he had time to do all else than work, eat and sleep. Bridget had been plotting and when they next arrived for their family visit, they were surprised to see that Jeanie was out, Katie and Annie Theresa were sent with the boys into the parlour, and James and his family were absent. Sal sensed some announcement which would not be a happy one. Peter and Bridget were seated in the front room, a fire lit, and two vacant chairs opposite them; she encourage her daughter and her husband to sit, and began.

"Well Sal, John has told me about his plan..." For a moment Sal thought that she had finally seen the back of this ludicrous scheme, surely her mother would not support this.

"And your father and I think it is an excellent idea..." Bridget paused, noting that Sal's look was not a happy one; John leaned over to her, trying to take her hand, but she snatched it away. Bridget continued, "John has also said that you are reluctant to do this? I do not see why? It is the best chance that your family has, your husband is right..." Bridget never told lies, as she always said, and she was not lying; this was the best chance that Sal and her boys had, apart from their father, and she intended to do all that she could to maintain this, if she could persuade her daughter to do so without arousing her suspicions of an ulterior motive.

"Your father and I...," she looked at Peter, who nodded she should continue, "...believe that this could be the answer to your prayers, and our wishes for you... John has said that he will go on a government scheme ahead of you and the boys and make all well for you to join him... We are willing to support you, we have decided to find a little money for you, John, to help you, so that you can get what you need to start... It won't be much, we need to keep some here, we do have three unmarried daughters... but Sal, you will need somewhere to live with the boys... and there is no better place than here, we are willing to extend our home to you, and support you, for however long is necessary... What do you say to that, Sal?"

Sal was seething inside; she felt that John had been dishonest approaching her mother behind her back, and not even revealing what he had done afterwards. And the prospect of being sucked back into the 'bosom of her family' – the family she had to fight to extricate herself from in the first place – was the last thing she had any intention of doing. But she knew that she had been manipulated by everyone, and her supporters were not there to help her fight her corner. She tried to explain why she did not think it was a good idea, that John should wait and things would change. Bridget countered by saying that she did not think that likely and what a good life they could have once they were all there.

Sal retorted, "But mother, we would have to live apart for two years... what about the boys not seeing their father? What if something happens to John or us, how would we get to one another? What if it does not work, what then?"

"Sal the whole world can be full of 'what ifs'... and what if he does not go? It could be the best thing he has ever done, and you could be saying 'what if' in ten years' time, because he had not gone... Soldiers and sailors live away all the time... people survive being apart, if it is for the right reasons."

Sal was lost. She knew there was no point trying to argue with her mother, her mind was intractable at the best of times; she knew that there was no changing her opinion. Besides which it was obvious to Sal that her father was absolutely in the same mind, he had spent the whole time nodding at every point that Bridget had made. It was John who she would direct her venom to, when they were back in their own home.

An uncomfortably quiet journey back to Comely Park Place was succeeded by a full volley against John in their kitchen.

"So you have forced the situation, have you! Left me no option but to let you have your way! How dare you go to my mother behind my back! How dare you force me to do this! I thought you were many things, John Flynn, but never dishonest!"

John sat at the table, his eyes cast downwards; he mumbled, "Sal I am so sorry, but I had to... You weren't listening to me, I had to do something... I know it's the right thing to do—"

"For you, maybe... but not for me! Not for the boys! And if anyone thinks I am going back to my mother's for two years, I just won't! I can't!"

"Sal, it's only a short time in the scheme of things and then you will be away from her... forever if you want... I can't see her interfering with us six thousand miles away... can you?"

"That's if it all works out! That's if you can make this foolishness work!... I mean come on John, nothing else has ever worked for you, even your mother does not want you to go!"

John felt very hurt by his wife's last remark, that was the first time in their marriage that she had ever made a direct comment that she found him inadequate as a husband. He swallowed hard with an even greater determination.

"Well, I have done it now... Your mother and father support my idea, they are even going to offer me some financial support... I know it is the right thing to do, and whatever happens I am going as soon as there are sailings available! You and the boys should take their offer and live with them while we are apart, at least it will be one less worry. I will know that you have a roof over your heads and are not struggling, I will have enough to do!"

"I can't, John, not now... I am pregnant again!"

John sat up suddenly, half with elation, half with unease. Another child, that was wonderful, it showed that there was still something worth fighting for between them despite all these months of dispute. But it meant, more than ever, that he had to make a better life.

"Another reason I should go then, I have another mouth to feed, and I can't make my way here... you are going to have to accept this, Sal, my mind is made up and I have done all that I can to make things right for you while I am away... If you want something else, that is for you to decide, but I am going to Canada as soon as I can!"

That Christmas was an unsettled one. Sal had to swallow much, including telling her mother that she was expecting again, but rather than the criticism of their carelessness, this time Bridget was far more cordial.

"Aye, well… at least your man will be making things better for your family while he is gone… I am sure we will manage somehow, once you move here."

That was last thing Sal wanted to do. She knew she could not manage on her own, she could not work, she would have three children to care for. She knew that she could not ask Mary and James to help, they already had two bairns with another due the following April; they barely had enough room for themselves. She appealed to Maggie, knowing that she too was stretched for space, and Maggie was highly apologetic. "Sal you know I would if I could… If there had just been the two we might manage, but three? I really dinnae' think I can… I am not happy with the way John has behaved, but now that your parents have offered some money to help him, it could be the best thing that has happened and it may well work out… I dinnae' think you have much choice, lassie, I think you must go to your mother's."

Sal had to face the reality of the situation. She was left in an intractable situation, she had to move to Mary Lea and live in one room with her three children. John had booked his passage for early March, she was due to have this baby in July. She had to move by the end of January somewhere, and Mary Lea Cottage was the only option that she had.

That final month, moving their belongings and preparing for John to leave was an awkward one. The weeks had flown by and she felt that she had been pushed too far by John; he tried in vain to placate her and make her see that it was for the best. They bickered constantly although discreetly in her mother's house, which led to feelings of tensions for everyone. Bridget was well aware of the discord between them, and did nothing to mediate; in fact she hoped that this would continue even after he had gone.

John's passage had been booked for the third of March from Liverpool; he knew he could only carry a case of clothes and that anything he needed to start his life there would have to be acquired once he arrived. He had registered to go to Saskatchewan where there were large tracts of unbroken land available. He knew it was not quite as simple as getting off the ship and taking a train, he would have to go through the immigration process once he arrived, and then somehow work his way across this vast country. Even if he could take the train directly from Halifax, it would still take him a week to get there. How monumental the whole exercise seemed the more he found out exactly what he had to do, but in his heart he was absolutely committed and he would do this, no matter what; he had to do it.

The parents and two boys shared a cramped room in the cottage; Sal had already assumed her new role. With Jeanie at work, and Katie an invalid, Sal was once again consigned to her kitchen duties. She resented her demotion to that of housekeeper to her mother, but muted her resentment by considering her two boys, whom she would have had to care for wherever she was. She felt that she no longer had any privacy and her life was no longer her own. The more she stayed, the more she resented John for putting her in this position, and the more they sniped at one another.

Then came the day he was to leave to take the train to Liverpool; he asked her to accompany him to the station, she made an excuse that she could not, because of the boys and her duties. John was hurt, he was going away for a long time, he had really hoped that when the day came that she would want to see him off and wish him well. As he boarded the train at Glasgow Central Station there were tears in his eyes, only witnessed by Maggie, who was the only one to wish him a safe journey.

"Oh laddie... I am so sorry... I really thought that she would come with you."

"She is so angry with me... Mama I dinnae' think I will ever see her again, I am scared, I really thought I was doing this for the best... why can't she see it?"

"Hey John... Dinnae' take on so... she will come to you, she won't let you down, she just needs time... you must take care of yourself... and please write to me, my bonnie boy?"

"I will, ma."

He leant out the window as the train steamed out of the packed station and he called back to Maggie, "Look after Sal and the boys, ma, please?"

He could not hear her answer yes, and she could not hear anything else he said. She had a heavy heart as she waved her son goodbye, she feared this would be the last time. He boarded the 'Canada' at Liverpool, and stood as far back on the deck of ship as he could to catch the last views of that mainland as the ship sailed onwards towards the vast empty horizon.

Back at Mary Lea a crumpled figure curled up on her bed and sobbed silently, wishing she had kissed him goodbye.

Chapter 15 –

The Pain of Parting

Life was completely changed for Sal. No longer was she free to organise her day as she chose; when she would go to see friends, shop, spend time entertaining the children, now her day and time were determined by the requirements of her mother's household. Bridget was not a young woman, and although she was no longer actively supporting Peter, she had developed quite range of social activities in between visiting her sons in different parts of Glasgow. She had a circle of women, mainly wives of Peter's connections in business, whom she made it her business to call on frequently. To her this was a mark of how much she had risen in her own society, and a way of maintaining Peter's position in the Glasgow network. She knew he was a member of the Masons – a subject she preferred not to discuss as it went against her Catholic beliefs – but she also knew that it was how the commercial network operated in Glasgow, and for Peter not to be an active partici-pant would have been foolhardy. So it was tolerated and never mentioned in conversation.

However, with all her absences combined with Katie's fragile condition, most of the daily chores now fell on Sal's shoulders. She envied Jeanie, leaving for work every day, so confident and carefree; that had been Sal six years ago, except when she returned from work she had been destined for the scullery, whereas Jeanie came home to a cooked meal and no chores. Annie Theresa was a precocious ten year old, she had an opinion about most things, and not all her opinions were agreed with. She had learnt a long time since that she must not share any of her wayward thoughts with her mother, but that had made her even more determined to sound out all others around her.

"Sal, do you think women should have the vote?"

"Sal, do you believe there is only one god who is a Catholic god?"

"Sal, do you think Socialism is a good thing?"

Usually, Annie Theresa had her own controversial answer already to contradict whatever response came, and she could be quite intense in attempting to win the debate. Sal was very thankful that she was at school most days; it gave her chance to rest from all the ethical and moral challenges that would be thrown in her direction. Annie Theresa was really good at entertaining Eddie and James, and both adored their young auntie and her extrovert character. Katie would quietly work in the back parlour, in the warmth; she never seemed to have the strength to want to go far from home, and when she would help in the kitchen she was a marvel with her baking skills. Sal did not like to see Katie doing too much and the confined space of the cottage scullery was quite restrictive as compared to the one that the McBrides had in George Street; Sal preferred to work alone in there.

Each day, she would shop for food for that evening. During the week it was just the women and the small boys. However, at the weekends Peter would return from his flat in London Street and on a Sunday James and Mary would join with their young children. Mary was heavily pregnant now, and was not expected to help in the house. That did mean that on those days, Sal found herself catering for six adults, four small boys and Jeanie and Katie. It was a mammoth task to prepare for this, never mind to shop for it all, but James would come to the rescue bringing groceries and provisions from his store, and Jeanie would be sent each Saturday to the local butcher, a task she seemed to quite enjoy.

Now John had gone, she had a little more space in her cramped little bedroom, but with both of her boys sharing, no privacy. She found that frustrating as she had always been a light sleeper, and their sleep noises disturbed her; she was herself waking up five or six times a night. In the wee small hours, when she could not get back to sleep, she would find herself thinking of John and missing him terribly. The blackness always heightened her fears that something terrible had happened to him, he had been gone three weeks and nothing had been heard from him. Her imaginations as she lay alone, were of awful events, him falling sick and being unable to find help, or being attacked by some robber and being left for dead. She would wake up weeping silently, wishing that she had parted with him on better terms, hoping that he had not given up on her and on their marriage. Her swollen belly would remind her that only a few months before, there had been some closeness, some love between them; she would lay both her warm hands over her growing form for comfort.

It was during one of these bad nights during the weekend of Easter that she noticed that James was making more noise than he normally did. He seemed snuffly and congested, sure sign that he was getting a cold. His first birthday was in in ten or so days' time; she hoped he could be over it, so that the little party that she had planned with his little cousins could go ahead. Her brother had suggested that it would be really good occasions to get them all together, and with Mary due any day now, it might be opportune to get his wee tearaways out of the house; Mary needed the rest.

As it happened, James sent word a few days later that Mary was in labour, and they would not be coming for a while. All in Mary Lea anticipated the arrival of the new baby. Mary bore a daughter a few days later. She was born most efficiently by all reports and mother and daughter were doing well. She was the first granddaughter born to Peter and Bridget; Peter showed uncustomary enthusiasm to this and sent flowers to congratulate the family. Sal wished that she could visit the new baby, but it was obvious by now that little James had developed a stinking cold and a hacking cough; the last thing that Mary needed was sickness being brought into the house, so Sal decided to wait until James was over the worst.

Five days later, little James was no better and his cough was deep in his chest, Sal was thankful he had not got that distinct whoop, whoop, that had come with Johnny's illness but still she fretted that this was more than a cold. Bridget told her she was worrying too much, that Katie had colds all the time.

"The little lad just needs more fresh air... You should take him out in the garden more... he will be fine."

Even with her outward reassurances, she made sure that Katie kept her distance.

"She is so frail... she could easily catch this and with her it could become something far more serious."

Little James turned one year old on the eighth of April. He was too sick and feverish to have a party, not that James had any intention of bringing Peter and Ernest to the house, especially as Mary needed him and with the added complication of the risk of the sickness coming back with a small infant for Mary to consider. Sal was sleeping even less, little James was waking her up most of the night with his persistent coughing and choking. He was beginning to refuse his food, and he complained and wailed when she tried to make him eat; she thought that he must have coughed his throat sore. She tried to ease his chest with steam and infusions, which brought some temporary relief, but then he would wake again with the explosive coughing which was becoming quite productive. Finally, after great insistence on Sal's part, Bridget sent for the doctor. He diagnosed bronchitis and laryngitis, he offered a linctus, and recommended beef tea and infusions. For the next four nights, Sal sat up nearly all night trying to soothe her small boy. Eddie had begun to complain that he could not sleep and wanted to go somewhere else. Sal was completely exhausted but had to keep going.

Jeanie and Katie took over more of the chores, knowing that their sister was at her wits' end and receiving very little support from their mother, who still rebutted the maternal fears as an over-reaction to a childhood sniffle. The night of the fifteenth, Sal lay her head on the pillow to try and catch just an hour's sleep, knowing that James would wake again very soon. She had made a bed for Eddie in the back parlour, just so that one of them would get a decent night's sleep. She slept deeply, and then dreamt terrible things about John; he was lying dead somewhere undiscovered, alone! This image shook her awake suddenly; it was just getting light, about seven in the morning. Initially, Sal was confused by the trauma of her dream, and her extreme fatigue made her forget why she was in that room, and why she was there at all. Then there was the dawning realisation that she had not heard James all night. *Thank goodness*, she thought, *he has slept, he is better.* But then she listened; she could hear nothing in the stillness of the morning.

She shot out of bed towards the cot bed where little James lay. He was lying still, his mop of red hair striking against his white skin. He was always pale, but he was unusually pale. Sal reached towards his face her hand shaking, she touched his skin, a pain shot through her body. He was stone cold. From somewhere she could hear screaming, uncontrollable screaming. The next she knew she was lying on the bed, voices all around her, the voice of a man she thought she knew.

"She has had a terrible shock Mrs McBride, she may not be in her right mind for a few days... I have given her a sedative... and I have written the death certificate... poor wee man... I did not suspect that this would take him, he seemed so strong and feisty... if I had thought for one moment that he needed to go to hospital..."

"We too, doctor... I thought he would be fine... it was just a cold... I am worried about Katie doctor, will she get this?"

"She's an adult now... Something like this would not be good for her, but I shouldn't think it would do any long term damage... but I will take a look at her before I leave."

In her dreamlike state, she could hear Eddie asking why mummy was asleep, and what was wrong with James, and she could hear her sisters trying to explain that little James had gone to god. Annie Theresa was sniffing back the tears as she did so. Jeanie was trying her best to comfort Katie who was sobbing uncontrollably. All the time in these first days, Bridget's voice was constant; it was a nagging insistent tone, telling her that she was needed. That Eddie needed his mother and the family wanted her to do things. She did not remember how many of these days passed in a blur; she had vague recollections of a funeral and a tiny coffin, she didn't cry, she couldn't, there were no more tears left. She vaguely remembered a christening for baby Mary, which had been delayed because of the tragedy that had occurred.

After a while she returned to her senses in some part, and then came the months of numbness. She would function but only on a basic level. She knew she must care. Care for Eddie, care for her family, and she would move around in a trance-like state, carrying out her duties in a mechanistic fashion. She did not enter into conversation or dialogue and only gave monosyllabic responses to questions asked of her. In her head the same thoughts kept repeating over and over.

Mary's comment when she was expecting Ernest, that they needed boys, boys grew into strong sons. Mary's would, both Peter and Ernest were still there, still strong and well, but Johnny and James had been lost. It must have been her fault, they should be alive. Then there was the protest that she had made to Annie as Johnny lay on his deathbed, that she didn't want the baby that she was carrying – that child being James – that she was being punished for not bonding with Johnny from the beginning; in her eyes, god was punishing her by taking away her beloved son. She had told Annie that she would give anything to save his life, meaning the infant she was carrying. Now she knew she was being doubly punished by god, that she did not deserve to a be a mother, she was not fit to be one. Poor Eddie, what would be his fate? And this new child she was carrying, would it even make its first birthday?

Her self-punishment continued well into June, and no one could reach her. Mary came often, bringing the boys to try and give some normality to the situation and Eddie desperately needed company. She would sit with Sarah, repeating the same mantra: "Sal, you must stop blaming yourself... you have to get on with life... James' death was not your fault, it could have happened to any of the children."

In Sal's heart that was just not true, it did not happen to Mary's boys because she kept them safe, they never suffered or struggled as her children had. She began to accept that both their souls were in a far better place; she had failed them, at least now they would never suffer anymore. Mary tried to give Sal a purpose.

"Sal, have you written to John?... Dinnae' you think you should?"

John, why write to John? She had been so hard to him those last days, and they had parted as strangers, he was better off without her, not that she knew where he was, having had no letters at all. When he knew that she had killed their youngest son by her neglect, he would never forgive her, why should he? And to think that one of the reasons he had been told why he should not go, was the danger that could befall the children when they were out in the wilds of Canada. For god's sake, she could not keep her children safe in a warm home with all the conveniences and a table of plenty.

Sal would sit in silence, barely acknowledging Mary's presence, lost in her self-recriminations, unable to vocalise them to anyone. Even Bridget's constant chiding made no difference; Sal relished the coldness and the nagging, she deserved all that she was getting. Yes, she was back as an unpaid skivvy to her family, again it was what she deserved; she had a chance to have a different life, but she would not support her husband when he had probably made the best decision of their married life together. She was trying to control things to go her way, she would not accept that there was a second person in the marriage who had rights too.

By the middle of July, she was very heavily pregnant, but determined to carry on with all her duties, even Bridget frowned on this martyrdom that she was obviously applying to herself, and encourage the other girls to take over as much as possible. It was Annie Theresa who finally made the change in her. She slipped into to Sal's room one afternoon while Sal was taking a rest.

"Can I come in, Sal?" There was no reply from Sal; she remained staring forward, not making any eye contact. Annie Theresa sat on a chair next to the bed, facing her. One of Annie's monologues began.

"Life's really unfair, isn't it, Sal? I mean there is Mary, all her children are well and strong and we have lost little Johnny and Jamie… I think that's really unfair… You and John have been such good parents, so much better than our father and mother have been… I mean, I know they want the best for us, but they have never come close to us or comfort us, I can never remember either of them playing with me, did they ever play with you?" There was no response. "…I mean you and John have been real parents, kind, loving and good… why did they die? It just does not make sense, don't you think so? …It makes me so angry that we have lost those two little boys… my two little nephews… do you know there are times I don't believe in god… I mean, what loving god takes away those lovely little boys, and lets old cranky people live? It's just not−"

Sal was suddenly rocked back to reality with a vengeance. To Annie Theresa's surprise, she rounded on her. "Don't you ever say things like that! Don't you ever say that you do not believe in god! If that's what you believe, then my little ones are nowhere! You must believe in god, for their sake!"

Annie Theresa smiled, slightly mischievously; despite her loud gaucheness, she had great insights and empathy to human soul, even at such a young age. She looked at Sal. "Of course I believe in god... and you do too... Just remember, they are always with you, they haven't really gone..." She rose from the chair walking towards the door. "And little Eddie is still here... and that little one inside you needs a Mama too."

Sal emerged from her withdrawn state and not a moment too soon. Towards the end of July, she was admitted into the Maternity Hospital – Bridget did not think it was appropriate for her to give birth at Mary Lea – the excuses that were given were her recent trauma and the cramped conditions. She would need some care before and after the baby's arrival and the hospital was considered to be the best place for her to be. Two days later, on the 26th July, she gave birth to a little girl. Sal was overjoyed with her new arrival; if it had been a boy that may have been different because of the loss of James and the reminders that might bring. She had a daughter, she was a good size despite all of the terrible times that Sal had been through in recent months. Her hair was fair, with the same stunning blue eyes of all of her children.

Sal felt a bitter-sweetness when she looked at her adorable little girl; she was the last connection to John, who had still not written. She did not blame John, after the way she had treated him on their parting, it would not have a surprise to learn that he was making a new life as a single man. She had not stood by him when she should have, or been there for him when he needed her. He was his own man now, but before her was the last semblance of the love that they had shared together. Sal pondered what to call the new arrival, she should really consider the mother's names – Margaret and Bridget – but calling her after one would offend the other; then there was Mary, but she couldn't call her after her because she had named her daughter so. She did not like her own name, Sarah, which is why she had always been grateful that her family had shortened it to Sal.

Then it dawned on her, there had been two others who had made a difference to her life; one was her friend back in Comely Park Place, who had always gone out of her way to help Sal when she was in difficulty and the other – though she would never realise how much she had helped – was her own young, but wise, sister. She looked at the little girl, asleep in her arms, and said softly:

"Hello Annie."

Chapter 16 –

Hard Cold Realities

Annie Theresa was thrilled that her new little niece had her name; ever the attentive auntie to Eddie, baby Annie received the same close affections. Bridget commented that her first daughter was called Annie, a fact Sal was only too aware of, because the comment that came next was, "But she didn't thrive... god rest her." Having lost two already, Sal had empathy for this, but she knew it was almost as if her mother was saying that calling her Annie was an ill omen. Sal put this aside, and her role as domestic was once more assumed. The pattern that had been established prior to the passing of little James continued unabated throughout the summer.

Meanwhile, Sal was very aware of the child mortality that had been inflicted upon her, and the slightest sniffle or cough in either of the two children, sent her into a spiral of over-care: wrapping them up, keeping them indoors and sitting up night after night to make sure. This irritated her mother, who considered all of this completely unnecessary.

"Children get colds... you must learn to put the past behind you and move on."

And these were not the only comments that Bridget was affirming about the past. She had been gleefully aware that John had not written. Maggie Flynn knew better than to come to Shettleston, and Sal had not been in any fit state to pay a call. Bridget thought that even if Maggie had heard from her son, she would assume that Sal had too, and would not make any great efforts to inform her daughter-in-law. And although Bridget did not wish ill on John, he may not have written to anyone for one reason or another. Bridget knew that her daughter was beginning to feel completely abandoned by her John, and that the loneliness of separation was setting in. She would choose moments to make less than subtle hints towards Sal.

"You should start to make a new life for you and your children."

Then another time, "He might have found someone else, you know."

After that: "Canada is a very long way away... It is easy to forget... distance creates distance, you know."

None of these choice remarks made Sal recoil or react; in her mind her mother was right, she had treated John dreadfully and deserved what had now obviously occurred. But Bridget overplayed her hand one day, when she covered old ground with the same spite that she had shown before.

"He was never good enough for you... you should move on... he never did anything to make a real difference in your lives, apart from when he was found wanting at the rail yard, for his dishonest handling of goods..."

Sal began to feel her venom rise. Bridget continued unabated, "... I always said that was a feckless family... and what did anyone expect but a feckless son... the only good thing he has done is to run away from his responsibilities; at least he has given you the right to change your life and make a new start."

Sal's anger was uncontrollable, she could no longer stay silent.

"Mother, you are right in many things and believe you me, no one knows more than I do that I deserve to have lost my husband, probably forever... but I will not have you destroying his character! And I won't have my children growing up here being told terrible things about him! He did not dishonestly handle anything, he was conned, he was stupid, yes, but not dishonest! And he worked all the hours that god sent to make me and the children comfortable and to give us a good life. No man was ever more attentive, or more caring, he was devoted to us! And if I pushed him away, that is because my stubbornness got the better of me! My stubbornness that is just like yours! You are unwilling to accept anyone else's opinion, or anyone else's way of life if it does not fit your own! Stop this maliciousness or you will lose me for a second time!"

Bridget froze momentarily: had her daughter had the audacity to make direct criticisms against her own mother, whilst defending her husband? It was unthinkable; Bridget considered her character beyond reproach. She contained her anger, stared Sal in the eye. "Well... if you think you can make a better life for you and yours away from us, then you had better take that course."

Another month passed. Bridget was not deterred from her sniping in any way. She was determined that her daughter was better off away from her husband; every day that she waited mourning her loss, was a day wasted. She thought that now was the time to make her daughter really face up to the realities of having been abandoned, that if she could convince her to strike out for her independence from her marital vows, that she would cleave to her own kith and kin as the only place she could be. Maggie would not be able to take her in, and without work, Sal could not afford to live elsewhere. Bridget took Sal's outburst as a meaningless threat, after all she had two children; one under four years old and the other not yet four months old; where could she go? Nowhere. The bombardment continued daily, until the post brought a much-wanted letter addressed to Sal, with a Canadian stamp.

It arrived on a Friday morning; the children were napping and everyone else was out of the house about their business. Sal's hands shook as she slowly opened it, in fear that it might be the final rejection in black and white. It was his handwriting, so at least she knew he was alive, at least he was one month ago, when she checked the date stamp. It was a letter of three pages, as Sal read it, tears began to fall down her cheeks. He was full of love towards her, and missing his little family dreadfully. He apologised profusely for not writing sooner, it had taken weeks to clear immigration once they had landed in Halifax, and the process of being naturalised had taken some time because of the bureaucracy. He was extremely grateful for the money that her parents had given him, for he had never planned on being detained at the port of entry for so long; the weather was hard and he needed to stay in a boarding house; it was just too cold to sleep elsewhere. This had reduced his capital considerably and he knew that making his way across Canada to Saskatchewan was going to consume even more. He had decided to work his way across, as best he could. He had a stroke of luck when passing through Ontario, travelling in the goods car – because he did not want to waste money taking a seat, and a sleeper was out of the question. He was in the car for three days, and made quite a friend of the goods guard. When he learnt that John had been one and was looking for work, he had an idea. As they arrived in

Winnipeg, in Manitoba, the guard had a chat to the foreman. The foreman said they could offer him some temporary work helping to load and unload, which would earn him a bit of money. So he had spent the summer months there. He wrote:

'I am in Winnipeg, it's a very beautiful place and the people are just fine. You will love Canada, it is so friendly and beautiful, but my goodness it is vast.

'It is now time to move on before the winter sets in, it gets very cold here Sal, and the snow lies deep for months on end. When the wind blows it is so cold that your skin can freeze. I have met a farmer from the other side of Manitoba, he has offered me some work for the winter, helping to tend his stock and mend the fences. I will have to buy some warm clothes, but I will manage.

'I hope from there to make it to Saskatchewan and maybe find some work on a wheat farm in the prairies, at least I can learn what I have to do from the farmers already here. I miss you Sal so much, I think about you all of the time, I hope you and the boys are well? Tell Eddie Papa misses him, and don't let wee James forget me.'

Sal swallowed hard. *Of course*, she thought, *he doesn't know*. She continued to read on:

'And the new baby, was it a boy or a girl? I hope that things were not too terrible for you, and that your mother is treating you well? Please could you go and see Maggie, and tell her I am well, I haven't had time to write.

'I don't know the full address where you can write to me yet, when I get to the farm I will write again.

'I love you very much and always will.

'Your John'

Sal sat on the bed, and read and re-read his words. She was ecstatic. He still loved her, he still wanted her! She had spent so many hard and difficult months alone, and gone through the terrible trauma of losing their little son alone, and she thought that she would probably be alone for the rest of her life. Now she had been granted a second chance, she would be able to see him, probably the end of next year! The last year had flown by, maybe the next would too and then they would be together as a family...

She stopped suddenly in her thoughts. She had to tell him about James, she had to write to him; how would he take the news? Would it be too difficult for him, so far away? It was a letter that she knew she must write and soon, but to where? He had no address yet that she could write to. And then there was little Annie, he had no idea that he had a baby daughter and how beautiful she was. Maybe that would be the solution to write the letter with all of the good news and maybe a photograph of their baby daughter, before telling him what had happened to James? But would he blame her for her carelessness? Sal was in a quandary, she could not keep all this from him, and her natural honest nature wanted to reveal all now, but she could not; there was nowhere to send it to. She would have to wait on the next letter, and content herself reading his cherished words over and over. And she must go and see Maggie, she must be terribly worried.

It was never going to be an easy exercise to visit John's mother, for many reasons. In all of the trauma of the recent months, she had not even considered going; her mind had been consumed by all of her conflicting problems and emotions. She felt terribly guilty, all she had to tell, the loss of James, the birth of Annie, why she had not come sooner. Then there was Bridget, who had been running her campaign of permanent separation of wife from husband. Sal knew that once her mother knew that she had re-established contact with John's family, she would have to deal with all of her wrath. She knew she would be unable to conceal a visit, Eddie was far too bright and intelligent not to say something inadvertently. But this is what John wanted her to do, and for his sake and her children's, it was what she must do.

She waited for the next quiet day to make her way into Glasgow with her two small children. She had not revealed to anyone that she had heard from John, though it was obvious to all in the McBride household that Sal's spirits had lifted considerably. She had decided to wait until after she had seen Maggie, as she knew that all sorts of objections and obstructions would come once she had disclosed the letter's contents. She took the train into the city and then walked back towards the Gallowgate, her walk was charged with memories, especially as she passed by the house in George Street – where she used to live – and down the High Street towards the Gallowgate; a walk that she had taken many times when she and John were courting.

She arrived at the Flynns' humble home and knocked on the door tentatively. Maggie opened the door and was so happy to see Sal, with Eddie and the baby.

"Oh dearie… I am so pleased to see you… are you alright, lass? Have you heard from John? Is James not with you?"

So many questions all at once. Sal drew breath. Maggie realised there was much to say.

"Forgive me… Please come in… I have been so worried… I nearly came to your mother's house… I was so desperate for any news… Please come in, you must be tired?"

Sal settled in the back room. Eddie was thrilled to be in a familiar place, with a warm and lovely woman whom he felt close to. Little Annie was wrapped tightly against the November chill in a shawl; she snuffled as she was lain on the couch, so that her grandma could take a good look at her.

"Oh she is a bonny one… and what fair hair she has."

Sal spoke uninterrupted for half an hour; Maggie, always an attentive listener, heard the awful tale of the loss of James and how it had affected Sal. Then the birth of Annie, which had lifted her out of her emotional turmoil. The problems that she was once again experiencing with her mother, and how she was now at her wits' end, but thankfully, she had heard from John. Maggie was overjoyed to know that John was fine and well, she had been so worried about him and not hearing, she too had begun to fear the worst. She told Sal that she understood the pain that she must have suffered losing James coming on top of John leaving for Canada. She worried that Sal was suffering living at Mary Lea Cottage.

"Sal, I wish I could help you dearie, but you know we have no room and very little money… I know that John will make good for you and the children if you can just wait out your time… It's not forever, just for another year… then you will be together as a family, with your own lives, and no one can try to part you."

Chapter 17 –

The Blackest Night

Sal made her way back to Shettleston, the feelings of doom mounting as she crossed the threshold; her mother had returned from her social visits. As astute as ever, Bridget had guessed that the change in her daughter could only have meant one thing.

"You have heard from him then?" It was a hard accusatory tone.

"Yes, I have, and I have been to see his mother because he asked me to."

"Well… seems like you are making other arrangements for your life… don't let us stop you… If you think that you can fare better elsewhere and meet our support and care with your ingratitude for taking you and the bairns in when your man ran out on you, then go and take your chances elsewhere… at least there will be less mouths to feed here and more room for the girls again."

Sal tried to ignore the challenge to leave, having considered Maggie's appeal for patience. She said nothing and continued about her duties for the next month or so, avoiding the sniping and chiding as best she could. It was the end of January before Sal finally felt that she could no longer go on. As Bridget was not getting reactions to her commentaries, her new tactic was to overload Sal with as much of the domestic tasks as possible, and create new ones. Christmas had been the final straw, with Sal expected to cater and clean for a houseful, including her brothers Peter and Hugh. She was completely worn out, with her nightly feeds to Annie, who was a very hungry baby. Each time she tried to get on top of the monumental feats that she was being expected to perform, fresh demands would be made.

One morning when all were gone, Sal was at her lowest ebb. She had not had the promised letter from John and after his comments in his first letter about the extremities of the weather, she had begun fearing the worst once again. She had descended into deep despair and decided that anything and anywhere was better than this. She placed Annie in the old pram that she had acquired from one of the neighbours in Shettleston, she folded some clothes for her and the children in a carpet bag and balanced it on the end of the pram. Then holding Eddie's hand, while pushing the pram with the other, she walked the four miles to Maggie's house, stopping every so often to let Eddie rest. It was bitterly cold and she had bundled the children into as much clothing as possible, in the hope that they would not get sick. She had told Eddie that they were going to their nice grandma's, and Eddie was going to have a little holiday there. He was excited at the prospect of grandma and a holiday.

She knocked once more on Maggie's door. Maggie knew when she saw Sal's face that there was something wrong, and hurried her inside, leaving the pram out the front. Sal quickly tried to explain how she had come to end of her tether, that

Bridget's demands and commentary were just too much to bear any longer. She was going to try and seek work.

"With the wee ones, dearie? Won't that be too difficult?"

"It would with both, Maggie, and Annie is still on the breast so she has to stay with me, but I was wondering if you could take Eddie in for wee while, just until I get on my feet... I am sure I can find somewhere to stay... There's my old neighbour in Comely Park Place, I am sure she will put me up temporarily... and I have saved a few pennies, if all else fails I am sure I can find a boarding house."

Maggie was very concerned that Sal was taking extreme actions, and worried that her depression was not allowing her to think clearly. Was she sure this was a good idea? Couldn't she make it work just for a wee while longer, at least wait until the warm weather? Sal insisted she had to, for the sake of the children as much as herself; she was in the darkest place that she had ever known and not hearing from John again, she knew that this was the only way. Maggie reluctantly agreed to take Eddie, but insisted to Sal that she must come back if she found things too difficult. Sal knew she would not; Maggie had barely enough to feed her own, she was doing a great favour by taking Eddie in, that was enough and she was very grateful for that.

After lunch, Sal made her goodbyes to Eddie, assuring him she would be back soon and that he was going to have a nice holiday with grandma. She said goodbye to Maggie, who wished her well, and pushed her pram back down the Gallowgate the mile to Comely Park Place.

Annie and Ellie were thrilled to see Sal, and welcomed her in. She poured out her heart to Annie over her small kitchen table, and a few cups of tea. Annie sat open mouthed at all that Sal had been through that last year.

"No wonder we dinnae' hear from you, lassie... I am surprised you are as well as you are... of course you can stay with us for a while until you find something, you are always welcome, you know that... and of course if any of the McBrides come calling, I have nae' seen you and have nae' heard from you... Dinnae' worry yer head, Sal... Ellie and I will be with you."

The month that Sal remained with Annie was a happy one, though more cramped than at Shettleston; she was grateful that Eddie was with Maggie. She had decided not to visit him, just in case it made him want to be with her. She thought it was best that if she was out of his seeing, she would be out of his mind. Every day Sal searched for work, but even when she didn't take Annie with her, there was nothing to be had, and seamstresses were ten a penny. She knew she could not make enough on home work and it had to be a factory or a tailor's that she must try. She tramped the streets of Glasgow for four weeks. Some tried to be helpful, telling her they knew of a position elsewhere, but as soon as she made her way to wherever 'elsewhere' was, she would find that the position had been filled.

She knew that Annie barely had enough to pay for herself and Ellie. Annie's man had died of a heart attack in the last year – and the only wage coming in was Ellie's from the weaving factory she was working in – there just wasn't enough to make ends meet. Poor Annie had been sharing her bed with her daughter, allowing Sal to have the other room with the baby. Sal was conscious she was becoming a burden, although that was never expressed, and nothing but kindness was shown to her. She tried to make a few things to sell, but she did not have the time in her frantic search for employment to make enough to make money.

Finally in March, with the better weather, Sal made up her mind to move on. She still had a few pennies and could find a room somewhere, she was sure. She would make it stretch for as long as she could and see what fate dealt her this time. She knew that Annie would never hear of her plan or accept it, so putting on a brave face, she told Annie that she was returning to Shettleston, and that she was not to worry.

Sal's search for room and board had not been a good one. Every place she found that looked clean and affordable would not let her take a room because of the baby. In desperation she had taken a room in a place where old men and drunks – generally down and outs of the city – would find shelter. It was a terrible place, full of rats and other vermin, stinking of vomit and urine. Over the week or so that she managed to tolerate these awful conditions, she had found herself threatened by a drunken molestation in the hall once or twice, and now she could not sleep for fear of attack. Not that the bed was particularly comfortable or clean.

That was when Sal took to the streets, still trying desperately to find work if she could, but after a few days sleeping in shop doorways and barely eating, her appearance had slipped. There was no employer who would even consider her. It was a particularly wet night in the middle of March; she had been out for ten days and had not eaten for three. Her milk was drying up, and little Annie wailed herself to sleep after hours of getting very little from her mother's breast. Sal had found a back alley down towards the Clyde that had a nook with a roof, where she could just about shelter out of the rain. It was a dark place with just one gas lamp at the end. She tried to rest, feeling sick with hunger and cold. She was barely in the world when she heard a young girl's desperate screams at the end of alley. She wanted to get up to help, but she was too lightheaded and scared, in case whatever was going on happened to her. She could tell from the noises that there was a man involved; she knew that he was forcing himself upon this poor wee creature, probably another waif and stray. She was screaming for him to leave her, for someone to help, but then her noises were muffled by the force of the man's hand clasped over her mouth. He was grunting and carrying on regardless. The screams had turned to muffled sobs. Then a slap, just to make sure she knew he would get her if she tried anything.

Then Sal heard footsteps staggering towards where she was. She froze in the darkness, fear gripping every inch of her being. The footsteps grew nearer and drew level. She tried to hunch herself back as far as she could, but he had seen her! He looked at the god forsaken bundle huddled in a doorway with a battered old pram, tutted and said, "Tramp!" and moved on. She could still hear the girl crying at the end of the street, she was alive at least. Then she too walked the other way.

Sal was at the bottom of the pit. How low she had fallen. Even a no good drunk despised her and saw her as worse than himself. And what had he been about? He had raped a girl at the end of the street without a care. She could be attacked anytime and Annie too. She fell into fitful dreams, warm fires, a comfortable bed, John's arms around her. She awoke at dawn sobbing. She knew she had to do something, this was no good for either of them. She tried to change Annie and make her look respectable, she gave her what little milk she had left to try and soothe her. For what Sal knew she was about to do, she had to depend on the kindness of someone to take a good looking little soul into their home.

She pushed the pram towards Glasgow Green and onto the river bridge and stood at the central point. The waters were grey and murky, it was a cold damp day; she could not be any more chilled to the bone than she was now after ten days on the streets, with little or no food. To her the cold water was quite inviting, even a relief to finally finish it all. The only thing that held her back was her Catholic soul; she was about to commit a mortal sin, she would be in purgatory forever, and she would never see her two wee boys. But why should she? She had brought nothing but trouble on both of them, she did not deserve to see them again. Eddie was fine, he was with his loving grandparents and she had not seen him for nearly two months. Little Annie would be taken somewhere, she had chosen this spot because many middle-class people walked their children on the Green, with any luck one of those nice, kind people would take the little foundling in.

Her hands gripped the capping stone on the bridge wall, she was building up the courage the climb on and sit, before making the fall. Her heart thumped in her chest, and tears ran down her cheeks at the thought.

"Now just stop, young lady!"

A familiar voice shook her back to reality; she turned slowly to be confronted with her mother before her.

"You weren't difficult to find... a woman pushing a pram... what do you think you are doing! Do you know how angry your father is with reports coming to him daily of his daughter walking the streets? Now you are coming back with me! You are in need of a good meal and bath by the looks of you... and this poor wee mite... did you give any thought to her with all your antics? And I suppose the little lad has been farmed out to the other family... well, you can get him back, he is your son and your responsibility... and you do have responsibilities, you know?"

Sal was all for carrying out her plan, but her mother said one thing that stopped her.

"There has been a letter waiting for you for over a month... from him!"

Sal was in no fit state to resist her mother's insistence that she must return to Shettleston. She was too starved and too weak to argue any more, she knew that Annie had suffered as a consequence; another child to fall victim to her bad role as a mother; it soon became obvious that Eddie had resented their forced parting, and resisted Sal when he was forced to leave the Flynns. Yet again, she felt that she had a lot to blame herself for. The only blessings were John's letter and the fact that Bridget had stopped with her constant back biting.

This letter had been written before Christmas, but had taken months to arrive; he had an address and pleaded with her to write, as he had heard nothing and was desperately worried about her and the children. But he had written that he had to move on in March and try and find work in Saskatchewan, as there was no more work for him where he had been. He said that the snow had lain six foot deep since November and the only way to travel now was on carts that had rails on them. He was at that time three hundred miles from the city of Winnipeg and fifty miles from the nearest post office, so they would have to wait for someone to pass by to take the letter. Every other line was another plea to Sal to reply, but he knew that if this letter did not reach her in time, he may well have moved on. He would try and write again when he could, and write to Maggie as well.

Sal felt thwarted. Maybe if she had not left when she did in February she would have been there to receive his letter and she could have replied as she should have. But yet again, she had acted rashly and not thought it all through; she should have listened to others, to have patience. Her only hope now was that she heard from him again soon, then she could reply and lay all of his fears to rest.

Mild-mannered Mary was none too happy with Sal when she finally saw her. In Mary's eyes Sal had not done herself any favours in the rash action she had taken and created a great deal of worry for everyone. Mary had gone looking for Sal early on in her disappearance and had visited Maggie, who had directed her to Comely Park Place, where Annie (as good as her word) had told on the two occasions that she had been there that she did not know of Sal's whereabouts. Mary was upset that Sal should have placed her in same mould as Bridget.

"You know that I would not have interfered, I just wanted to know that you were alright. I would not have revealed your whereabouts to anyone, not even James if you had told me not to. I have worried myself sick over these passed two months, and I don't understand why you dinnae' come to us... and when Bridget told me she thinks that you were about to do away with yourself! Well... what were you thinking! Don't you realise you would have broken my heart!"

Sal had not considered at any time that Mary would have been so stricken by it all, but on reflection, she realised that Mary cared for her deeply and that she had put her through needless worry and stress. Sal apologised over and over for her thoughtlessness, and begged Mary to forgive her. She told Mary about that terrible last night, and how she thought that it was best for her children if she was no longer around. She sobbed, and Mary placed a motherly arm around her shoulder.

"Please try and remember that you are loved and very needed... Sal, you must try and make this work, for the sake of your little children."

Chapter 18 –

The Greatest Distance of Separation

Sal waited month after month for another letter. She would visit Maggie on occasion just to see if she had any news. Both would sit there in mournful silence and worry, and then try to pretend that it was just the vagaries of the Canadian postal service and maybe letters had been sent that had never reached their destination. But in their heads they worried constantly, Maggie especially as she had not heard from him at all since he had left in March 1910. It was now late October 1911; he had said that it would be a year or two and they would all be together, yet, they had no news that he had even made it to Saskatchewan.

Back at Shettleston, Sal had readjusted into her life as the family domestic, thankfully less had been expected from her than before she had left; Bridget was only too aware that her demands had probably been the last straw for Sal, and that other members of the family were judging her for pressurising her daughter. Time was the best level to all, the longer that he stayed away, the less contact that Sal had, maybe that would tip the balance in Bridget's favour. Eddie had barely known his father when he left, and now hardly mentioned him at all. Baby Annie, now sixteen months old, did not even know who he was; time would be triumphant for Bridget's plans.

Sal was allowed to come and go relatively freely as long as her jobs were done. Bridget had considered her miscalculations previously, and if Sal was to consider that her quality of life was better if she remained, then she should be allowed to visit others as she saw fit. On the days that she could, she took Annie and Eddie to see Maggie, and other days, Ellie and Annie, or Mary. It was a chance to have contact with others. Sal had also grown closer to Katie, who needed some companionship, finding herself confined to the four walls of the cottage because of her health. She shared more of the baking and cooking with Sal, enjoying the camaraderie of the kitchen. Jeanie was out at work every day, and apart from her trips to the butchers, she remained mainly at home, though there were one or two occasions when she would request to spend an afternoon walking with friends. Unlike Sal's experience of the iron grip of the McBride parents, Jeanie was permitted to walk out with others, "As long as they were lasses, mind." But Sal recognised more in Jeanie of herself. *Was there a boy?* she thought, whenever she returned from these infrequent sojourns, a little pink and smiling happily.

Eddie was now rising five years old and very big for his age. Maggie could see the resemblance to John, both in looks and stature. He was as bright as a button, but inclined to rebelliousness; that is where the likeness faltered. Sal and Bridget recognised that trait, the McBride stubbornness. Bridget concurred that it would get him far, or end badly. Not something Sal wanted to dwell on, having lost two boys already. She tried her best to curb Eddie's wilful streak, but she recognised that without the firm hand and guidance of a man, he was going to do things his own way, and often. Mary was far more charitable.

"At least he will be dependable when you need him to be, Sal... and boys always cleave to their mothers."

Sal took heart in this long term promise of Mary's, she knew that whatever direction her life took, as long as she kept him safe, he would be there for her.

Annie was a quiet child, unlike her namesake. She was inclined to tantrums and needed to be corrected once or twice for screaming uncontrollably when she did not get her own way; a toy she wanted to play with, or refusing her food, and so on. She would on occasion lie on the floor, hammering her little fists on the floor boards, a lot of noise but no tears. Annie Theresa would remark, "She's having a paddy again."

A comment Bridget would despair at, paddy being a derogatory name for an Irish dimwit.

Finally, in late November, the long awaited letters arrived almost simultaneously, one to Sal and one to Maggie. Sal was overjoyed to receive the familiar handwritten envelope, and the Canadian stamp. She opened in front of Katie, smiling as she did so.

"What does he say, Sal... what does he say?"

Sal's hope was that it had been the long awaited invitation to join him next spring and her mind was rushing with all the things that she would have to do before they could leave. She began to read quickly. 'Sorry', he had written, she skipped the excuses and read on. He was somewhere now, can she write to this address. She moved on quickly, second page. How hard a summer it was, and all the thing he had learnt, she skipped the page again. Then as she read the next page, her smile left her face and she began to turn ashen in colour. Then with a sudden exclamation she threw

the letter down on the floor and headed for her room, raging
and crying all at once. Katie was flabbergasted by her sister's outburst and did not want to pry, but she could see that
Sal was in no fit state to tell her; she picked up the letter from
the floor, reordering it as she did so. She briefly scanned the
first three pages and then got to the crux of the matter that
had just sent her sister into a down spiral of despair. It read:

'Sal, I have learnt a lot this past year, and it is not going to be
as easy as I first thought. You can't just pitch up in Canada,
stake your claim and start farming; you need capital, money
to get you going and much more than I thought. I have been
working for a man in the north east of Saskatchewan now
for these past six months, he has taught me a lot, and given
me considerable advice.

'What most tend to do, is work like I am for a few years as
hired hands, planting and harvesting, working as stockmen.
They save what they earn and move from place to place to
find work. Then when they have enough to buy tools and
seed and survive for a year or so, then they stake their claim
to a parcel of land.

'You see, once you have that land you only have so many
years to break what is required to get the title; that does not
leave much time, with all the work that you have to do. Also,
you have to build a house fit to live in (most build a soddy –
like they used to in Ireland – to live in during the first years,
then they build a shack of lumber). Only when you have done
all of that and broken what is expected can you get the title.

'I know now that I will have to work at least another year
to have anything near enough money to start and then it will
be another year or so before I might have built a home fit for
you and the children to come over.

'I know that I promised that you would be here next spring, but I haven't got anything yet. I am going to have to ask you to be patient for another year or so, then we can all live together...'

Katie stopped reading, she could see that the rest was personal and she did not want to intrude further, she made her way with the letter to Sal's room, and knocking gently let herself in.

"Oh Sal... are you alright?... You must feel so disappointed?"

Sal was lain down staring upwards her tear streaked face drying now.

"Katie, he is expecting me to wait another two or three years!"

"Yes, I know... sorry, I had to read, I just wanted to know what had upset you, but I have read nothing else."

"Burn it! I don't want to read any more!"

"But Sal you can't do that, it has his addr-"

Sal had shot off the bed, snatched the letter from Katie's hands and thrown it in the fireplace, so fast that Katie had been unable to finish her sentence.

"...But Sal, how are you going to write to him now...You do not have an address?"

"And I don't want one!" she snapped fiercely. "He made a promise, two years he said, just two and now he is making me wait another three! Katie it will be 1914 before I get out there, I will be over thirty! What does he expect of me? Miracles?... and what about Eddie? He will be nearly seven the next time he sees his father, he will barely remember him and Annie... she will think he is a stranger!"

"But Sal, you have managed this long, just a few more years... what is the difference?..." Katie paused, unsure if she should even ask the next question. "You do love him… don't you?"

"I don't know any more, Katie…" Sal quietened. "We've been apart so long, and I have been through so much alone. I hardly hear from him and when I have he has moved, gone somewhere else and I can't write back… We don't share anything anymore!… it's like we are two different people… I don't even know who is now, he is a stranger to me… I am going to have to think about all of this… could you just leave me alone for a while, please?"

A week or more passed. Sal did not discuss with anyone the letter that she received, and asked Katie not to divulge its arrival, especially not to their mother. She was facing a Christmas yet again and knew that it would be busy; she could bury herself in her work and that would help to take her mind off everything. She knew that she had acted with her normal impetuosity, throwing the letter on the fire the way that she had; she had not read half of it, she certainly had not read on after the shock of his revelations. She knew now where her children had learned their behaviours from and felt slightly ashamed that she had not thought first and acted later. Now she had no address to write to. She had not told him about the death of James, Annie's birth; he had a right to know, he also needed to know how she felt. He needed to realise that he was placing an enormous expectation on her, one that she probably could not meet. Maggie would have received a letter by now surely. She needed to go and see John's mother and tell her the frightful news and ask for a return address; this had to be done and before another Christmas passed.

Maggie was not in the least surprised to see Sal, or, it seemed, angered by what John had written to Sal. She understood why Sal had been so dreadfully upset, and by the second cup of tea, she began her counsel.

"Sal, John did write to me too, and he told me more than you realise… He knew that his letter might upset you and asked me to try and talk to you the best I could to try and help." Maggie paused and drew breath.

"He is my son, my boy… as Eddie is yours, and I love him deeply, he is doing his best Sal, but he cannot do more than he can. He is working so hard to save the money that he needs as fast as he can, but the money is not that good for hired hands, once they have their board and lodgings. You have to see that he is doing his best for all of you… He also asked me how you are and the children… I am sorry but I have already replied, I have told him all that has happened and what a hard time that you have had… but I have tried not to worry him unduly, he is thousands of miles away and completely alone… You must try and see it from his point of view too… it is not his fault that things are working out the way that they are, no one has tried harder than my son for you… You have to try and have some sympathy for him."

Sal sat quietly by listening to Maggie's soft voice. Yes, she had behaved in a rash manner yet again, and John deserved a chance to prove that this could be so. But she was not prepared to wait on false promises. She made up her mind to reply, not to tell him all of her news, because that had been done, and it was always going to have been too painful to write. She would put her point across, that five years would be long enough and she would not be prepared to wait a moment longer.

She had sent her letter in late December; again there was no reply for some months, and if Maggie had received one, she was not prepared to tell Sal that she had. Eventually in March a letter came back; again all were out, including Katie, who had taken Annie and Eddie for a short walk. Sal sat once more on her bed in her small room, opening a letter from John. This time she read carefully, curbing her impulsiveness as much as she could. He was thrilled to have finally heard from her and to know that she was alright. He was very sad to hear of the death of little James from his mother, and expressed his deep love to her for shouldering it all and managing to get through. He wanted to know about baby Annie, how she was growing, what she was like. Then he moved to the bone of contention.

'Sal, I understand that you are not happy having to wait five years instead of two, no one feels more unhappy about this than I do. I really miss you so much and know now that you have gone through some terrible times alone. I wish that I had been there when you needed me, and I wish none of that had happened, but it is done now, and no deep regrets are going to change any of it.

'I will do my best to make sure that in 1914, you and the children come to me at last. I will build the finest home that I can and make you safe again. I have really tried and if I could make more money then it would be faster, but there are only so many hours in one day that a man can work.

'I hope that you do not give up on us? I hope that you will see that it is for the best and it will all be worth it? Please write to me as soon as you can, I will be moving on again in the summer, so I will ask the farmer to forward on to wherever I am.

'All my love
'John'

It was the best she could expect, she knew that. She had to give this her support, especially as the alternative would be to admit to her mother that she had been right after all that 'distance creates distance'. It was not the best of times for her, but she had been through much worse and what was another two and half years in the scheme of things? She had waited so long now, there wasn't much difference in waiting a while longer. She did not tell Bridget all that had gone between her and John in their letters, but thought it pertinent to ask if she could remain a while longer – for another few years. Bridget was very supportive.

"Of course, Sal... where else would you be? This is your home."

Secretly, Bridget was gleeful at this turn of events: two years had turned into five. It could change again and become, six, or seven, surely Sal's patience would run out? Or maybe she would be too long apart and not be able to return? All she had to do was wait and time would do its mischief for her.

Another letter had passed each way by the end of September. John was so glad to be finally in contact, Sal's listing events and happenings. His full of love and devotion, hers the characteristic coldness from when they were first married. She was bottling up her emotions, knowing that if he failed her again, she would have to break free from his hold, as she could no longer envisage making their lives work together if the time apart extended beyond that she had stipulated.

Then came a terrible day in early October. Sal had gone about her business as normal, her routines fixed: mothering two small children and keeping food on the table at Mary Lea Cottage. It was a Monday, and as normal her father had left for his business and flat in London Street; Sal did not expect his return until Friday evening. Katie was in the parlour, making scraps with Eddie and Annie, Jeannie was at work and Annie Theresa was at school. All of a sudden a procession of the McBrides, Peter, Bridget and James, were walking through the gate of the cottage. Bridget was visibly upset and her small diminutive frame was being comforted by her son. She came in first, asking for a glass of water and a seat. The children were whisked away to the bedroom by Katie, who sensed a deep trouble. Sal stood questioningly as the men having removed their hat and coats, followed after. James looked at Sal solemnly.

"It's terrible news Sal, just terrible... Peter has been found dead... poisoned..." Bridget let out a muffled sob, restraining herself as much as she could. Sal stood aghast.

"How? Where? What do you mean poisoned?"

"We don't know all of the details yet... He was found on last Tuesday at his lodgings... he had been dead for a while... the doctor thinks it was accidental... but because it has been a few days it is impossible to tell...We have just been to the mortuary to identify him...it is Peter."

Sal looked at her mother, who was sitting in shock. She felt an enormous pity for this old woman, normally so strong and unshakable. What a terrible thing to have any child die, but in such tragic circumstances and not to be found for days? What she must be feeling right now was beyond comprehension. Sal crouched down next to her mother and did something that she had never dared to do: she put her arms around her, and drawing close to her, allowed her to bury her face in Sal's shoulder while she let go her contained grief.

Chapter 19 –

Jeanie's Story

Whether it had been the tragic turn of events, or it had been Sal's reaction to her mother's grief, something changed in Sal that day. It was as if a switch had been thrown in her mind, and the whole world seemed different to her. The plans she had seemed superficial, even artificial; against this backdrop of shared grief, everything else was pointless. The McBrides collectively mourned Peter's passing, never understanding why or how this awful thing had happened, but no one daring to raise the prospect that he may have taken his own life. The death certificate read that it was accidental, which was enough for a catholic burial in Dalbeth Cemetery on London Street. But still some feared that it may have been the family's disposition to depression that may have taken him away.

Sal had grown closer to Bridget through this troubled time, and Bridget needed the support of her eldest daughter to steady her. Nothing now seemed more important to Sal than her family, the family who had been there for her through all her difficult times; now they needed her support, even her own mother. Why was she even considering leaving them? she thought. What would she achieve by taking this ridiculous risk for her children? Surely it would be too long apart to ever make it work for both of them again? The more she considered the prospect, the more it became an alien one. She needed to make a 'once and for all' decision, not just for her, but for John too; she was no longer being fair with him.

At the same time, there were other happenings in the McBride household, which took everyone by surprise, an unannounced visit from James brought the news that was least expected. He came in surreptitiously and asked his mother to join him in the front parlour. All that Sal could make out were indistinct words, with Bridget's voice raised occasionally. After half an hour, she came out of the parlour took her hat and coat and headed out of the house, obviously intent on an important mission. James came through to the scullery, and asked Katie to go to her room. Sal wondered why he was determined to see her alone. Had something untoward happened? Had she done something to cause problems for the family without knowing about it? She looked at him, worry written all over her face.

"No, Sal… it's not you this time, no need to worry, it's Jeanie… That's why I asked Katie to leave, the fewer people know about this the better… especially as Mama is away to see father, he does not know yet and she has taken it better than I expected, but she is none too happy." He stopped. Sal was curious, what could Jeanie have done that could have caused such a hiatus? She had worked in a local shop for a while, maybe she had said something out of turn? James continued.

"She came to see Mary and I on Sunday last, to ask for our help… she has a young man…" Sal smiled and laughed.

"Oh is that all! You had me worried for a moment."

"No, Sal… it's not so simple… she has been seeing him secretly for some time now…" Sal remember the flushed-

faced girl returning from her Sunday walks, suddenly horrified and she came back quickly, "She's not... she's not
expecting, is she?"

James laughed, if only she were, it might have been an
easier conversation that the one he had just been through
with their mother:

"No Sal, it's much worse than that... he's a Methodist."

"Oh good god!"

"Exactly... to Mama that is next to being a worshiper of
Satan, or an Orangemen... the only reason I managed to
calm her was by reminding her that father was a protestant...
All we can hope is that father has less objections to the union."

"But who is it? I had no idea?"

James smiled again. "Remember I told you about the
butcher's boy that we called young Ernest after? Well his
real name is Arthur Ernest Allan, but he thinks that Arthur
is rather old fashioned, so he just calls himself Ernest... it is
him. He is a nice young man in his twenties, and doing well
for himself, like me he will probably make a go of it as his
own man. She has been seeing him."

Sal knew now why going to the butchers for the meat had
been Jeanie's chosen task, and why she was working in the
haberdashery only five doors down from the butchers, it all
made sense. But she could see why she had kept it a secret...
a Methodist? How was Bridget ever going to come to terms
with that? She asked her brother.

"Well I should think if Jeanie's got any sense she has
convinced him to marry in St Andrews."

"No unfortunately, that is not going to happen. He is a
devout Methodist. His parents are both dead, but his father
had been a congregational minister, he is set in his beliefs
and expects Jeanie to marry as a Methodist."

"Oh, I see... that explains why she went to you, you are the only person who may be able to talk mother round... have you managed to, do you think?"

"Well, not right now... she is fiercely against it, and has gone to see father to tell him... I think she believes he will support her and stop this... that's why I am seeing you alone... I really believe, and so does Mary, that if they try and stop them they will do something rash... they have been together for a few years... they were going to tell us before Christmas... but of course with Peter's death..."

They both stood in silence, remembering the pain of their brother's passing. James continued, "I know that you have not got the best of relations with our mother, but you do understand what Jeanie is facing... Mary's worried that if I involve you it will cause trouble for you again, and I know things have been better for you recently, but I really need your help with this... If you can just find an opportunity to raise the subject with her... just anything to try and sway her opinion?"

Sal thought for a moment. Did she really want to create conflict when she had just settled things with her mother? In her own mind she was struggling to come to terms with her marriage, a marriage that she knew she was beginning to believe was a mistake; did she really want to see her own sister make a similar mistake, and then have to bear all of the problems that would bring down on her? But Jeanie was different, and Ernest sounded a determined young man, with frank views and good prospects; who was she to criticise them or come between them? She assured her brother that she would try to mediate for Jeanie and Ernest, but she was not sure if her influence would have any bearing on the matter.

An awkward few days passed in the McBride household. Jeanie sheepishly came and went, unsure what the reaction would be. To her and Sal's surprise nothing was said, although there was some obvious tension emanating from Bridget toward her husband. Then came the summons to Jeanie to bring her young man; Sal knew what was to be expected and tried to reassure Jeanie that all was not lost. Sal made an attempt to speak to her mother two or three times, but each time her approaches were dismissed; Bridget had too much to do and had not the time for idle chatter.

That Sunday, James and Mary arrived with their children as always and after lunch there was a knock at the door. Peter had already assumed his chair in the front parlour and Bridget sat with him. Sal met a very nervous young man. He was not of great stature, but fair and well-presented; he recognised Sal from the few visits that she had made to his employer's shop, it eased him slightly, especially when he saw Jeanie hovering behind her nervously. They exchanged a loving smile between them and he was summoned into the parlour, all others were excluded and sat waiting in the back room. After a while Jeanie was called for. Sal and James wished her luck.

A relatively short time after, a jubilant Jeanie emerged her beau trotting behind her. Their parents had agreed, they were to be married in April, when she turned seventeen. Much congratulation was exchanged by all the younger members of the family, and James and Sal were quite naturally relieved, but somewhat shocked that whole process had been so easy. Jeanie said that their father had done most of the talking, another thing that surprised all, and Bridget had sat by, not as involved as she might be. James speculated, "It's because you are in the trade, lad... Father sees a good meat supply coming through." All laughed, and spent a nice afternoon together before parting. Bridget remained with her husband in the front room for most of that time. James took Sal to one side in the scullery before he left.

"I know why... can you not work this one out?... It's business, Sal... Ernest works in retail and is going somewhere... father has told mother to put her feelings aside, his business interest always come first... Mama has no choice but accept this union on any terms."

Sal could see that her brother was right. Bridget was a reluctant participant in all of the preparations for her second daughter's wedding, but nonetheless she had to do it. Jeanie was ecstatic and relieved not to have to conceal her relationship anymore, it was obvious to all that she loved Ernest a great deal and the feeling was mutual; they made a very handsome couple and were devoted to one another. Sal was genuinely pleased that all had gone so well for her younger sister, but in her quiet moments, did feel slightly resentful that yet again, everyone else had been able to do things that she would not, just because of this young man's prospects. Her father showed some warmth towards Ernest, more in fact than he had towards his own sons, and never to his daughters.

Sal and John had exchanged one more letter over that winter. His – as always – full of love and longing, hers, a list of the happenings with the children and her family; the loss of Peter and the joy of Jeanie's impending marriage. She had contained her emotions. Over the ensuing months, she felt herself making the break. Before the nuptials in April her decision was made: she was no longer being fair to him or herself, and she could only see her children suffering as a consequence. She wrote another matter-of-fact letter, but this time she laid her cards on the table.

'I think the time has come to admit to one another that this cannot work as it is. You are no nearer bringing me and the children over, you know that it would be impossible this year, and probably the next. I cannot go on living a life in hope that we will be together. With Jeanie and Ernest marrying shortly, it has made me realise that I want what they have, being together, not alone facing life without a companion and friend.

'You too might find life more bearable if you had not got the responsibilities towards us, and could find someone to share all that you plan who is there without the added complications of children. You are a lovely man, and you deserve more than we are, more than I have ever given to you. Fate has dealt us some terrible blows and it is almost as if it has been a signpost that we should not continue trying to keep things together.

'I am very sorry and I know that you will not be best pleased with me to have kept you hoping these past three years, but you must realise that what you are expecting of me is just too much. I think it is best we try to make our lives apart.'

Sal never received a reply to the letter in the months and years that followed; what she had written had made the facts plain, and if John was suffering as a consequence, she was never to know. When the wedding came, Sal stood by as Jeanie's witness, and as if to make a proclamation to the world without a big fanfare, she signed her name, 'Sarah McBride'. Bridget's dispute with her second daughter's choice of husband was eased that day, by the glee at her first daughter's actions.

The rest of 1913 and early 1914 passed as if there had never been a different life known by all in Shettleston. Sal was settled with her children, Eddie was rising seven and still as headstrong and bullish as he always was. Now at school, he was forever receiving some punishment or other for various misdemeanours, usually from his refusal to obey something asked of him, or do something expected. Sal hoped that the force of the schoolmaster's cane might curb his rebellious nature. He possessed so much charm that whenever she tried to punish him at home, he would smile or laugh, or say, "But I love you, Mama."

Her heart would melt and so would her anger.

Annie was another story. Although she was as pretty as an angel, she was predisposed to moodiness, and though still only quite small, would sit and sulk when she did not get her own way. These sulks would last for hours and no one could make her forget her mood. Everyone realised it was best just to let her get on with it. She had also acquired a new name, which she seemed to like. Eddie had taken to calling her 'Cissie', as he said, Annie Theresa was Annie, Cissie was his sister. Sal knew that he had picked up the derogatory term 'you're a sissy' at school, and as much as no one else appreciated her moods, he did not; so Cissie she became and the name 'Cissie' stuck.

Katie seemed much healthier in these years. Bridget was beginning to hope that her childhood invalidity was a thing of the past, and gentle domestic work might be sorted for her somewhere so that she could have a purpose in her life. Hugh too had made a new life for himself, not that he appeared much these days. He had been living in Coatbridge for some years, working in the railyard there, first as a fireman and then as a shunter. He had taken a wife Charlotte, who had been in service. Bridget did not much approve of his choice, or how it was done. It was not so much a secret, he just did not feel inclined to tell anyone, why should he? He was a man, he could do what he wanted. He neither sought nor wanted his family's permission. He married out of the faith without a care in the world and had proceeded to have two daughters, Jemima and Catherine, without any family interference. Unlike James and Mary, who valued their families and would go to extraordinary efforts to maintain their relationships too where necessary, even if it meant they spent more time visiting others than being alone together.

Sal had made infrequent visits to Flynns, especially after revealing to Maggie what she had written to John. the relationship between the two women had become quite distant, and if Maggie had a strong opinion she kept it to herself. She may have considered that for Sal to have kept going through so much for so long alone, it was to be expected that she would now feel that making her own life was the only way forward. Maggie loved her son deeply, and although Thomas was still close by, John had been her firstborn a very treasured little boy, and in her eyes, a man that could do no wrong – he was her son. Now she knew he was out there alone, the only person that he was writing to was her, and it was up to her to support him come what may. At least if these meetings between Sal and her could be maintained she could report back to her son as to how his children were thriving and growing.

With all gone except her two smallest daughters, Lizzie and Sarah, she had a much quieter home. Eddie and Cissie loved to see their other family, although Cissie still was inclined to her moody outbursts even there. Thomas had made a friendship with the daughter of the man he worked for, and Maggie hoped that they would marry one day. At least then, there would be more grandchildren and they would be closer by for her contact.

No one thought then that all the strange 'goings on' over the sea in Europe would have any great impact on their lives, although there was much talk of war and the jingoism that goes with it. No sooner had the conflicts started to erupt, as various governments declared war on their neighbours, than soldiers were being mustered in regimental colours and marching through George Square. Sal felt that this was an ominous sign. She knew that the younger members of the family were talking about nothing else, especially Ernest, who was feeling that it was his patriotic duty to enlist and go and fight the Hun. She heard from Maggie that Thomas had the same desire, but Maggie had tried to counsel him against it; she had some experience of army life, having married her husband when he was serving in India, but she could not have possibly imagined the hardship that this new conflagration would cause, for so many and so widespread.

By the end of 1914, both young men in their early twenties had enlisted; Ernest was away to the 11th Battalion Highland Light Infantry, Thomas Flynn to the 8th Battalion Seaforth Highlanders. Jeanie had got quite caught up into the patriotic romance of the situation, especially when Ernest had finished his basic training and came home on leave in his fine uniform; as with all the Scots regiments, the splendour of the tartan and sporran. Jeanie brought him to say his farewells to the family that last Sunday that they were together in 1915. Peter was quite vocal towards Ernest.

"Well done, lad… you make sure that ye give as good as ye get."

Bridget, too, had warmed to this young man, and patted his shoulder as he sat in the parlour. "That's a fine uniform, on a fine young man."

James had been quite envious, he had tried to enlist, but his fitness and age had gone against, as too his occupation; someone had to keep those at home fed, and grocers were important for the population of a large city. Sal did not see Thomas before he left for the front. Maggie said that it had been a difficult goodbye, and he had been very happy to go. It would all be over soon, and he would come home and she very much hoped that he would.

As that first year of war passed, it became clear that this was not going to be over soon by any stretch of the imagination. More and more men were mustered in the city centre, boys, older men. Sal thought as she saw some go how young some of these lads looked, and how proud their parents seemed to be waving them off as they marched; pipes stirring the heart, Souters blowing in the breeze. There were posters and banners all over the city and everywhere felt part of what seemed so far away.

Peter's business thrived. Having dealt in rags and woollens for many years, he had a fine network of supply and distribution. The army could not get enough uniforms and blankets, they needed much more and their demand was now outstripping their supply. They began to turn to men like Peter McBride to help plug the gaps. Peter was able to source serge and wool, fabric and manufactured garments; the more the war grew in intensity, the more the demand grew, the more money Peter made. Never a spendthrift, all was reinvested to grow his capital; he knew that it would all end one day, and he had to reap the benefits now, rather than make any fanciful purchases.

Chapter 20 –

Sal's War

Christmas 1915 was a very patriotic one in Glasgow; people celebrated the few victories that the Highland Regiments had made during the war's duration and supported those poor unfortunate men who were arriving back daily, maimed and shocked, from the front lines. It would all be over soon, we would win and everyone would come home, despite the ever growing casualty and fatality lists which were posted around the city.

Sal got caught up in the waves of celebration and enthusiasm that were sweeping Glasgow. She had taken to walking daily to see as much as she could, especially now that both children were at school. One day she turned south away from George Square and headed for Glasgow Green, where she found a place to sit and rest from all of her exercise. Just then, a man in his mid-thirties asked if he could sit on the bench. He introduced himself as Robert McLeod, "But my friends call me Robbie."

Sal introduced herself, and they chatted pleasantly. He was an engineer and unmarried; he had lived with his elderly mother who had passed in the last year. He had just been to enlist, he felt that it was the right thing to do. He paused.

"...I notice you are not wearing a wedding ring... but a beautiful woman such as yourself... have you lost your husband on the front?"

"No... no...," Sal began slowly, "... He is fighting his own war... with the elements."

Sal explained her story, and how after three years apart and all of the trouble she had taken the decision to make a new life. Robbie looked at her with great sympathy.

"It's easy to forget with the war going on, that lives continue with all their troubles and tribulations... It does not sound like you have had an easy one, Sal..." He paused. "... Look, I don't have to leave for a week... This may seem very forward, but... shall we meet up again?..." Seeing Sal's shocked face, he quickly added, "... There is nothing bad meant in this... it's just I have no family now... well, no close family... and there is something about you... I mean, we get on... I would like to have someone to write to... it would be nice if we could do this again, just walk and talk."

Sal had not been shocked by his approach, she had been knocked off her feet that anyone had found her interesting. She had been alone so long that she had not even considered that anyone ever would. War is a strange time and makes people feel an urgency to hang on to something, 'any port in a storm'. She looked at him, so different to John; he was small with brown hair, greying round the temples, and his eyes were brown. He was very softly spoken, and despite his forwardness was really quite shy, all of a sudden she felt his loneliness – he needed for a friend.

"Yes, Robbie, that would be very nice… but we are just friends… I mean, it would not do for anyone to think anything else… I do have children to consider."

Robbie was really pleased and replied quickly, "Of course, that is to be expected… just as friends."

Sal felt flattered by these attentions, but genuinely surprised that someone would find her attractive. Over the next four days, she repeated the trip to Glasgow Green to the same bench at the same time, and there was Robbie waiting for her. They chatted away about this and that, her complicated life, his life less dramatic and more mundane. He told her that his father had died when he was a lad, and he had been determined to give his mother a good life and had worked hard to train as a civil engineer; he had been employed by Glasgow City Council, mainly bridges and roads. His mother had died in the last year and he felt that he had to do his duty, especially when he saw all these young lads going off to fight, and now many more returning maimed and injured.

Sal asked which regiment he was enlisted in.

"The 7th Seaforth," he replied.

"That's incredible, my brother-in-law Ernest is in the 8th, maybe you will see him?"

"I doubt it, I am not sure they keep all of the regiments together, but there is a strong chance because of my age and experience that I will be a Corporal, so if I do, I will make him jump to attention." He laughed.

He was to leave soon and had formed a strong attachment to Sal. He told her he was very glad that he had met her, that he thought his mother was watching over him and had brought them together so that he would have a reason to look after himself and come home. Sal was a bit taken aback by his forthrightness, but excused it as the urgency that is instilled in people during those dark times. Sal felt very at ease and relaxed with Robbie, just as she had known him all her life, and it was her that he was leaving tomorrow. To any onlookers on the Green that day, they looked like any normal husband and wife, before he departed for his training and then the front. After a while, Robbie asked nervously, "I know it is a great deal to expect, Sal, but would you come and see me off tomorrow at the station?"

Sal drew breath, she nearly said yes immediately, but her guilt at not seeing John leave years before suddenly reawakened. She felt a prick of conscience and wondered what others would think if she were seen. But then she looked at his deep brown eyes, just like a puppy, how could she say no? He really needed a friend. "Yes I will be there Robbie..." And then in a lighter tone, "...But you make sure that you write to me, or I won't do it again." She giggled.

On the packed station, there was the now very familiar sight of many young men; some mere boys, making tearful farewells mainly to mothers. There were a few women like Sal, in the arms of a beau, or a husband. The picture of Robbie and Sal did not quite fit. A man and a woman with two small children, but there was a shake of hands and a brotherly peck on the cheek, no overfamiliarity, just that. Inside, Sal was a turmoil of emotions; she felt drawn to Robbie and if she had been single or a widow, would not have thought twice than to step over the line of contact. But something held her feet firm, something that she thought that she had put aside. Whether Robbie felt more, or felt cheated by not having the farewell he may have hoped for, he said nothing, and was charming and a complete gentleman. He told Sal that he would write and come and see her on his embarkation leave; Sal said she would count the days until she could meet her friend on the Green.

Sal made a reluctant visit to Maggie in January 1916; she was feeling the guilt of her recent association although she had no reason to, she had not indulged in anything inappropriate, but there were moments when she wished that she had. She felt different; she thought that others, particularly Maggie, might sense the change in her, her paranoia was ever-present. But Maggie had other things on her mind and a great deal to tell. Tom had been home on leave at Christmas. Without telling anyone, he and the girl that he had been courting – Sarah – had got a special licence and married on the last day of the year before he had embarked once more. Maggie told Sal she was very glad for him, but worried about her son, who looked terrible; he was obviously going through some very frightening things, and was not eating properly, his facial expressions had lost their boyishness and hardened considerably.

In those early months of 1916, the atmosphere of patriotism changed to a tiring of the austerity of war. Only those that could make money out of making goods that supplied the front, such as Peter McBride, could now have any benefit from all that was going on over the channel. There were shortages everywhere: food, fancy goods and fabric were all now difficult to get, as more and more of the manufacturing capacity turned itself towards the needs of the war. Hemlines visibly shortened, and the volume went out of skirts, as clothes needed to be made with less fabric when shortages became more acute. Young women relished the freedom, older women such as Bridget frowned and tutted at the immodesty that was being shown. Both Katie and Jeanie donned the new fashion and showed their ankles; when questioned about this by their mother, the answer was a simple one, we have to do our bit to save on things that are needed Mama. Bridget could not contest this, although she expressed 'a hope' that they would return to adopted traditions when war ceased.

Jeanie was receiving letters from Ernest from time to time. They were heavily censored, in case of interception by the enemy, and also by the army so that morale at home was not influenced by the terrible conditions of life on the front lines. Soldiers could not reveal where they were, or any problems that were too difficult for those at home to imagine. Rats and water-filled trenches were not recorded, neither was the scabies, and the foot rot. Basic information could be exchanged, never 'what battle', or 'how many dead or injured', or 'the inadequacy of officers'. He wrote as many did, about the love he had for her, the desperate wish for it all to be over and peace to come, so that they could be together again.

Jeanie would reply with a complete account of all that had happened in the intervening period since he had been gone. She tried to give him a sense of home, a sense of normality. The more that the lists of fatalities grew in length, and the more that the young men and boys came back with limbs missing, blinded and suffering shell-shock, the more apparent it had become to the general population, that this was a new and more horrific type of war. Millions were dying, all over Europe and there seemed to be no end in sight.

Robbie had embarked in July and within a few months a letter arrived in a strange hand, addressed to Mrs Sarah McBride. Bridget had been at home that day and had greeted the postman, she read the address; someone had written to Sarah from the front who did not know her married name was Flynn? She turned the letter over to read the sender's details, it read:

'Cp R Mcleod
S/35795
7Th Seaforth Highlanders.
Loos'

She smiled to herself as she handed Sal the letter. It was a
very long letter, despite the fact he could not give any details.
It was cleverly written, she was able to understand that he
had seen plenty of action already, that there were no breaks
from the unremitting shelling from enemy lines. He was
tired but his spirits remained high, as he knew that one day
he would be coming back to Glasgow. He reminisced about
the few short times walking on the Green with a lovely lady,
who had given him a reason to carry on and keep going.
Before signing off, he asked Sal if she might send a photograph just so that he might remember her face better. He
was careful with his closure, just in case this may cause her
embarrassment if it was read by others, he signed simply,
'affectionately yours, Robbie'.

Sal was genuinely touched by the sentiment that he had
expressed in the letter, and set to replying to him, knowing
that morale of the troops was only kept up by the support of
their family and loved ones, and Robbie had no one except
her. She went to Glasgow in her best hat and coat, and had
a photograph made; this was a thriving business as many
were doing the same. She wrote a long letter of normality to
him; the weather during the summer, how Eddie and Cissie
were growing and becoming very feisty. She talked of the
changes around Glasgow, knowing that as a municipal engineer this would be of interest to him. She did not mention
the hardship or shortages, compared to horrendous conditions of the trenches – which were widely known by now –

the difficulties experienced at home were minor. Then she, too, wished for those so few days to be again. She wrote:

'I had a lovely time those days that we spent on the Green. You made me feel like a lady for the first time in my life. Before I was a daughter, then a wife, then a mother, and then a mother alone. It was so nice to be valued as me, you will never know just how wonderful that was.'

She ended the letter in the same way as he had, but added a postscript, 'please write soon, if you can.' She added the photograph and sealed the enveloped and took it to post.

Indeed, his letters did come frequently, which for Sal was a joy after the limited and rare contact she had received from John during the years that she had tried to carry on regardless. She entered into a regular dialogue with Robbie, where they shared their dreams and desires for peace and how their lives would be so different. Neither was too forward or direct, both respected that they barely knew one another, and that would be the main wish: to spend more time together so that they might. All the time their friendship grew, as they exchanged more and more stories of their childhoods and anecdotes of funny things that they had done.

During the closing months of 1916, everyone was wrapped up in their own experiences of war. Bridget and Peter were about business, the substantial nest egg had been building and discussions about investing in property became a common-place topic. Katie was putting her sewing skills to good use, having become a Woman Volunteer making uniforms that were desperately needed. Annie Theresa had left school and was working in a munitions factory. Sal was on her own trying to be father and mother to her two strong-willed offspring.

Partly because of this flurry of activity, partly because she no longer lived in the family home to have regular surveillance, no one had noticed Jeanie's failing health. She had a succession of colds in that year, which had left her with a persistent cough. Not to be tarred with the same brush as her sister, and marked as an invalid, she had failed to see a doctor or visit a hospital, pretending it was nothing and continuing to work as she always had – she was most like her mother out of all of the McBride girls.

When the family came together to share their Christmas – a quiet one, as no one felt that it was right to make a big spectacle – James and Mary were very concerned that Jeanie had lost so much weight and was coughing almost continuously, breathlessly. Bridget was immediately alerted, truth be known more concerned for the effects that this may have on Katie. She sent for the doctor, who wasted no time and admitted her to Glasgow Infirmary. Jeanie was diagnosed with endocarditis, a severe condition of a failing heart; Bridget was told to contact Ernest immediately as she was not at all well.

Fear gripped the family. Jeanie could not be that sick. Nobody had known that she was even ill, she had brushed it all aside as a cold, she would be fine soon. Even now, sitting up in bed, her cheerful disposition and her insistence that they (the doctors) must have their diagnosis wrong, she would be as right as rain in a week or two. Bridget was of the same mind, and delayed writing to Ernest; there was no point in alarming her husband, he had enough to do at this present time. The Western Front was at its peak of fighting, with overwhelming numbers of fatalities and casualties.

Then all of a sudden, Jeanie began to fail. Her breath became so laboured she was given oxygen through a mask, she had stopped eating. The last day of the month of January, she was barely in the world. Bridget and Sal were sitting with her, expecting Mary and Katie to come so that they could get some rest. The men were told not to be there, this was a woman's place. Jeanie lay still. Each breath rasping and wheezing through the sound of the hissing mask. Just then she lifted her right hand shakily and pushed the mask away. Sal leapt up.

"No, Jeanie, you must keep that on, it is helping you." She leant over to push it back on, Jeanie weakly grabbed her arm, and whispered, "No."

Sal stopped, she could see that she was trying to speak, but her voice was barely audible. Sal leant her ear towards Jeanie's mouth, and listened.

"Te-ll... Ernest... I am so sorry... Bu-t... I have to go now... Tell hi-m I... I... love... him."

And with that last word, her breath stopped. Jeanie's heart had failed.

Ernest was brought back on compassionate leave for his wife's funeral. He seemed lost, half the man that he had been. He was completely devastated and could not bring himself to talk to anyone, though James did try once or twice. The shock of losing Jeanie so suddenly had left everyone numb, Bridget especially, now only five of her children were living; she had lost a much-loved daughter.

On his last day of his leave, he came to say goodbye; he was withdrawn and his uniform was hanging off his reduced frame through lack of nourishment. It was only Sal that he really spoke to before he left. She tried to wish him well, and told him that she would be there for him when he returned, and that he must try to keep going. He looked at her through tearful eyes.

"Sal, I shan't come back… without Jeanie I have no reason anymore… this will be the last time that you see me…"

Sal tried to dismiss his comment, telling him that he mustn't talk like that, Jeanie would want him to keep himself safe. But no matter what she said, his facial expression was fixed and unchanged, he asked to leave and for no one to come with him, he wanted to be alone.

The telegram came at the end of March addressed c/o Mrs B McBride. Everyone knew before she even opened it what it would say, but everyone hope that it would not.

'I am sorry to inform you that Pte Arthur Ernest Allan – 31365, has died of his wounds during the Battle of Scarpe.'

That was not quite the end of it. Sal had not heard from Robbie for a few weeks and her concerns were growing. The telegram had brought home to her the fact that he had no next of kin, that she would not be informed if he was wounded, or killed. She began to scour the lists daily in the newspaper for any news, as each day passed with no news she would give thanks that he was still safe. She took the children to see Maggie; with Jeanie's sudden demise and death, the funeral and all that had ensued, she had not been for a few months. What greeted her when she arrived at the Gallowgate left her in no doubt what had happened even before she knocked on the door. A bow of black ribbon was nailed to the door; a simple sign of loss. Tom had been killed a few weeks after Ernest in the same action. Sal knew now that their family had not escaped the tragedy of this bloody awful war.

It was on her journey back that she passed a church with a casualty list pinned up; now almost second nature to her, she scanned the eight pages of tightly typed script, coming to the 'Mc's', which were many. There it was. No fanfare, no sorry but… just Cp R McLeod – Killed – Scarpe.

Her shock now was absolute! She felt nothing all was just a blur. How could this all be happening at the same time? Why was there such a fruitless waste of life? Why was she wasting her life…? That thought appeared from nowhere as she stared at the church door. Yes, that was it. She had been stupid, bloody minded and stupid. She had treated John despicably. She must make amends towards him. Somehow and someway, she must pull her family back together again. Life was too short to waste it, and she had wasted too much through her own stubbornness!

Part II

A Canadian Life

Chapter 21 –

The Longest Journey

"Stop pulling my hair!" the girl whined. "Mama, Eddie's bullying me!" And with that, she poked the young lad in the eye for good measure. A scuffle of hair pulling and shoving then ensued on the lower bunk, with screams and harsh retorts. Sal awakened suddenly on the upper bunk, to rebuke her unruly offspring, who were both thoroughly bored with their weeks of travelling.

"You two are making me tired! I have a good mind to turn round and go back! Now just sit quietly, or read or look out of the window, but behave!"

Silence resumed. Sal felt slightly annoyed with herself for losing her patience with Eddie and Cissie; it was hardly their fault, they had been very good all things considered. She craned her neck to see what she could through the top part of the small window, which just topped the edge of her bunk. Just a bleak whiteness met her gaze, stretching endlessly, flat and monotonous, just like the train journey itself. They had been on this train for over a week, crammed into a two-bunk sleeper in a very draughty corridor.

The cold was unremitting. Despite preparing the best that they could for the presumed Canadian extremes, it was simply impossible to carry enough clothing to suffice, or wear enough it seemed. The inactivity of being captured in a confined space, unable to move, to exercise and get warm, made the coldness even more pronounced. Her bones ached and her hands could barely grip anything, and she had not felt warm since the last day onboard the ship. As the lub-dub of the slow train continued, her heart echoed a response and she drifted off into her memories; the decision to come, the last days in Scotland, the tensions and excitements of the impending adventure. The confrontation with Bridget…

That had not been quite as she had expected. She had made the decision to go, when the tragedies of the deaths of Tom, Jeanie, Ernest and Robbie had been all-consuming. She had realised that life was too short to waste more of it waiting for things to change for the better. She had the 'better' already waiting for her in Canada, at least it must be better than that which she would leave behind in war-torn Europe. She had seen too many young boys return scarred and mutilated, suffering immense mental tortures, for all that they had witnessed and all that they had been through. Eddie was 11 years old now; the thought that if he had been 6 years older, he could have been one of those hopeless shell-shocked souls returning, or worse, not returning, had really impacted on her. She was also conscious that the environment that her children were growing up in was not a healthy one.

Although Bridget was still yearning for the next move, the larger house, more in fitting with her rising status in life, and Peter's ascent in the business world, which had not yet been fully realised, Eddie, Annie and Sal still slept in the same room, in the tiny cottage. Sal still skivvied for the family and her children knew that. Her authority with them was meaningless and dismissed by them, as much as it was undermined by others around her. They had a father, a lovely man, who would have done anything he could to make a life for his family and he had done; she was the one that had rejected all. And her mother had used all of her efforts to ensure that her daughter never really considered going to her husband as an option. With that in mind, the day that she announced what her intentions were was filled with a great deal of fear and trepidation. Her anxieties had been further pronounced through months of delicate and covert communications with John.

That had not been straightforward either. She had been to see Maggie to ask whether it was the right thing to do. Unsurprisingly, Maggie was very protective of her son's feelings; having just lost her only other son, she was not prepared to put John through the same pains he had suffered over the last few years, now that he truly believed that his marriage was over and that he had lost his family. Maggie had been his only anchor, his only rock to cling to in his storm of emotions. With the complicated and broken communications which punctuated the pioneer life, Maggie had handled her son with considerable care and love, piecing his broken heart back together again. With every letter she had reinforced the need for him to look after himself, to make a new life and a future, and find a new companion; someone who understood the life out there and could support him properly.

Maggie was reluctant to allow Sal to have any further contact, she was certainly not going to supply his latest address to her.

"I am sorry, Sal, my son is a broken man, you have damaged him… I think you know that… I am not having you pick him up to drop him again on a whim… or worse, when your mother dictates that you should."

Sal pleaded with Maggie, telling her that she knew now that it was the right thing to do, that John and her were meant to be together and she had been so stupid not realise that. She begged Maggie to give her a chance to try, that she would make it work and the children would be safer and more happy with both their parents than they were now. Maggie was unmoved, until Sal said the words, with genuine feeling and emotion, that Maggie needed to hear.

"I love him deeply, Maggie… It's taken me a long time to realise how much I actually do love him, and it was a friend who has gone that has made me realise how precious that love is and how lucky I was to have John."

Maggie relented slightly. She was prepared to write to John on Sal's behalf, but just to see in the first instance whether he had already changed his life. In that case, she insisted that she was not going to mention Sal's desires, she was not prepared to turn his life upside down if he had another life, a new love.

The wait for John's first reply to his mother's enquiries seemed to last an eternity. After a month Sal had visited Maggie again, who had news. John had settled, and there was no one else in his life. It was at that point that she revealed to Sal, that John had homesteaded in the last year finally; he had a piece of land that was his own and he had built a small place on it. Sal was thrilled, that meant that once the war ended, she could join him… when the war ended. It was the autumn of 1917, there seemed to be no end in sight, but Sal knew she had to go to John as soon as she physically could, as soon as he would agree, as soon as the civilian ships would sail the North Atlantic again. She implored with Maggie to intercede for her with John, Maggie agreed, seeing the tears of joy in her daughter-in-law's eyes when she did so.

Another month had passed; John's letter had come for his mother, but he had not written directly to his wife, despite the fact that her address had remained unchanged; an ominous sign. As Maggie explained John's reply, Sal felt deflated. Maggie did not quote from it, but rather, made a précis of all his concerns; it had obviously been a very severe reply and she was doing her best to mediate between a broken couple.

"He is worried, Sal… he thinks that he will build his hopes up and you won't come, or that your strength of feeling now will leave you. He is also concerned that you will find the life too hard. It is very harsh there in the winter, much more than you can ever imagine, and very hot in the summer. The home he has is very basic, he thinks that you will not be able to cope with not having the things that you have now, even running water. But the thing that seems to worry him most is that Bridget will talk you out of going, she has too much influence over you…"

Sal was lost. He would not write to her directly, and obviously what he had written to his mother was so extreme that his mother had felt it more tactful to couch all in more delicate terms. Maggie could see that she was deflated and hopeless, and she had realised that Sal's wishes to join John were genuine and she believed that this time she would stand up to her mother and make this happen. Maggie offered to try again, and told Sal to be patient.

"All things come to those who wait," she said, doing her best to try and reassure this broken women.

Another two months passed. It was now coming up to Christmas, the war still raged incessantly, Peter still worked tirelessly; maximising his potential to exploit the conflict. The cottage had an air of sadness; Katie continually plagued by health problems, Bridget still reeling from the loss of Jeanie. Eddie and Annie were quiet and withdrawn, only showing signs of normal childhood pastimes on the rare occasions when their much-loved cousins would stop by with Auntie Mary. It was on one of those days shortly before Christmas, when Bridget was out on one of her social jaunts and Katie had taken to her bed, that Sal and Mary sat in the back parlour chatting about this and that, as the children played in scullery, then the postman knocked at the door. Sal went, as she always had, to receive the various letters that would be addressed to her parents.

As she waved the postman goodbye, she glanced at the top letter in her hand, and she felt the hairs of the back of her neck quiver as a cold shiver passed through her. It was his writing! It had a Canadian stamp! Her legs buckled, just as Mary came through to see what was taken her so long.

"You look like you've seen a ghost! Quick, sit down."

Sal's arm was still shaking and extended, tears in her eyes, a smile on her face… he had written to her! But, it could be a letter to her like the one that he had written to Maggie, she could not bear to read is final rejections. She blurted all out to Mary, as she sat shaking still staring at the unopened letter.

"Well, open it… you are not going to know anything unless you do… I cannae' open it… it is your letter."

Sal slowly took the letter out of the envelope, and she began to read. The first paragraph was cold and aloof, how he had heard from his mother, he understood that she was trying to get in contact with him and he thought it best to write to her directly rather than go through his mother. Then there was a weather report, the snow had come it was falling very deep this year and he would probably get cut off in January and there would be no chance to get any letters to anyone until March. She felt that he was trying to put her off, prepare her for the fall. She read on in silence, Mary watching her nervously.

He wrote that he loved her very much and that despite his mother insisting that he found someone else, that he just could not look at another woman, which, he further qualified, were few and far between and most already married. He missed her, and was deeply saddened because he knew that neither that of his children would know him now, and that brought some fear into his heart that it would be too difficult for everyone to try and make a life together. But... that Maggie had been very determined, that she felt that Sal was of one mind now to make a go of things; the war in Europe having made everyone realise how precious life was. He felt detached from all of the turmoil that was ripping the world apart, as to him his own war was battling with the land and the elements every day. Sal stopped reading for a moment and looked up. Mary looked at her quizzically.

"It is not the news that you hoped for then?"

Sal resumed the last page and a half, tears falling down her cheeks causing the ink to smudge. John continued that he was being honest, to stop her doing anything without thinking it through. He asked her to find out as much as she could about the 'real' life in Canada, to really understand what she was letting herself in for. Then in his final paragraph he wrote just one sentence that made a difference to all else that had preceded those few words:

'My love, if you really feel after all that you know that you can make this work, and will manage with whatever you come to, you know that will make me the happiest man in the world.'

He signed it simply, 'yours, John'.

Sal was ecstatic. He wanted her there, she was sure of it, she threw the letter at Mary and dashed into the scullery to hug her two children, who were totally taken aback by their mother's sudden display of emotion. She bit back her enthusiasm with them; she knew that she had to contain everything until she had told everyone, knowing that her greatest nemesis in all this was her own mother. She returned to the back parlour to be greeted by a concerned Mary.

"Sal, are you sure about all this? I mean he has tried to discourage you, you must realise that you are doing something that you cannot undo once it is done, are you sure?"

Sal rushed to her, kneeling in front and grasping both of Mary's hands in hers.

"I have never been more sure of anything in my life, Mary, I will battle through anything, anyone to be with him again. I don't care what he says, I know it will be hard and I know I will have a harsh time there, but I will be with him, we will have hope, and no war."

Sal was rocked in her bunk as the train pulled into yet another station for a needed stop to take on water and empty the overfull lavatories; at least the wretched smell would subside for a while. It was also a chance for the children and their mother to stretch their legs. She swung herself out of her recline and slithered down onto the lower bunk. Eddie was already pulling on hat, coat and scarf, and Cissie was huddled up in the corner in a sulk.

"Are you coming with us, Cissie?"

Cissie pouted and looked away. "It's too cold."

"You are being very silly, you need to stretch your legs. Come on, come with me and Eddie, you need to see your new country."

Cissie pouted again. "It's not my country, I don't want to be here, I want to be in Scotland, I want to go home."

"Oh leave her Mama, she is in one of her moods. Come on, let's go."

As the door to the big CPR locomotive was opened, a sudden gust of biting cold greeted them. Sal was glad that she had wrapped her shawl around her face, over her head and under her hat. She took a deep breath and stepped off. The snow had been cleared directly around the platform, but they could see it was at least waist height. Eddie restrained his urge to throw himself bodily into a pile, having been severely reprimanded by his mother for doing this the day before; getting too wet, with nowhere to wash or dry clothes. They surveyed the flatness; they were in Saskatchewan and the joke that the guard had chortled when he had first met them days before and had asked their destination hit home to both.

"Ahh Saskatchewan, where you lose your dog on Monday and can still see him running on Thursday."

It was so vast and flat, nothing to break the monotony for miles and miles. Caked in snow, the horizon was subsumed into the snow filled sky; all seemed endless. It seemed so stark and lifeless in contrast to the bustle of Glasgow and the industrial city of Liverpool where they had embarked four weeks before. Sal wondered how many more hours until they would reach Saskatoon and changed their train to head south down this vast province. The cold had seeped into her bones, Eddie's lips were turning blue. They climbed back onto the train to try and find what little warmth there was in their tiny corridor sleeper. Cissie had dropped off to sleep, the scowl now gone from her pretty little face. Sal thought how sweet she could look with her bobbed mousy-brown hair over her flawless pale skin. She hoped that when she finally met her father, she would begin to adjust. Eddie stayed in the corridor watching the guards doing all of their duties. Sal climbed her ladder sliding back onto the bunk, pulling a blanket over her. She drifted back to her thoughts of those last months.

Bridget had been angry, no matter how strong Sal had felt when she took it upon herself to tell her mother her plans; her mother's outburst had been more than she had expected. She was furious, did Sal not know how much trouble it had been for them all these years with her living in their small cottage? That they had supported her and her children, despite everything? A reference to her moment of madness when she had taken off with Cissie as an infant and had been found attempting to end her life. And then there was the time when all had thought that she had come to her senses and had put all this romantic nonsense behind her. And how long would they be expected to house her for now? No one knew how long the war was to go on, she was not being fair to anyone.

Sal took it all, even though she felt very roughly handled. She told her mother that she was adamant that there was a better life for her and the children waiting for her in Canada. She was going on the first sailing that she could as soon as the war was over and that was that. Sal fell into a deep sleep, while the great Canadian giant trundled on across the icy flat terrain.

Chapter 22 –

Journey's End

"Mrs Flynn, we are coming into Saskatoon in half an hour."

Sal was awakened by the guard calling up to her. It was dark and she knew that she had to gather all of her things and the children together as quickly as she could, as another train would be leaving an hour or so later for the two day journey south. Wearily, she slipped down the ladder, pulling her packed carpet bag with her. Thankfully Cissie had woken in a happier mood, and Eddie was already standing up in the corridor. Both children looked highly relieved to be leaving their prison of the past few weeks and were keen to get moving as soon as they could.

Their collective enthusiasm was soon dented when the next train had no sleeping room; in fact, all three bodies were crammed into two seats, which would be the best that they could expect for the next twenty-four hours. Luckily for Sal, by the time all luggage had been collected and transferred to the local service, and they had negotiated the biting cold – which had made breathing painful – they were grateful to get into whatever comfort they could. Soon exhausted by the anxiety of the move, the two young people fell fast asleep as the train moved slowly out of Saskatoon. Sal lost herself in her thoughts once more.

After Bridget had adjusted to the idea that Sal and the children were leaving eventually, what planning that could be done was made. It would all be dependent on the war ending. At that time in January 1918, it seemed as far away as it had been for the previous three years. No one knew how long this mass conflagration could go on, but Sal knew that she had to be ready, whenever it came, to book her passage. She had sent a letter to John to tell him that she was to come, and that nothing would stop her; she did remember that he had said that it was unlikely any communications may get through till February or March. She had mused over his new address:

'J.C.Flynn, C/O PO Lidgett, Fir Mountain, Saskatchewan.'

She had visions of purple-topped mountains, heather and coniferous trees. She wondered how he could farm on slopes, and what sort of place he had built; knowing that his skills in that area were unsophisticated. She knew that she and the children would be travelling alone; Cissie at that time was eight and Eddie 11, they would carry what they could but they were only small people; she would have to think carefully about the limited possessions that she could take, ever mindful of the climate. She hoped it would be winter, so that they could wear all of their heavy clothes, leaving room to pack more things to take with them.

Eventually, in early April, John's reply came. He was still somewhat detached and aloof; he feared another rejection, no doubt, and was arming himself against more hurt. He said that he was glad, and that as soon as the passenger ships started again, that she was to book a passage from Liverpool. He advised her to save what money she could, as she would have to pass through immigration in Halifax – which should be straight forward as they were married, but it might mean a night or two boarding there. He suggested that while she was there she visit Eaton's and get a set of warm clothes for each of them, particularly warm boots (fur-lined), she would need them. As soon as it had been booked she was to write to him directly, he estimated that it would take three weeks once they entered Halifax to make the progress to their meeting place – Lafleche Station. The trains were at set times, and a telegram could be sent to Lidgett Post Office to inform him of their time of arrival, and he would be there to meet them all.

'I do hope the war ends soon Sal, it will be nice to have you all here, and I am looking forward to meeting my little girl. Yours, John.'

That had been the unexpected event in her planning, the reaction of her children. She had not wanted to over-excite them, but by the summer rumours were circulating that the war may end, and she thought it best to prepare them, expecting that when she did there would be genuine joy. Indeed, Eddie was thrilled by the prospect; he vaguely remembered his father, and being a boy, the whole idea of a big adventure was all-consuming, fuelled by the comic strips he had seen of cowboys and Indians. Cissie was not so impressed.

"I don't want to go, I want to stay here with Grandmamma and Katie. I want to be with Auntie Mary and my cousins… I won't go and you can't make me."

It was a battle that Sal knew that she could not win with her stubborn daughter, she hoped that after a time of adjustment that Cissie would change her mind and the thought of a new life, and meeting her father, might appeal. Cissie was adamant, she did not want to see her Papa, she did not know him and he was a stranger. Maggie and Mary did their best to persuade her, but the more they tried, the more resistant she became. Bridget observed from the outside; this could be the way to make her daughter stay, she thought. She was not going to make the offer to take the child, she was far too wilful and difficult and Bridget was feeling too old to take on another difficult girl. But in her mind, if Cissie created enough discontent and the offer were not made to take her in, then Sal would have to reconsider her plans to leave.

Sal was not going to let anything stand in her way, she knew that as long as she had Eddie's support, that Cissie would follow, however reluctantly. Like all close siblings, they could dislike each other intensely, but they were lost without one another, and Cissie idolised Eddie; where he went she would go. Sal had made it her strategy to involve Eddie in every aspect of her plans. Eddie's schoolboy visions grew, riding horses (something that he had never done in his life), helping his father till the land, tend the livestock, and not have to go to school. Sal did not want her son to forget his education and hoped that things were a little more civilised to make sure both of her children continued with their schooling.

Peter was surprisingly supportive; all done through Bridget as usual. He offered his daughter and her children a new set of travelling clothes each and some warmer things that he had reserved in his warehouse; there would be a sum of money to help them make their long journey, that amount was undecided. Peter was always careful not to offer too much to anyone, generosity was never his first motivation, he was a businessman after all. James and Mary commented to Sal that this uncustomary offering from their father, was more to do with removing yet another drain on his finances; Eddie and Cissie would be costing more to care for. Peter was scaling down his responsibilities to his family, it would just be Bridget, Katie and himself; Dunoon was becoming a realistic prospect.

Then in November, the Armistice came. The celebrations and relief were everywhere, soon all of those men and boys would come home, soon the world would be reshaped after the ravages of a colossal war. Sal wasted no time, and went straight to Glasgow to book passage for her and the children on the Canadian Pacific Railway Atlantic Steamship Line. She secured a third class birth for them on the Melita, departing Liverpool on the 10th December 1918.

The remaining time was a blur, despite her months of thought and planning, heaving suitcases had to be reduced, precious items of their old life removed. Only those things that were absolutely essential could be taken; this added to Cissie's gloom as a favourite doll was removed.

"You can only take one Cissie, there just isn't enough room, but I am sure that Papa and I will get you another one."

Sal had calculated that the sailing would be a week, and then another week in Halifax, clearing immigration, then two weeks on the CPR across to Saskatchewan, followed by two days on the local service to Lafleche. She hoped that they would be meeting John at the end of the first week in January and wrote to him telling him so. She would send him a telegram from Halifax when she knew her exact date of arrival.

The small family had stood on the platform of Glasgow Central station, waiting to board the large train to Liverpool. Only James and Mary came to see them off. Bridget had become totally detached from Sal and her offspring over the previous nine months, making her feelings clear that she did not approve, but as Peter had supported the idea, she would do the same. There were to be no false or tearful goodbyes, she considered that Sal had been ungrateful and that whatever she had coming in her life she had brought on herself. Her final conversation with her daughter a week before she had departed had been strained and cold, apart from one statement which she had made.

"Faraway hills look green, Sal, always remember that. Life can always seem better elsewhere when you look from a distance, it does not mean that will be how it will be."

Sal had dismissed these last words with the same contempt for her mother's philosophies that had punctuated her life with doom and gloom. *They could be green, they will be green,* she thought, *John's there, and they are not just hills it is a mountain, my mountain, my mountain home.*

Peter had been as good as his word, all were in a fine set of travelling clothes. Sal had been taken to an outfitters in the centre of Glasgow. Eddie was fitted with a pair of heavy brown tweed trousers, matching jacket, cap and muffler. Sal and Cissie had identical dresses made in the same deep green woollen tweed. As they stood on the station, Mary had a concerned look on her face as she gazed at mother and daughter. *Didn't Sal know that green was unlucky,* she thought to herself. But green was Sal's favourite colour and it suited her well.

Sal clung tightly to her carpet bag, knowing that all that she had of value in the world was contained within; her modest savings combined with a reasonable amount of travelling and boarding expenses provided by her father was all that she had to get them all there. She knew she would have to plan for all unexpected happenings and be frugal to make it last; she was used to penny-pinching, that was all she had known in her married life. Sad goodbyes were made, no one knowing whether they would ever see each other again, but hoping that they would.

The sailing had been terrible, with awfully stormy seas, delays, and sickness. All three spent most of their time confined to their cabin, trying to sleep through the waves of nausea that made it impossible to keep food down. When they had finally disembarked at Halifax, it was to a strange large world, of enormous buildings and wide boulevards; the immigrants were herded like cattle through the processing station, and sent to find lodgings while their applications to remain were processed. Nothing would be immediate, facts had to be checked and double checked, and there were thousands arriving weekly.

Sal had managed to find a reasonable room in a small guesthouse owned by a Mrs Jaques; a women with a strange accent that Sal could not place. She had managed to change her pounds to this new money of dollars, nothing made sense, values of things were not able to reconcile with what she knew. She just hoped that she could keep the costs down and that they would only be there for a day or two. It was not to be. Too many people had flooded in from ships from all over the world, as desperate as she had been to make the first passage that they could as soon as war had ceased. The immigration authorities had been completely overwhelmed by this deluge of persons from many places and cultures; they were understaffed and struggling to make their checks, with the communications problem of weather and the impending Christmas holidays.

A very bleak two weeks passed. Despite the festive feeling that pervaded this wealthy city, bedecked with trees, lights and tinsel, there were no celebrations for mother and children. There was barely enough money for food, as Sal found the new currency did not go as far as she had first assumed. The wait for their papers was becoming a drain on their mental resources as much as their financial ones. Cissie was as awkward as ever, Eddie was just desperate and impatient to get moving, Sal worried constantly about how long it might take, and what she would do if the money ran out. The only highlight came on Christmas Day, when Mrs Jaques took pity on the forlorn family and invited them to take a meal with her. She turned out to be a lovely lady, a second-generation Canadian, her father having come from France. She said that she never had a desire to venture west, it was too remote and uncivilised for her. She much preferred to remain in the city, and since her husband had passed, it had become a necessity in order to earn a living and keep the support of friends.

Finally, on January 4th, Sal was given the family's papers and they were all naturalised as Canadians. She was free to travel, and take the Canadian Pacific Railway train to Saskatchewan. That itself had not been easy; it was a further three days, before they could book their sleeper. She sat both the children down before they left Halifax explaining that she had sent a telegram to their father, asking him to meet them at Lafleche on 19th January. They were going to be travelling a long time, and money would just stretch for food, but they must be careful, it would mean eating only once a day. Eddie agreed with a serious nod of his head; he knew he was the man of the family and must be responsible, so he could show his father how mature he was. Cissie pouted her dark scowl back in her mother's direction.

The CPR was enormous! Far bigger than any train they had ever seen before. For the first few days, the children found the experience of being in their own little sleeping place with a window to look outside very exciting. But as the train chugged on, stopping here and there to take water, supplies, parcels and crates, the monotony of their confined space, and their small framed view ate away at their high spirits. Small readers were read and re-read. I-spy played until boredom set in with the featureless wide expanses of land. And the primitive over-used portable toilet at the end of the corridor, reeked with the stench of constant human visitation. Then as they left Toronto the cold really began to bite; there weren't enough clothes to wear to stay warm, or enough blankets to bundle under. Sleep became disturbed by freezing limbs, which could not get warm no matter how much they tried. Two days through Ontario, and then another through Manitoba; they had been travelling for ten days, and there seemed no end. The relief at stepping out onto a freezing Winnipeg Station, just to stand in the extreme cold and breathe fresh air, was wonderful.

Now they were on the last leg of their journey. Sal was beginning to lose faith in her big adventure, her big plans. They had journeyed for another twenty-four hours, in con-fined chairs. The children had even lost interest in fighting, and the interest of looking out of the window had left them a long time since, especially as their journey south had the same view of nothing and flatness, that they had seen for days. The only punctuations on the snowy landscape the occasional granary at the side of the rail line. Moosejaw was the final stop before Lafleche. Sal stepped off the train alone; Eddie was no longer interested, Cissie was complaining that she was hungry and cold. Sal thought to herself, what a funny name Moosejaw was, mind you she had seen so many funny place names on this long journey. As she stood there a cold chill passed up her spine. There was something about this place that was uncomfortable; she did not know why, she could not place what it was that was troubling her, but she needed to get away from Moosejaw.

The final miles to Lafleche dragged. She had been right in her assumptions, it was the 19th January. She dreamed of John's smiling face waiting for her on the station. She was getting used to the local form of transport, that being carts with runners on to pull across the snow behind a tired old horse. He would be there waiting for them, blankets and furs, bedecked on the cart, they could all snuggle up and he could take them to their new home. It would be warm and welcoming, there would be some hot food, waiting for them, and they could sleep in a bed! A bed that did not move with the jolts of the train; a bed that would be hers forever, and she could get warm next to her man – her lovely man.

It was mid afternoon when they finally pulled in, bright and sunny thankfully. They had got up and stood next to the door, trying to get a glimpse of their new world, the children trying to get the first sight of their father; for Cissie really the first sight. But as they rolled in there was not one soul on the station. The snow lay crisp and perfect, swept by the guard from the platform, but undisturbed around the station perimeter; no carts on sledges had passed this way before this last fall of snow, the station was totally deserted.

The dismayed party stood on the platform, gazing aimlessly around them, not sure what to do next. Stomachs rumbled, Cissie tearful from the cold, sniffed stubbornly. The kindly guard enquired where they were headed. Sal explained that her husband should be there to meet them.

"Where's he coming from, miss?"

"Lidgett... Fir Mountain."

"Ooo... that's a ways from here... there's nobody been here today."

Just at that moment Sal's spirit broke. After all that she had done to make this happen, after all that they had been through to get here. Where was he? Why had he not come as promised? Cold, tired and very hungry, her eyes welled over, and the hot tears fell into the virgin snow.

Chapter 23 –

No Warm Welcome

The guard was kind and gentle; he brought the family into the warm waiting room, and made them some tea with a slice of cake each. Sal insisted that she had no money and she could not pay him for it, the guard brushed her concerns away.

"We don't let no strangers suffer, miss... we all help one another... we'll find a way to get you to your husband."

The children devoured the cake in their famished state.

"Looks like you could all do with a decent meal inside you, miss... you wait here a moment, I'll be right back."

Within in few minutes the guard had returned, with a smile.

"I have just spoken to my wife, and we think that you should come and stay in our place here overnight... No one will be coming through today, although we have a break in the weather, the postman should be through tomorrow and I am sure he can get you as far as Glentworth at least. I don't know your man but someone will help, we all help round these parts... we haven't got much room mind, so you will all have to share one room, but by the looks of you, you need that and some food. My wife has put the copper on to boil... I think the children might need a good bath..."

Sal was too tired to be ashamed, she knew they all must be looking frightful and two weeks without a decent wash, probably a little on the high side. She gratefully accepted, although she concealed her anxieties that they had come all of this way and John was not here for the promised meeting. After a hearty meal, and a good wash, the children were tucked up in the large bed, leaving their mother just enough room to squeeze in beside them, after she had managed to rinse some much-needed underwear out in the remains of the bath water, leaving them by the warm range to dry overnight. The guard and his wife did all that they could to make the weary travellers welcome, and tried their best to reassure Sal that she was not the first to have found herself stranded.

"I wouldn't say it happens all the time, but it has before... It's the time of year, and the weather you see... it's very hard to make arrangements and stick to them. It's been terrible here for weeks, this is the first decent day that we have had, and no doubt it will close in again in the next day or so. You have been more lucky than you realise, either side, you could have been here for weeks, but I have no doubt you will be with your husband tomorrow."

Sal tried to take some comfort in his kind words, but knowing how difficult her scant communications had been with John, and knowing his strength of feeling, she was concerned that he may have had a change of heart and had decided that she should not be here after all. Maybe he had written to tell her so, and she had not received the letter, or it had arrived after she had left. Either way, she had travelled many thousands of miles and she was here, she had no money, two children and no way of surviving. She had to see him, just to know, and then somehow contact her parents and fall on their mercy to bring them back to Scotland; that was the last thing that she wanted to do, having already vowed to herself that she left for good, and had no intention of ever returning. But she knew in her heart that if she were faced with the inevitable rejection that she would have absolutely no choice. She climbed in next to the children; although cramped, the bed was soft and still, and all slept the deepest sleep that they had since leaving Scotland.

The next morning after a fine breakfast, the three sat with their baggage in the warm waiting room. The guard was right, about mid-morning the postman arrived to collect the sacks of mail to deliver to the outlying communities. The guard waylaid him at the end of the platform and after a brief discussion, both entered the waiting room to greet Sal. The postman was a man in his fifties, clean shaven, and wrapped from head to toe in various animal skins, he introduced himself as Sam and enquired of Sal where she was trying to get to.

"Mr John Flynn... Lidgett... Fir Mountain?"

Sam looked a little confused.

"Fir Mountain, you say... Mr Flynn? Is that Mr and Mrs, or Mr John Christopher?"

Sal was surprised. "Do you mean there are two John Flynns living on Fir Mountain?"

Sam laughed. "Well not exactly... and not exactly on the mountain... you see, Mr and Mrs live up that ways... but Mr John Christopher lives between Glentworth and there... you say Lidgett? That will be the name of the man who keeps the post office nearby... It's not uncommon for communities that have no name, to have everything sent to the local postie... that's why everything goes to Lidgett... or Mr Lidgett, should I say."

"Can you get me somewhere near, then I can try and walk the rest of the way?"

"I will do better than that, I will take you there... and you won't be able to walk, the snow is laying too deep."

Soon all three were gathered on the post wagon with Sam, who had covered them in furs. The sun glinted on the snow as they passed the many miles to the outlying homesteads. Sam knew the urgency of the situation and had decided to take Sal and her children directly to John's section, just in case he had to bring her to somewhere else to stay; he too had an ominous feeling about the failed rendezvous. As they had left Lafleche, the few homes that could be seen became more and more scarce until all that could be witnessed in the snowy landscape was the very occasional small wooden shack. These places looked more like workman's huts that any human habitation, but the curls of wood smoke that rose through the makeshift chimneys were the witness to life within. Sal thought to herself how pitiful lives must be in these tiny places, in these awful conditions. She enquired of Sam if they were just poor workers living in these places.

"No ma'am, there are all homesteaders, some have families of five or six living there... don't forget, everything can look small in this big place."

She was amazed at how people managed, the snow having come in early November and according to Sam, sometimes not easing until March or April.

"Well, people learn to stock up good for the winter... it's just a case of staying in and keeping warm... That's what gets people, the cold I mean... it's a nice day today, only about minus twelve, but you get a bad day, minus twenty-four or thirty even, and the cold will kill you."

"But what do people do all those days?"

"Oh they keep themselves busy... reading... making things... passing the time... It's the kids that lose out, they can't get to their schools if the weather's bad."

Eddie grinned, at the prospect of not being forced to go to school, to be able to do as he pleased for days and days. Neither of the children had picked up on their mother's anxiety at the absence of their father; she had not made mention, choosing to cross that bridge if and when she had to.

After a while the flat landscape had changed quite miraculously, to a more featured landscape of gently rolling hills, Sal thought how much the terrain reminded her of the shape of the hills that surrounded Glasgow, not as large or prominent, but very familiar all the same. She still could not see a mountain though and wondered how much further they would have to travel to be at their destination.

"Yes, well, ma'am, it's not exactly a mountain, not by your standards anyways... but to us here it's the biggest, highest place there is... you see over there towards the south west?"

Sal could see a large ridge about two miles away, sparsely covered with trees.

"That's Fir Mountain ma'am, few folks are homesteading there... it's close enough to life, but far enough away from the Indians, over that ways on Wood Mountain..."

"Indians!" Both Sal and Eddie chimed together, one rather alarmed, the other thrilled.

"They're all right ma'am, been here a long while now, since Sitting Bull brought them... not as many as there used to be... he had the whole Sioux nation here after the Little Big Horn... He came north thinking that the Canadians would give them sanctuary... well, that was a while back, and nobody wanted to help... they had a terrible time, starving and getting sick, many died. Their only friends were the RCMP... Royal Canadian Mounted Police... they were sent to keep an eye on them... well, after a while, old Sitting Bull went south to make a treaty, taking nearly all with him... course he got assassinated by the US government, but he had left his own tribe here, the main tribe, the Hunka Papa... they are a friendly lot... but always getting into problems here and there. We let them live there now, on a reserve, they come and go, and do what they can to make a living. But they still live their lives like they always have, they can be a bit scary when you see them all in their Indian finery, but most wear our clothes now. It's like everyone ma'am, some good, some not so good."

Sam could see that Sal was far from reassured by his tale, so he qualified himself further.

"And there is still an RCMP post that way, so they are kept in order ma'am, there's no need to worry... and they have ways that we don't know... I mean knowing how to get food and make special medicines, I can tell you a few people owe a lot to the Indians, even their lives."

For a few more miles the wagon slid on, over the gently undulating snow, deeper now, the horse team struggled at a walking pace, their load much heavier than normal, and their journey to the homestead more challenging what they were used to. Just then Sam alerted Sal to a distant speck just over the ridge to left that they were on.

"That's Mr Flynn's place, ma'am."

Sal could barely make out the tiny wooden construction, they were still a good half a mile away; it was rough and wooden as the others had been and seemed so much smaller. As if that did not cause her alarm, the absence of smoke reinforced her fears. They had made a wasted journey she thought, he was not even there. All these days, all these many miles, and she could not even talk to him to find out why? And what she and the children should do now? Sam, too, had spotted the sign of desertion, he knew that they had to go on just to make sure, and his fears were growing with every ten yards they made forward; fears that he dared not share with Sal, and definitely not with the children.

There were no marks on the virgin snow, no sign of any human passage, and very few animal tracks. No one had passed this way for quite a while. The sun still shone thankfully, they had another hour or two of daylight, enough time to make it back to somewhere safe for the evening if necessary; the horses stumbled on through the ever-deeper snow.

As the little rough shack grew on the vast landscape, Sal could make out two doors and a window to one side, both firmly shut. The snow was a good two feet up the front of the doors, it had not been cleared for a few days. Her anxiety grew, what was she to do now? Fall on the charity of others, yet again? She began to grow quite angry with the predicament that she now found herself in. Why had he consented to them coming, if he had serious doubts, and knowing that they were on their way? A journey that he knew himself was of immense struggle. Why had he not been there to explain himself? He would have to help, he could not just run away from his responsibilities in this fashion.

Sam pulled the two horses to a halt, and quickly put feedbags onto the flagging horses and blankets over their sweaty backs; when a horse meant the difference between getting somewhere and not, they were to be protected at all costs. The children were wanting to leap down, but Sam stopped them, sensing a problem.

"Listen, ma'am, it's probably best I go and check this out, you wait here."

Getting down from the wagon, he armed himself with more vital tools of his trade: he donned his snow shoes and grabbed his shovel and headed for one of the two doors. Quickly and expertly, he cleared the door enough to open it to squeeze through, Sal could see him recoil slightly at the odour that greeted him, then he squeezed himself in, after a minute or two, he came out quickly and headed back to the wagon without shutting the door; a horse's whinny could be heard emanating from inside the shack. Sal was suddenly caught in an icy paralysis. Why had he left the door open? What was the smell that made him hesitate? She managed to pull herself together enough to quickly dismount, her boots sinking fast into the knee-deep snow, she hitched her skirts up. She knew she had to talk to him out of earshot of the children, something was wrong, something terrible had happened; dread filled every inch of her being. Sam nodded to her to wait, and he shuffled towards her on his shoes.

"Ma'am, I think your husband has left something for you…wait there, I shall carry you over." He tried to sound nonchalant, so as not to alarm the children, who were growing evermore impatient with their forced incarceration in their fur-lined seats.

"Snow's too deep young 'uns, let yer ma just come see."

At that point he had reached Sal, and swept her up in his arms to carry her back, Sal was petrified.

"What is it, Sam? Is it… Is it… bad?"

"He's alive… just… It looks like he's very sick… we need to get a doctor to him… the place is cold, ma'am… he's let the burner go out… and his two beasts look half-dead too… I am going to get you in and see what can be done… I will be away to fetch the doctor… I think it's best if the children come away with me and the doctor can bring 'em along…

he is in a bit of mess… you will have some cleaning up and sorting out to do… sorry ma'am… this happens… but at least he's alive."

Sam put Sal down at the door's entrance, the putrid aroma of animal waste and rotting food made her want to wretch. She swallowed hard, and opened her mouth so that she could breathe without smelling the foul stench. The two animals, a half-dead cow and starving horse, lay together for warmth on the right side of the divided homestead. Sam went quickly to them, breaking the ice of their trough inside, trying to encouraging them to drink, he found a sack of animal mash and sat with handfuls under their mouths, while Sal crossed the floor of the tiny shack to the left side, where John lay on his bed. He looked dreadful, swollen and blue. He was barely breathing, and the breaths that he made were troubled and rasping. She could smell that he had messed himself, a dried pool of vomit lay on the floor next to the basic wooden couch. The blankets – what they were – stained and holed.

She touched his face lightly; he had a fever, yet his lips and hands were blue with the extreme cold. He was not in this world, she knew there was no point trying to rouse him; he needed warmth quickly; he needed medicine. She looked around her to see what she could do. To the back of the shack was a rough curtain, and she could make out two more rough wooden beds; he had obviously prepared for their coming, to the right about five feet away was a black combustion stove which had been cold for days; a huge pile of fire wood sat to its immediate left, with a tinderbox and kindling placed by. Her hands could barely grip with the cold but she knew she must make a fire and she set about the task. Sam called through.

"I've done what I can with the beasts, sorry ma'am I have to go… I will head back to Glentworth with the children and find a doctor for you. I will tell the children, that you are sorting some things and they will see you later… I am sorry I can't do more, but we have to get you a doctor."

Chapter 24 –

The Comfort
of Strangers

Sal did what she could. Within an hour the black combustion stove was giving off good heat – the place being so small and well-insulated by a covering of heavy snow, two feet deep around and about. The icy chill began to leave the air, and the temperature became more bearable. She had found the largest stew pot that she could and had gathered handfuls of snow from near the door to melt on the wood burner; she knew that she would need to get him as clean as she could. She searched around for some soap. It was at this time she began to take in the ramshackle surroundings in more detail.

John had put his heart and soul into making his small home, no matter how basic it appeared. She assumed that he had needed some help to build it. He had managed to construct a small rectangular place, that measured about thirty feet in length by about fifteen feet in width. It had been further divided into two parts to accommodate the two pitiful beasts that been without food and water for a good few days in the bitter cold. They had a portion that was ten feet by fifteen feet. The walls were overlaid wooden planks, roughly sawn and nailed together, there was a partition wall dividing the main part from the animal shed. The combustion stove stood in the one corner, far enough away from the wooden wall not to damage it with the heat. He had made a makeshift store, for the firewood and the tinderbox to the left of the stove. On the opposite wall was the rough wooden bed, just large enough for two, that he now lay on in his dreadful condition, then behind a small curtain two smaller wooden beds, side by side, made ready with rough blankets. It was there Sal found what few clean clothes that he still possessed. All washed and neatly folded after a fashion. She knew he needed changing, but he was a large man, and in his present unconscious condition a deadweight to move. At the far end was another door, which she had not noticed when they had pulled up in the post wagon, because a large drift of snow had concealed that end of the shack. As she surveyed clockwise back round the combustion stove, she saw a small rough table sat under a window, with two home-made wooden chairs. The remains of what had obviously been the last meal that he had taken lay dried up and congealed on some tin plates; an enamel mug and tea pot sat beside.

There was a piece of log sawn off in a thin slice lying on the table, the poker from the wood burner lying abandoned by the chair of the floor. There was something burnt in on the wood, she moved closer to see what it was. Half finished, John had been using the red-hot poker to burn in two letters; 'J' and 'S', entwined. She winced at the sight, all the terrible thoughts and anger that she had felt for the past day or so, when he had failed to meet her and the children, and his last act before taking to his bed with his terrible illness had been to make her a homecoming present.

She turned back to the couch were he lay still unsightly, his face dreadfully swollen with the dropsy. His lips and fingers were now ashen white, and not the blue colour that she had first seen. His breath was rasping and low. She took up part of her dress, and ripped her cotton petticoat, and dipped it in the now steaming water on the stove. She squeezed the dampened cloth and made her way over to the couch. She began to mop his very feverish face, and clean the dried vomit from his cheeks. She was trying to work out how she was going to roll him to strip him and clean him, when she heard the noise of an approaching sledge and horse. It was still light and two voices were making their way to the cabin door.

Sam had been a treasure. The doctor had arrived, minus Eddie and Cissie who had been persuaded by a nice spinster with a good larder in Glentworth to stay the night. Fears and concerns were placated, Sal would join them soon; the temptations of the tea table had been enough to convince them all would be well. The doctor was accompanied by a matronly looking woman, who introduced herself as Mrs Purdy; she knew John in passing and had been shocked by the news that Sam had recounted and knew that Sal would need help. She had also bought a pile of warm blankets and a picnic basket of food. Sal was overwhelmed by her generosity and relieved, as this strong woman set to immediately helping her remove John's soiled clothing and blankets to clean him.

The doctor, who had introduced himself as Doctor Cameron – a first generation Canadian hailing from Scottish parents – began his examination of the unconscious John. His temperature was very high, he was malnourished, his chest was full of fluid, and a red rash was covering his upper torso. The doctor diagnosed rheumatic fever. He was amazed that John had lasted this long; his stove must have gone out a good two days previously and they had recorded minus twenty-five on both those nights. The doctor looked at Sal and said that John was gravely ill, he had to tell her that he could not guarantee his chances and the next twenty-four hours were going to be critical to his survival. Sal stood frozen to the spot, she had come all these thousands of miles, she had as good as broken with her family, she had no money left in the world and two children to support, and she was here at the journey's end in the cabin of her dying husband. What was she going to do?

Mrs Purdy had finished making John comfortable and could see that Sal was distressed but contained. She moved over to her, and in a motherly fashion, the like of which Sal had never known, she put her arm around her shoulder and spoke gently to her.

"Mrs Flynn... all will be well... your man, he's a strong one... he's mighty fine and tall and strong...Everyone says he is the hardest worker that they know, he does the work of two most days, he never complains and always keeps going... he's a fighter, Mrs Flynn... if anyone can win this battle, he can... and with your help and love he will..."

Then, more softly, "He knows that you're here... you may not think it... but he knows... he knows you have come to him at last... that is the best medicine that you can give him... just sit a while next to him there... talk to him, let him know you are with him."

Mrs Purdy manoeuvred Sal gently back towards the bed couch, and encouraged her to sit. Sal took John's hand in hers and began to squeeze it lightly. With her right hand she took the flannel with the cold water they were using to bring his fever down, and she began to wipe his brow. She looked at his grossly swollen face, mottled with the red rash of the fever; he was still a handsome man, but she could see the last seven years had taken their toll. His face had weathered and lined, there was a hardness to his skin. She began softly to speak to him.

"John… it's me, Sarah… it's Sal, John?… I have come, I am with you, and the children too… Eddie and Cissie are here… we've come…"

Just for a split second his eyes flickered and opened, the enormous pools of blue, stared wildly, then they shut. Sal was overjoyed at this sign of life, Mrs Purdy was encouraging and positive that all was good sign. She moved towards the door as Doctor Cameron made his way to go, they spoke in a low tone so as not to be heard by Sal.

"She's got nothing, doctor… the poor lamb's come all this way and she has nothing left… we have all got to help."

"Mrs Purdy, you know I waive my fees for those on hard times, and you can't get much harder than this lady. I will be on by tomorrow to see how he is… will you be coming back with me or are you planning to stay?"

"I will stay doctor, he is such a nice man, and she seems pleasant enough, and there is no doubt she needs someone right now, she is completely worn out. You better stop at Evelyn's and tell her that she may have a couple of small house guests for a few more days, just till we get things sorted here either way."

"Right you are."

A little while later, the two women were sat either side of small table. They had cleaned up the place as best they could, washing the plate and mug in a pail next to the stove. Sal had found a few more plates, and Mrs Purdy was taking out the contents of her basket, to try to get Sal to eat something.

"I see your man's got a sack of flour and a sack of oats, he was obviously planning to survive on dropped scones and porridge this winter… aye but you won't get far now the old girl's stopped milking… I think you will have to receive

what we give you… and don't take badly at folks' charity…
it's what we do in these parts, neighbour helps neighbour,
when the needs arise… you will do the same, I'm sure."

Sal felt warmed by the care shown her. She smiled, tears
in her eyes. She knew that she must eat to try and conserve
her strength. She gazed over at the couch where John lay
motionless, his breathing laboured and raw. Mrs Purdy
sensed her fears.

"Now dear, there is nothing that either of us can do right
now to make yer man more comfortable… we will attend
to him through the night, but the fight is his, he is in god's
hands, and at least we got to him now… I am a great believ-
er that everything happens for a reason, and you got here
just in time… let him fight his fight, and we will do our best
to help but first you must eat, then sleep a little."

She unloaded her basket of bread and cheese, preserves
and cold meats. A hot coffee pot sat on the table, a drink that
Sal was not used to, but it was warm and lifting. Soon the two
women sat getting accustomed to one another, learning each
other's stories, although Sal was careful not to tell all too soon.
She listed her life in brief and how John and she had struggled
to live in their native city. She spoke of the short lives of her
two wee boys, and her rough progress apart from her husband during the war. Mrs Purdy sat listening attentively and
spoke only briefly to offer encouragement for the brave step
that she had made coming all this way. Mrs Purdy explained
that the war seemed so far away from Canada, though many
of their boys and men had gone to fight, but that the fight in
Saskatchewan was day to day, just learning to live with the
extremes of the climate and unpredictability of nature. The
winters were hard and unforgiving, everything happened
within the home then, generally no one ventured out unless

absolutely necessary – it dawned on Sal how much that this woman had done for her this day, when she would never normally leave the warmth and safety of her hearth and home.

Mrs Purdy continued that the summer was short and sharp, it could get very hot and screen doors were necessary against the invasion of insects, mosquitos and the like. That farmers could find that all would be well one season, with good crops and plenty sell, yet other seasons, droughts or failing crops could ruin even the most experienced, and then there were the prairie fires... Sal froze visibly; Mrs Purdy continued, "It's part of life, my dear... I was born here, my parents came from Scotland and they had to work hard to break their land. I married a neighbour, a lovely man that I had known since childhood, my Tom. He passed two years ago now, he was older you see. We were never lucky enough to have children, we were too busy trying to keep going. We lost all our possessions one year when a prairie fire took hold on our land, and although all the folks round here rushed to help, it was too quick... we all help in a fire, because if you don't stop the fire it will just go on, eating its way through the land. But me and Tom started again, with the help of all the kind folks, we built it all back up again. That's why I am here now, we all help each other dear, no one can live alone here," she looked over at John, "though the young men when they first get here try to, he did. But he has probably not told you of the hard times he has had, of the time three years ago, when even as he was breaking his land he could not make enough to make ends meet, so another farmer offered him work so that he could pay his way and continue. But like all the young bucks he had to learn that we all have to lean on each other from time to time... and when I lost my Tom, young John helped me a great deal, I am so sorry to see him like this, if it had not been winter I would have checked on him sooner, but he is always so determined to carry on…"

Sal nodded, she knew John, she knew his stubbornness and diligence, she recognised all that Mrs Purdy said about him.

"… And there is one thing I will say about him, he is a hard worker, he broke all his first section himself, with barely any help, until Paul moved in next door…"

Sal puzzled for a moment, she had not seen any other place, where could she be speaking of? Mrs Purdy corrected herself.

"… When I say next door, I mean the neighbour a mile away, young Paul Valentine, he is a German man. We have Scots, Irish, Ukrainians, Norwegians, I think Paul is our only German though, not that I will hold that against him…" She looked at Sal, whose eyelids were beginning to droop heavily.

"Listen my dear, you are weary, go and lie down on the kiddies' beds, you need a rest, I will wake you when it's your turn, you go rest now."

When Sal awoke finally, light was breaking through the blanket that had been hastily hung from the window; she started, unsure of her unfamiliar surroundings, and then the sudden fear that she had left John and not nursed him. She sat up quickly, Mrs Purdy swung round on the chair that she had placed by John's bed.

"Oh, there you are dear… do you feel better now? I let you sleep, it was no trouble for me to sit a while with him… I think his fever is less… he is breathing better… come and see."

Sal felt terrible, she had slept for hours, she had been unable to rouse herself to do her duty; she climbed off the bed, seeing that the table was tidy, in fact, much in the cabin had been put in good order. This wonderful woman had done much more than nurse her ailing husband.

"I am so sorry Mrs Purdy, you should have awoken me, really you have done too much… I feel terrible to have taken advantage of you in this way."

"Now listen dear… I won't say it again, we help you so when we need help you help us… it's no trouble… and he has been no trouble at all, come and see him."

John lay still and quiet; the gross swelling of his face and limbs seemed to be reducing, he looked more at peace and a pink colour was beginning to tinge his sallow skin. She leant over to feel his forehead, it was cooler and less moist, Mrs Purdy was right; the fever was lessening.

"We will see what the doctor has to say when he comes, but I think you will be better tonight once you have yourself sorted a little. If you don't mind I will go back with the doctor and organise a thing or two, and check on your young children, but I will come back a little later."

"Mrs Purdy, you have already done more than enough, more than I ever expected, I feel totally in your debt and I know that you have gone out of your way to help us, I just don't know how I would have managed without you."

"Oh I think you would have, my dear, I can see you are a strong one too, but isn't it so much better when you have those around to help you? And call me Leila…" She paused, looking at Sal questioningly.

"I am Sal, Leila… it has been a great pleasure to meet you and thank you for everything."

A little later Doctor Cameron came by. He was not a little surprised to see the good changes in John's condition.

"He's a fighter, Mrs Flynn," he said admiringly.

He and Mrs Purdy left together just before lunch, the basket containing the food remained on the table, an open invitation for Sal to eat and take care of herself. Sal found herself alone, and stoked the wood burner as best she could, preparing for the rest of the afternoon, and (she assumed) an evening and night to follow. She sat on and off by John, wiping his face, talking to him softly. She had learnt that, without the luxury of flushing conveniences, you made do with the barn hay on the bad days and then on better a pit outside, until the outside lavvy could be used again. It was not the best of conditions and she was very glad that the children were not there at that time. But as Mrs Purdy said, "The animals do all their doings in there and we muck them out, it's no different for you, my dear."

It was getting on for mid-afternoon when Sal heard a distant commotion, the noise growing as it came closer to the cabin. She peeked out of the door. A hay cart on runners, with two horses pulling, was heading up the tracks, she could make out Mrs Purdy and another on the front, she was surprised that she was back so soon, but grateful for the help. The wagon pulled to a halt outside. Mrs Purdy descended quickly, the man, dark-skinned, hopped off quickly, another young man of a similar complexion suddenly appeared from under the fur skins in the back; both men set to gathering bundles of skins together, which were parcelled around things. They stood waiting for permission to enter while Leila quickly explained.

"These are two of my Indian friends, just call them Pete and Wade, they have helped me gather from others things that you need, can we come in?"

Sal's jaw dropped, she stood to one side as load after load was brought through the door, and as quickly as they had come the two men – who had said nothing – leapt back on the cart and headed back the way that they had come, leaving Sal and Mrs Purdy surveying the large pile of accumulated bundles which now littered the cabin floor.

"Everybody has helped, my dear... word has got round of your troubles, everybody has made a contribution. We will get you through the winter and get you back on your feet."

Not for the first time Sal's eyes welled up and she cried with relief. Whatever troubles she had come from and whatever new troubles that she had come to, she had never known such wonderful kindness in her life; the kindness of strangers who she had not even met yet.

Chapter 25 –

New Beginnings

It was now the end of April 1919. The previous months had been very difficult for the young family, with all the upheaval of John's illness, and the adjustments that had to be made to a new way of life.

John's recovery had been a slow one; the rheumatic fever had taken its toll on him. He had finally regained consciousness ten days after Sal's arrival, he was weak but extremely happy to see that what he thought had been a dream was a reality.

"I thought I was in heaven... I just could not get up to stoke the fire, I really thought it was over for me..."

"Shush... I am here and the children are too... but they are staying in Glentworth until things are a bit more settled."

"Bring them home, Sal, it is the best medicine that I can have, to have you all here..."

Sal did not have the heart to say that she did not think that things were ready enough to have two boisterous young people there, never mind the fact that she did not know how she was going to cope in such a confined space, with them unable to go anywhere, or be entertained.

"I will go to see them… and Leila, she has been so help-ful. You must not worry, just get well."

Sal knew that the post wagon may come past in the next day or so, she was learning all about the difficulties of even trying to get anywhere within a small distance without transport. Even though the plough horse was recovering from his enforced famine, she had no idea how to ride; she would have depend on the arrival of others to help. She was lucky, that same day Leila chose to call. She was pleased to find John awake, and immediately sensed Sal's concerns about having the children return too soon.

"Now John, your young 'uns are having a marvellous time after their long journey. There is no need to worry yourself about them, or about any imposition, we like hav-ing them in Glentworth, Eddie, especially, has charmed all of the ladies, he is your son that's obvious. They know that you have been unwell and that their mother is nursing you, they understand, all will be well."

This had to be said, it was no use telling either parents the truth, that the resentment at being parted so near their journey's end had manifested itself in both. They were angry and felt abandoned; no matter how much Leila had tried to explain, particularly to Cissie, they had reacted badly and become distant and withdrawn. But everyone knew that until Sal and John had adjusted, the possibility of another two or three months' forced captivity in a small shack, with no access to anyone, would just lead to more trouble and probably add to John's illness.

Mrs Purdy had a way of making everything seem fine, and even Sal felt settled by her story and asked if she could come back with her just to check on things. Leila knew that would create even more difficulties for the folks who were trying to keep them stable, especially when their mother left again to return to their father and hurriedly made an excuse.

"I don't think that's a good idea Sal, Cissie has a small cold, only a light one mind, but if you get it you could bring it back here... you don't need to be sick right now with all you have to do... and John does not need it on top of everything else."

Sal was troubled to think that her daughter may be sick, especially after losing two sons to childhood conditions, but she took Leila's reasoning to heart and agreed to let a few days pass before going to see them. Leila hoped that in that intervening period there might be some improvement in Eddie and Cissie's disposition.

With each cup of broth, and hunk of bread that John managed to consume over the next few days, he began to regain his strength enough to sit up and talk. Sal and John spent many hours reacquainting themselves, and John also began his education of Sal of living in such a place.

"It is not easy Sal, there is much to do in the summer, and as you can see in the winter you have to learn to live in a small space and keep busy. Getting anywhere means hitching up the horse, and going only small distances. There isn't much in Glentworth, a shop or two, a shoemaker, a post office, a butcher. In the summer I try to get there once or twice a week, just for the company. But there is our neighbour, young Paul... I think you will like him... he's a bit quiet, but I have helped him a lot with his land and house and he helps me in return. I think he is finding life hard here, but I know that he has had a harder life elsewhere. We only have the milker and the horse now, I plan to get some more livestock in the spring, maybe some hens too."

Sal listened intently to all that he had to say; she knew that life was going to be very different. She had concerns now about the schooling of Eddie and Cissie. Schools only opened when the children could get there and when the snow was too deep – as it was in the winter months – they would have to learn at home. She was also concerned about the sparseness of their small environment; there were only the basics here, enough for a single man to survive; the toilet conditions were not marvellous, washing of themselves – never mind laundry – seemed nigh-on impossible. There were no decorations or items that make a home a home. Cooking for her was confined to the simple wood burning stove, which meant all had to be done on top in one pot. There weren't even enough plates and pans. These were all things that she needed to talk to him about, but not now, she would wait until he was on his feet.

By the following week when Doctor Cameron called to check on John, he was able to pronounce that the patient was on the mend. Sal took the opportunity to ask for a lift back to village, she knew she could probably ask Leila or another to get her back, but she must see her children. When she arrived in Glentworth, the doctor took her straight the house of the young spinster who had taken them in on the first day. Miss Evelyn Tasberry was shocked to find Sal had arrived unannounced, but had a look of relief to see her standing on the snowy step of her house. She hurriedly introduced herself, ushering Sal inside out of the cold, she was just about to try and explain her difficulties, when two excited voices yelped exclamations and dashed from the kitchen to greet their mother.

"Mama!" they jointly exclaimed.

Eddie threw his arms around Sal hugging her so tightly she thought she would burst, Cissie stood, somewhat unusually with a smile.

"You've come! You've come to take us home, we can see Papa!" Eddie shrieked.

Sal was somewhat overwhelmed by their overexcitement and desperation. Evelyn interjected.

"Let's all go into the kitchen where it is warm… your Mama looks half frozen."

At that point Sal realised that her visit had perhaps not been her best idea, the children were obviously desperate to come home, but to what home? How would she explain? How could they all live in such a difficult situation while their father was still so unwell?

She sat with them at the table, and began to tell them of what she had found that day, and how sick their father had been.

"But he is better now, isn't he Mama?… I mean he is not going to die, is he? You have come to take us home, right?"

Sal asked Eddie just to listen a while, Evelyn busied herself making a pot of coffee and getting out the cookies which she had tried again, and again, to tempt the children with over the last few days. Sal attempted to explain that John was still sick and the conditions were very difficult back at the cabin, and that it would be best if they remain where they were for the time being.

"It won't be for long, just another week or so… please try to understand."

Cissie's eyes welled up with tears and she ran out of the room and thumped up the stairs.

"Cissie," her mother called, to no avail. Then seeing that Eddie was somewhat crestfallen, "I am sorry Eddie, but you do understand, don't you? It is really not a good place for you two right now."

Eddie lifted his face, and looked very seriously at her. "Yes Mama… I understand… but I can help you, please can we come back? Please?"

"No, Eddie… it is not good for your father right now… but I promise as soon as I can I will take you back…"

"Oh." Again his face fell.

Sal looked searchingly at Evelyn. "Oh you know young folks, they just want to be with you… but we will make sure they are OK… maybe you had best go try and talk to Cissie, though? And maybe Eddie will help me in the kitchen a while?"

Eddie nodded, reluctantly.

Sal made her way through the small but neat little wooden house. She noticed how well-maintained it was, with all the knick knacks of home; pictures on the wall, samplers of cross-stitch and embroidery, an empty vase or two, rugs on the wooden floor. *How nice*, she thought, how different to the basic living that she now faced. She climbed the short stair where there were just two bedrooms, almost attic-like. She could hear the stifled sobs from the room on the left, she knocked on the door post, and went in through the half-open door. Two little beds and a chest of draws was about all the pretty little room could accommodate, but it was warm and cosy. Cissie sat on the bed hunched up, her arms round her legs, her tear-stained face buried in her knees. Sal spoke gently.

"Cissie, I know you are disappointed and I wish I could take you home now, your Papa can't wait to meet you finally and get to know you, and if he was well enough, I would take you there, I mean it. But it is very simple there, there is no toilet, nowhere to wash, and the beds are not as comfortable as here, and if it hadn't been for all the charity that the people round here have given to us, we wouldn't have food. You are in the best place for now, honestly… but it won't be for long."

The frustrations in Cissie had been bottled-up to bursting point; whereas in her normal way, a scowl or pout would have been a sufficient acknowledgement of disdain, today she bit back.

"You are always saying this… you don't think about us! You and him are together, you don't care about us anymore!"

"Cissie! What a terrible thing to say! That is just not true! It's because I care about you that you are not there."

"No it's not! You just care about yourself and what you want! I didn't want to come here, I wanted to stay at home, with grandma and auntie Katie. You made us come! You told us it would all be wonderful, it's horrible, I hate it here! I hate the snow and the cold, I miss my family and auntie Mary! I hate you and I want to go home!"

Sal took a sharp intake of breath. Cissie's words were cutting and harsh, but she was a child letting off steam, she had to remember that. She was obviously not going to get anywhere trying to reason with her, it was best just to leave her be to think it all through. She went back to the small kitchen. Eddie was still sitting where she had left him, looking dejectedly at the table in front. Evelyn looked at her sympathetically. Sal sat down in front of Eddie once more; she knew Cissie's outburst had been clearly overheard in such a small house.

"Eddie, you don't really believe this, do you? That I don't care about you, that I have taken you somewhere terrible."

"No." His reply was short and sharp, he remained fixed on the table.

"I will come back you as soon as I can…" She modified that thought quickly. "…In a few days I mean… as long as Miss Tasberry doesn't mind having you a few more days?" She looked at Evelyn beseechingly.

"Oh sure, it's no problem, they are no bother. They barely make any noise."

Sal spoke to Eddie once more. "I have to go back to your Papa now, he is still very sick and I have to keep him warm, but I will come soon, I promise."

As Sal made her way back, wrapped up on another farmer's sledge, she thought about what she had just been through with the children, how damaged they had been by all this; she wondered whether she would ever be able to get Cissie to accept Canada, or restore Eddie's faith. She also thought about the bleakness of the cabin. Something had to be done and quickly, even if it was a difficult way to live; the four contained in one small space, only the basic standards of living. She would have to make things work, somehow, and soon. She knew that she could not leave them in Glentworth much longer, it had become obvious they had already outstayed their welcome with their moody frustrations.

Over the next few days, she set about between helping John get back on his feet and making the best she could of the cabin. She found a wooden hay tub in the small barn that she scrubbed at with some soda and a scrubbing brush; it leaked a little, but would make a good wash tub. The various furs and blankets that had parcelled bundles of goods were put to good use, either on the small beds and chairs, or hanging over the two windows as make-shift curtains. Leila caught Sal's need to nest and once again made a collection, which was brought over by Sam in an old tin bath (a very needed piece of equipment). People had donated old bits of bric-a-brac; vases that weren't wanted, a collection of un-matching crockery, a few cooking pans, old sheets that had been 'middled'. A skein of calico, and the best thing Sal could have hoped for: a hand-operated sewing machine, complete with an assortment of threads and needles. She could put the calico to good use, she knew that, as it would be a while until the snow left.

The day came when she went with Leila to fetch the children. They were not as pleased to see her as they had been the previous week, and they now clutched two bags each, rather than just the one that they had arrived with. Evelyn explained that a few items of clothing and some old school books had been donated.

"They are just readers... I am not sure what level they are at... they wouldn't read with me, but hopefully I have guessed it right... I teach at the school house... I hope to see them there in the thaw?"

"Of course," Sal responded, not noticing that Eddie was scowling hard at the prospect of a return to over-restrictive schooling. Cissie surprised everyone, by shaking Evelyn by the hand.

"Thank you very much for having us Miss Tasberry, I hope we haven't been too much trouble?" Her tone exuded genuine charm, the only evidence of the contrary, was the look that she threw back at her mother as she did so. She was making it clear that the only person that she had any respect for right now was the stranger that had extended her hospitality for the past few weeks.

The meeting of father and children was joyous and happy. John, still frail, managed to stand to greet them. Eddie was not sure whether to hug him, or shake him by the hand – being a 'man' now. John pulled him in for a hug, father toward son. Then he looked over at the mouse that was smiling sheepishly at him, in her hand-me-down woollen, brown coat.

"And is this my wee girl now? Aren't you a beauty," he said. Cissie's smile broadened and she shuffled towards him, she was unsure what to do next; he was her father, but she did not know him, she had been brought up in grandmother's restrictive environment where outward displays of affection were frowned upon. She looked up at him and replied in her soft, scots tones.

"Hello."

"Well hello, my bonny girl… we have plenty of time to get to know one another, but I have to sit down right now." He resumed his seat, Cissie stepped backward, eyeing him carefully, and gazing around the tiny place – which since Sal had worked her magic was beginning to look quite homely.

"You have to choose which bed you want, Cissie. The one by the window or the one next to it?"

Cissie ignored her, continuing her scrutiny of this man, who she knew that she must recognise as her father.

"Do you want a warm drink?"

Again Cissie blanked her mother. John realised that there were some tensions. "Aye, cat's got her tongue, Sal… I am sure she'll be fine in a wee while… I will have to organise a couch to sit on in the spring, but why don't you both sit at the table?"

Cissie obeyed happily, it was yet another open protest against her mother; everything that Sal tried to ask was either ignored or dismissed, but she would be ever-dutiful to her father's requests. Sal did her best to swallow the snubs as the act of a spoilt little girl.

A quiet supper of dropped scones and coffee was consumed. Sal longed for tea, John knew that she was missing it and said that in the spring he would get some from the general store in Glentworth. That night the two youngsters were sleeping soundly behind their curtained area. Sal had managed to suspend a curtain over their own bed; one that she had quickly made out of part of the skein of calico that had been donated. This was the first time that they had shared a bed together since her arrival, and the first time in over eight years; both felt an awkwardness at being confined in an intermit situation after spending more years apart than they had shared as a normal husband and wife. So much had happened to them both as individuals that had made changes emotionally, but also the physical transformations had brought their toll. A certain amount of embarrassment and awkwardness ensued as Sal shuffled in next to him.

The hay-filled grains sacks that served as mattresses were lumpy and uncomfortable, but cosy. His body next to her was warm. She felt comforted and she moved closer in, she felt safe, she felt happy, the smell of him felt like home; she was home. John had missed her immensely, the children were sound asleep, he rolled over to nestle her in his arms. They were together again, warm and snug in their little cabin on the prairie, his cabin, his prairie, all his.

Two tumultuous months had passed, the children had settled and resumed their normal childhood behaviours; irritated by one another's presence, but inseparable. Sal did her best to sit them down once a day to do sums and read a little. Eddie resented this enormously, but John would look at him in a stern fashion and he would quickly comply. Cissie set about trying to do everything she could for her father, so much so that it became almost suffocating for John. He loved her attentions, but he felt even more the need to assume his role as provider. Little by little, he would move around more, walking daily as much as he could from one end of the cabin and back. He tended the two animals, noting that Bessie the cow had passed her best.

"She's good for meat," he told Sal out of earshot of Cissie, whom he knew had become very attached to her.

"It's what we have to do," he said. "It will be good salt-beef, and I have enough to get a few head of cattle in the spring, or some more tools and another horse, but we do need hens."

Eddie loved 'Old Jack', the plough horse that John had acquired three years before, but he had been old then. He took it on himself to tend him; 'Old Jack' had never had so much attention. By and by, people would drop by knowing that John was on the road to recovery; they would not stay long, just introduce themselves, say how glad they were to see things were getting sorted out and the familiar phrase 'if you need anything just ask, always will to help, neighbour helps neighbour.'

One neighbour came to see John, a medium-size (compared to John) man with a strange accent. He came through the door without knocking, it was obviously normal for him to do so.

"Hello Paul... Sal, this is Paul Valentine, our neighbour and good friend."

Paul shook her hand. "Good day," he said in his strong German accent, shaking her firmly by the hand.

"I thought you weren't around till spring... Meet the family, Paul...my son Eddie..."

Eddie returned the handshake with a, "Hello sir."

"And my beautiful girl over there..." Cissie was standing back in the corner, with her scrutinising look.

"And what is your name, young lady?" Paul asked.

"Cissie."

Chapter 26 –

And Then There Were Five

My mother's nursing of my father must have been successful; I was born the fifteenth of November 1919. I was delivered by my father in the cabin; we had been snowed-in for two months. I was told later that it was all surprisingly fast, not just my birth, all of the months that had passed in between. Too fast for one person in particular, my sister – Cissie.

I think she resented my sudden arrival enormously, she had only just got to know our father herself, and she had been 'his special girl' as he told her all the time. If I had been a boy, I don't think that she would have had a problem, but I was a girl and a small quivering infant, whom he felt very proud and protective of; and he had brought me to life, a bond that must have been very strong for him indeed. People have often doubted the story that I now tell, claiming that a small child could hardly have remembered first-hand in such detail; that I must have pulled the story together from what others have told me since. I believe that when one so young experiences such momentous events, it becomes an imperative to hold onto whatever memories that you have, because sometimes that is all you have.

My first memories are of being wrapped in a shawl by my mother, obviously then I was still very small indeed. I remember sitting on the rough wooden floor, playing with an old enamel mug; I know that I could not walk then and I was told that I could walk and talk well before my first birthday. I remember our simple home, my little cot, a rough wooden structure that must have been full of splinters that a small child could get in their skin, but it never brought me harm. I remember the sensation of pain when I would try to touch the black combustion stove, I know I was only crawling then. I remember as clearly as if it were yesterday, my mother's soft voice, singing me to sleep.

"Shall Mama and Rita sing a song? What do you think, Rita?"

"Speed bonnie boat, like a bird on a wing, onward the sailors cry…"

That's what I was called, Rita, not Margaret, my given name. Like Cissie and my mother Sal, we had 'our' names, and mine was Rita. My mother was very attentive and caring, I only ever remember joy when I was with her; that is not to say she did not discipline me, because all good parents have to, just like a mother cat cuffs a kitten that gets out of its place or does something that may cause it harm. But children have more respect for parents who are fair but firm; attentive to your education as well as your fun, and Sal certainly was.

I remember my lovely big brother Eddie too. Though to me he was a man, not a boy, he towered above me and seemed so strong. He always smelt of sweat, from all his labours out in the fields, most of the time alone. Cissie did not like me. It was something that I instinctively knew, I almost accepted it as a fact, as a part of life. I can understand why now, looking back. It must have been such an enormous undertaking for her at the age of seven, to have travelled all those thousands of miles from a very different – more convenient – life; to this prairie wilderness. Knowing that she was going to meet her father for the first time, but not knowing what he was really like. Having had all those terrible stories about him from grandma, yet very different accounts from other people; she must have been confused and very scared, scared that he might not like her, that they might not get on. Then when they had eventually met, to be the apple of his eye, to feel such an affinity with him for such a very short time; to have had that attention that she had needed for so long snatched away, by a small baby. She must have been so angry. And unfortunately, I then took the brunt of her anger and her teasing.

But the one person who I remember always with a tear in my eye, was my wonderful father John. My first memory – when I must have been a little over a year old – is sitting on his lap by a window while he shelled a brazil nut. It was our little window, where you could see out towards the rolling hills that reminded Mama so much of the lowlands of Scotland. In fact, she used to say that Papa had travelled all across Canada until he had found a place that looked just like home, especially for her.

It was a winter; to me the white was normal, the cold – extreme cold the like I have never known since in my life – was normal. As I sat on his lap we were looking out of the window, and he was talking to me about this and that, when a big beast with antlers came out from behind a thicket way across the field – I know now it was my first memory of a moose. But again all of this was normal to me. What people can not understand is that to my brother and sister this was an alien life that they had to adjust to, but to me it was my life, all that I knew. I was born a Canadian on a Saskatchewan prairie farm.

I remember my father's smell, eucalyptus and camphor, always the same strong smell. I remember each evening when my mother used to put a steaming basin of water on our table, and she would make my father sit with a blanket over his head, over the bowl to clear his lungs, and how he would cough, wheeze and gasp for breath. He was such a mountain of a man, yet so gentle and dexterous, he would sit for hours with a sharp woodsman's knife whittling away at a piece of wood, carving some kind of intricate shapes or other.

Our lives had some sort of rhythm; once the snow had lessened, around about March, Cissie had to make the mile or so trek on a small pony to school; she seemed to resent this too, that Eddie was not forced to go yet he was still of school age, I just remember the fights about it between them and Eddie putting her in her place time and again.

"You know I'm needed here, Papa can't do it all anymore, someone's got to keep the place going... tell you what, sis, you can muck out the beasts in the morning, plough the fields in all weathers, see if you like that more than a warm school room?"

You see, that was the biggest problem that Sal now faced. My father had not fully recovered from his illness. The doctor had been back and forth over the previous year and half, always the same routine. John would be sat on a chair with his shirt up, the cold stethoscope applied to his back making him jump; he was told to breathe then stop, breathe then stop. Cough then stop. Then the stethoscope would be applied to his chest and it would be the same drill. Now and then the doctor would bring new inhalations for him to try, or another medicine that had worked on a TB patient and may help. But it was not TB that my father had; the rheumatic fever had left him with a heart condition, one all thought would resolve given time. But as time passed and he got more breathless, he had less energy.

Whereas before my mother's arrival he could go out all day every day, and work like three men, now he would struggle to be out for more than a few hours. So when Eddie protested that he was not going to school, neither of my parents disagreed. He was thirteen now, and very much a young man with his own mind and feelings. He had never liked the rigorous discipline of school life, as he had proven by his trouble in Glasgow; he needed to learn farming and quickly. Everyone hoped that some kind of cure could be found, that with plenty of rest that my father could recover.

So Eddie set to work doing as much as he could, he learned what was needed quickly and was very good with the animals; by that summer, we had acquired a small pony called Jock, and. a replacement for the milker called Maisie, and a coop full of laying hens. But they had a lot to make up, for the summer before my birth had been a particularly bad one for my father. Despite all of his grand plans during the height of his illness and considerable help from our neighbour Paul, he was unable to do half of what he had done previously; land quickly turns back to rough ground if left untilled for a season. That and the added problem of a very hot and dry summer, which had led to a prolonged drought and a plague of insects, which had ravaged much of the wheat that had been planted; as a consequence, we barely had enough to sell, never mind see us through those bleak winter months; not that I was aware of any of this, being only just new. Once again that tough winter, neighbours had rallied around us to support, and also desperate to see the new arrival; Leila Purdy had been particularly taken with me by all accounts, when she had brought Evelyn and a few timely bundles of food for our winter stocks.

"Oh Sal… she is a pretty little thing… and how nice to have a baby here in your new home."

Cissie had scowled in her customary fashion; something that all accepted as Cissie's way and to be disregarded as anything of consequence. Evelyn had held me and cooed. She was a spinster by choice, women were in very short supply in Canada, and she could have found many suitors, but being second-generation and having known the tough existence of many a farmer's wife – like my own mother – she had chosen to stay single; opting rather for the professional life of the school mistress. Everyone knew that she was very maternal and it must have been hard for her to sacrifice the chance of motherhood because she did not want the drudgery of being a wife; she would make do with frequent visits to hold the new baby instead.

To me these ladies became the maiden aunts that Cissie and Eddie had known in Katie and Jeanie, that I would never know as I lived in Canada thousands of miles from my own kith and kin. That is not to say that members of the family were totally absent from my life, indeed they were not. Although Mama and grandma never exchanged letters; excepting the one time just after I was born to inform her of the 'sad passing of Katie' – of little consequence to me as I was only a few weeks old, and although upset by the news, my mother, brother and sister had somewhat expected that letter would come one day. My grandma Maggie would write once or twice a year and my mother would dutifully write back and tell her all of the happenings in our lives. When my mother was singing, I knew that she had received the timely arrival of a letter from Auntie Mary and that always lifted her spirits, especially on the particularly bad days. Another letter writer from her old life was the young girl who had lived next door to my parents in court – Ellie; her mother Annie had died, and I think my mother had become the nearest to family that she had. My mother wrote frequently to her, always offering the opportunity for her to try a new life in Canada.

Thinking back now, I suspect that my mother knew in her heart that my father's condition was a serious one, and it was almost like she was mentally preparing herself for the inevitability that he would be an invalid for the rest of his life; I think she hoped despite everything that it would be a long life though, and that she and Eddie would have to carry the farm and that was going to be their lives. Cissie did her bit, but Mama considered that it was far more important that Cissie finished her education, despite Cissie's protestations that she should be allowed to remain at home and help on the farm just like her brother. No, my mother was adamant, she wanted her daughter to have a different life, to get on and not be tied to the kitchen.

It was a combination of that desire coupled with the fact that we had very basic and limiting conditions to live in, that my mother never actively encouraged Cissie to cook all the time; not that much could be made on the old black combustion stove, if it did not go in a pot, or fried on a griddle, it just could not be made. That is why it was always such a treat when Evelyn or Leila would turn up with a freshly baked loaf of bread, or better still a cake! It was such a joy to taste the sweetness and lightness of something that had been oven-baked, rather than our standard diet of dropped scones, eggs and scotch pancakes. Looking back we were quite spoilt by these two lovely ladies, who could not get enough of their regular visits to our home.

By that second winter of my life while I sat on father's lap observing that skilful shelling of the Brazil nut and the funny beast with antlers, things had improved markedly. We had not had to depend on the charity of others, rather we had been in the position to help people ourselves. In no small thanks to my brother's considerable efforts to adapt quickly to the farming life; in fact, Eddie was thriving on it! He had sprouted in height and was going to be the same height and build as our father; he still had a little way to go. His shoulders were broadening, and the hard summer had given him a very muscular frame, and with his feats of strength and daring, he would love to show off frequently.

That winter Paul Valentine, our quiet young neighbour had been sick, he had contracted influenza; a very serious condition in 1920, for it was still the Spanish flu that was passing person-to-person that had killed many millions across the world the two seasons previously. My mother took it upon herself to nurse Paul, as he had not married and was determined to carry on as a happy bachelor. Cissie and my mother would ride on wee Jock the mile to his homestead twice a day, and attend to his needs. Once or twice, Cissie came home alone; Mama had been so worried about his fever, she had stayed through the night to be at hand if needed.

The second act of kindness that my mother had extended had started in the summer. There was an old Indian woman who used to come knocking, her name had been too diffi-cult for western tongues to pronounce – and as many of the remaining Sioux had – she had adopted a white name of Brenda. She had lost her husband and her sons, probably to the Spanish influenza, and had made her living passing from homestead to homestead doing what she could; as an Indian she was very adept at most manual tasks and livestock work;

I remembering watching her ease at wringing the necks of three of our hens, and she then slit their throats in seconds, and she proceeded to have them bled and plucked in no time. When Old Jack had got an infection in his foot, and my father had been convinced he would have to shoot him – because bills for animal doctors can't be afforded when you can't afford a human doctor – it had luckily coincided with Brenda's arrival – in her broken English she had asked to let her try and heal the sick horse.

She had squatted outside our barn, making a small fire and boiling up in a small pan a mixture of mud and various prairie herbs. Then when this foul-smelling mix had cooled slightly, I remembering watching her applying this mud pie to poor Old Jack's very painful hoof; she sang an old Indian chant as she did so. It was soothing and hypnotic, it almost sent me to sleep, it had certainly calmed the poor old boy. Then she had left without a word, returning a few days later, she chipped off the remaining dry mud, on the inside was now dried yellow pus and blood, as this poultice had worked its magic and pulled the infection out of the horse's hoof, leaving a visible hole where it had been. Again Brenda mixed a different mud pie and packed it into the crevice of the hoof, then turning to my mother and father said simply, "It's OK now."

And off she popped again.

So when Brenda turned up barely able to walk, leaning on a stick, my mother had been quite concerned; she was obviously struggling and as she could only eat by going place to place, she was going to suffer from her own lack of mobility. My mother managed to communicate with her after a fashion, through broken words of English and the few words that my mother had learnt from the Indians; Benda had fallen and she had damaged her leg, my mother asked her if she could look and was shocked to see that her leg was extremely swollen; strong evidence of a fracture, yet, the old lady was still walking around. My mother knew enough to know that it should be completely immobilised and she was not going to let Brenda walk one more step.

So for the next month or so, we had a house guest. She refused to take Eddie's bed – Eddie now slept on the Winnipeg couch, as he had long since out-grown his old bed. I was moved next to Cissie, and with a bit of moving around of our few sticks of furniture and piles of hay sacks with furs, we made a makeshift bed for her. She was not a good patient and most days would get up and move around a little too much for my mother's liking. Thankfully the winter came later than normal, and being the determined soul that she was, by November, she had decided that she was well enough to carry on her nomadic life. She walked with a limp the rest of the time that I knew of her, a consequence of having walked on the fracture for too long, and probably for getting on her way too soon at the end, but that was Brenda.

We passed the remainder of that winter confined to our four walls, as was the way in this part of the world. My mother would busy herself making what she could, both for the home and for sale when the spring came. She had bottled preserves in the summer months, and now she made small bags of herbs to freshen clothing drawers, as well as cloth peg pockets and mittens for cooks. There was not much of that wonderful skein of calico – which had been one of our first donations – left eventually.

My father whittled away until our Christmas Day, the first Christmas that I was actually aware of. Cissie and Eddie had one gift each; money had been used to purchase those from the general store. For Eddie, it was a much needed pair of workmen's boots, several sizes bigger than he required now, but they would last and that was what was needed. Our feet were as hard as leather having spent most of the summer barefoot on the rough prairie terrain, but it was not safe for Eddie to work with the machinery and scythes barefoot, so this had been 'a must' to purchase.

For Cissie, my mother had decided that she needed a decent dress – she had long since outgrown the green travelling dress, which had seen her from Scotland to Canada, and she needed a good dress as she was become a 'young lady'. She had been thrilled to receive this wonderful present; that was, until I received mine. Her face froze as my father handed me my little gift; his whittling and hand polishing had produced a little wooden rabbit, small enough for a little toddler's hands.

I remember now the shape and the softness of the curves and the form of this rotund bunny. It had a smiling expression and its ears were smoothed to its back, it was very tactile and had a lovely aroma of pine and polish. I fondled it lovingly all Christmas time; Cissie's intense jealousy of me grew. Although it was nothing special, well not to anyone else anyway, and it had been poor parents' solution for a gift for their youngest child, by the very fact that it had been lovingly made by my father over many weeks, gave it an extra-special appeal. In her eyes, he had spent hours over my present, which must mean that he loved me more. Oh Cissie, I wish you could have seen things differently.

Chapter 27 –

The Long Hot Summer

My short life continued as it had started. I watched as my sister took the little pony backwards and forwards to school each day and my brother threw his all into trying to be the strength of our father. Meanwhile I was my mother's shadow. Where she went I was with her. Whether it was outside in all weathers feeding hens, sitting on the floor of our little cabin whilst she cooked or made something, or a special treat was hitching up the newly acquired buggy to go visiting.

John had realised that Sal needed to get around under her steam, without having to be over-reliant on the generosity of others. I have no idea where the money was found, or if had been yet another of the many kindnesses that had been shown to us, but a buggy became our mode of transport. Our little barn now held 'Wee Jock' and 'Old Jack', and the smaller livestock shed, the 5 or so heifers and another larger pony – Minchie – who had been bought to pull the buggy. He was not the only new arrival that winter. My mother was always rescuing poor unfortunate creatures that she came across, like the little bird she found starving and frozen to the ice; most would have let nature take its course, but not my mother. She carefully released the half-dead bird from the icy prison, and wrapping it in her muffler, she brought it into the cabin, and made a nest of fur and hay. She then painstakingly fed weak chicken-broth through an eye-dropper for days and days.

I wanted to pet and stroke it, but I was told very sternly that all wild creatures were wild, and not to be tamed. It was not fair to make a wild thing into a pet, it would never survive when released back into the wild; they would become too dependent and unable to look after themselves. I would sit and watch this poor motionless soul for hours, then one morning it was perched, as if to fly, on the edge of the make-shift nest. My mother smiled, and careful clasped her hands around it, and standing at the open door, she opened her hands and threw the grateful bird into the sky.

That was one of many wild things rescued, some saved, some not; we had a little graveyard outside the door in a small flower bed of those fatalities. In May 1921, when I was rising two years old, we had been out visiting, and great fun that had been. As usual the trek had been made to the general store in Glentworth, for 'a few extras'. We had wheels on the buggy, the snow for that winter had gone, and spring flowers were appearing everywhere; being such short seasons, spring would happen with urgency and what had been a complete covering of snow two weeks ago was now a burst of crocuses and sweet little flowers.

The little gardens that surrounded the front porches of the Glentworth homes, were a mass of different pinks and yellows, fascinating to a little girl. We had been away to see Evelyn, and Leila was there too; I was the complete centre of everyone's attention, and a big syrup cookie was placed before me, while the three ladies chatted about this and that. Time passed quickly, and no sooner had we sat down, than

I was whisked away again. My mother pointed out homes on the horizon as we made the few short miles back to ours. Then just up ahead, sitting in a ditch to the side of the road, was a black bundle of something. My mother pulled Minchie to a halt, she had to see. I saw her gently touch the little bundle, which seemed to quiver ever so slightly. She took her shawl off and wrapped the black bundle tightly in her shawl and placed it on her lap as we made the last half mile home.

She didn't say what it was and placing it on the table she poured some warm water into a bowl, and began to gentle sponge the bundle. A little yelp was made as she tried not to make the pain of the injury worse. Then she took a bit of cotton with some mild disinfectant, and applied it to the wound site; a second little yelp could be heard. Then she poured a small bowl of the chicken broth, and found her glass eye-dropper. Then she sat down next to the half-wrapped bundle, and beckoned me over to the table, placing her finger over her pursed lips; a signal for complete hush. I came over and scrambled onto the chair next to her, and pulling myself up on my knees, leaned towards her, while she put her arm around me to steady me, I grasped the table edge tightly.

My mother carefully pulled the corner of her shawl back, a little nose raised slightly in the air, but with very little interest in much. Mama took the glass dropper and carefully filled with the chicken broth, and then touched the animal's nose lightly. The nose sniffed, then sniffed again, more animated this time. Then a little pink tongue appeared, and began to lick the drops off the bottom of the dropper. Then again more, as my mother squeezed the dropper, this time more urgency. My mother could not fill the dropper fast enough, and now she just squeezed it into a little open mouth. After a while, with a contentedly full tummy, the little black bundle of fur curled up asleep. I still could not work out what it was, and I couldn't really see it properly, despite standing on my tippy-toes and nearly over-balancing a couple of times.

My mother carefully lifted me onto her lap so that I could get a better look at it; I did not reach to touch, having been told other times not to.

"Look Rita, isn't he lovely?... It's a wee black doggy..."

I made one of those little child exclamations. "Yes, he is wonderful, isn't he?..."

"Yes, Mama..."

I was a bit unsure of why we had a very small doggy on our table, not having had any association with puppies, only ever having seen full grown farming dogs running around other properties. But my mother had given me the cue that this was something very special indeed.

The little bundle was placed in a wooden box that was once again lined with fur and hay and placed on the floor. He slept for a few days; Mama had discussed him with Papa, she thought it might have been a stray bitch collie that had whelped and died, leaving just the one, or maybe there had been more, but the coyotes had seen to them. It might have explained the horrible bite mark on his back. He could even have been carried some distance from an outlying place and dropped there. But luckily the right person had found him at the right time. He was obviously a little black collie dog and he could be very useful addition on the farm; my father had been unsure, as he had no intention on sheep rearing. But my mother was ever-persuasive and they both agreed as long as he recovered fully he could be kept.

"Maybe he will make a good ratter, or catch rabbits?" My father had said optimistically.

The little bundle didn't stay still for long. He became a normal bumptious little puppy and he had sharp little teeth, which I felt once or twice when I tried to pat him. Every now and then he would forget himself, and leave a little smelly present on the floor, which my father would sometimes step in and curse the black minx. My brother christened him Jimmy and as we entered the hot months of July and August, when school was closed, all four of us, Eddie, Cissie, Jimmy and myself, were inseparable.

That was a hot summer indeed. My father barely came out at all, except to sit in the shade of the cabin; he found the heat combined with his problems with his wheezing chest just heightened his fatigue still further. If It had not been for Paul Valentine we would have never got the crop in. I remember the last few days of the harvest, when I was so hot, my mother had given up trying to keep any clothing on me as I would just strip it off. I was turning into a wild prairie child; my feet never saw shoes, not that I needed them, my baby skin had long since become leather-hard and immune to the small sharp stones that littered the ground. Cissie was impatient with me and embarrassed by my lack of inhibition.

"Mama, can't you put something on her... she can't run around like that... say if anyone comes visiting, what will they be thinking?"

Mother felt very firmly put in her place by the indignity of her eldest daughter, but also found it highly amusing that Cissie had moved from the sulking petulant child that no one could reason with about anything, to an opinionated little madam, who had now reversed the tables on her parents. But I was left to run naked, it saved on wash day and mother had enough to do.

We were lucky we had got the crop in when we did, for two days later a black pall of smoke could be seen rising over the ridge about two miles away – a prairie fire! A farmer's worse nightmare! Any homesteader would dread this happening, for if you had anything left on your fields – that by August were tinder dry – with the winds that would blow, the fire animal would spread, eating all in its path. This is why farmers would keep the ground free as far as they could around their houses in the hope of saving their home if they were unlucky. But fire could jump large distances, either a gust of wind or a spark on the breeze, and before you knew there was not one prairie fire but three or four in a moment.

All of a sudden there was a great commotion around me, I was being swept up by my mother and bundled into the hastily-hitched buggy. My father and Eddie had told Sal to take us girls to safety into Glentworth. Eddie had headed off bareback, on 'Old Jock' in the direction of the fire; for he knew that was expected, all who could would get there with spades and shovels, anything that could help make a fire break. My father set about wetting the ground around our property and around the barn; he hoped that our clear fields would lessen the risk to us. My mother, Cissie and I headed as fast as we could to Leila's place (it was the furthest away). Mama knew that Leila would need help, she would always take in those who suddenly found themselves homeless during disastrous times like these. She would be rushing around making temporary places to sleep and wash, and food for those who would need it that night.

Leila's house was much bigger than anyone's; it was like a palace to me, though Cissie used to say that it was much smaller than grandmamma's. I used to imagine that grandmamma must be very rich indeed to live in a place such as that. Leila lived chaotically, despite her ability to organise everyone; it was because she spent all of her time caring for and visiting others that she never had much time to organise her own place. It was fascinating for a small child, all the many things that she seemed to squirrel away. Piles of books, heaps of clothes and linen, ornaments by the bucket load; she was a bit of a hoarder, but she would always hand on what she could. I suppose she collected all that she did, because she always knew that someone could eventually need it.

My mother directed Cissie into the kitchen to help her and Leila prepare a big pot of soup and bake bread. It was a screechingly hot day, but it was better to be inside with the fly screens shut away from the clouds of mosquitos, which now plagued the prairies day and night. They could bite like anything and my whole body was one mass of fiercely itching, red lumps. While the women set-to in the higglety, pigglety kitchen, I mooched through the piles, pulling things out that caught my attention; a piece of emerald green silk, a bright red Indian rubber ball, a picture book with bright colours.

Eventually it was coming onto evening, we all were collected in a space round the table in the kitchen. There was a strange orange light, like a glorious sunset; to me it was a nice thing, but I sensed the anxiety in the others. The orange glow was the raging fire on the horizon. The fire that could not have been witnessed from our vantage point upon our arrival, but was now obvious to the women and my sister – and more worryingly to them than to me – it was heading in the general direction of our homestead. They tried to keep each other's spirits up as best they could, and my mother did not wish to unsettle me or Cissie and pretended to ignore what was going on outside in the distance, but every now and then she would be caught glancing in the general direction of the window.

It was dark when we heard the rattle of a cart coming down the road, Leila rose immediately to see who it might be; she was gone a while, but was then back with a woman and her husband who lived five miles further from our homestead. They had lost their cabin that afternoon, and were the first victims of the outbreak. Paul had directed them to Leila's as they had nothing remaining; they had been completely burnt out. I thought that they looked funny with their sooty black faces, legs and arms and I giggled, Cissie hit me to get me to stop, I yowled and was removed quickly from the kitchen. I could still hear the woman sobbing uncontrollably, and Leila's calming voice, telling her that all looked dark now, but they would get through; very wise words, after all she had known.

Leila had found we three a small space in what had been a bedroom once. We all bundled into the tiny bed, at least I think we did, because I was first to sleep and when I awoke the next morning, Mama and Cissie were already up and moving about down in the kitchen. Leila had given her own room to the distraught couple and had spent the night on the couch.

"I am very thankful that there has been no more... I watched the fire until the early hours, but I think they may have stopped it... mind you, the smell in the air is horrible," she announced at breakfast.

"Have you heard anything?" my mother had enquired, trying not to look overly concerned in front of us two girls. Leila knew what she was enquiring.

"No I haven't, Sal... but you know what they say, no news is good news."

My mother could not contain herself much more and she knew that she had to get back as soon as possible. We were hastily assembled back in the buggy, behind Minchie, and were soon heading back the few miles to our homestead.

Claggy, acrid smoke hung in the air, and a strange fog seemed to cover most of the view, but as we drew nearer home, the charred black smoking earth to one side of the road became clearly visible. Every so often, there was evidence of human intervention to try and break the path of the rampaging fire; soaking wet black earth, old damp sacks that had been physically used to beat the ground. A trench hastily dug filled with sloppy mud. Soon a clearer view to the right, smoking and black, nothing standing where once there had been mile after mile of un-harvested wheat. My mother and Cissie were silent; I knew that I should be quiet and sat still sensing their collective panic.

As we pulled onto our land, the fire seemed to have come quite close – very close to the barn by the look of it – because the heifers had been moved out into a corral on the other side of the cabin. Minchie was uneasy as we pulled to a halt, smelling the danger of fire and the scent of dead livestock that must have hung in the air from other places. We slid off the buggy ankle-deep in mud, and squelched our way to the cabin; a time my mother was probably quiet grateful that I refused to wear shoes. The sun was already well up, and I remember the contrast of the very warm sun on my skin, and the squelching cold mud between my toes.

We opened the cabin door, expecting Papa and Eddie to be inside, but there was no one. It had a strange feeling – there would normally have been a low warmth from the stove, especially after a family breakfast at dawn – but it felt quite desolate. Two things panicked me there and then, not the unusual absence of my father and my brother, but the whereabouts of our puppy dog Jimmy, and the location of my Bun-bun – my little wooden treasure that I normally carried everywhere, but had been completely forgotten in our the rush to leave. I now felt very upset by the lack of the familiar special things, and I began to howl. I was inconsolable, and Cissie became very impatient with me, knowing that Mama had much more serious concerns on her mind just at that moment.

"Shut up, you big baby… stop carrying on… you are too spoilt, you need to grow up!"

Chapter 28 –

The Changing Life

I had been very firmly put in my place by my elder sister and I bit my lip hard. Mama was not willing to settle and wait, fearing the worst we were bustled outside again, and herded to the waiting buggy. Just then Eddie could be seen coming from the south on Old Jack. My mother dashed forward to meet him, leaving us in the buggy. Cissie hissed at me, "You better learn soon little miss, you can't always get your own way… Mama is very worried about Papa… stop thinking about yourself all the time… you are not a baby anymore!"

Silent tears ran down my face, I just wanted Mama and Papa to hug, I wanted Jimmy to lick my face, and I needed to hold my comforter – Bun-bun.

Then Mama dashed back to the buggy, and Eddie rode past us towards Glentworth without stopping.

"What is it, Mama?" Cissie's voice was filled with anxiety. I sat in misery.

"It's Papa… he's been taken ill, he is at Paul's, we will go there now, Eddie's away to fetch the doctor."

With that, we headed down the back road of our property towards Paul Valentine's homestead.

Papa was in a terrible state. He was slumped on Paul's dishevelled bed, black from the soot of the fire. He was barely conscious and his breath was rasping and catching in his chest. My mother looked at Paul searchingly for answers; Cissie and I stood back, horrified at the state of our lovely father.

"He worked hard trying to keep the fire away… I was not there, I was with the others beating it back from the crops. He was found yesterday late evening by another farmer who had passed along the road to douse down anything that was left. Thank goodness he did, and had the sense to bring him here directly. I got back early in the morning, but I did not dare leave him, Eddie came looking this morning when he couldn't find him at your place… the rest you know… I don't know what to do, Sal… I have tried giving him some brandy, but he seems to have no breath…"

Paul's face was ashen, he was completely worn out from his own exertions, and dreadfully worried about his friend. Paul was a strange man, a bit of a hermit. There were all sorts of rumours about him; jumping ship at New York, having been shot -off his previous claim by a rival family, he did not mix with anyone, my father was the only man he trusted that he had anything to do with. I surveyed Paul's cabin, much like ours in construction, but that was no surprise; my father had helped him build his as he had helped my father build ours. The only difference was there was nothing there. My mother had made our place so homely and pretty – we had nothing special and any ornaments we had were home-made, or chipped donations – but it had a feeling of home. Paul insisting on his sole existence needed nothing, and he did not want the interference of a wife (not that they were easy to find). He was determined to live his committed bachelor life, which meant scarcity of anything in the house, and total clutter and disorganisation of what was.

My mother was crouched down next to my father trying to rouse him, while Cissie fetched a cloth and some water to help clean him up a little. Paul stood nervously by, not sure what to do or say, shifting from one foot to the other. My father managed to wheeze some low conversation to my mother, inaudible to everyone else; just then there was a recognisable whining from outside the door.

"Jimmy!" I squealed excitedly and I headed to open the door.

"I don't want that mutt in my house," Paul growled, then seeing my face, relented. "Well, you watch him," he said fiercely. "I don't want him chewing and messing."

I opened the door and was bowled over by the boisterous pup, who proceeded to lick my face as I lay sprawling on the floor.

"Mr Halderson... the farmer who found your husband, brought the pup too... but he has been a bit skittish, I had to put him outside," he said to my mother.

She had very little interest in his explanation, her concerns lay with my ailing father. Cissie was now boiling some water in a pan, in an effort to get some steam going. On my mother's instructions they were going to try and get my father to sit over the steaming bowl to try and help his smoke-clogged passages. A chair was brought over beside the bed and my father brought to a sitting position, his legs off one side and held by my mother, a blanket over his head, while the steam did its work. Ten minutes later, my father's explosive coughing was met by my mother's handkerchief, after it had subsided she brought the white cotton away from his mouth and nose; it was now black from the smut that had been inhaled at the height of the raging father. His breathing was easier; he was once again lain down to await the arrival of the doctor. My father wheezed, "Rita... come here angel..."

I righted myself from Jimmy's enthusiasm and stumbled my way to the side of the bed. My father was fumbling in his workman's trousers and his enormous hands concealed what he passed to me. My joys were complete, it was Bun-bun! Slightly charred to one side – a new smell. I examined it, slightly puzzled.

"I rescued him," he whispered. "The fire nearly got him, I found him on the ground in the yard." The charring left black carbon on my hands, but I didn't care: I had him back. I turned to re-join Jimmy in our game on the floor, and caught Cissie's angry expression as I did so. She was still mad at me about Mama, I could tell.

The doctor and Eddie finally arrived, and now there were too many bodies inside the small confined cabin. Mama told me and my siblings to go outside with Jimmy and wait there, and Paul followed us; he felt more awkward inside than he did waiting outside. I busied myself running with Jimmy in the hot sun. My feet were black and mud-stained, my hands black from the soot, but I didn't have a care in the world. Cissie and Eddie stood shuffling their feet near Paul. Eddie was the first to break the silence.

"I hope he's alright, Cis?... He doesn't look good, does he?"

Cissie nodded in agreement and then sniped, "And it's all because of her." She threw a vicious look in my direction.

"Why, what's she done?"

"If he hadn't got so close to the fire to rescue her toy, he would be fine now!"

"No, you can't say that… it was bad for hours, he must have been fire beating for a long time… there was lots of smoke… it was a terrible night."

Paul grunted in agreement. Cissie tutted at the lack of support she was receiving from the two. I thought nothing of it, I was happy.

After what seemed like an age, the doctor and my mother emerged from the cabin and began to chat to Paul. The decision had been taken not to move my father that day; the doctor considered that even the short journey back to our homestead might be too much for him. They had managed to relieve his breathing, but only just, and he needed to rest up a bit. Paul agreed to have the houseguest one more night. My mother was extremely grateful for his courtesy and said that she would send some cooked food over later, to save Paul the trouble of trying to make something for himself. Cissie offered enthusiastically to act as porter. Eddie was grateful, he had a lot to do to try and bring some order back to our yard, plus the horses and heifers needed feeding.

So back we went in the buggy, Eddie just behind on poor Old Jack, who was tired from a day and night working without rest. Jimmy sat on my mother's lap, as she skilfully manoeuvred Minchie and the buggy back down the homestead's rough track that divided neighbour from neighbour. An hour or so later, I can remember being painfully scrubbed by my mother, who did not seem the normal happy person that I knew and loved. In my childlike way I tried to give her comfort.

"It's alright, Mama… Papa home soon… It's alright…"

I watched my mother's face for a rewarding smile, but instead one silent tear rolled down her cheek. I had no idea then, and not till sometime later in my life, that my mother was reeling from shock – the shock of it all.

Papa was brought home by Paul the next morning, and put straight to bed. He was exhausted and breathing badly. Doctor Cameron visited each day, and when he did he would have conversations with Mama outside, where none of us could hear. It was so hot, and the cabin was the only cool place to be, that I was kept in, away from the biting mosquitos and the fierce sun. Mama and Cissy would take care of Papa, who slowly began to make a slight recovery. He did not go out much especially the month of August, but by September, Mama would place a chair outside the door in the cooler evenings to allow him to get some fresh air and a change of scene. His skin was very pale, and there were dark circles around his eyes; his clothes hung off him like a badly made scarecrow; he had lost so much weight and was barely eating.

Eddie now handled most of the farm work alone. The crop had been in early, not that there was much that year. But there was a lot of ground to clear and plough for the planting; Old Jack was literally on his last legs, and over several days, Paul brought his plough shear and horse over to help. Mama and Cissy managed the few cows, and mucked out the horses and hens daily; we always had eggs, we always had milk, and if times got really tight that winter – a hen or two for our staple meal, chicken broth. Mama had a little vegetable garden on the other side of the house from where the fire had been; just a few potatoes and carrots, that was all. She could make the most amazing food out of nothing.

One evening an unexpected visitor came calling, unexpected to me anyway. My mother had decided that one kindness deserved another, and she was so grateful to the farmer from Fir Mountain who had found my father and got him away to the safety of Paul's that she had written a note of thanks to him, extending an invitation to come and share a simple meal with us, when his own farming duties has lessened; tonight was the night that was chosen.

Mr Halderson stood very tall, like my father, the same broad-shouldered build. But he was blonde, not dark, and he was softly spoken in a strange accent; just like Paul, but not as gruff. We all crammed round our tiny table for a really nice chicken stew and fresh dropped scones. My mother exuded gratitude to this stranger for saving Papa's life.

"Aw, Mrs Flynn, anyone would have done the same… I hope someone would do it for me if ever I was in difficulty."

He was a very modest man, and full of stories. He told us that he came from a place called Oslo in Norway. He told us it was very pretty with mountains and much snow in the winter, just like our Saskatchewan winters. His father and mother had seen him off at the port in Norway, as many parents had done; when he had taken passage to Canada to try and make a better life. He had learnt how to make boots in Norway, and as he had crossed the provinces, this trade had kept him in money to survive before homesteading. Papa and he laughed about my grandpa John being a bootmaker too.

"It's a good trade," noted Papa. "It kept food on our family table… people always need boots," he said. "Just like they always need undertakers…" An awkward silence hung for a moment, as my mother swallowed hard.

It was a lovely evening, and when it came time for Mr Halderson to leave, he was asked to join us again when he was free; he acknowledged kindly that he would, and offered Eddie some tools and help for the farm. Eddie was not too proud to receive assistance, the workload for him was stressful, any help offered by anyone was always gratefully accepted. Cissie had been very quiet throughout the whole meal, but nobody thought anything of it; she was just in one of her moods again.

The end of the summer passed as the previous year; Eddie struggled on with the farm work, Cissie was back on Wee Jock backwards and forwards to school. I stayed at home with Mama and Papa, he sat most of the time unable to do much. I would help Mama with the chores; feeding the hens, collecting the eggs, and churning the butter. Every week, we would go to Glentworth on the buggy and Mama would sell the extra eggs and butter, and buy a little meat to feed us; Eddie needed the energy to work, and Papa's ailing health meant he ate little, but she would try and tempt him with special food.

The doctor would come week after week to see him, and still the quiet chats between him and Mama would happen outside, as I sat with Papa passing the time. Jimmy would follow Mama and me everywhere. He was a big collie dog now, as bright as a button. He had stopped chewing everything that he used to find. Bun-bun now had a few sharp little teeth marks; war wounds from various encounters with Jimmy's mouth, but that just added to my treasure's tactile qualities.

When Mama could, she would write her letters to Scotland, and every now and then a long letter would arrive from grandma Maggie, or auntie Mary, and sometimes Ellie. Mama had got to know quite a few of the farmers by now that lived in the outlying homesteads, who, like us, used to visit the general store for provisions. One such man, who seemed quite old to me – but everyone seemed old to me – had let it be known he was looking for a wife. Mama had written to Ellie and in a half-hearted manner; she had mentioned this. Ellie had replied very enthusiastically wanting to know more, so Mama had passed the farmer's name and address to her, thinking no more of the matter.

Auntie Mary wrote about the family to Mama; the cousins that I had never met, uncle James and his business and grandmamma and grandpa. They had fulfilled their plans and moved to Dunoon. Grandpapa Peter had made a great deal of money with his trade during the war, and was able to invest in a couple of properties there; one that they lived in called Mary Catherine Villa, and two that they rented to tenants – Charleston and Greenbank. Mama tried to describe to me how different these places were to our own humble little wood cabin, but as there was nothing slightly like these stone buildings anywhere in my world, they meant very little to me. I dreamed one day when I was a grown girl that I might go and see grandmamma and grandpapa, but I knew I would have to be very grown up to make that journey.

But life didn't stay the same as summer changed to winter. My father's conditioned worsened and he got a chest infection; the doctor was now very concerned, but I was kept out of it all. It was as if they all shared a secret that I was not to know. Cissie was tearful and forever moping around, she wouldn't play with Jimmy or me, and Mama would tell her off for being so miserable in front of everyone. Eddie looked like a man now, and he did the work of a man. His voice was low and his shoulders and frame broad; he looked like Papa, but he did not have all the silver in his hair that Papa had now.

One day in November, I think it was near my birthday, but I don't really remember, I am not even sure if I had a birthday that year, there was a great deal of commotion in the cabin. My father was getting ready to go on a long holiday, I wasn't even sure what a holiday was, but Mama explained that Papa needed a rest in a hospital to make him better and that he would be away for a long while and I had to say goodbye to him. Paul and Mr Halderson stood waiting outside; they were to take him to Lafleche, where he was to catch a train to a place called Moosejaw. A nurse was to meet him from the train and transfer him the City Hospital, where he was to 'convalesce'; Mama explained it was a big word for rest. Cissie stood sniffing in the cabin, Eddie had his arm around Mama, who looked very pale and shaking. Papa called me over to him, as he struggled to get his breath to stand, I climbed on the bed next to him, my legs dangling over the side, covered in rough woollen stockings to keep out the cold.

"Now, wee Rita, you be a good girl for Mama, you hear? No naughtiness…" I nodded with my most serious face on. "You do what she tells you to do, and don't let her work too hard, you must help like the other two…" I nodded again, and then thinking it all rather strange and not having any concept of what a long time was, I said, "When you come back Papa, you'll be all better and we will go and see the cows, won't we?"

"Yes, little one… when I am all better we will go and see the cows… and play, too."

I smiled at that; it was all going to be fine, we were all going to be together again, that was that.

Chapter 29 –

The Winter's Chill

It was a very bad winter in lots of ways. Firstly, Old Jack died; one morning my mother found him lain down, eyes tightly shut. It took four men to get him out of the barn and onto the back of a cart. Mama said they were going to take him somewhere to bury him, I believed this story in my childish innocence, but knowing now that the ground would have been frozen very deep, he was obviously destined for the abattoir to be rendered down. Cissie just seemed to be in abject misery all the time; that day she was particularly bad, but to me death of animals was part of life, having watched chickens having their necks stretched and knowing that cows would be meat one day. But Old Jack was a friend, and that was sad that he wouldn't be there in the barn every day.

When Mama mithered about how they were going to manage with the spring ploughing, Eddie would sit her down and say that they would find a way.

"There's enough money to buy another old boy like Jack, we'll wait and see, Mama."

Paul would visit from time to time, mostly to share a meal with us; he missed the creature comforts of a home life.

Sometimes Mr Halderson would stop by and enquire after papa. Mama hardly heard anything from the hospital, but would try and be cheery and say, "No news is good news, Hjalmer."

I thought he had a really funny name, I couldn't say it like the others did and I would repeat it like a parrot calling him Elmer, he would laugh affectionately and his blue eyes would sparkle.

Most of the time a black shadow would fall over the house, no one would talk or laugh. My mother busied herself with her winter-making; the old sewing machine clicking away, as she fashioned oven gloves, herb bags and aprons that she would sell in the spring; Cissie helping by pinning up, applying running stich and trimming the loose threads on the finished garments. Eddie would endlessly leaf through farm catalogues, dreaming of the time that he could make the farm pay that his father had worked so hard to establish. He had barely managed to farm the first quarter and the second was fast turning fallow again; he had a spring plan to try and work that half as much as he could.

I was still only small; just two years old. But I would try to pretend to read picture books; Mama said that I reminded her of auntie Katie when I was like that, but when I was chatting nineteen to the dozen, I was more like auntie Annie. Every day I would hope that day would be the day that Papa would come home from his 'rest'. Mama used to try and placate my constant enquiries by saying, "When the snow goes, Rita, you must watch out for your Papa, he will be back when he can get through the snow."

But the snow had not gone when Mama got the news. It was March 1922 and Doctor Cameron paid an unexpected visit to our homestead. He looked very serious as he came in. I was sent with Cissie to sit in the bedroom area with the curtain around us. Cissie protested, but Mama insisted that we do this; Cissie was very angry and told me to be quiet or she would hit me. We heard Mama let out a gasp, and then Eddie's voice thanking Doctor Cameron for coming and he understood how difficult it was for him. Cissie let out a yowl, I wondered what was going on with all this pandemonium around me. Mama drew back the curtain and sat on Cissie's bed doing her best to try and comfort my distraught sister. With her other arm she pulled me in close to her other side. I was confused and too small to understand, but I knew I had to give comfort somehow.

"What's wrong, Mama?... It's alright, when the snow goes Papa will be back... It will all be alright..."

Cissie yowled again, and buried her head into my mother's arm. I looked appealingly at Mama, whose face was wet with tears; she looked at me pitifully knowing that she could not make me understand, but she would try.

"I am sorry, Rita... but your Papa has died..."

Cissie sobbed uncontrollably.

"He's gone to heaven to be with god."

I knew this story that they used to tell me about god, but we never went to church when we there, so it didn't really mean anything to me. Papa had just gone to another place for his rest, and he was coming home, he had told me that he was coming home and that we would see the cows and play.

"He'll be home soon, Mama... when the snow goes... Rita see him come... when the snow goes?"

Mama knew that I could not grasp the concept of him never coming home, that it was something to leave to explain another time, so she humoured me, just to stop the questions.

"Yes, Rita... when the snow goes."So everyday I waited

and waited; the snow had long since gone and life carried on as it had the previous spring. It might have helped a small child's understanding to have attended a funeral, or even to have seen my father's corpse. But he was so far away, and we were poor and in the grips of winter; my mother just could not find a way to get us there. The small money that she had she sent to the sisters at the hospital, to arrange for my father to be interred in the city cemetery, but she did not have enough to pay for a headstone.

One day she was out, visiting or something; it was spring, she knew that she would be late back and had instructed Eddie to make some food for us later, the best he could. He never had much idea about this, and used to drop potatoes straight into the stove, then fish them out black and charred, but he would try. He was off with our replacement for Old Jack – we had christened this one Tom. I was left alone with Cissie, who had no school that day. I took up my normal position on my bed peering out of the window waiting for my father's return from his 'long rest', Bun-bun lying by my side on the bed, my only connection with the man I missed so much.

"What are you doing?" hissed Cissie.

My childhood innocence, showed its face again. "Waiting for Papa... the snow has gone..."

Cissie was incandescent. She shot off the chair by the table where she had been sitting, and hurtling towards me she snatched Bun-bun from the bed where it lay.

"You stupid little brat," she spat. "Papa's dead... don't you get it... he is dead and he is not coming back..."

By now I was screeching as she held my treasure in her hand menacingly.

"Give me my Bun-bun... I want Bun-bun!" I screamed.

"No," she hissed.

"It's all your fault... you and this stupid thing... if he hadn't rescued this he would be here today... You made him sick... this made him sick... and it's going where it should have gone then... in the fire!"

With that she opened the wood burner and threw him in. I was screaming wildly and trying to get past her to the fire; she held my wrists tightly and would not let me go. She picked me up and threw me back on the bed, she was quite scary and she kept shouting at me.

"If you don't shut up, you will go where Bun-bun's gone... and you tell anybody and I will smack you so hard!"

I was scared and I knew she meant it. I sat quivering on my bed, biting back stifled sobs.

"I would shut up if I were you... or you will get a good smack... I have had enough of you being so spoilt... you don't know how spoilt you are... I am not going to let it be that way anymore... I am older than you and you are going to listen to me and respect me... just like you do Eddie and Mama!"

For another hour or so, I sat shaking and scared. Cissie resumed her reading at the table, every now and then throwing accusing looks at me, just to reinforce that she meant what she said. Then Eddie came back, and after seeing to Tom, entered the cabin.

"What's wrong here then?" he said, as he washed up in the bowl.

"Oh, it's her..." Cissie hissed. "She's been moaning and complaining again... I have just put her in her place."

"Oh," he said, somewhat disinterested. I slid off the bed and waited for what I knew he would do next.

"Better put some potatoes in then." He lifted the lid; I could just about see inside if I stood on my tip-toes from where I was. The orange fire was blazing with the sudden rush of oxygen, all I could see was orange. I knew that Bunbun was no more. I sank to the floor in abject silent misery. I think it was that moment that made me dislike my sister; I would never trust her again, no matter what we went through.

Mama was as strong as ever. If she was grieving she tried not to display it in front of us, and for the most part, my life carried on as it had, just waiting for Papa's return; I knew not to mention it again, as it caused too much trouble for me. Eddie was the man of the house now, and the muscles of the farm; a huge expectation of one so young, but he just got on and did what he had to. Paul would lend what help he could and was a regular visitor to our homestead, but more so Mr Halderson. He would come often and spend a morning or and afternoon with Eddie out on the prairie and Mama would always reward him with a shared meal, which he was always truly grateful for. I liked him a lot; he used to make me laugh and Eddie and he seemed to get along just fine, but Cissie was always distant when he was around and a little offhand. Mama decided as he was doing so much to help us, that she had to do something more for him than just cooking food. She would go to his place once a week and lend the woman's touch to his property; we never went, she felt it was not right for him to have children running around when he was a very solitary man, who valued his independence. She told us that he lived high up on a hill in a bigger house than us. That was hard to imagine for me, as our vast expanse of land was so flat, and I had only really known the tiny cabin.

Just before the summer we had one of those days which stays in my memory for the right reasons. Firstly, the postman came by with a letter for Mama. She was thrilled, she had received a letter from Ellie, who had written that a romance of sorts had blossomed between her and the farmer that Mama had introduced her to. So much so that he had asked her to marry him without even meeting her, she had agreed and she was to arrive in a month at Lafleche. She asked Mama if she would be there too, just in case the man changed his mind. Mama laughed to herself all morning, knowing that there were so many lonely farmers who were desperate for a wife to keep home for them, and Ellie was such a nice person that this match could not fail.

Later in the morning a familiar silhouette could be seen in the distance making her way across the prairie; Brenda the Indian. We had not seen her for a long while, and Mama had worried that some serious misfortune had befallen her. She was overjoyed to see her, and went quickly to meet her and give her some help on her progress. She was limping badly, but as proud as she was, would struggle on regardless without aid; just leaning on a walking cane that some kind soul had not doubt donated to her at some time. She came to offer any services that she could, for a meal and a place to sleep.

There was not much to do, as we were managing pretty well ourselves, with Paul's and Mr Halderson's help of course. We all had our set chores; Cissie would help with food and cleaning when she was home from school, my jobs with Mama were still the chickens, the milking and butter churning. But my mother knew that Brenda would not stay unless there was a genuine need for her to work, to do things; Mama found some chores that could keep her busy for a day or so; she looked like she needed a good meal or two.

In the afternoon, as we sat out of the heat next to the cabin, Brenda reached into her small bag and pulled out a small skin package, which she offered to me in broken English.

Mama told me to say thank you, and was intrigued at what a poor old soul like Brenda could possibly give a small child. I opened the skin and inside, were the softest pair of beautiful beaded shoes; little hand-made moccasins like all the Indians wore. There were the colour of the sand mud that surrounded our house and soft calf's leather, with little coloured beads all painstakingly sewn on by hand. Mama gasped at their beauty, I was excited and immediately put them on; they were slightly big, but so soft and so pretty. I sat looking at my mud-stained legs with these pretty shoes on the end for ages and then I ran around like a mad thing, pretending to be a wild Indian. Mama and Brenda laughed at my antics. I may have lost my Bun-bun and these would never replace what that little wooden treasure meant to me, but they were a truly treasured gift, so much so that I wore them constantly; that is, apart from night time when I would hide them under my pillow, away from my sister's envy and spite.

This time there had been a gift for Cissie, which drew her fire away from me. Brenda had made her a beaded necklace, which she wore most days, except to school. Some people were not keen on those who were friends with the Indians and wearing a necklace like that could bring a great deal of hostility on one; my sister knew better than to get on the wrong side of her friends.

Brenda stayed for a day or two, and then thanking my mother moved on as she always had. I loved that old Indian woman, I loved her singing that she would do all day long while she worked. Sometimes at night she would sing me to sleep and the memory of that hypnotic chanting has stayed with me all of my life.

Then came the day I went with Mama in the buggy to Lafleche to meet her friend Ellie, who was nervously anticipating her meeting with her potential future husband. Mama had arranged things so that she would arrive to meet Ellie, give her a chance to draw breath and make herself presentable before the farmer's arrival. We waited for the train to roll into the station, and Mama was worried in case she had changed so much that she wouldn't recognise her; indeed that Ellie might not recognise my mother. But as the door swung open on the end carriage there was an instant and very excited reunion. Mama cried with happiness to see this woman, who had been such an important part of her life at a particularly bad time.

She was quite round, and bit like Mrs Purdy with a very homely happy face, she smiled all of the time, and had a cheery sing-song voice. I know that she was a lot younger than Mama, but to me they looked the same age, her face had that look of a hard life, even though her red hair did not grey. She looked at me and said, "Oh Sal, what a little angel she is."

Mama laughed, "Oh she can have her moments, can't you Rita?... She can be a little devil... but she is always a happy child."

We sat in the waiting room for a short while, Ellie and my mother taking excitedly about memories and happenings; the farmer was not due for another hour, or so my mother thought. But he must have been eager too, for just then, he ambled into the waiting room, taking everyone by surprise. Mama and Ellie fell into instant silence. The farmer grunted, "Afternoon."

Ellie stood up to shake his hand, which he ignored and saying nothing he began to walk round her. He was eyeing her up like a heifer he was considering purchasing from the livestock sale. He hummed and grunted and made three full circles of her, making Ellie quite dizzy, then he looked her up and down, and announced, "She'll do."

And with that he left.

Mama and Ellie were flabbergasted! He obviously approved and he was a well-to-do farmer, but she had expected a few more simple courtesies than that. Mama laughed, "Well, you've passed then... looks like you're getting married!"

Arrangements were made quickly, Ellie only stayed with us for a few days, before visiting the pastor and making it all official; then she was installed in the farmer's house. She was not worried at all, he seemed civil enough and she knew that she would want for nothing, it would suit her just fine to marry him. Mama visited her often in the first few months, just to make sure. Ellie was perfectly content, and said to Mama that 'all things take time'. He was a very affable man, who treated her with a great deal of respect; they would get to know each other, she thought, and maybe something more between them would come, but if it did not it was of no matter, they would make fine companions. Mama used to say some of the best marriages of all are not based on love but on friendship.

"Rita, it is more important to like someone than it is to love them... if you stop liking someone, the love soon goes."

Chapter 30 –

The Pain That Will Not Heal

But nothing stays the same for long. My short life had already been a rollercoaster of extremes; and the end of the summer was the last truly happy time for Mama.

We seemed to manage with the help of our good neighbours and friends through that harvest time; Eddie had done well, all things considered, and had made a little money to see us through the long winter, which would start to bite in November. Mama had conserved food and flour, for the times when we would be consigned to 'staying in' throughout December to March. Plans were being made with Paul and Mr Halderson to work up more of the land that was quickly falling back into the wild since my father had gone. Still I would sit and hope that he would come one day, and all I had to do was keep looking out of that window.

My little moccasins sat snuggly on my feet, my toes were warm, and soon Mama said I had to have some boots on because it would be too cold to wear them. Every night I safely concealed my skin shoes out of the sight of my sister, when I thought she was not looking; I had never told Mama about Bun-bun's terrible demise. My third birthday came, and I remember it well. Mrs Purdy came with her young cousin from Winnipeg; she was blonde and looked like an angel, her skin was flawless and pale, not like ours which was dark as a consequence of a hot summer mainly spent outside. She wore pretty clothes and did not quite fit with all of us rough-farming people.

Evelyn came with a selection of cakes and cookies. Mama made a special birthday tea and we all sat together on whatever chairs and couches that could be assembled. My brother told jokes and made us all laugh, even Cissie. I was given a picture book from my family and a little teddy bear; I think that it had belonged to someone else – one of the things that Mrs Purdy had reclaimed and kept in her piles of conserved objects that filled her house – but it was small and cute – I called it Billy bear, and it was not going to be left out of my sight; I had learnt my lesson and Cissie was not to be trusted. Eddie was now fifteen, tall and strong, very much a man, Cissie was rising thirteen, she was getting more particular and pushy; Mama said it was her age and she was going through changes; I hoped that they would be nice changes.

A week later it was cold outside and I stayed in the warm with Mama; she had started her winter sewing and making, the sewing machine clattered and the scissors snipped at threads. I leafed through my picture book for the umpteenth time. The book was an alphabet book; A is for Apple and so on; to me it was twenty-six double pages of beauty. The images were colourful and bright and interesting. The beautiful red and green apple was in a little girl's hand as she sat cross-legged on the floor; I really wanted to eat that apple so badly.

Then there came a terrible wailing and commotion from outside, with a cart and horse moving quickly from the other side of the property. Cissie was shouting, "Mama! Mama!"

Mama rose quickly spilling her pins all over the floor, and dashed for the door. She opened it to see Cissie running towards her gabbling nineteen-to-the-dozen, very distressed, Paul carrying Eddie in a lift over his shoulder from the back of his trap.

"Oh my god!" my mother exclaimed, clasping her hand over her mouth.

"Mama Mama!" Cissie grabbed Mama tightly. "Eddie's been hurt! He's fallen from that wild horse! Quickly, Paul!" she shouted back as Paul struggled to carry the large unconscious lad on his shoulder. Mama dashed to help, leaving Cissie standing shaking uncontrollably. Mama was focussed only on her fallen son, as she struggled with Paul to get him lying on the couch. All the time Cissie was trying to tell what she had seen, what she had witnessed.

"He was trying to break that horse, that's been on our property, he was on him riding and he shouted back 'look Cis see what I can do!' and just then the horse reared and threw him, he fell off and hit his head, and then the horse kicked him in the head and bolted... he wasn't moving... I was screaming... Paul heard... Mama, he's going to be alright, isn't he?"

Mama wasn't listening much, she was trying to see where he was hurt; there was no blood, just stillness, he was completely out cold. Paul said he would ride to Glentworth quickly and get the doctor. The time he was away seemed to last forever. Mama got Cissie to get some cold water and a cloth, and Mama knelt next to him, speaking softly, mopping his face, trying to wake him up.

"Come on Eddie... wake up please... you have had a fall, but you are home now, you must wake up..."

Cissie stood helplessly by watching all, I sat nervously on the bed, watching for any sign of movement from my brother's still body.

Eventually, there was the noise of ponies and buggies dashing towards our place. The doctor hurried in without knocking; he knew common courtesies were not needed, urgency was the order of the day. Then a second buggy and women's voices, Mrs Purdy I recognised, accompanied by her cousin, I could make out the voices of Ellie and Brenda the Indian woman. All four hushed their voices as they came in, shutting the door carefully behind them to keep the wind out of the cabin. Mrs Purdy came quickly to Mama, her cousin Ellie and Brenda staying back by the door.

"How is he, Sal?"

"I don't know Leila, he won't wake… doctor, please do something, he won't wake!…"

Mama's voice was high-pitched and stressed, Mrs Purdy tried to guide her away.

"Let the doctor do his work, Sal… we need to stand back a little…"

I shuffled off the bed, my intention was to go to Mama for comfort, but Mrs Purdy looked at me and shook her head silently. I remained standing where I was; I felt like I was no longer in the room, like it was a dream that I could not wake up from, where nobody could see me.

Then there was the screaming and the crying, Brenda singing softly in the corner. I could not hold back my need for comfort anymore, I tried to go to Mama, as Mrs Purdy pushed me towards her, but she screamed, "I don't want Rita, I want Eddie."

I was scared. Mama was crying, Cissie was crying, the doctor was so solemn, slowly packing his bag on the table. All the while Eddie lay still on the couch, now there was blood running from his nose, but that was only thing that looked different. Mama was inconsolable, Mrs Purdy was having a quiet word with the doctor, the doctor was nodding and agreeing; I could not hear, there was too much commotion and distress, too much noise.

The next thing, the doctor was pouring some medicine for Mama and Brenda was trying to guide her to the bed, all the time she was fighting to return to the couch. Cissie was being comforted by Ellie, who was talking to her. Meanwhile, the doctor was pulling a blanket up over my brother's body and face. Then the doctor was guiding me to the door, towards my sister and 'angel face'; I just wanted to be with Mama, she was sobbing and sobbing; Mrs Purdy was sitting with her on the bed, the cup of the medicine now empty on the chair, Mrs Purdy looked at my frightened face.

"It's OK, Rita, I will look after your Mama with Brenda… you go with Marguerite and your sister… I will look after your Mama."

A day turned to two days, then four, then a week. Me and my sister were now at Evelyn's as there was no room in Mrs Purdy's house and she was not there, she was staying with Mama. Nobody would let me see her, I just wanted to be with my Mama. Every night I would cry myself to sleep, and Cissie too. Evelyn tried so hard to make me feel comfortable, but I missed my home, I missed my Mama and Eddie, and more and more I wished my Papa would just come home.

One day in December, Mr Halderson came to see us. I asked if Mama would come.

"No, Rita… the doctor thinks that your Mama needs a rest…"

Alarm hit me, that's what they had said to me when Papa went away, now I was really scared… if Mama went for a rest, it might be like Papa and I may never see her for a long time.

"I want my Mama!" I wailed. Cissie sat silently, she had barely spoken to anyone for weeks. Hjalmer tried to explain.

"It's OK, Rita… it's just a rest, she will be back… but she needs to have some special medicine to make her better… she is not well at the moment."

"What about Eddie?" Cissie finally spoke.

"Eddie's been buried… up at Mountain View."

Cissie's expression changed to anger. "But why didn't we go!"

Hjalmer was caught with a difficult question; it had not been his fault, it had not been anyone's fault. Mama had been so distressed she could not do anything, and she did not want to let Eddie go, it had been decided by others that it had to be done before the ground froze. Everyone had just got on with doing what was necessary and trying to limit any further damage and upset. Hjalmer stuttered. "He… he… had to be buried… I was not the one who did this… it just had to happen… your Mama has been sedated for weeks. It was for the best."

Cissie stormed from the table, up the stairs to the familiar room where she had cried once before, when Mama had told her she was not coming back when Papa was sick.

Hjalmer tried to comfort my fears.

"I promise you, Rita, I will look out for your Mama… and as soon as she is well I will make sure she comes home to you… I promise."

It was a terrible Christmas despite the fact that Mrs Purdy and Evelyn tried to raise our spirits. I was desperately unhappy and did not want to eat or play, it didn't matter how much kindness and gentleness was shown; I was beside myself. Cissie would swing from desperate anxiety to anger, this did not help me, as I picked up on her extremes and began to display the same mood swings. I think our dear friends were at their wits' end by the end of January. All the time the snow stayed deep and although being in Glentworth there was more to do, and more activity to keep us occupied, we were both completely disinterested. Every so often, Hjalmer would come on by to see us, not that it made a difference. He would try and talk to us and calm our fears, but we would not respond; it was the one time that Cissie and I were as one. We felt lost and alone, angry that we were not home and safe, nothing would take that away. During one of those visits, Cissie and I had left the kitchen table, feeling that our duty was done so we left for our bedroom. I climbed all the way, but Cissie sat on the bottom stairs.

"Cissie?" I said.

"Shhhh… I'm listening."

I crept back down the stairs to hear. There were low voices barely audible in the kitchen, where Hjalmer sat with Mrs Purdy and Evelyn. Every now and then we would catch snippets of conversation.

"She's in Waverley, you say…" Mrs Purdy's voice, expressing concern.

"That's what I have been told…"

"That's not a good place, Mr Halderson… People go in and never get out…"

I was filled with fear and let out a yelp. Cissie put her hand firmly over my mouth.

"Shhhh…" she whispered. "They'll hear us."

Mr Halderson spoke again. "I have been hearing this… I am worried for Sal too… she has been through so much… we have got to get her back as soon as we can… but the weather… I just can't get through…"

"And these poor children…" Evelyn's voice now. "What's to be done? Have they any relatives?"

"She has broken with her mother… she has a brother I know of… but let's hope we can sort this all soon and have them back together…" Mrs Purdy said, and she continued, "And is Paul managing with the farm?"

"Not really… I can't do much… we've let the beasts go to good homes… we just could not keep up with it all… and she'll never manage on her own with two small girls… she has to move somewhere, or return to Scotland… or…" Mr Halderson paused. "…marry."

Then there were footsteps; we crept quickly up the stairs as the kitchen door shut firmly. I did not understand much, the adults seemed worried, yet they kept telling me not to. I tried to ask my sister what was happening. Cissie hissed back, "They're just keeping us away from her… she doesn't care about us… if she did she would be here… and I don't trust him at all!"

I was now very worried, all of these conflicting stories and emotions sent a three year old mind into complete turmoil.

"But Mama's coming back… Elmer says so?"

"And you believe him?" she scoffed. "For all we know she is staying at his place… she could be anywhere… they are all just telling lies!" These mixed stories played on my thoughts all of the time. My resentment grew and my lack of communication and resistance with it. I became highly resentful of everyone around me, and reluctant to communicate with anyone, except Cissie. She was the only constant in my life. I was beginning to understand death now, and I knew that Papa was dead and never coming back, and so was Eddie, but what about Mama? Nobody had told me she had died, everyone kept saying she was coming back, but was she? Or was Cissie right, had she given up on us? Had she taken to living somewhere else, with Mr Halderson, like Cissie said? I was in complete turmoil.

Then came the day, that Mrs Purdy said she was taking us somewhere special, that we would be really happy. We scowled a lot as we forced to put on coats and boots and wrap up to take a buggy ride. The snow was still lying thick, so it was a buggy and runners, but Mrs Purdy was more than a capable driver of the sledge. She took us on an unfamiliar road out of Glentworth, a longer journey than it would have been to our home. I was sad, because I had thought for a short while that was where we were going; it would have been nice to see familiar things. In my young mind, our home would be warm and welcoming and smell of cooking. This was far from the truth, of course, because it had lain abandoned for some months, and all it smelt of was death.

We climbed up the hills; Mrs Purdy had a strong horse pulling, but even he struggled a few times to get a foothold on the uneven snow-covered tracks. Then we were on a ridge, looking down at a small icy creek, and on the other side on high ground stood a house, wooden, bigger than ours. Mrs Purdy told us we had arrived and made us get out and follow her. I remember slipping down the path on the ice, and having to pick myself up once or twice. We reluctantly climbed the other side, Mrs Purdy marching on ahead, calling back to us.

"Come on, you two... we are nearly there... journey's end!" She sounded relieved and happy, we were just fed up.

Then she was at the door, knocking. Hjalmer opened it, Cissie looked and me and I at her, our expression said it all; this was the last place that we wanted to be. We were motioned into a kitchen, Hjalmer looked at us both and smiled. "Well, you are finally here... welcome home!" He exclaimed, and, "I will go and fetch their things."

Cissie turned to run, she was not staying here for five minutes, this was not home. Mrs Purdy held her fast.

"Now now, young lady... you just hold your horses, there is somebody here you need to see..."

Just then the door in the far corner of the kitchen opened, and a familiar figure stepped into the room.

"Mama!" I exclaimed and I ran to her, grabbing her round her skirts and legs.

"Hello girls... I am sorry it's been so long... I have not been well... but I am better now..."

Cissie stood and stared, no emotion on her face. Mrs Purdy tried to encourage her forward; I didn't care, I just clung to my Mama, who had squatted down next to me and was hugging me. Cissie spoke, a hard edge to her voice.

"You're back then... and what are we doing here? Why haven't we gone home, to our place?"

"Let me explain..." Mama tried, but I was quite emotional and kissing her wildly.

"This is your home now... OK Rita... OK... let me just tell Cissie..."

"This is not our home... this is HIS home!" she spat back just as Hjalmer came through the door. "I want to go back to OUR home."

Mama tried again.

"But this is our home now Cissie, you see—"

Hjalmer jumped in quickly, "We are married, Cissie... this is your home, now... my home is your home... isn't this good?"

Chapter 31 –

The Last Days
of Summer

I was ecstatic: I had Mama, I was with my Mama. And that was not all, some other familiar things were there too; a chair, a table, and lots of ornaments and things that had been in our cabin, and Billy bear, and my picture book. But Cissie was not so happy – in fact, she was mad. She felt as though she had been betrayed by Mama, and would not get the thought out of her head that Mama had not been away in a hospital at all, but had been here all the time living with Mr Halderson and not bothering about us; she didn't even believe they were really married.

"Well, if they are…" she hissed at me. "Why weren't we there?"

Mama tried to reason with her again and again. "You are making it all sound so terrible, Cissie… it wasn't… isn't like you think it is… let me try again… I got sick… I couldn't think properly… losing E… Ed… Eddie…," she bit back the tears, the grief still raw and transparent, "… was a terrible thing… I couldn't face it… I didn't want to face it… I didn't want to live anymore…" She paused, sniffing back even more tears and breathing hard.

"I knew that your Papa was dying long, long before he did... it does not mean I did not care for him as much as Eddie... I just had a long time to get used to the idea that he would be going and there was nothing that I could do about it... with your... brother... it was a complete shock... an absolute tragedy and I fell apart..."

She paused again, trying to recollect the hazy events, which had been confused by time, treatment and sedatives and all that had happened to her since. I sat and listened quietly, while Cissie fixed her with her eyes, searching for any flaw in her story. Mama began again.

"If it hadn't been for Leila... and Brenda and Doctor Cameron of course... I don't think I would be here now... They made me keep you two in my thoughts, all the time... they told me I had to live... I had to be responsible for you two... but I wouldn't eat and I couldn't do anything... so the doctor thought it was best that I go to special hospital where they treat people who have what is called a break-down... that's what I had, a breakdown of myself... anyway, no one knew the place really, they just thought it was the best thing to do... but it wasn't very nice... and I did pull myself together very quickly, especially with all the bad treatments... I asked again, and again, if I could leave, come back... but they kept insisting that I was not well and that I had to stay... that only a relative who was responsible for me could take me away... I haven't got anybody in this country except you two, who was going to come for me? I was not allowed to write to anyone, and if people did send letters, I did not get them."

Cissie spat out her response. "So why didn't you just walk out? I would have done, especially if I knew that I had two children waiting for me."

"It wasn't that simple, Cissie… it was like a prison, high walls, and locked doors everywhere… I had no money… not even any clothes… I didn't even know where I was…"

Cissie grunted, a reluctant acceptance for that part of the story. Mama continued.

"I was thrilled when Mr Halderson… Hjalmer… came in February… His was the first friendly face that I had seen in over two months… the hospital let me out for a day, because he gave them reassurances that he would take me back… I didn't know that he had made a plan… not until we sat in a café near the hospital… that's when he asked me about what I was planning to do, and I told him that I couldn't do anything, that they were not going to let me go till they were ready… that's when he told me that he had arranged a special license and that we could be married if I consented to it… and that the hospital would have to release me then, because he would insist as my husband…"

Cissie came back harder this time. "But you don't love him, do you? Maybe you did not love Papa either?"

"Cissie, how dare you!…"

Mama was not happy with Cissie's comment one little bit. "Of course I loved your Papa very much… why do you think we came all this way from Scotland?… No, I don't love Hjalmer yet, but he is very kind and very good to me, and from these things, love can grow… as I have said to you many times, it is more important to like someone… and I like Hjalmer and we work together well… if you would give him a chance, you would see that too… he has always been very kind to us all… and here we are…" She looked around the separate kitchen – so much bigger than our kitchen had been (not that we had a kitchen, it was all one room for us). She added, "He has a lovely house, you two have your own special place in the attic... all the animals live in a separate barn, he's bought me a little range with an oven! I can bake my own bread and cakes for the first time in years!"

Cissie snarled, "It's just things... that's all, just things! Meanwhile our home lies empty, that's where we should be, not here!"

"And how would we manage? Tell me that, Cissie? Poor Paul and Hjalmer could barely keep their own places going because of all the help they were giving us... who would farm it now? Hjalmer has a big place here and his house is so much roomier... you two are growing fast... this was the best choice we had, now you either learn to live with it or you don't... I am sure Rita will be perfectly happy... you will be fourteen next year and soon you will be old enough to make your own decisions and your own way in life... I would rather that we all learned to get along properly... like a family."

Cissie never really accepted any of it, and despite my mother's constant attentions towards her, she seemed determined to be as difficult as she could; my mother despaired of her and was very glad that she was back to school, as at least it distracted her from her constant gripes and complaints and gave us all peace. At least for me the transition was more simple, just the things that were special to me; my moccasins, Billy bear and thankfully Jimmy the collie – Hjalmer had taken him in when my mother had been taken to Waverley Hospital. These were all I needed to feel safe. I fell in love with the house and became very attached to the mountain of a man, who was always so kind. He wasn't my Papa and I knew that, no one could ever replace him, but was very attentive towards me, when he was around; Hjalmer had a big place and a great deal to do, it was early spring and he was out from dawn until dusk every day.

My mother had made the place as much like home as she could, she had painted little flowers on the old furniture, hung curtains on the windows. The house consisted of three main rooms; the kitchen, a small sitting room and then my mother and Hjalmer's bedroom. Cissie and I slept in an attic, which was so big it was like a house of our own. Under the house was a grain cellar; this was very unusual for us, never having had a cellar beneath our old house, it was also very unusual to everyone else as houses did not have cellars. But Hjalmer had built his house the way he would have made one in Norway, and for him, a high pitched roof so the snow did not weigh the roof down and a grain cellar were absolutely necessary.

He had brought my mother three things as wedding presents: a little white range that she loved, a replacement couch (we left the old one because it had been Eddie's bed and the place he had died), and her most treasured possession, a little piano. She had played her parents' piano on occasions, when her brothers and sisters would let her, and she had a real talent for singing and making music. My strongest memories at Hjalmer's place are the daily smell of fresh baked bread in the morning, the smell of cakes being baked in the afternoon, and the sound of my mother singing and playing in the evenings. After all that we had been through, it was absolutely blissful to suddenly have smells and sounds that brought joy and happiness.

My daily routines with my mother of feeding hens, milking and helping with the butter had been restored too, Jimmy always with us wherever we went. I began to feel safe and secure, and however awkward Cissie might be towards me, I was not going to let any of that spoil my time.

It was now the end of April, and although the thaw had started the creek below the house hadn't quite thawed out from the deep winter frost. It was like a fairy glen, with all the little rivulets of ice that had little trickles of water running through them. I imagined all sorts of tiny worlds with tiny people, living in and among the magic little place. One day my sister was not at school, and she had followed me down to my special spot. I stood next to the icy brook, I felt her shove me so hard that I skidded onto the ice, then I heard a slight cracking sound.

"Run," she taunted.

I tried to move but slipped and fell; she laughed at me.

"Run," she said again. "Or you'll fall through."

Panic gripped me. I tried to get to my feet, but slipped again, she laughed more. I started to cry.

"You big baby..." she snarled, grabbing the back of my coat and hauling me onto the bank. "It was only a game." She took off back up the hill, leaving me miserable, cold and angry. I knew now that I did not like my sister at all.

By May the summer storms had come. Being on a rise in the land it left us vulnerable to a lightning strike; my mother would be very nervous when a storm started and would shoo me to the ladder into the grain cellar, she and Jimmy following quickly. I used to love the feeling of the warm, silky grain as we sheltered till the thunder passed, my mother's nervousness as electric as the storm. I have been frightened of thunder ever since, it must have been those few anxious times with my mother that have stuck in my consciousness.

The days were long and lovely, it was cooler on the mountain and there were fewer insects because of the breeze, but we had fly screens on all the doors and windows just the same; a blessed relief from the swarms that would come from time to time. Sleeping in our attic was less stuffy than it had been confined to our little curtained sleeping area in my father's cabin. In the heat of the summer, there was still a breeze blowing through the attic. The house was festooned with prairie flowers that I would pick every day when Mama and I went out for our afternoon walk with Jimmy.

One such day came in early July. It was late afternoon, our shadows were long and the summer sun made us feel lazy, as I and my mother, with Jimmy of course, ambled on the high prairie next to the homestead. My mother was wearing a tammy hat with a white pom-pom on it to keep the heat of the sun from her head. I was in my little moccasins, which were now so snug, it would not be long until I could no longer fit it into them. My mother carried her wicker basket, she was looking for mushrooms for supper, and trying to teach me what we could pick and what we shouldn't. I remember finding a beautiful puffball and bringing it excitedly to Mama. She snatched it away in a hurry.

"No, no, Rita, that's a bad one, you should never eat that." And with that she threw it away, Jimmy running excitedly after the mushroom's trajectory. As it hit the ground it burst into many pieces and blew on the breeze, the confused collie came running back hoping for a new game. That evening Mama cooked a beautiful meal of bacon with the mushrooms and fresh bread. We all sat down to eat them, Hjalmer causing me to giggle uncontrollably with some funny faces he was making at me across the tea-table, much to Cissie's disapproval of course.

Then my mother grabbed her stomach and whimpered loudly.

"Are you all right, Sal?" Hjalmer's voice was full of concern.

By now my mother was screaming and had gone very pale.

"Cissie, quick take Mama to the bed. Rita fetch a glass of water." I fetched the water and ran in sloshing drips of water through the kitchen and sitting room. Hjalmer had lit the paraffin lamp, my mother was curled up moaning in pain on the bed, unable to speak with the intensity of the cramps that were overtaking her. Hjalmer looked at Cissie.

"Maybe it's the mushrooms," he said.

"No," said Cissie. "Mama knows mushrooms… and we are all OK. She must need a doctor. I can ride into Fir Mountain and find the doctor."

No sooner had she said it than she was dashing for the door. Hjalmer was trying his best to comfort Mama, who was in a lot of pain; he pulled me up onto the bed, in a hope that he could distract her a little. Every now and then the pain would pass for a few minutes and she would try to speak a little, then she would be gripped by another wave of cramping and would start screaming again. I don't know how long it was, it felt like forever, but Cissie came back leading the doctor to Hjalmer's place. Cissie was told to take me into the kitchen with Jimmy. Hjalmer waited apprehensively outside the bedroom door. After a few minutes the doctor came out with some urgency.

"Mr Halderson… I suspect your wife has an appendicitis… she needs an operation… it means a long journey to Moosejaw…"

Then he looked most serious, and tried to say the next part as quietly as possible, but Cissie and I heard.

"It's a long way, I am not sure she will make it… I can't tell how advanced it is… she tells me she has been having pains for a few days."

Hjalmer was determined. "But we have to try, doctor?"

"If you are willing to do the journey, sir, I am too... but we will need a flat cart so that I can make your wife as comfortable as possible."

While Hjalmer rushed around outside, moving out his flat-bed wagon and hitching a good horse, the doctor gave Mama a sleeping draught to try and help with the pain; she held it down for two minutes and then it all came up. She was trying so hard not to make noises, knowing now that both Cissie and I were very scared. The doctor looked seriously at Cissie.

"Mr Halderson and I are going to try and get your Mama into hospital." Cissie nodded. "You must take care of your sister until we return." Cissie nodded again; a command from a doctor was one to be respected at all times. Hjalmer carried Mama out of the bedroom wrapped in blankets out into the dark night and laid her on the trap; a light had been attached to the back. I could see him gently touching her forehead and stroking her, he was talking to her, but I could not make out what he was saying through the closed window.

The doctor and Hjalmer made out on the road, which left the house on the high prairie, almost the same place my mother and I had walked earlier. It was a flat and endless expanse of land; in the darkness the only thing that Cissie and I could make out from our window was the light swinging two and fro on the back of the trap. We watched in silence as the little light got smaller and smaller, finally becoming a pinprick in the darkness. We were just about to come away from the window, when we noticed that the light had stopped, and then after a while it was growing in size again. We were both filled with horror; what had happened? Why were they coming back?

The short journey that they had made on the bumpy farm tracks, had just been too much to bear for my mother, who found it far too painful. The doctor had decided it was best to bring her back and try giving her the strongest painkillers that he could. My mother was lain back in her bed, and a strong dose of morphine was administered; the doctor and Hjalmer sat talking in the sitting room, both the doors closed. When they emerged, Hjalmer looked slightly red-eyed, the doctor looked beaten.

"I will be back first thing in the morning, Hjalmer, to give your wife some more relief for the pain."

"How is Mama?" Cissie asked; her enquiry was genuine. Hjalmer looked at her, then at me. It was late, there was too much to think about.

"We will see in the morning... you two should go to bed now, please."

Mama passed a bad night, I could hear her moaning with the pain that would come again, and as the morphine wore off, the moans turned to cries. Hjalmer sat with her all night. I could hear them talking, but I could not hear what they said. The next morning, Cissie and I sat in the kitchen. Neither of us wanted to eat, we both knew that things were bad. The doctor came back early, he looked tired and solemn. He went through with a bottle of morphine to Hjalmer and Mama and gave strict instructions when it should be given, then without saying a word to us walked out through the kitchen door. After a while, Hjalmer came into us and sat at the table. He was worn out and his eyes were sunken and red, his face was puffy, he had been crying.

"Your mother is sleeping now, when she wakes up she wants to see you both, but we must let her rest now."

Cissie was surprisingly concerned for Hjalmer. "Can I make you something to eat?"

He looked up, for a moment I thought he was going to say something, but he just shook his head and looked down once more at the table.

News travels fast in such a small community and those that needed to know of yet more Flynn misfortune soon arrived, namely Mrs Purdy. She came mid-morning and stopping outside to talk to Hjalmer first, then she came into the kitchen.

"And how are you two doing?" she said, trying to sound her normal self, but we knew that things were far from normal. Cissie said nothing, but I could not contain myself anymore and the tears began to roll down my face.

"Mama's sick," I blubbered. "She's not going to have to go to hospital again, is she?"

"No, Rita... Mama's not going to hospital, she is staying here." Then she qualified her statement. "When she wakes up... she will talk to you both, I am sure... now you are both going to eat something or your Mama will be angry with me... then I am going to see some friends of mine here in Fir Mountain, but I will be back and I am going to stay with you for a day or so."

Eventually, Mrs Purdy had gone, but not before she had spoken to Mama. Hjalmer told us it was time to see Mama. We both went in as quietly as we could. Mrs Purdy had sat Mama up on lots of pillows, her skin was so white, she was gripping her tummy tightly. Two chairs had been set up by the bed. We sat down and waited for her to talk, we knew she was sick, we knew we should not make a fuss. Mama began slowly, her speech slurred by the medicine, as she began to talk her eyes began to well up with water and flooded her face.

"Now, you two are going to have... have to be... my two strong... strong and clever girls..." She stopped and winced as another pain gripped her tightly. "I am very sick... I am not going to get well..." She stopped again. "I am dying..." Cissie started to cry.

"Hush now, Cissie... there are things that I have to say and you have to listen. Leila has gone to see some friends, a nice couple nearby... Hjalmer can't look after you two on his own... he has enough to do and it's not right... I... I have decided... to write to your grandmamma... my mother... I am going to ask her to take you both in..."

Cissie gasped. "No Mama... please don't make us go back?"

Mama tried to make light of it. "Well that's a shock... I thought you loved Scotland and hated Canada? Never mind... it can't be changed... We... we have no family here... you have to go back... I am sure grandmamma will take you in..."

The enormity of what Mama was saying did not sink in. She was dying? But she couldn't be, she was here, she was alive? And grandmamma, my grandmamma... surely not Mama's mother? And leaving Hjalmer? Staying with other people? But who were these other people? I did not know what to think, my little head could not take it all in, I was in shock. This was yet something else that had happened in my short life which was just too much to understand, and my mind had developed a new way to deal with all the extremes; just to block it out. If I just did not think, it could not be real.

After Mama had finished talking, Hjalmer came in and told us to go back to the kitchen. It seemed a very long time until he came back to us. He sat again silently, then Cissie said, "Why can't we stay here... with you?"

Hjalmer was tongue-tied, he tried to speak, but Cissie continued. "Or is it that you just don't want us around?"

Hjalmer looked hard at Cissie, his eyes moist, the pain showing on every line of his face.

"I wanted you to stay... but your mother says that would not be good for you... I don't want you to go... as much as I don't want your mother to die." Having put Cissie very firmly in her place, he got up and left the yard. I knew that Cissie was wrong to say what she had, and I too got up and followed Hjalmer outside. I called to him, "Elmer."

He turned to me, his face wet, mine wet too. He scooped me up in his arms, and his body shook as he sobbed into my shoulder, as I in turn sobbed into his.

Chapter 32 –

Full Circle

Two terrible nights passed. We could hear Mama's cries and moans and were terrified for her, she could not get enough relief from the pain that wretched through her body. Mrs Purdy said that it wasn't good for us to see Mama the way she was, and that she was not in the world now because of all the morphine and it would be too distressing for us. All we could do was listen and pray, not that I understood much about god and church, as it had not been present in my life, not as it had been in Cissie's. Hjalmer kept a constant bedside vigil with Mama; he took no rest. We would hear him talking softly to her, trying to reach her and bring her comfort.

Mama died in the early hours of the 6th July 1923. The house fell silent. We were awake and came down and waited for a while, until Mrs Purdy brought us through to see Mama. Mrs Purdy had attended to her; combing her hair, sponging her down with lavender and adding some powder to her face. She looked lovely, really peaceful. All the lines of pain had disappeared and her mouth was slightly open and in a half smile. Mrs Purdy looked at us both.

"I am so sorry, my dears… but your Mama is at peace now."
The few short days after that we stayed at Hjalmer's were
punctuated by many visitors coming and offering their
condolences to the big man, and to us. People would smile,
and say how lovely she was and how sorry they were, but then
we would catch aside conversations, such as, 'those poor we
mites, what's going to become of them now?' 'That family has
had more than its fair share of pain and tragedy, when is it
going to end?' and one particular comment, which affected
me deeply: 'You know they have no one left in the world?'

We were introduced to another Mr and Mrs Flynn, no
relation to us whatsoever, but he was called John and she was
called Sadie. They were a lovely couple who seemed very
kind, they had no children and had offered to take us in until
contact could be made with Scotland. It was thought better
for us and better for Hjalmer if we stayed close by while we
waited, but too much for him to have the responsibility of
having to take care of us. He was so deeply engulfed in his
own grief, he could barely take care of himself. We were told
that after Mama's funeral we would be staying with these
other people for a while; I didn't quite understand. Cissie as
always was resentful at the whole prospect, feeling that we
had once again been abandoned by those we trusted.

The day of the funeral was bright and sunny. Quite a few
of Hjalmer's friends were there to escort my mother's body
to her last resting place at Mountain View Cemetery next to
our lovely brother. Cissie was outside in the pasture crying;
someone said, "Shouldn't we go and comfort her?"

Then someone else answered, "No it's best to leave her be."

Soon we were all gathered on the road; a car had been
hired to take Hjalmer, Cissie, Mrs Purdy and I. It was such a
novelty that a crowd of men had spent the last hour standing

and admiring it. I felt like a princess, and although I knew we were going to bury Mama, I still did not quite understand what that actually meant. Mrs Purdy thought it was a good idea to keep me distracted.

"Why don't you gather some flowers for your mother along the way... when you see some, we will stop the car."

I was amazed at my power to bring all to a halt, because I had seen another pink, or blue, or yellow flower. Soon I had gathered quite a bunch and we had finally arrived on the high ridge that looked over the lower prairie. A grave had been dug next to our brother, someone showed me his name on the little metal T plaque that marked his grave; they had another lying face down on the ground ready to be installed.

There were many people gathered, I had no idea that we knew so many, and that Mama had so many friends. Looking back now that was the way it was round there, we had been through so much in our short time, that many people felt connected to our tragedy and wanted to show their sympathy. One person stood far at the end of the cemetery on the outside; it was the old Indian lady Brenda. I wished she would come and stand with us, but she remained on the outside, paying her respects her way.

Mama's coffin was laid next to the grave and the lid removed for one last time. There she was dressed in her best dress; navy blue with white polka dots. Her hair was beautiful done, and she looked young and lovely, her eyes shut. I placed my flowers next to her folded hands and while the pastor read the service, I stood transfixed while they replaced the lid and slowly lowered her into her grave.

The next few months of our lives seemed to last an eternity. No matter how hard Mr and Mrs Flynn tried to raise our spirits, we were both silent and moody; we must have been truly miserable house guests. I remember being dressed up one day in a white frilly dress with socks and shoes and being made to stand outside holding Billy bear to have my photograph taken. Little did I know at the time that grandma had replied and asked for a picture of me and Cissie to be sent; Cissie had refused point blank, with no discussions. I remember feeling very silly in this dress, I was too warm and the shoes were too tight on my feet; not like my little moccasins that had eventually fallen apart with age.

Finally the day came when we were to leave Saskatchewan. A passage had been booked for us by our grandparents from Montreal; Hjalmer was to accompany us there and see us safely onboard. I was very excited, the waiting was over, we were going somewhere new and different. Cissie had said to me that we were going to cross the sea and live with our grandparents near the sea. I had no idea what the sea was and no one could describe it to me, to help me make sense. Cissie tried to explain that there was sand and sea shells, and that we could swim in the water. In my childish imaginings, I had visions of me walking on the seabed collecting shells.

The goodbyes were difficult. Mrs Purdy and Evelyn came with us to the station at Lafleche, and Mrs Purdy knelt down to talk to me.

"Well little Rita, you have a very big adventure ahead of you, and you are going to live with your family in Scotland."

Evelyn added, "If you are good girl, maybe your grandmamma will let you come back for a visit one day?"

I stared at Evelyn long and hard. I did not want to come back, I was too excited about my new life and my big adventure. I made up my mind there and then not to be a good girl.

I had never been on a train, and the train from Lafleche to Saskatoon fascinated me, and as we crossed the vast flatness of the province heading north, the sun shone and we could see for many miles all the little homesteads dotted around in the distance. On being transferred to a massive Canadian Pacific Railway monster of a train to head east to Montreal, I was aghast at the size of the train. Grandpapa had not stinted on cost, we each had our own corridor sleeper (including Hjalmer) and a place to sit in a carriage. The first day or so of the journey I absolutely loved it, especially going to bed in a bunk that moved. The noises of the train covering the tracks, the thumpty-thump, the hiss and the smell of the engine, became a soothing rhythm and every now and then when the guard blew the train klaxon I squealed with delight.

But as the days drew on, boredom set in. A small child who had been used to the freedom of the prairie – in fact our last five months we had been practically let to run wild – felt over-constrained and trapped. I couldn't be sat to look at picture books and magazines and my questions over and over again to Cissie and Hjalmer, were that of any small child on a journey that never seems to end.

"Are we there yet?"

"You'll be there when you see the sea!" Cissie spat back for the hundredth time.

"But what does it look like?"

"I have told you again and again, it is water that goes on forever, like the prairie."

So I would scour the horizon in hope of my first glimpse, as we crossed Manitoba and then into Ontario and expanse of water that, to me, had to be the sea.

"Is that the sea?"

"No that's just a lake... see, you can see the other side," Hjalmer replied. But I wasn't satisfied or sure. Again and again, I would spot water and ask.

Then we began to cross the Great Lakes, I was sure this had to be the sea, I couldn't see all the way across.

"This must be the sea?" I shrilled.

Then came a joint, "No!"

That was it for me, I gave up looking and resumed my bored impatient travelling face.

But eventually, we did arrive in Montreal, and I was flabbergasted by the grand, high buildings and how big it was... and how many people there were... and how busy it was... I was, for the first time on the journey, completely speechless; a blessed relief to my step-father and sister. We made our way from the station to the ship quite close by, but we passed a small jewellery shop on the way and Hjalmer asked us to wait outside a moment. He returned with two beautifully tied parcels. We sat on a bench and unwrapped them enthusiastically. Cissie had a beautiful pendant on a gold chain with a light blue stone on it.

"It matches your eyes," he said. Cissie was polite and said thank you. Mine was a golden ring with a dark red stone in it, he placed it on my index finger, it fitted perfectly.

"Just so you don't forget me," he said. I threw my arms around his neck and said, "I'll never forget you, Elmer."

The jewellery must have been real gold and stones, probably semi-precious, because we were to find out later that our grandMama was very particular about jewellery and would never let people wear fakes; she let us keep Hjalmer's gifts.

Then came the sad moment, as he led us both up the vast gangplank to board the S.S. Melita; just the biggest thing that I had ever seen. I could see the water lapping so far below and I was scared that we would fall in, so he held my hand tightly. At the top we were met by a porter to take us to our cabin. Cissie barely acknowledged Hjalmer and began to walk off in the direction to which the porter had pointed we would be heading. Hjalmer picked me up for one last time, and I hugged his neck tightly.

"You will come and see me at grandma's, won't you?" I said.

"I will if I can, you know that, and Rita…" He paused. "You know that your mother loved Canada, don't you?"

"Yes," I said.

"And she will always be here, but she will always be in your heart too, with Eddie?"

I added, "And Papa."

With that he put me down and the porter took my hand. As I was led away, I tried to turn and say goodbye again, but there were so many people gathering I couldn't see through the wall of legs and bodies. I never saw my step-father again.

The voyage was long and stormy. I must have had good sea legs, because I was not sick at all and neither was Cissie, but many people were. We had been assigned to a shared third class cabin. There were four bunks and a lady and her son who was about my age were sharing the voyage with us. Cissie and the lady took the one set of bunks, the boy and me the other; I was placed on the lower bunk in case I fell out. He was a spoilt little brat, that boy! He always got his own way, and his mother always gave in to him. I had been so used to fighting my own corner and being independent, especially since my mother had died – I had become quite feisty. He would try to pick on me, and he would prod and poke, until I would hit him, then the waterworks would start and immediately his mother would order Cissie to take a firm hand.

"That child is out of control! You do something about her or I will!"

Cissie didn't like them much either and happily ignored her, thankfully.

Then it was my fourth birthday. I had made a few friends of the adults on the ship by then, and when they heard of my special day and they gave me a little purse with some money in it. Strange money, so different from our dollars and cents. The grand total was four pennies and one halfpenny. Cissie took me to the shop on board and told me to choose something. I saw this beautiful gold rubber fish; that is what I wanted and I called it 'Goldie'. Later when we got back to the cabin, the little brat had a tantrum and insisted he should have a fish. His mother dutifully went to the shop, but there were only green ones left, she offered it to her son in hope.

"I don't want that one!... I want a gold one!" he snapped. Then, looking at mine, "I want hers!" He snatched for my fish. "Give it to me!"

I held firm. Then his mother chimed in, "They're just the same, really... why don't you have the green one and give my son yours?"

"No!" I still held firm.

Then Cissie tried. "Go on Rita... let the little boy have yours?"

"No!" I stubbornly hung on. The little boy started crying and let go. I held on to my fish; he was not having it, he howled till he made himself sick. I was glad!

The last night of our voyage we were allowed up to the upper decks to have our meal. I had never seen such beautiful things in all my life. White linen table cloths, beautiful chairs, crystal chandeliers, and the beautifully dressed gentlemen and ladies: full evening wear, long dresses and sparkling jewellery. I think we were allowed up because it was such a rough night there was hardly anybody in there and they had a great deal of food going to waste. The waiter brought me my dinner. As the giant ship rolled, and rolled, being tossed around like a matchstick. With the motion of the great vessel, my plate moved from side to side, so I couldn't actually eat anything. The waiter seeing my dilemma, brought a jug of water, lifted my plate and splashed some onto the cloth – a very effective solution.

Finally, we were at Port Glasgow after our long journey. It was cold, damp and foggy and getting on for late evening. We were sat on the station on our luggage, as a porter walked up and down the station calling out, "Mr and Mrs McBride... Mr and Mrs McBride." We seemed to be there for ages and we thought that no one would ever come for us. Then we saw two old people walking towards us, both in black. I stood up, expectantly, and Cissie became very proper.

"Hello grandmamma, hello grandpapa," she said in her best voice, reluctantly.

Grandmamma seemed tiny as compared to the corpulent frame of Mrs Purdy. Grandmamma wore a long black dress with little black polished boots; her waist was so tiny confined in her corsets. Grandpapa seemed gruff, with stern clothes and an expression to match; wearing a black suit, his silver moustache flashed in the lights on the station. He did not smile.

"We thought you were never coming," Grandmamma said starchily. She continued, "There were delays with your crossing? I expect it was stormy? We stayed at your grandfather's flat and have been backwards and forward these past few days waiting for you."

She reached into her handbag and pulled out two silk scarves; a blue one for Cissie and a green one for me. She placed them round our necks and embraced us; this, we were to find, was a very unusual display of affection, never to be repeated.

"Well, it's time to go home then."

With that we made our way to the tiny boat train to Dunoon, to our new lives and our new beginnings. As this part of my life story ended, another eventful chapter began.

CPSIA information can be obtained
at www.ICGtesting.com
Printed in the USA
LVOW10s0403040117
519674LV00001B/192/P